The Best AMERICAN SHORT STORIES 2007

GUEST EDITORS OF

THE BEST AMERICAN SHORT STORIES

1978 TED SOLOTAROFF

1979 JOYCE CAROL OATES

1980 STANLEY ELKIN

1981 HORTENSE CALISHER

1982 JOHN GARDNER

1983 ANNE TYLER

1984 JOHN UPDIKE

1985 GAIL GODWIN

1986 RAYMOND CARVER

1987 ANN BEATTIE

1988 MARK HELPRIN

1989 MARGARET ATWOOD

1990 RICHARD FORD

1991 ALICE ADAMS

1992 ROBERT STONE

1993 LOUISE ERDRICH

1994 TOBIAS WOLFF

1995 JANE SMILEY

1996 JOHN EDGAR WIDEMAN

1997 E. ANNIE PROULX

1998 GARRISON KEILLOR

1999 AMY TAN

2000 E. L. DOCTOROW

2001 BARBARA KINGSOLVER

2002 SUE MILLER

2003 WALTER MOSLEY

2004 LORRIE MOORE

2005 MICHAEL CHABON

2006 ANN PATCHETT

2007 STEPHEN KING

The Best AMERICAN SHORT STORIES® 2007

Selected from
U.S. and Canadian Magazines
by STEPHEN KING
with HEIDI PITLOR

With an Introduction by Stephen King

HOUGHTON MIFFLIN COMPANY
BOSTON • NEW YORK 2007

www.houghtonmifflinbooks.com

ISSN 0067-6233
ISBN-13: 978-0-618-71347-9 ISBN-10: 0-618-71347-6
ISBN-13: 978-0-618-71348-6 (pbk.) ISBN-10: 0-618-71348-4 (pbk.)

Printed in the United States of America

VB 10 9 8 7 6 5 4 3 2 1

"Pa's Darling" by Louis Auchincloss, from *The Young Apollo and Other Stories.* First published in *The Yale Review,* January 2006, Volume 94, No. 1. Copyright © 2006 by Louis Auchincloss. Reprinted by permission of Houghton Mifflin Company. All rights reserved.

"Toga Party" by John Barth. First published in *Fiction,* Issue 19, No. 2. Copyright © 2006 by John Barth. Reprinted by permission of The Wylie Agency, Inc.

"Solid Wood" by Ann Beattie. First published in *Boulevard,* Volume 21, Nos. 62 and 63. Copyright © 2006 by Iron & Pity Inc. Reprinted by permission of the author.

"Balto" by T. C. Boyle. First published in *The Paris Review,* Winter 2006, No. 179. Copyright © 2006 by T. C. Boyle. Reprinted by permission of Georges Borchardt, Inc.

"Riding the Doghouse" by Randy DeVita. First published in *West Branch,* No. 58 Spring/Summer. Copyright © 2006 by Randy DeVita. Reprinted by permission of the author.

"My Brother Eli" by Joseph Epstein. First published in *The Hudson Review,* Volume LIX, No. 3. Copyright © 2006 by *Hudson Review.* Reprinted by permission of the author.

"Where Will You Go When Your Skin Cannot Contain You?" by William Gay first appeared in *Tin House* magazine's All Apologies issue, which came out in winter 2006. Copyright © 2006 by William Gay. Reprinted by permission of McCormick & Williams.

"Eleanor's Music" from *The Stories of Mary Gordon* by Mary Gordon, copyright © 2006 by Mary Gordon. Used by permission of Pantheon Books, a division of Random House, Inc.

"L. DeBard and Aliette: A Love Story" by Lauren Groff. First published in *The Atlantic Monthly,* Fiction Issue 2006. Copyright © 2006 by Lauren Groff. Reprinted by permission of the author.

"Wake" by Beverly Jensen. First published in *New England Review,* Volume 27, No. 2, 2006. Copyright © 2006 by Middlebury College Publications. Reprinted by permission of *New England Review;* Jay Silverman.

"Wait" by Roy Kesey. First published in *The Kenyon Review,* Fall 2006, Volume XXXVIII, No. 4. Copyright © 2006 by Roy Kesey. Reprinted by permission of the author.

"Findings & Impressions" by Stellar Kim. First published in *The Iowa Review,* Winter 2006/2007 36/3. Copyright © 2006 by Stellar Kim. Reprinted by permission of the author.

"Allegiance" by Aryn Kyle. First published in *Ploughshares,* Fall 2006, Volume 32. Copyright © 2006 by Aryn Kyle. Reprinted by permission of the Denise Shannon Literary Agency Inc.

"The Boy in Zaquitos" by Bruce McAllister. First published in *Fantasy and Science Fiction,* January 2006. Copyright © 2006 by Spilogale, Inc. Reprinted by permission of the author.

"Dimension" by Alice Munro. First published in *The New Yorker,* June 5, 2006. Copyright © 2006 by Alice Munro. Reprinted by permission of the author.

Eileen Pollack, "The Bris" from *In the Mouth: Stories and Novellas.* Copyright © 2006 by Eileen Pollack. Originally from *Subtropics* 1 (Winter/Spring 2006). Sue Standing. Reprinted with the permission of Four Way Books, www.fourwaybooks.com.

"St. Lucy's Home for Girls Raised by Wolves" from *St. Lucy's Home for Girls Raised by Wolves* by Karen Russell, copyright © 2006 by Karen Russell. Used by permission of Alfred A. Knopf, a division of Random House, Inc.

"Horseman" by Richard Russo. First published in *The Atlantic Monthly,* Fiction Issue 2006. Copyright © 2006 by Richard Russo. Reprinted by permission of the author.

"Sans Farine" from *Like You'd Understand* by Jim Shepard, copyright © 2007 by Jim Shepard. Used by permission of Alfred A. Knopf, a division of Random House, Inc.

"Do Something" by Kate Walbert. First published in *Ploughshares,* Winter 2006/2007. Copyright © 2006 by Kate Walbert. Reprinted by permission of the author.

Contents

Foreword

I'VE NEVER BEEN much good at hiking solely for the sake of inner peace or exercise. I wish I could be such a person, but I find myself wanting to know how many feet I climbed, how long it took, and what distance I covered. To immerse myself in thousands of short stories has been a strange, wonderful thing this year, a little like climbing the highest, rockiest mountain around. For the first six months or so, I kept track of the number of stories I read. One thousand! Two! Three!

Maybe it's the braggart in me (tell someone you read four thousand short stories in one year and watch their eyes widen), or at least the braggart's close cousin, the attention-starved child. At any rate, with each five hundred or so stories came a greater sense of accomplishment, as if I'd reached a new, hard-earned vista from which to see the landscape in a completely different way. And the more I read, the foggier this panorama appeared — at the risk of stretching a metaphor too far.

During this, my first year as series editor, I was tempted to watch for trends in theme and style, but the more I read and the more I tried to fit these stories into discrete boxes — minimalist stories about good parents and bad children; maximalist stories about bad parents and good children; lyrical or plainspoken or experimental stories about history, war, travel, disease, being single, married, divorced, widowed — the more I came to see that they resisted neat categorization. A story ostensibly about a child starting school bloomed into an extended metaphor for a country adopting democracy. A story about a civil war came to explore warring factions within a strained marriage. I was also tempted to develop my own definitions of what made one story successful and another less so. In the end, I found this business of success a shifty prospect as well. A story that met my initial requirements — say, a story that could be considered risky, profound, and deft — often just didn't rise off the page for me, while a safer, seemingly more quiet story stayed with me on a deeper level, even months later. In the end, my observations and requirements changed and faded and all but disappeared.

One basic thing did stay the same: I was drawn to stories that transcended something. Whether it was a particular cliché of character — the doting mother, the gluttonous dictator, the wise child — or language or situation, the stories I chose twisted and turned away from the familiar and ultimately took flight, demanding their own particular characters and structure and prose. I was pleasantly surprised by the volume of such stories this year.

Lauren Groff's mesmerizing story, "L. DeBard and Aliette," explores a love affair between a girl in a wheelchair and an Olympic swimmer. In the end, it is her strength that undoes the man and his weakness that emboldens her. Stellar Kim's moving story, "Findings & Impressions," begins as a radiologist's report and ends as a meditation on the unique intimacy that comes with proximity to the dying. In "Dimension," Alice Munro brings to life a classically abusive marriage, but in her masterly hands, both husband and wife seem utterly original and sympathetic. Perhaps, in the end, what makes a story successful is just such a surprise — one that quietly taps the reader on the shoulder and then takes her breath away without revealing any of its secrets.

What an honor to join the esteemed ranks of past series editors Edward J. O'Brien, Martha Foley, Shannon Ravenel, and Katrina Kenison. They have discovered or been among the first supporters of writers such as Ernest Hemingway, Willa Cather, William Faulkner, Dorothy Parker, F. Scott Fitzgerald, Thomas Wolfe, Richard Wright, Saul Bellow, Philip Roth, and Eudora Welty. The series editors have observed nearly a century's worth of American fiction, serving as witnesses of a constantly changing country and its evolving aesthetics and values. Katrina Kenison held this position for the past sixteen years and was an early champion of writers such as Amy Bloom, Robert Olen Butler, Andrea Barrett, Pam Houston, and

Aleksandar Hemon. To say she left me with big shoes to fill is an understatement.

I am also honored to have worked with Stephen King, whose dedication, unflagging hard work, and enthusiasm for excellent writing shone through on nearly a daily basis this past year. Typically, the series editor reads thousands of stories and culls 120 deemed to be the finest. The guest editor then reads these and selects twenty to include in the book. Mr. King opted to read along with me during the year, and, bless him, climbed a good-sized mountain himself. We agreed, disagreed, and in the end very much concurred on the merit of the twenty stories chosen. Mr. King was also instrumental in choosing the one hundred notable stories for the back of the book, again rising far above and beyond the call of duty. Thanks are also due for the work of Reem Abu-Libdeh, Nicole Angeloro, Michael Borum, Susanna Brougham, Ken Carpenter, Deborah Delosa, Carla Gray, and Janet Silver.

Back to the rather tired mountain-climbing metaphor. After a year spent looking out over vista after vista, I do not claim to hold any secret knowledge about what makes a story better than the rest. Having edited books for many years, I am often asked for recommendations, but every reader is different, thank God, and in the end I usually find myself asking more questions of the reader than I answer. Admittedly, mine is a job based on subjectivity — my own particular taste and that of the current guest editor. I do hope that the stories collected here provide as much inspiration, provocation, and sheer emotional and intellectual enjoyment to readers as they have to the editors.

I'm proud to report that I finally stopped counting the stories I read. Eventually I found myself reporting on their quality rather than my stunning endurance at climbing Mount Fiction. Maybe this job will be good for me after all. Maybe reading a lot of fiction, and a lot of excellent fiction, could humble a person just this much.

The stories chosen for this anthology were originally published between January 2006 and January 2007. The criteria for consideration are (1) original publication in nationally distributed American or Canadian periodicals; (2) publication in English by writers who are American or Canadian, or who have made the United States their home; and (3) original publication as short stories (excerpts of novels are not knowingly considered). A list of magazines consulted for this volume appears at the back of the book. Editors who would like short fiction from their publications to be considered for next year's edition should send them to Heidi Pitlor, c/o The Best American Short Stories, Houghton Mifflin Company, 222 Berkeley Street, Boston, MA 02116.

HEIDI PITLOR

Introduction

THE AMERICAN SHORT STORY is alive and well.

Do you like the sound of that? Me too. I only wish it were actually true. The art form *is* still alive — that I can testify to; I read hundreds of stories between December 2005 (when the first issues of '06 periodicals came out) and January 2007, and a great many of them were good stories. Some were *very* good. And some — you will find them in this book — seemed to touch greatness. Or so I felt, and in most cases Heidi Pitlor, my excellent coeditor, felt so too. But *well?* That's a different story.

I came by my hundreds — which now overflow several cardboard boxes known collectively as THE STASH — in a number of different ways. A few were recommended by writers and personal friends. A few more I downloaded from the Internet. Large batches were sent to me on a regular basis by the excellent Ms. Pitlor, probably the only person in America who read more short stories than I did in 2006 (in addition to reading all those stories, The Amazing Heidi also published a novel and gave birth to twins: a productive year by anyone's standards). But I've never been content to stay on the reservation, and so I also read a great many stories in magazines I bought myself, at bookstores and newsstands in Florida and Maine, the two places where I spend most of the year.

I want to begin by telling you about a typical short-story-hunting expedition at my favorite Sarasota mega-bookstore. Bear with me; there's a point to this.

I go in because it's just about time for the new issues of *Tin House* and *Zoetrope: All-Story,* two *Best American* mainstays over the years. I don't expect a new *Glimmer Train,* but it wouldn't surprise me to find one. There will certainly be a new issue of *The New Yorker*— that's the fabled automatic — and perhaps *Harper's Magazine.* No need to check out *Atlantic Monthly;* its editors now settle for publishing their own selections of fiction once a year and criticizing everyone else's the rest of the time. Jokes about eunuchs in the bordello come to mind, but I will suppress them. (And besides, the one fiction issue that *Atlantic* does publish is richly represented here.)

So into the bookstore I go, and what do I see first? A table filled with best-selling hardcover fiction at prices ranging from 20 to 40 percent off. James Patterson is represented, as is Danielle Steel, as is your faithful correspondent. Most of this stuff is disposable, but it's right up front, where it hits you in the eye as soon as you come in, and why? Because money talks and bullshit walks. These are the moneymakers and rent payers; these are the glamour ponies.

Bullshit — in this case that would be me — walks past the bestsellers, past trade paperbacks with titles like *Who Stole My Chicken?, The Get-Rich Secret,* and *Be a Big Cheese Now,* past the mysteries, past the auto repair manuals, past the remaindered coffee-table books (looking sad and thumbed-through with their red DISCOUNT PRICED stickers). I arrive at the Wall of Magazines, which is next door to the children's section. Over there, Story Time is in full swing. I sort of expect to hear *"Once upon a time there was a poor little girl who wanted to be a pop singer,"* but Goldilocks is still dealing with the Three Bears rather than prepping for *American Idol.* At least this year.

Meanwhile, I stare at the racks of magazines, and the racks of magazines stare eagerly back. Celebrities in gowns and tuxes, models in lo-rise jeans, luxy stereo equipment, talk-show hosts with can't-miss diet plans — they all scream *Buy me, buy me! Take me home and I'll change your life! I'll light it up!*

I can grab *The New Yorker* and *Harper's Magazine* while I'm still standing up. There's that, at least, although *New Yorker* fiction is almost always at the back of the book, hiding in the shadow of an Anthony Lane movie review, and the *Harper's* short story will be printed in type so small that by the time I finish it, I'll feel like my eyeballs have been sucked halfway out of their sockets. Still, I can make these selections without going to my knees like a school janitor trying to scrape a particularly stubborn wad of gum off the gym floor.

For the rest of what I need to complete this month's reading, I must assume exactly that position. I hope the young woman browsing *Modern Bride* won't think I'm trying to look up her skirt. I hope the young man trying to decide between *Starlog* and *Fangoria* won't step on me. I also hope some toddler bored with Story Time won't decide I want to play horsie and climb aboard.

So hoping, I crawl along the magazine section's last display module, making my selections from the lowest shelf, where neatness alone suggests few ever go. And here I find fresh treasure: not just *Zoetrope* and *Tin House* (both with wonderful covers those browsers unwilling to assume the position — or incapable of it — will never see) but also *Five Points* and *The Kenyon Review.* No *Glimmer Train,* but there's *American Short Fiction* . . . *The Iowa Review* . . . even an *Alaska Quarterly Review.* I stagger to my feet (the prospective modern bride gives me a suspicious look) and limp toward the checkout, clutching my trove and reaching for my wallet. I will gladly take my Frequent Shopper discount; the total cost of my six magazines runs to over eighty dollars. There are no discounts in the magazine section.

So think of me crawling along the floor of this big chain store's magazine section with my ass in the air and my nose to the carpet in order to secure that month's budget of short stories, and then ask yourself what's wrong with this picture. A better question — if you're someone who cares about fiction, that is — what could possibly be *right* with it?

Well . . . the magazines were *there,* at least. There's that.

We could argue all day about the reasons for fiction's out-migration from the eye-level shelves — people have. We could hold symposia, have panel discussions — people have done that too. We could marvel over the fact that Britney Spears has become a cultural icon, available at every checkout, while an American talent like William Gay labors in relative obscurity. We could, but let's not. It's almost beside the point, and besides — it hurts.

Instead, let us consider what the bottom shelf does to creative writers — especially the young ones, who are well represented in this volume — who still care, sometimes passionately, about the short story. What happens to a writer when he or she realizes that his or her audience is shrinking almost daily? Well, if the writer is worth his or her salt, he or she continues on nevertheless — because it's what God or genetics (possibly they are the same) has decreed, or out of sheer stubbornness, or maybe because it's such a kick to spin tales. Possibly a combination. And all that's good.

What's not so good is that writers — even those who claim to spurn Shakespeare's bubble reputation — write for whatever audience is left. In too many cases, that audience happens to consist of other writers and would-be writers who are reading the various literary magazines (and *The New Yorker,* of course; the holy grail of the young fiction writer) not to be entertained but to get an idea of what sells there. And this kind of reading isn't *real* reading, the kind where you just can't wait to find out what happens next (think "Youth," by Joseph Conrad, or "Big Blonde," by Dorothy Parker). It's more like copping-a-feel reading. There's something *ucky* about it.

In 2006 I read scores of stories that felt . . . not quite dead on the page, I won't go that far, but *airless,* somehow, and self-referring. These stories felt show-offy rather than entertaining, self-important rather than interesting, guarded and self-conscious rather than gloriously open, and — worst of all — written for editors and teachers rather than for readers. The chief reason for all this, I think, is that bottom shelf. It's tough for writers to write (and editors to edit) when faced with a shrinking audience of readers-for-pure-pleasure. Once, in the days of the old *Saturday Evening Post,* short fiction was a stadium act; now it can barely fill a coffeehouse on Saturday night, and often performs in the company of nothing more than an acoustic guitar and a mouth organ. I read dozens of short stories that felt airless, and why not? When circulation — to use a word particularly apropos when discussing magazines — falters, the air in the room gets stale.

And yet.

I read plenty of kick-ass stories this year. There isn't a single one in this book (or in the Roll of Honor at the end) that didn't delight me, that didn't make me want to crow "Oh man, you *gotta* read this!" to someone (last year that someone was Heidi Pitlor; this year it's you). I knew it would be that way. That's why I took the job. Talent does more than come out; it *bursts* out, again and again, doing exuberant cartwheels while the band plays "Stars and Stripes Forever." I think of such disparate stories as Karen Russell's "St. Lucy's Home for Girls Raised by Wolves," John Barth's "Toga Party," and

"Wake," by the late Beverly Jensen, and I think — marvel, really — *They PAID me to read these! Are you KIDDIN' me???*

Talent can't help itself; it roars along in fair weather or foul, not sparing the fireworks. It gets emotional. It struts its stuff. In fact, that's its job. And if these stories have anything in common — anything that made them uniquely *my* Best American stories — it's that sense of emotional involvement, of flipped-out amazement. I look for stories that care about my feelings as well as my intellect, and when I find one that is all-out emotionally assaultive — like "Sans Farine," by Jim Shepard — I grab that baby and hold on tight. Do I want something that appeals to my critical nose? Maybe later (and, I admit it, maybe never). What I want to start with is something that comes at me full-bore, like a big hot meteor screaming down from the Kansas sky. I want the ancient pleasure that probably goes back to the cave: to be blown clean out of myself for a while, as violently as a fighter pilot who pushes the EJECT button in his F-111. I certainly don't want some fraidy-cat's writing school imitation of Faulkner, or some stream-of-consciousness bullshit about what Bob Dylan once called "the true meaning of a peach."

So — American short story alive? Check.

American short story well? Sorry, no, can't say so. Current condition stable, but apt to deteriorate in the years ahead.

Measures to be taken? I would suggest you start by reading these stories, part of a series that is still popular and discussed. They show how vital short stories can be when they are done with heart, mind, and soul by people who care about them and think they still matter. They *do* still matter, and here they are, liberated from the bottom shelf.

STEPHEN KING

LOUIS AUCHINCLOSS

Pa's Darling

FROM THE YALE REVIEW

PA'S DEATH, in the cold winter of 1960, at the age of eighty-seven, was a crucial event in the lives of his two daughters, but particularly for myself, the supposedly most loved, the adored Kate, the eldest. As I sit in my multichambered apartment, the last of my many wasted efforts to impress him, looking out on the strangely white and oddly dreary expanse of Central Park, with the newspaper clippings of his laudatory obituaries in my lap, it seems a timely if unsettling opportunity to review my own life, no longer, I can only hope, in the shadow of his, unless it will be even more so. For people, I know, always think of me not as the widow of the brilliant young attorney Sumner Shepard, gallantly dead in the 1940 fall of France, nor even as the present wife of Dicky Phelps, senior partner of his distinguished Wall Street law firm, but as the daughter of Lionel Hemenway, the great judge of the New York Court of Appeals, renowned sage and philosopher, author of provocative books on law and literature, and the witty deity of the Patroons Club. God rest his soul if it be capable of resting.

I have decided to write up this assessment of my past, to make a probably vain attempt to get it off my chest. Whether I shall ever show it, or to whom, I do not know as yet. I am sure, however, it will not be to my husband, fond of him as I am. Perhaps to my daughter. Or to a grandson, if I ever have one. But that needn't concern me now.

As I have already suggested, I was always supposed to be Pa's favorite daughter. He made a good deal of me, particularly before company; he liked to show me off — he was proud of my good looks, of what he called my "pale-faced, raven-haired beauty." But he was like a financial magnate showing off a master painting he has just acquired, inwardly confident that the owner of the picture is superior to both the work and its artist. There was always a distinct vein of sarcasm in his ebullient mirth. Did he really value me very much? Did he even value women very much? Oh, he had to make a fuss over them, of course; he had to be the gallant gentleman who elevated the fair sex to the skies and left them there, but when it came to a question of real work, the real thing . . . no, give him a man.

But I have now just learned that all of this may have been the cover-up of doubts as to his own masculinity. This exploded before me last night at a family gathering in this apartment. It erupted from what Uncle Jack Sherman, brother of my other, also now deceased, parent, told me when he and I, after dinner, were sitting apart from the others in a corner of my living room, discussing who among Pa's surviving friends and disciples might be the best qualified to write his biography.

After considering and discarding several names, Uncle Jack paused and glanced cautiously about the room, as if to be sure that none of the others was within earshot. This, I knew, was his usual prelude to some particularly odiferous piece of gossip. He was a tall, thin, rather emaciated old man, a lifetime bachelor, who wanted to bring down any man who had done more in life than he, which was almost everyone. He liked to pretend that he and I were the only truly sophisticated members of the family.

"The first job of your father's biographer," he told me emphatically, "will be to explain why he lived for so many years on such intimate terms with his wife's lover."

"Oh, Uncle Jack! That old canard! Surely you didn't believe it. Of your own sister?"

"My dear, I had it from Sam Pemberton himself. One night when he was in his cups."

"The filthy braggart! And you credited him?"

"I did not. At first. But when I warned your mother about what he was saying, she explained the whole matter to me in her own cool, measured way. Your father, it appeared, had become impotent while only in his forties. He had agreed to her finding an outlet to her very natural desires in this unconventional but by no means unique fashion. She assured me grimly that she would see to it that Sam Pemberton should hold his tongue in the future. And indeed he did, to the very day he died. He even became a teetotaler! And your mother pledged me to silence in your father's lifetime."

Some cousins at this point crossed the room to bid me good night. The party was over, and Uncle Jack departed, leaving me to my troubled thoughts.

Perhaps the strangest thing about Uncle Jack's revelation was that it gave me a nasty kind of exhilaration. Of course, I knew perfectly well that a certain number of family friends and relations believed that there had always been something more between Mother and Sam Pemberton than an *amitié amoureuse.* But my sister and I had both firmly repudiated the idea. That Mother, so tall and straight, so grave, so unbending, so somehow chastely beautiful, with her prematurely snow-white hair, her lineless face, high cheekbones, and noble brow, could ever have shared her couch with a man as unimpressive as Sam was unthinkable. Sam, however grinning and good-natured, however accommodatable, was still a balding, rotund little bachelor who taught French at a fashionable private day school for girls. We thought Mother liked him because he read Gallic plays and poems aloud with her and that Father put up with him because he listened, seemingly impressed, to Pa's monologues. It was true that he was a household fixture but such a harmless one!

And why should all this now titillate me when all three participants were dead? I suppose it is possible that I felt in Pa's humble acceptance of the eternal triangle some settling of an old score between him and me. He, who had been so superior, despite any effort he may have exerted to condescend, whose towering masculinity had seemed to relegate his daughters to a kind of mock respect and reverence, had in reality allowed a silly little man to be his pal, his constant houseguest, and the lover of his wife!

How the past now unreeled itself through my mind, like a film played backward! I saw Mother passing serenely through the years, calmly going about her domestic tasks, efficiently organizing the social gatherings that Pa required for an audience, attending to the myriad problems of complaining daughters, always in control of everything, yet always placidly aware of the respite that awaited her in the arms of her lively if diminutive bedmate. Mother was never unreasonable in her requirements; she rarely raised her voice because she rarely had to: there was something ineluctable in her tone and demeanor. Her daughters knew — and Pa knew — that she revered the rule of reason and that if ever reason was ousted by emotion in her house, she would simply walk out and never return.

I can remember a party that Dicky Phelps and I gave for a visiting English economist who expounded after dinner on the subject of a novel theory of taxation. Pa took extreme objection to some of his points and even heckled him, to the poor economist's obvious embarrassment. Mother at last spoke up in her fine, clear tone that everyone heard: "Lionel, if you make another objection, we're going home." That was the way she could do it, without a trace of anger or even criticism in her voice. And when Pa *did* make another crack, she simply rose, went over to him, and told him: "We're leaving now," and he followed her out of the room like a dog with its tail between its legs.

It was probably in the same fashion that she had put to him her proposed solution for their more intimate marital problem. I am sure that she never reproached him for his bullying manners at parties or for his sexual inadequacy; she simply took the steps she deemed appropriate for the situation at hand. She was always a realist, but one doesn't always relish so much realism in a wife or in a mother. Pa, of course, must have blamed himself for his impotence, if that was what it was. I don't think many men could have helped that, no matter how fiercely they told themselves it was not their fault. And I don't blame them. I even think I might have admired Pa more had he smothered Mother with a pillow, like Othello. What I suppose I resented was that, however small he may have come to think himself, he still thought he was bigger than me.

It was like him to overdo his role of *mari complaisant.* There was always something of the ham actor in him. Was it his way of recapturing the lead from his wife? Surely otherwise he wouldn't have made such a pal of Sam Pemberton. He wouldn't have invited him for long visits to our summer camp in Maine or made him a member of his elite men's discussion group, the "round table," at the Patroons Club. Was it even his way of taking Sam from Mother? What she thought of her lover and husband being such friends I cannot imagine. Perhaps it amused her. She would have been capable of that.

Sumner Shepard, my first husband, and the only real love of my life — which reminds me, I must hide this manuscript from Dicky Phelps, who is utterly amoral about reading things not addressed to him — was one of Pa's golden boys. He had been first in his class at Harvard Law and editor-in-chief of the *Review*, and on graduation could have gone to any of the great Wall Street firms (which, of course, he eventually did), but he chose instead to go first to Albany and clerk for a year for Pa. This was not, in 1927, considered the bright choice it is today, but Sumner was in love (there's no word more fitting) with the luminous prose of Pa's judicial opinions and yearned to sit at the great man's feet. And it was no surprise to anyone that Pa rejoiced in an esteem so flattering and reveled in a brilliant and handsome young assistant who saw, as he did, the law as great literature.

Pa stayed in Albany only while his court was sitting; the rest of the time, except for our Maine summers, he was in Manhattan in our East Side brownstone. In order to have Sumner available for discussions, particularly in the evening, he arranged for him to occupy a spare bedroom on the top floor whenever they worked late, as a result of which he was frequently present at our family board. I was attracted to him at once, for he was not only bright but beautiful. But at first I and my sister, Edith, were cast in the role of rather dumb listeners while he and Pa argued about law and Ma and Sam Pemberton, another constant guest, discussed French literature. Of course, my ears were open only to Sumner. To me the law was mere nitpicking, something men adored and women had little use for. But I noted that Pa and Sumner seemed to be looking for beauty, even when they worked on the draft of one of Pa's opinions; you might have thought they were carving a statue out of marble. I couldn't for the life of me see why it was such a big deal to dress up a dry legal opinion in purple prose. Who but other lawyers was going to read it, anyway?

I should make it clear that I was no philistine. If I cared too much for dancing parties and smart clothes, if I spent too many weekends visiting rich friends in chic resorts like the Hamptons, if I had a bit of a yen for gambling and casinos, I was still up on the latest novels and plays and served three afternoons a week as a docent at the Metropolitan Museum of Art. It was not from a lack of appreciation of the finer things in life that I found Pa and Sumner's ecstasy over some silly little phrase excessive.

Of course I had the ancient weapon of sex, and I decided it was time to wield it. I began to ease myself into their discussions. One night, when they were making rather heavy weather over how best and concisely they could phrase the excuse of a defendant who had severely damaged a plaintiff while pulling him out of a burning house through the jagged glass of a shattered window, not having noted that the same room had an open door to the outside, I had a bright idea.

"Peril blunts caution!" I suggested in one of my rare flashes. I had always been clever at parlor games.

"Peril blunts caution," Sumner repeated slowly and thoughtfully. He turned to Pa. "It's perfect! Just three words. Let's start the opinion with them."

"Out of the mouths of babes and sucklings!" Pa murmured approvingly, and he pulled out his notebook and jotted down my suggestion.

I didn't have to say another word, and I had the sense not to. I had gained Sumner's full attention, and that was all I needed. He looked at me; he really saw me, for perhaps the first time, and Pa thereafter got only his second glances. I won't say that I caught Sumner with three words, but they gave me a start. To keep up his image of the bright and thoughtful woman he had idealized for himself I had only to let him develop his own conception. I wouldn't have to do a thing until we were married. Then, of course, I could relax. Hasn't that been the story of millions of women?

We were married right after the completion of Sumner's year's clerkship with Pa and enjoyed a glorious honeymoon in Hawaii before he started work in the great law firm of Harris & Eyer of which he and his friend and ultimate successor to my hand, Dicky Phelps, were to become partners. Pa had wanted to keep him as his clerk for another year, and Sumner had wanted this too, but I had pointed out that we might as well get started on a career that would bring him eventually the income we were both going to need. It was the first time that I had to take a firm position in my share of the direction of our joint lives, and it was not by any means to be the last. Sumner always had a tendency to espouse the ideal as opposed to the practical, but he was at the same time generous and malleable, particularly with a woman he loved. And he certainly started by loving me. By loving me almost to distraction.

Yes, I'm getting to it. Getting to the point. Sumner in time discovered that he had attributed qualities to me that I did not have. He had assumed that I was much more my father's daughter than I really was, and I had certainly, at least until our marriage, done my best to sustain that illusion. I daresay he agreed that it was all very well, to some extent anyway, for a woman to be of the earth, but he had expected this to be counterbalanced by something more ethereal, and there was very little of the sky in my nature except the suspicion that those who claimed it bordered on the hypocritical. Yet I have to admit that he never breathed a word about this; he was always the perfect gentleman, and, yes, the perfect husband. I could nonetheless feel his concealed disillusionment at finding that I did not share my father's tastes and appreciations and that our life together was not going to be a joint search for all that was glorious and inspiring in the universe. However, he put the best possible face on it.

We never quarreled about it; we did not even talk about it. We had many friends, and we went out and about socially, at least on weekends, for he worked too hard to do so on weekdays, and we both loved and fussed over our only child, Gwendolyn. We were considered a well-matched, happy, and attractive couple, and to some extent we were. But now I think I can see that the reason he worked so hard was not only that he loved the practice of law, which he did, but because he wished to bring me the worldly success that he knew I wanted. At least, he may have generously thought, he could do that much for me.

And he did. He became a partner in the firm at twenty-nine, and it was evident to all that he was destined to be one of the leading lights of the New York bar and no doubt, when his fortune was made, a judge on a high court.

Oh no, I had nothing to complain about, but that never stops one from complaining. I fretted constantly at the notion that I was not the woman he had dreamed of, and tended more and more to resent the fact that he had presumed to have such a dream. I offer this memory of the kind of thing that used to exasperate me. It was on a night when Pa and Mother were dining at our place — just the four of us — and Sumner and Pa were discussing John Gielgud's performance as Hamlet over which they were both lyrically enthusiastic. Mother had preferred John Barrymore's earlier interpretation of the vengeful Dane, but they had almost violently disagreed with her.

"Nobody," Pa murmured in his most velvet tone, "has a voice

as musical as Gielgud's. The poet Alfred de Musset is supposed to have fainted dead away when he heard the divine Sarah utter that exquisite line in *Phèdre* with the two *accents circonflexes: 'Ariane ma soeur de quel amour blessée / Vous mourûtes aux bords où vous fûtes laissée.'* I felt almost that way in the final scene where the dying Hamlet addresses the staring onlookers: 'You that look pale and tremble at this chance / That are but mutes or audience to this act.'"

"Yes, what glorious lines those are!" Sumner exclaimed. "It is as if Hamlet is suddenly breaking out of the play and addressing not only the gaping Danish court but the audience at the Globe Theatre. We have been sitting on the edge of our chairs for two hours, and now, at last, at the end, we are with him!"

That was one of the times that I spoke up. "How can you both go on so about a simple sentence? One that anyone might have written. 'You that look pale.' What's so great about that? 'And tremble at this chance.' Oh, come off it, Sumner! And you too, Pa! It's really too silly to make so much of that."

Sumner said nothing, but Pa turned on me. "Aren't you exposing something of a tin ear, Kate? Though perhaps your reaction would have been shared by some of the great ladies of the Tudor court. I seem to see you as one of Holbein's pale, grave beauties playing the deadly game of power because it's the only game to play even if you end with your head on the block. Isn't Lady Macbeth one of them? Resolute, realistic, eager to shake her husband out of his inhibitions and fantasies? Of course, my sweet, I don't accuse you of murder."

"Lady Macbeth had no imagination," Mother commented. Mother would. "She could not foresee what guilt would do to either of them."

Of course, it was a crack at me. But Mother was wrong. I had quite enough imagination to see the flaw in my marriage.

The great grief of my life — at least as I have always tried to see it and make others see it — was Sumner's death as an officer in the British army in the evacuation of Dunkirk in that grim spring of 1940. But what I can now privately inscribe is that the blow to my pride was as heavy as that to my heart when I learned that Sumner had confided to my father but not to me all the tumult and agony of his decision to leave his wife and child and country to enlist in what was still a foreign war. To his "beloved Kate" he had presented only the "kinder and quicker" last-minute announcement of a fait accompli. Quicker it certainly was; kinder it was not.

Of course I had known that Sumner was following with the most intense interest every item of European news from the Munich Pact to the invasion of Poland and that he passionately believed that we should have been in the war from its start. And of course I was aware of his keenness for military training; he belonged not only to the Seventh Regiment but to the National Guard. But it never crossed my mind that he would do anything so rash as to desert his family and the great firm of which he was so valued a young partner to rush abroad to join a fight to which his nation was still neutral. He simply came home from the office one night, grim and tense, poured each of us a stiff drink, and told me he was leaving for Montreal on the morrow. He had already assigned all his work in the office to Dicky Phelps.

"I knew, dearest," he told me in a thick voice, "how violently you would have opposed me. I just couldn't face the argument. I can't now. For God's sake try to accept this. Tell yourself that you married a madman and let it go at that."

Well, for some time I *did* take it that way. After the first shock of his departure had worn off, I even began to take pride in what he had done. I was unique among my friends in actually having a soldier in the war. In the riotous discussions that soon broke out between the interventionists and the sponsors of "America First" I noisily joined the former and found myself seated proudly on the dais at pro-war rallies. Like Teddy Roosevelt I took "my stand at Armageddon to do battle for the Lord."

The elation so evoked helped me to endure the bleak news of Sumner's death from a strafing plane on a beach in northern France. I even gained a wide reputation for nobly accepting grief from a letter that I wrote to the *Times:* "In a day when many young men on this still unassaulted side of the Atlantic are asking why they should be concerned with ancient European animosities, it may be illuminating to cite the example of one who, without a word of reproach to those who felt otherwise, silently shouldered a gun and joined an alien army to fight for the patch of civilization we have left on the globe." Oh, yes, as the widow of one of the great war's first American victims, I had a fine role to play.

What changed all this for me was an article that Pa wrote for *The Atlantic Monthly* as a memorial tribute to Sumner. That it was a beautiful piece, nobly expressed, can be taken for granted. But the article revealed something that had, no doubt, been deliberately concealed from me: the long heart-to-heart talks that Pa had had with Sumner before he had given his blessing to his son-in-law's proposed enlistment in the British army.

Could anything have told more clearly that I was not of the intellectual or spiritual stature to share those Olympian conferences?

I had not been a widow for long before Dicky Phelps began to show me a marked attention. Dicky was not only Sumner's partner; he had been a law school classmate and a deeply admiring friend. Yet I had always been aware that, however loyal a pal Sumner was of Dicky — and Dicky's openly demonstrative nature inspired affection — he did not return Dicky's admiration to anything like the same degree. The circumstances of Dicky's divorce from his dull little first wife were probably responsible for this. Dicky had explained to Sumner, at the time both had been made partners in Harris & Eyer, that the improvement of his legal position called for a corresponding improvement in his social one and that his wife had failed to understand this. She had clung stubbornly to the old bunch from which he now sought to detach them, which had led ultimately to their separation and a bitter divorce.

It is certainly at times embarrassingly true that Dicky has always been absolutely shameless in admitting his social ambitions and the steps he is willing to take to effectuate them. But he honestly believes that they are shared by everyone and that it is perfectly proper to make no bones about them. And it's quite possible that he may be more often right than wrong in this assumption, but it nonetheless startles and sometimes shocks people. Pa used to say that Dicky was like a character in O'Neill's *Strange Interlude* who uttered the thoughts on his mind when he stood motionless on the stage and the thoughts that were socially acceptable when he moved.

Some people, like his first wife, deeply resented this trait in Dicky, but more found it amusing. It seemed so natural from this big, stalwart, black-haired, bushy eyebrowed, impressive male who embraced all the world with the same hearty candor. And of course Dicky, to boot, was a great corporation lawyer whose astute handling of the most complicated mergers and reorganizations was to carry him to leadership at the bar and the presidency of the New York State Bar Association.

Dicky virtually took charge of my widowhood. He telephoned me several times a week; he took me to plays and concerts; he sent me flowers and the newest books; he insisted that Sumner would have wanted me to enjoy a full and entertaining life. He showered with expensive gifts my eleven-year-old daughter, whose dislike of him he blandly ignored, and worshipfully cultivated the favor of my father, who made ribald fun of him. When he proposed that we should become lovers, and I at length agreed, it was as if he were paying the ultimate tribute to Sumner. But he proved himself as good a lover as he was a lawyer, and what could I better do than marry him? Which of course I did.

Mother, who was already ailing with the breast cancer that was to kill her, dealt me her final blow in her cheerful recognition that Dicky was just the man for me. Pa had his doubts, but he was fascinated by this new son-in-law. When Dicky told him frankly that he was postponing the wedding for two weeks so that his richest client who was abroad would be back in town to attend the small reception (small because of my widowhood), Pa said to me: "Imagine his telling *me* that reason! When he could have invented a dozen more innocuous ones! But that's Dicky all over; he puts things just as they are. Your man's unique, Kate. We should keep him in a jar!"

Yet Dicky seemed sublimely unconscious of the fact that Pa was laughing at him. When he heard Pa describe hilariously at a dinner party his first visit to the newly redecorated offices of Harris & Eyer, Dicky laughed as hard as the others. Yet Pa had said: "As I stepped into the reception hall where my son-in-law's handsome likeness hung in all its painted glory, I tottered and gasped. I had sunk knee-deep in carpet!"

But in the years that followed my marriage, Pa and Dicky's joshing relationship began to develop into something like a real friendship. Pa must have found some kind of consolation for the doubts that his frequent melancholy moods cast over even his fame, in the fulsome compliments of this big, bluff son-in-law who professed to deem his own accomplishments and wealth as only trivia in contrast to the golden law opinions of this great but meagerly salaried judge. Indeed, Dicky appeared to regard his greatest claim to notice his connection with my sire. And Pa, who was beginning to show his age and to repeat himself, who was, if the truth be told, already something of a garrulous bore at dinner parties, was depending more and more on the uncritical and vociferous support that he received from my spouse.

But did Dicky ever aspire to emulate or even comprehend Pa's never-ending search for beauty in words, in art, in music, in history, in philosophy? Never. He wished to be crowned by the Muses, without imbibing their products. He wanted success, but success in *all* its manifestations. The world might admire power and money, but it also esteemed the arts. By associating himself with Pa, might he not borrow a few rays of Pa's aura? To Dicky appearance and reality were the same. If he looked as if he had everything, why, then, he had everything. It was why he was perfectly happy. I had again been married to my father.

Dicky irritated me by taking on Pa's death as if he had lost his own father. He wore a long face for weeks and insisted on sporting the black tie and black armband that had gone out of fashion years before. I was just able to refrain from sarcastic comment until he stipulated that we should turn down an invitation to what promised to be a stimulating dinner party and to which I had particularly looked forward. "Really, Dicky, aren't you carrying things a bit far? It isn't as if we were being asked to a dance or some sort of jubilee. It's just a small circle of interesting friends sharing a few drinks and a meal. We'll be called hypocrites if we stay home on the excuse of mourning."

"Kate, I don't think you realize how broad a shadow your father's demise has cast over his family. Our friends, even our closest friends, tend to see us in relation to him. Therefore more in the way of mourning is expected of us."

"Do you think I don't know about that shadow? Haven't I spent my life in it?"

"Then you should know how to act."

"Acting is just the word for what you want me to do! Well, I'm going to that dinner party! With you or without you!"

"It may be acting for you, my dear. But it won't be for me. I feel as if some of the light had gone out of my life with your father's passing."

"Don't be more of an ass than God made you!"

Dicky at this rose from the breakfast table without a word and departed for his office. He will think things over as he always does, and when he comes home tonight he will utter no word on the subject. He has always been a great one at putting unpleasant things behind him. But I shall have a job to do in learning to live with his absurd faith that he enjoyed a unique accord with a father-in-law who actually found him an amiable fool. He is the second husband that my greedy parent has taken from me. Pa has done me two evil turns: he has made me feel unworthy of Sumner and worthy of Dicky. Why did he have to take out on me his bitterness over Mother's infidelity? Just because he was mortally afraid of her and I was the nearest available vulnerable woman?

JOHN BARTH

Toga Party

FROM FICTION

IF "DOC SAM" BAILEY — Dick Felton's long-time tennis buddy from over in Oyster Cove — were telling this Toga Party story, the old ex-professor would most likely have kicked it off with one of those lefty-liberal rants that he used to lay on his Heron Bay friends and neighbors at the drop of any hat. We can hear Sam now, going "Know what I think, guys? I think that if *you* think that the twentieth century was a goddamn horror show — two catastrophic world wars plus Korea and Vietnam plus assorted multimillion-victim genocides, purges, and pandemics plus the Cold War's three-decade threat of nuclear apocalypse plus whatever other goodies I'm forgetting to mention — then you ain't seen nothing yet, pals, 'cause the twenty-first is gonna be worse: no 'infidel' city safe from Jihadist nuking, 'resource wars' for oil and water as China and India get ever more prosperous and supplies run out, the ruin of the planet by overpopulation, the collapse of America's economy when the dollar-bubble bursts, and right here in Heron Bay Estates the sea level's rising from global warming even as I speak, while the peninsula sinks under our feet and the hurricane season gets worse every year. So really, I mean: What the fuck? Just as well for us Golden Agers that we're on our last legs anyhow, worrying how our kids and grandkids will manage when the shit really hits the fan, but also relieved that we won't be around to see it happen. Am I right?"

Yes, well, Sam: If you say so, as you so often did. And Dick and Susan Felton would agree further (what they could imagine their friend adding at this point) that for the fragile present, however, despite all the foregoing, we Heron Bay Estaters and others like us from sea to ever-less-shining sea are extraordinarily fortune-favored folks (although the situation could change radically for the worse before the close of this parenthesis): respectable careers behind us; most of us in stable marriages and reasonably good health for our age (a few widows and widowers, Doc Sam included at the time we tell of; a few disabled, more or less, and/or ailing from cancer, Parkinson's, MS, stroke, late-onset diabetes, early-stage Alzheimer's, what have you); our "children" mostly middle-aged and married with children of their own, pursuing their own careers all over the Republic; ourselves comfortably pensioned upper-middle-classers, enjoying what pleasures we can while we're still able — golf and tennis and travel, bridge games and gardening and other hobbies, visits to and from those kids and grandkids, entertaining friends and neighbors and being by them entertained with drinks and hors d'oeuvres and sometimes dinner as well at one another's houses or some restaurant up in nearby Stratford — and hosting or attending the occasional party.

There now: We've arrived at our subject, and since Sam Bailey's *not* the one in charge of this story, we can start it where it started for the Feltons: the late-summer Saturday when Dick stepped out before breakfast as usual in his PJs, robe, and slippers to fetch the morning newspaper from its box at the end of their driveway and found rubber-banded to their mailbox flag (as would sundry other residents of Rockfish Reach to theirs, so he could see by looking up and down their bend of Shoreside Drive) an elaborate computer-graphic invitation to attend Tom and Patsy Hardison's TOGA PARTY!!! two weeks hence, on "Saturnsday, XXIV Septembris" to inaugurate their just-built house at 12 Loblolly Court, one of several "keyholes" making off the Drive.

"Toga party?" he asked his wife over breakfast. The house computer-geek among her other talents, between coffee-sips and spoonfuls of blueberry-topped granola Susan was admiring the artwork on the Hardisons' invitation: ancient-Roman-looking wild-party frescoes scanned from somewhere and color-printed as background to the text. "What's a toga party, please?"

"Frat-house stuff, I'd guess," she supposed. "Like in that crazy *Animal House* movie from whenever? Everybody dressing up like for a whatchacallum . . ." Pointing to the fresco shot: "Saturnalia?"

"Good try," Doc Sam would grant her two weeks later, at the party: "Especially since today is, quote, 'Saturnsday.' But those anything-goes Saturnalia in ancient Rome were celebrated in December, so I guess *bacchanalia*'s the word we want — after the wine god Bacchus? And the singular would be *bacchanal*." Since Sam wasn't breakfasting with the Feltons, however, Dick replied that he didn't know beans about Saturnalia and Animal Houses, and went back to leafing through the *Baltimore Sun*.

"So are we going?" Sue wanted to know. "We're supposed to RSVP by this weekend."

"Your call," her husband said or requested, adding that as far as he knew, their calendar was clear for "Saturnsday, XXIV Septembris." But the Feltons of 1020 Shoreside Drive, he needn't remind her, while not recluses, weren't particularly social animals, either, compared to most of their Rockfish Reach neighborhood and for that matter the Heron Bay Estates development generally, to which they'd moved year-round half a dozen years back after Dick's retirement from his upper-mid-level management post in Baltimore and Susan's from her office administration job at her alma mater, Goucher College. To the best of his recollection, moreover, their wardrobes were toga-free . . .

His wife's guess was that any wraparound bed-sheet kind of thing would do the trick. She would computer-search *toga parties* after breakfast, she declared; her bet was that there'd be a clutch of Web sites on the subject. "It's all just *fun*, for pity's sake! And when was the last time we went to a neighborhood party? Plus I'd really like to see the inside of that house of theirs. Wouldn't you?"

Yeah, well, her husband supposed so. Sure.

That less-than-eager agreement earned him one of Sue's See-Me-Being-Patient? looks: eyes rolled ceilingward, tongue checked between right-side molars. Susan Felton was a half-dozen years younger than Richard — not enough to matter much in her latter sixties and his midseventies, after forty-plus years of marriage — but, except at work, he inclined to be the more passive partner, content to follow his wife's lead in most matters. Over the past year or two, though, as he'd approached and then attained the three-quarter-century mark, he had by his own acknowledgment become rather stick-in-the-muddish, not so much *depressed* by the prospect of their imminent Old Age as *subdued* by it, de-zested, his get-up-and-go all but gotten up and gone, as he had observed to be the case with others at his age and stage (though by no means all) among their limited social acquaintance.

In sum (he readily granted whenever he and Sue spoke of this subject, as lately they'd found themselves doing more often than formerly), the chap had yet to come to terms with his fast-running mortal span: the inevitable downsizing from the house and grounds and motorboat and cars that they'd taken years of pleasure in; the physical and mental deterioration that lay ahead for them; the burden of caregiving through their decline; the unimaginable loss of life partner. . . . The prospect of his merely ceasing to exist, he would want it understood, did not in itself much trouble him. He and Sue had enjoyed a good life indeed, all in all. If their family was less close than some that they knew and envied, neither was it dysfunctional: Cordially Affectionate is how they would describe the prevailing tone of their relations with their grown-up "kids" and growing-up grandkids; they could wish it better, but were gratified that it wasn't worse, like some others they knew. No catastrophes in their life story thus far: Dick had required bypass surgery in his midsixties and Sue an ovarectomy and left-breast lumpectomy in her mid-menopause. Both had had cataracts removed, and Dick had some macular degeneration, luckily of the less aggressive "dry" variety, and mild hearing loss in his left ear, as well as being constitutionally overweight despite periodic attempts at dieting. Other than those, no serious problems in any life department, and a quite satisfying curriculum vitae for each of them. More and more often recently, Richard Felton found himself wishing that somewhere down the road they could just push a button and make themselves and their abundant possessions simply disappear — *Poof!* — the latter transformed into equitably distributed checks in the mail to their heirs, with love . . .

These cheerless reflections had been center-staged lately by the business that he readdressed at his desk after breakfast: the periodic review of his and Susan's Last Will and Testament. Following his routine midyear update of their computer-spreadsheet Estate Statement and another, linked to it, that Susan had designed for estimating the distribution of those assets under the current provisions of their wills, it was Dick's biennial autumn custom, in even-numbered years, to review these benefactions, then to call to Sue's attention any that struck him as having become perhaps larger or smaller than they ought to be and to suggest appropriate percentage adjustments, as well as the addition or deletion of beneficiaries in the light of changed circumstances or priorities since the previous go-round: Susan's dear old all-girls prep school, e.g., had lately closed its doors for keeps, so there went Article D of Item Five in her will, which bequeathed to it 3 percent of her Net Residual Estate after funeral costs, executors' fees, estate taxes, and other expenses. Should she perhaps reassign that bequest to the Avon County Public Library, of which she and Dick made frequent use? Estate lawyers' fees being what they are, they tried to limit such emendations to codicil size, if possible, instead of will-redrafting size. But whatever the satisfaction of keeping their affairs in order, it was not a cheery chore (in odd-numbered-year autumns, to spread out the morbidity, they reviewed and updated their separate Letters to Their Executors). The deaths in the year just past of Sam Bailey's so-lively wife, Ethel (cervical cancer), and of their own daughter Katie's father-in-law out in Colorado (aneurysm) — a fellow not even Dick's age, the administration of whose comparatively simple estate had nevertheless been an extended headache for Katie's husband — contributed to the poignancy of the current year's review. Apart from the dreadful prospect of personal bereavement (poor old Sam!), he had looked in vain for ways to minimize further the postmortem burden on their grown-up daughter and son, whom they most certainly loved, but to whom alas in recent years they'd grown less than ideally close both personally and geographically. Dick couldn't imagine, frankly, how he would survive without his beloved and indispensable Susan: less well than Sam Bailey without Ethel, for sure, whose lawyer son and CPA daughter-in-law lived and worked in Stratford, attentively monitored the old fellow's situation and condition, and frequently included him in family activities.

For her part, Suse often declared that the day Dick died would be the last of her own life as well, although by what means she'd end it, she hadn't yet worked out. Dick Jr. and Katie and their spouses would just have to put their own lives on hold, fly in from Chicago and St. Louis, and pick up the pieces. Let them hate her for it if they chose to; she wouldn't be around to know it, and they'd be getting a tidy sum for their trouble. "So," she proposed perkily when the couple reconvened at morning's end to make lunch and plan their afternoon: "Let's eat, drink, and be merry at the Hardisons' on X-X-I-V Septembris, since tomorrow et cetera?"

"Easy enough to say," her grave-spirited spouse replied. "But whenever I hear it said, I wonder how anybody could have an appetite for their Last Supper." On the other hand, he acknowledged, here they were, as yet neither dead, disabled, nor devastated like the city of New Orleans by Hurricane Katrina just a week or so since: No reason why they *shouldn't* go to the party, he supposed — if they could figure out what to wear.

Over sandwiches and diet iced tea on their waterside screened porch, facing the narrow tidal creek of Rockfish Reach agleam in end-of-summer sunshine, "No problem," Sue reported. She'd been on the Web, where a Google search of *toga party* turned up no fewer than 266,000 entries; the first three or four were enough to convince her that anything they improvised would do the trick. It was, as she'd suspected, an old fraternity-house thing, made popular among now-middle-aged Baby Boomers by John Belushi's 1978 film version of *The National Lampoon's Animal House.* One could make or buy online "Roman" costumes as elaborate as any in such movies as *Ben Hur* and *Gladiator,* or simply go the bed-sheet-and-sandals route that she mentioned before. Leave it to her; she'd come up with something. Meanwhile, could they be a little less Gloom-and-Doomy, for pity's sake, and count their blessings?

Her husband thanked her, wholeheartedly, for taking charge of the matter, and promised both her and himself to try to brighten up a bit and make the most of whatever quality time remained to them.

Which amounted (he then honored his promise by *not* going on to say), with luck, to maybe a dozen years. No computer-adept like his wife, Dick nonetheless had his own desktop machine in his study, on which between his more serious morning desk chores it had occurred to him to do a little Web search himself. *Life expectancy,* entered and clicked, had turned up nearly fourteen *million* entries (more than a lifetime's worth of reading, he'd bet), among the first half-dozen of which was a questionnaire-calculator — age, ethnicity, personal and family medical histories, etc. — that, once he'd completed it, predicted his "median quartile" age at death to be 89.02 years. In (very!) short, fourteen to go, barring accident, although of course it could turn out to be more or fewer.

Only a dozen-plus Septembers left: how assimilate it? On the one hand, the period between birth and age fourteen had seemed to him of epical extent, and that between fourteen and twenty-eight scarcely less so: nonexistence to adolescence! Adolescence to maturity, marriage, and parenthood! But his thirties, forties, and fifties had passed rather more swiftly decade by decade, no doubt because his adult life changes were fewer and more gradual than those of his youth. And his early sixties — when he'd begun the gradual reduction of his office workload and the leisurely search for a weekend retreat somewhere on Maryland's Eastern Shore that could be upgraded to a year-round residence at his and Sue's retirement — seemed the day before yesterday instead of twelve-plus years ago.

So: Maybe fourteen years left — and who knew how many of those would be healthy and active? "Eat, drink, and be merry" indeed! About what?

Well, for starters, about not being a wiped-out refugee from the storm-blasted Gulf Coast, obviously, or a starving, gang-raped young African mother in Darfur. "*God's only excuse is that He doesn't exist,*" Sam Bailey liked to quote some famous person as having said (Oscar Wilde? Bertrand Russell? Don't ask Dick Felton, who anyhow regarded it as a pretty lame excuse). But here they were, he and his long-beloved, on a warm and gorgeous mid-September afternoon in an attractive and well-maintained neighborhood on a branch of a creek off a river off a bay luckily untouched (so far) by that year's busier-than-ever Atlantic hurricane season; their lawn and garden and crape myrtles flourishing; their outboard runabout, like themselves, good for a few more spins before haul-out time; their immediately pending decisions nothing more mattersome than whether to run a few errands in Stratford or do some outdoor chores on the property before Sue's golf and Dick's tennis dates scheduled for later in the day.

So they would go to the goddamn party, as Dick scolded himself for terming it out of Susan's hearing. Some hours later, at a break in whacking the yellow Wilson tennis balls back to Sam Bailey on the Heron Bay Club's courts (since Ethel's death, Sam had lost interest in playing for points, but he still enjoyed a vigorous hour's worth of back-and-forthing a couple of times a week, which had come to suit Dick just fine), he mentioned the upcoming event: that it would be his and Sue's first toga party, and that they'd be going more to have a look at their new neighbors' Loblolly Court mansion and get to know its owners than out of any interest in funny-costume parties. To his mild surprise, he learned that Sam — although an Oyster Cover rather than a Rockfish Reacher — would be there too, and was in fact looking forward to "XXIV Septembris." As a longtime board member of the Club, Sam had met Tom and Patsy Hardison when they'd applied for membership even before commencing their house construction. And while he himself at age eighty could do without the faux-Roman high jinks, his Ethel had relished such foolery and would have loved nothing more than another toga party, if the goddamn nonexistent Almighty hadn't gifted her with goddamn cancer.

They resumed their volleying, until Sam's right arm and shoulder had had enough and the area behind Dick's breastbone began to feel the mild soreness-after-exertion that he hadn't yet mentioned either to Susan or to their doctor, although he'd been noticing it for some months. He *had* shared with both his life partner and his tennis partner his opinion that an ideal way to "go" would be by a sudden massive coronary on the tennis court upon his returning one of Sam's tricky backhand slices with a wham-o forehand topspin. "Don't you *dare* die first!" his wife had warned him; all Sam had said was "Make sure we get a half-hour's tennis in before you kick."

"So tell me about toga parties," Dick asked him as they packed up their rackets and balls, latched the chainlink entrance gate behind them, and swigged water from the drinking fountain beside the tennis-court restrooms. "What kind of high jinks should we expect?"

The usual, Sam supposed: like calling out something in Latin when you first step into the room . . .

"Latin? I don't know any damn Latin!"

"Sure you do: *Ave Maria? Tempus fugit?* After that, and some joking around about all the crazy getups, it's just a friendly cocktail-dinner party for the next couple hours, till they wind it up with some kinky contest games with fun prizes. Susan will enjoy it; maybe even *you* will. *Veni, vidi, vici!*"

"Excuse me?"

"You're excused. But *go,* for Christ's sake. Or Jove's sake, whoever's." Thumbing his shrunken chest, "*I'm* going, goddamn it, even though the twenty-fourth is the first anniversary of Ethel's death. I promised her and the kids that I'd try to maintain the status quo as best I could for at least a year — no major changes, one foot in front of the other, et cetera — and then we'd see what we'd see. So I'm going for her sake as much as mine. There're two more passwords for you, by the way: *status quo* and *et cetera.*"

Remarkable guy, the Feltons agreed at that afternoon's end, over gin and tonics on the little barbecue patio beside their screened porch. In Dick's opinion, at least, that no-major-changes-for-at-least-the-first-year policy made good sense: Keep everything as familiar and routine as possible while the shock of bereavement was so raw and overwhelming . . .

But "Count me out," said Sue: "Twenty-four hours tops, and then it's So long, Susie-Q. But what I *really* want is the Common Disaster scenario, thanks" — a term they'd picked up from their estate lawyer over in the city, who in the course of this latest revision of their wills had urged them to include a new estate-tax-saving gimmick that neither of them quite understood, although they quite trusted the woman's professional advice. Their wills had formerly stipulated that in the event of their dying together (as in a plane crash or other "common disaster") in circumstances such that it could not be determined which of them predeceased the other, it would be presumed that Dick died before Susan, and their wills would be executed in that order, he leaving the bulk of his estate to her and she passing it on to their children and other assorted beneficiaries. But inasmuch as virtually all their assets — cars, house, bank accounts, securities portfolio — were jointly owned (contrary to the advice of their lawyer, who had recommended such tax-saving devices as bypass trusts and separate bank and stock accounts, not to the Feltons' taste), the Common Disaster provision had been amended in both wills to read that "each will be presumed to have survived the other." It would save their heirs a bundle, they'd been assured, but to Dick and Sue it sounded like Alice in Wonderland logic. How could each of them be presumed to have survived the other?

"Remind me to ask Sam that at the party, okay? And if he doesn't know, he can ask his lawyer son for us."

And so to the party they all went, come "XXIV Septembris," despite the unending, antifestive news reports from the Louisiana coast: the old city of New Orleans, after escaping much of the expected wind damage from Hurricane Katrina, virtually destroyed by its levee-busting storm surge and consequent flooding; and now Hurricane Rita tearing up the coastal towns of Mississippi even as the Feltons made their way, along with other invitees, to the Hardisons'. The evening being overcast, breezy, and cool compared to that week's earlier Indian-summer weather, they opted reluctantly to drive instead of walk the little way from 1020 Shoreside Drive to 12 Loblolly Court — no more than three city blocks, although of course Heron Bay Estates wasn't laid out in blocks — rather than wear cumbersome outer wraps over their costumes. The decision to go once made, Dick had done his best to get into the spirit of the thing, and was not displeased with what they'd improvised together: for him, leather sandals, a brown-and-white-striped Moroccan caftan picked up as a souvenir ten years earlier on a Mediterranean cruise that had made a stop in Tangiers, and on his balding gray head a faux-laurel wreath that Susan had found in the party-stuff aisle of their Stratford supermarket. Plus a silk-rope belt (meant to be a drapery tieback) on which he'd hung a Jamaican machete in its decoratively tooled leather sheath, the implement acquired on a Caribbean vacation even longer ago than the caftan trip. Okay, not exactly ancient Roman, but sufficiently oddball-exotic — and the Caesars' empire, as they recalled, had in fact extended to North Africa: Antony and Cleopatra, *et cetera.* As for Sue, in their joint opinion she looked Cleopatra-like herself in her artfully folded and tucked bed sheet (a suggestion from the Web, with detailed instructions on how to fold and wrap), belted like her husband's caftan with a drapery tieback to match his, her feet similarly sandaled, and on her head a sleek black costume wig from that same supermarket aisle, with a tiara-halo of silver foil stars.

Carefully, not to muss their outfits, they climbed into "her" Toyota Solara convertible, its top raised against the evening chill ("his" car was their VW Passat wagon, although both vehicles were titled jointly) — and got no farther than halfway to Loblolly Court before they had to park it and walk the remaining distance anyhow, such was the crowd of earlier-arrived sedans, vans, and SUVs lining the road, their owners either already at the party or, like the Feltons, strolling their costumed way toward #12.

"Would you look at that?" Dick said when they turned into the tree-lined keyhole drive at the head whereof shone the Hardisons' mega-McMansion: not a neo-Georgian or plantation-style manor like its similarly new and upscale neighbors, but a great rambling beige stucco affair — terra-cotta-tiled roof, great arched windows flanked by spiral pilasters — resplendent with lights inside and out, including floodlit trees and shrubbery, its palazzo design more suited, in the Feltons' opinion, to Venice or booming south Florida than to Maryland's Eastern Shore. "How'd it get past Heron Bay's house-plan police?" Meaning the Community Association's Design Review Board, whose okay was required on all building and landscaping proposals. Susan's guess was that Tidewater Communities, Inc., the developer of Heron Bay Estates and other projects on both shores of the Chesapeake, might have jiggered it through in hopes of attracting more million-plus-dollar house builders to HBE's several high-end detached-home neighborhoods, like Spartina Pointe. She, too, thought the thing conspicuously out of place in Rockfish Reach, but "You know what they say," she declared. *"De gustibus non est disputandum"* — her chosen party password, which she was pleased to have remembered from prep-school days. "Is that the Gibsons, ahead of us?"

It was, Dick could affirm, when the couple — she in a bed-sheet toga like Susan's, but less appealing, given her considerable heft; he wearing what looked rather like a white hospital-gown set off by some sort of gladiator thing around his waist and hips — passed under a pair of tall floodlit pines flanking the entrance walkway. Hank and Becky Gibson, Oyster Covers like Sam Bailey, whom the Feltons knew only casually from the club, he being the golfer and she the tennis player in their household.

"Et tu, Brute!" Sue called out (she really had been doing her homework; that "Bru-tay" phrase sounded familiar, but Dick couldn't place it). The Gibsons turned, laughed, waved, and waited; the foursome then joked and teased their way up the stone walk beside the Eurocobble driveway to #12's massive, porte-cochèred main entrance: a two-tiered platform with three wide, curved concrete steps up to the first marble-tiled landing and another three to the second, where one of the tall, glass-paned, dark-wood-paneled double doors stood open and a slender, trim-toga'd woman, presumably their hostess, was greeting and admitting several other arrivals.

"A miniskirt toga?" Hank Gibson wondered aloud, for while the costume's thin white top had a fold-and-wrap toga look to it, below the elaborately figured multi-paneled belt were a short white pleated skirt and sandal-lacings entwined fetchingly almost to her knees. "*Amo amas amat!*" he then called ahead. The couple just entering turned and laughed, as did the hostess. Then Sam Bailey — whom the Feltons now saw stationed just inside the door in a white terrycloth robe of the sort provided in better-grade hotel rooms, belted with what appeared to be an army surplus cartridge belt and topped with a defoliated wreath that looked a bit like Jesus' crown of thorns — called back "*Amamus amatis amant!*" and gestured them to enter.

Their sleek-featured hostess — more Cleopatran even than Sue, with her short, straight, glossy dark hair encircled by a black metal serpent band, its asplike upper body rising from her forehead as if to strike — turned her gleaming smile now to them and extended her hand, first to Susan. "Hi! I'm Patsy Hardison. And you are?"

"Sue and Dick Felton," Sue responded, "from around the bend at Ten-Twenty Shoreside? What a beautiful approach to your house!"

"And a house to match it," Dick added, taking her hand in turn.

"I *love* your costumes!" their hostess exclaimed politely. "So *imaginative!* I know we've seen each other at the club, but Tom and I are still sorting out names and faces and addresses, so please bear with us." As other arrivals were now gathering behind them, she explained to all hands that after calling out their passwords to Sam Bailey, whom she and Tom had appointed to be their Centurion at the Gate, they would find nametags at a table in the foyer, just beyond which her husband would show them the way to the refreshments. "Passwords, please? Loud and clear for all to hear!"

"*De gustibus non est disputandum!*" Sue duly proclaimed, hoping her hosts wouldn't take that proverb as any sort of criticism. Dick followed with "*Ad infinitum!*" — adding in a lower voice to Sam, who waved them in, "or *ad nauseam,* whatever. Cool outfit there, Sam."

"The Decline and Fall of the You-Know-What," their friend explained, and kissed Sue's cheeks. "Aren't *you* the femme fatale tonight, excuse my French. Ethel would've loved that getup."

Hugging him, "I can't *believe* she's not in the next room!" Sue said. "Sipping champagne and nibbling hors d'oeuvres!"

"Same here," the old fellow admitted, his voice weakening until he turned his head aside, stroked his thin white beard, and cleared his throat. "But she couldn't make it tonight, alas. So carpe diem, guys."

Although they weren't certain of the Latin, its general sense was clear enough. They patted his shoulder, moved on to the nametag table on one side of the marble-floored, high-ceilinged entry hall, found and applied their elegantly lettered and alphabetically ordered stick-on labels, and were greeted at the main living room step-down by their host, a buff and hearty-looking chap in his late fifties or early sixties wearing a red-maned silver helmet, a Caesars Palace T-shirt from Las Vegas, a metallic gladiator-skirt over knee-length white Bermuda shorts, and leather sandals, even higher-laced than his wife's, on his dark-haired, well-muscled legs. With an exaggeratedly elaborate kiss of Susan's hand and a vise-hard squeeze of Dick's, *"Dick and Susan Felton!"* he announced to the room beyond and below, having scanned their name stickers. "Welcome to our humble abode!"

"Some humble," Dick said, his tone clearly impressed, and Sue added, "It's *magnificent!*"

As indeed it was: the enormous, lofty-ceilinged living room (what must it cost to heat that space in the winter months? Dick wondered), its great sliding glass doors open to a large roofed and screened terrace ("Lanai," Susan would later correct him) beyond which an even larger pool/patio area extended, tastefully landscaped and floodlit, toward the tidal covelet where the Hardisons' trawler yacht was docked. A suitably toga'd pianist tinkled away at the grand piano in one corner of the multi-couched and -cocktail-tabled room; out on the lanai a laureled bartender filled glasses while a mini-toga'd, similarly wreathed young woman moved among the guests with platters of hors d'oeuvres.

"Great neighborhood, too," Dick added, drawing Sue down the step so that their host could greet the next arrivals. "We know you'll like living here."

With a measured affability, "Oh, well," Tom Hardison responded: "Pat and I don't actually *live* here, but we do enjoy cruising over from Annapolis on weekends and holidays. Y'all go grab yourselves a drink now, and we'll chat some more later before the fun starts, okay?"

"Aye, aye, *sir,*" Dick murmured to Susan as they dutifully moved on. "Quite a little weekend hideaway!"

She too was more or less rolling her eyes. "But they seem like a friendly enough couple. I wonder where the money comes from."

From their husband-and-wife law firm over in the state capital, one of their costumed neighbors informed them as they waited together at the bar: Hardison and Hardison, very "in" with the governor and other influential Annapolitans. What was more, they had just taken on their son, Tom Junior, as a full partner, and his younger sister, just out of law school, as a junior partner: sort of a family 4-H Club. And had the Feltons seen the name of that boat of theirs?

"Not yet."

"Stroll out and take a look." To the bartender: "Scotch on the rocks for me, please."

Susan, "White wine spritzer?" And Dick, "I'll have a glass of red."

The barman smiled apologetically. "No reds, I'm afraid. On account of the carpets?" And shrugged: not *his* house rule . . .

"Mm *hm.*" The living room wall-to-wall, they now noted, was indeed a gray so light as to be almost white: poor choice for a carpet color, in Sue's opinion — and for that matter, what color *wouldn't* be stained by a spilled merlot or cabernet? But *de gustibus, de gustibus.* "So make it gin and tonic, then," Dick supposed.

"*Ars longa!*" a late-arriving guest called from the hallway.

Sam Bailey, behind them, asked the bartender for the same, predicted that that new arrival was George Newett, from the College, and called back, "*Vita brevis est!*" His own *vita,* however, he added to the Feltons, had gotten *longa* without Edith than he wanted it to be. Raising his glass in salute, "Fuck life. But here we are, I guess. *E pluribus unum.* Shall we join Trimalchio's Feast?"

The allusion, or whatever, escaped them, but to make room for other thirsters they moved away from the bar, drinks in hand, toward the groups of guests chatting at the hors d'oeuvres tables at the lanai's other end, and out on the pool deck, and in what Susan now dubbed the Great Room. As Sam had foretold, once the admission ritual was done the affair settled into an agreeable Heron Bay neighborhood cocktail party, lavish by the standards of Rockfish Reach and Oyster Cove if perhaps not by those of Spartina Pointe, and enlivened by the guests' comments on one another's costumes, which ranged from the more or less aggressively noncompliant (the bearded fellow identified by Doc Sam as "George Newett from the College" wore a camouflage hunting jacket over blue jeans, polo shirt, and Adidas walking shoes; his wife an African dashiki), through the meant-to-be-humorous, like Tom Hardison's casino T-shirt and Dick Felton's caftan-cum-machete, to the formally elaborate, like Patricia Hardison's and some others' store-bought togas or gladiator outfits. Although not, by their own acknowledgment, particularly "people" people, husband and wife both found it a pleasant change from their customary routines to chat in that handsome setting with their neighbors and other acquaintances and to meet acquaintances of those acquaintances; to refresh their drinks and nibble at canapés as they asked and were asked about one another's health, their former or current careers, their grown children's whereabouts and professions, their impression of "houses like this" in "neighborhoods like ours," their opinion of the Bush administration's war in Iraq (careful stepping here, unless one didn't mind treading on toes), and their guesses on whether Maryland's Chesapeake Bay, in places still recovering from the surge-floods of Tropical Storm Isabel two years past, might yet be hurricaned in the current superactive season.

"Just heard that Rita's blowing the bejesus out of Gulfport and Biloxi. I swear."

"Anybody want to bet they'll use up the alphabet this year and have to start over? Hurricane Aaron? Tropical storm Bibi?"

"As in B. B. King?"

"C. C. Ryder? Dee Dee Myers?"

"Who's that?"

"E. E. Cummings?"

"Who's *that*?"

"I can't get over those poor bastards in New Orleans: why didn't they get the hell out instead of hanging around and looting stores?"

"Did you hear the one about Bush's reply when a reporter asked his opinion of *Roe versus Wade?* 'I don't care how they get out of New Orleans,' says W, 'as long as it doesn't cost the government money.'"

"*George Newett,* is it? At my age, I wish *everybody* wore nametags . . ."

"On their foreheads. Even our grandkids."

"*Love* that headband, by the way, Pat: right out of *Antony and Cleopatra*!"

"Why, thanks, Susan. Tom's orders are that if some joker says I've got my head up my *asp,* I should tell them to kiss it. Now is that nice?"

"Some cool djellaba you've got there, Dick."

"*Caftan,* actually. Some cool yacht you've got out there! Is that your RV too, the big shiny guy parked down by your dock?"

It was, Tom Hardison readily acknowledged. In simple truth, he and Pat enjoyed *owning* things. Owning and doing! "What the hell, you only get one go-round."

George Newett's wife (also from the College, and with a last name different from her husband's) explained to Susan, who had asked about Sam Bailey's earlier reference, that Trimalchio's Feast is a famous scene in the first-century *Satyricon* of Petronius Arbiter: an over-the-top gluttonous orgy that became a sort of emblem of the Roman Empire's decadence. "The mother of all toga parties, I guess. But talk about 'over the top' . . ." She eye-rolled the sumptuous setting in which they stood. The two women agreed, however, that Patricia Hardison really did seem to be, in the best sense, *patrician:* upscale but good-humored, friendly, and without affectation; competent and self-assured but in no wise overbearing; as Amanda Todd put it (i.e., Mrs. George Newett, poet and professor, from over in Blue Crab Bight), superior, but not capital-*S* Superior.

"I like her," Susan reported to her husband when they next crossed paths in their separate conversational courses. "First poet I ever met, actually. Is her husband nice?"

Dick shrugged. "Retired from the College. Describes himself as a failed-old-fart writer. But at least he's not intimidating."

"Unlike . . . ?"

Her husband nodded toward their host, who was just then proclaiming to the assembled "friends, Romans, and countrymen" that the dinner buffet (under a large tent out beside the pool deck) was now open for business, and that Jove helps those who help themselves. "After dinner, game and prize time!"

En route past them toward the bar, "Me," Sam Bailey said, "I'm going to have me another G and T. D'ja see their boat's name? Bit of a mouthful, huh?"

Sue hadn't. She worried aloud that Doc Sam was overdoing the booze, maybe on account of his wife's death-day anniversary; hoped he wouldn't be driving home after the party. "I doubt if he cares," Dick said: "*I* sure wouldn't, in his position." The name of the boat, by the way, he added, was *Plaintiff's Complaint.* Which reminded him: Since both Hardisons were lawyers, maybe he'd ask Emperor Tom about that "each survives the other" business in their wills, and Sue could ask her new pal Cleopatra. Or was it Sheba?

"Come on," his wife chided: "They're friendly people who just happen to be rich as shit. Let's do the buffet."

They did it, Sue chatting in her lively/friendly way with the people before and after them in the help-yourself line and with the caterers who sliced and served the roast beef au jus and breast of turkey; Dick less forthcoming, as had lately more and more become his manner, but not uncordial, and appreciative of his mate's carrying the conversational ball. Time was when they'd both been more outgoing: In their forties and fifties they'd had fairly close *friends,* of the sort one enjoys going out with to a restaurant or movie. By age sixty, after a couple of career moves, they had only office lunch colleagues, and since their retirement not even those; just cordial over-the-fence-chat neighbors, golf/tennis partners, and their seldom more than annually visited or visiting offspring. A somewhat empty life, he'd grant, but one that, as afore-established, they enjoyed more than not, on balance — or *had* enjoyed, until his late brooding upon its inevitably approaching decline, even collapse, had leached his pleasure in it.

So "I'll fetch us another glass of wine," he said when they'd claimed two vacant places at one of the several long tables set up under the tent. And added in a mutter, "Wish they had some *red* to go with this beef."

"Shh. Mostly club soda in mine, please." Then "Hi," she greeted the younger couple now seating themselves in the folding chairs across from theirs: "Dick and Sue Felton, from down the road."

"Judy and Joe Barnes," the man of them replied as they scanned one another's nametags: "Blue Crab Bight." He extended his hand first to seated Susan and then to Dick, who briefly clasped it before saying "Going for a refill; back in a minute."

Speaking for him, "Can he bring you all anything?" Sue offered. "While he's at it?"

They were okay, thanks. He ought to have thought of that himself, Dick supposed, although he'd have needed a tray or something to carry four glasses. Anyhow, screw it. Screw it, screw it, screw it.

Some while later, after they'd fed themselves while exchanging get-acquainted pleasantries with the Barneses — Sue and Judy about the various neighborhoods of Heron Bay Estates (the modest low-rise condos of Egret's Crest, the look-alike "villas" of Oyster Cove, the over-and-under duplex "coach homes" of Blue Crab Bight, and the detached-house complexes like their own mostly mid-range Rockfish Reach and the high-end Spartina Pointe), Dick and Joe about the effects of global warming on the Atlantic hurricane season and the ballooning national deficit's impact on the stock market (Joe worked in the Stratford office of a Baltimore investment-counseling firm) — "Aren't *you* the life of the party," Susan half teased, half chided her husband, who on both of those weighty questions had opposed Joe Barnes's guardedly optimistic view with his own quite darker one. The two couples were now on their feet again, as were most of the other guests, and circulating from tent to pool deck and lanai.

"Really sorry about that, hon." As in fact he was, and promised her and himself to try to be more "up." For in truth he had rather enjoyed meeting and talking with the Barneses, and had had a good postdinner conversation with young Joe out by the pool while Susan and Judy visited the ladies' room — "On the jolly subject of that Common Disaster provision in our wills."

"You didn't."

"Sure did — because *he* happened to mention that his clients often review their estate statements with him so he can help coordinate their investment strategies with their estate lawyer's advice, to reduce inheritance taxes and such."

"Oh joy."

"So naturally I asked him whether he'd heard of that Each Survives the Other business, and he not only knew right off what I was talking about but explained it simply and clearly, which Betsy Furman" — their estate lawyer — "never managed to do." What it came down to, he explained in turn to not-awfully-interested Susan, was that should they die "simultaneously," their jointly owned assets would be divided fifty-fifty, one half passing by the terms of *his* will, as if he had outlived her, and the other half by hers, as if she'd outlived *him*. "So you make us up another computer spreadsheet along those lines, and we can estimate each beneficiary's take."

"Oh very joy." But she would do that, she agreed, ASAP — and she appreciated his finally clarifying that little mystery. Nor had she herself, she would have him know, been talking only girlie stuff: When Pat Hardison had happened to speak of "her house" and "Tom's boat," upon Sue's questioning their hostess had explained that like most people she knew, the Hardisons titled their assets separately, for "death tax" reasons: Their Annapolis place was in Tom's name, this Stratford one in hers; same with the boat and the RV, the Lexus and the Cadillac Escalade, their various bank accounts and securities holdings. *So* much more practical, taxwise:

Why give your hard-earned assets to the government instead of to your children? Weren't Sue and her husband set up that way?

"I had to tell her I wasn't sure; that that was your department. But my impression is that everything we own is in both our names, right? Are we being stupid?"

Any estate lawyer would likely think so, Dick acknowledged: Betsy Furman had certainly encouraged bypass trusts and such, and had inserted that Each Survives the Other business into their wills as the next best thing after he'd told her that they were uncomfortable with any arrangement other than Joint Ownership, which was how they'd done things since Day One of their marriage. He was no canny CPA or estate lawyer or investment geek: one of those types who tell you it's foolish to pay off your mortgage instead of claiming the interest payments as a tax deduction. Probably they knew what they were talking about, but it was over his head and not his-and-Susan's style. "If the kids and grandkids and the rest get less of the loot that way than they'd get otherwise, they're still getting plenty. Who gives a shit?" What he *really* cared about, he reminded her, was not their death, much less its payoff to their heirs, but their Last Age and their dying. It required the pair of them in good health to maintain their Heron Bay house and grounds and the modest Baltimore condo that they'd bought as a city retreat when they'd retired, sold their dear old townhouse, and made Stratford their principal address. The day either of them joined the ranks of the more than temporarily incapacitated would be the end of life as they knew and enjoyed it; neither of them was cut out for long-term care-giving or care-getting. A Common Disaster, preferably out of the blue while they were still functioning, was the best imaginable scenario for The End: Let them "each survive the other" technically, but neither survive the other in fact — even if that meant making the necessary arrangements themselves.

"My big bundle of joy," Susan said, sighing, and hugged him to put a stop to this lately-so-familiar disquisition.

"Sorry sorry sorry, Doll. Let's go refill."

"*Hey, look at the lovebirds!*" Sam Bailey hollered, too loudly, across the deck from the lanai bar. The old fellow was, pretty obviously, overindulging. A few people paused in their conversation to glance his way, a few others to smile at the Feltons or raise eyebrows at the old fellow's rowdiness. By way of covering it, perhaps, Tom Hardison, who happened to be standing not far from Sam, gave him a comradely pat on the shoulder and then strode behind the bar, fetched out a beribboned brass bugle, of all things, that he'd evidently stashed there, blew a single loud blast like an amplified, extended fart, and called out, "Game and prize time, everybody!" The "Great Room" pianist underscored the announcement with a fortissimo fanfare. When all hands were silent and listening, perky Pat Hardison, holding a brown beer bottle as if it were a portable microphone, repeated her husband's earlier "Friends, Romans, and countrymen," politically correcting that last term to country-*folk:* "Lend me your ears!"

"You want to borrow our *rears?*" Sam Bailey asked loudly.

"We've got those covered, Sam," the host smoothly replied; he too now sported a beer-bottle mike in one hand, while with the other he placed the bugle, bell down, on his interrupter's head, to the guests' approving chuckles. "Or maybe I should say *un*covered, since tonight's Special Olympics consist of Thong-Undie Quoits for the ladies, out on the pool deck, and for the gents, Bobbing for Grapes wherever you see them, as you very soon will. I'll be refereeing the quoits" — he held up a handful of bikini-briefs for all to see — "and Pat'll oversee the grapes, which every lady is invited to grab a bunch of and invite the bobber of her choice to bob for."

"Here's how it's done, girls," Pat explained. Out of the large bowl of dark grapes fetched up by the bartender from behind his station, she plucked a bunch and nestled it neatly into her cleavage. "You tuck 'em in like so, and then your Significant Other, or whoever, sees how many he can nibble off their stems — *without using his hands,* mind. The couple with the fewest grapes left wins the prize." Turning to her husband: "Want a no-grope grape, sweetiepie?"

"Yummy! Deal me in!" Doffing his helmet, he shmushed his face into his wife's fruited bosom and made loud chomping sounds while she, with a mock What-are-you-going-to-do-with-men? look at the laughing bystanders, uplifted her breasts with both hands to facilitate his gorging, and one of the hors d'oeuvre servers began circulating with the bowl among the female guests. A number of them joined in; as many others declined, whether because their costumes were (like Susan's) non-décolletaged, or they preferred watching the fun to joining it, or chose the quoits contest instead. More disposed to spectate than to participate, the Feltons moved with others out to the far side of the pool deck to see how Thong-Undie

Quoits was played. Tom Hardison, his grape-bobbing done for the present ("But save me a few for later!" he called back to Patricia), led the way, carrying a white plastic bin full of varicolored thong panties in his left hand while twirling one with his right. On the lawn just past the deck a shrubbery-light illumined a slightly tipped-back sheet of plywood, on the white-painted face of which were mounted five distinctly phallic-looking posts, one at each corner and one in the center: six-inch tan shafts culminating in pink knobs and mounted at a suggestively upward angle to the backboard.

"Here's how it's done, ladies," Tom explained; "not that you didn't learn the facts of life back in junior high . . ." Holding up the robin's-egg-blue underpants by its thong, from behind a white-taped line on the deck he Frisbee'd it the eight feet or so toward the target board, where it landed between pegs and slid to the ground. With a shrug, "Not everybody scores on the first date," he acknowledged, and then explained to the waiting contestants, "Three pairs for each gladiatrix, okay? If you miss all three, you're still a virgin, no matter how many kids and grandkids you claim to have. Score one and you get to keep it to excite your hubby. Two out of three and you're in the semifinals; *three* out of three and you're a finalist. All three on the same post and you win the Heron Bay Marital Fidelity Award! Who wants to go first?" Examining the nametag on one middle-aged matron's ample, grapeless bosom, *"Helen McCall,"* he announced: "*Spartina Pointe.* How about it, Helen?"

The lady gamely handed her wineglass to her neighbor, fetched three panties from the bin, called out *"We who are about to* try *salute you!"* and spun the first item boardward, where it fell two feet short. "Out of practice," she admitted. Amid the bystanders' chuckles and calls of encouragement she tossed her second, which reached the board but then slid down, as had the host's demonstration throw.

Somebody called, "Not everybody who drops her drawers gets what she's after"; to which someone else retorted, "Is that the Voice of Experience speaking?" But Ms. McCall's vigorous third toss looped a red thong undie on the board's upper-left peg, to general cheers. Tom Hardison retrieved and presented it with a courtly bow to the contestant's applauding husband, who promptly knelt before her, spread the waistband wide, and insisted that she step into her trophy then and there.

"What fun," Susan sighed, and took Dick's hand in hers. "I wish *we* were more like that."

"Yeah, well, me too." With a squeeze, "In our next life, maybe?" He glanced at his watch: almost nine already. "Want to hang around awhile longer, or split now?"

Incredulously, "Are you *kidding?* They haven't awarded the prizes yet!"

"Sorry sorry sorry." And he was, for having become such a party-pooping partner to the wife he so loved and respected. And it wasn't that he was having an unenjoyable evening; only that — as was typically the case on the infrequent occasions when they dined out with another couple — he reached his sufficiency of even quite good food and company sooner than Susan and the others did, and was ready to move on to the next thing, to call it an evening, whatever, while the rest were leisurely reviewing the dessert menu and even considering an after-dinner nightcap at one or the other's house. To his own surprise, he felt his throat thicken and his eyes brim. Their good life together had gone by so fast! How many more so-agreeably-routine days and evenings remained to them, even at best, before . . . what?

Trying as usual to accommodate him, "D'you want to watch the game," Sue asked him, "or circulate a bit?"

"Your call." His characteristic reply. In an effort to do better, "Why not have a go at the game yourself?" he proposed to her. "You'd look cute in a thong."

She gave him one of her Looks. "Because I'm *me*, remember?" Another fifteen minutes or so, she predicted, ought to wind things up gamewise; after the prizes were handed out they could probably leave without seeming discourteous. Meanwhile, shouldn't he maybe go check on Doc Sam?

Her husband welcomed the errand: something to occupy him while Susan made conversation with their hostess, a couple of her golf partners, and other party guests. He worked his way barward through the merry grape-bobbers, their equally merry encouragers and referees ("How many left down there? Let me check." "No, me!" "Hey hey: no hands allowed . . ."), and the occasional two or three just talking politics, sports, business. Couldn't immediately locate his tennis pal, in whose present position he himself would . . . well, what, exactly? Not hang around to *be* in that position, he hoped and more or less re-vowed to himself. Then he heard the old fellow (but who was Dick Felton, at age five-and-seventy, to call eighty "old"?) sing out raucously from the living room, to the tune of *O Holy Night:*

"*O-O-O ho-ly shit! . . .*"

Sam stumbled out onto the lanai, doing the beer-bottle-microphone thing as the Hardisons had done earlier, but swigging from it between shouted lines:

"*The sky, the sky is fall-ing! . . .*"

Smiling or frowning people turned his way, some commenting behind their hands.

"It is the end . . . of our dear . . . U-S-A! . . ."

Dick approached him, calling out as if in jest, "Yo, Sam! You're distracting the thong-throwers, man!"

"And the grape-gropers, too!" someone merrily added. Thinking to lead him back inside and quiet him down, Dick put an arm around the old fellow's bony shoulders. He caught sight of Pat Hardison, clearly much concerned, heading toward them from the food tent. But as he made to turn his friend houseward, Sam startled him by snatching the machete from its sheath, pushing free of its owner, raising it high, and declaring, "If there's no red wine, I guess I'll have to Bloody Mary."

"Sam Sam Sam . . ."

Returning to his hymn parody, *"Fall . . . on your swords!"* Sam sang: *"O hear . . . the angels laugh-ing! . . ."*

Too late, Dick sprang to resnatch the blade, or at least to grab hold of its wielder's arm. To all hands' horror, having mock-threatened his would-be restrainer with it, Sam thrust its point into his own chest, just under the breastbone. Dropped the beer bottle; gripped the machete's carved handle with both hands, and pushed its blade into himself yet farther; grunted with the pain of it and dropped first to his knees, then sideways to the floor, his blood already soaking through his tunic front onto the lanai deck. Pat Hardison and other women screamed; men shouted and rushed up, her husband among them. An elderly ex-doctor from Stratford — whose "toga" was a fancied-up set of blue hospital scrubs and who earlier had complained to the Feltons that the ever-higher cost of medical malpractice insurance had pressured him into retirement — pushed through the others and took charge: ordered Tom Hardison to dial 911 and Pat to fetch a bunch of clean rags, towels, anything that he could use to stanch the blood flow; swatted

Sam's hands off the machete handle (all but unconscious now, eyes squinted shut, the old fellow moaned, coughed, vomited a bit onto the deck, and went entirely limp); withdrew and laid aside the bloody blade; and pressed a double handful of the patient's robe against the gushing wound.

"Bailey, you idiot!" he scolded: "What'd you do *that* for?"

Without opening his eyes, Sam weakly finished his song: *"It was the night . . . that my dear . . . Edie died . . ."*

"We should call his son in Stratford," Sue said, clutching her husband tearfully.

"Right you are." Dick fished under his caftan for the cell phone that he almost never used but had gotten the habit of carrying with him. "Where's a goddamn phonebook?"

Pat hurried inside to fetch one. "Tell him to go straight to the Avon Health Center!" the doctor called after her.

Men led their sobbing mates away. A couple of hardy volunteers applied clean rags to the blood and vomit puddled on the deck; one even considerately wiped clean the machete and restored it to its owner when Dick returned outside from making the grim call to Sam Junior.

"Jesus." But he gingerly resheathed the thing. The EMS ambulance presently wailed up, lights flashing; its crew transferred the barely breathing victim from floor to stretcher to entranceway gurney to vehicle without (Susan managed to notice) spilling a drop of his plentifully flowing blood onto the carpeting. The ex-doctor — *Mike Dowling,* his name label read, *Spartina Pte* — on familiar terms with the emergency crew from his years of medical practice, rode with them, instructing his wife to pick him up at AHC in half an hour or so. The Feltons then hurried to their car to follow the ambulance to the hospital, promising the Hardisons (who of course had their hands full with the party's sudden unexpected finale and the postparty cleanup) to phone them a report on Sam's condition as soon as they had one.

"I can't believe he'll live," Sue worried aloud en route the several miles into Stratford, the pair of them feeling ridiculous indeed to be approaching the hospital's emergency wing in their outlandish costumes. "So much blood lost!"

"Better for him if he doesn't," in Dick's opinion. The sheathed machete, at least, he left in the convertible, cursing himself for having included it in his getup but agreeing with Susan that in Sam's desperate and drunken grief he'd have found some other implement to attack himself with, if not at the party then back at his house in Oyster Cove. Their headdresses, too, and any other removable "Roman" accessories, they divested before crossing the parking lot and making their way into the brightly lit ER. The few staff people they saw did a creditable job of keeping straight faces; the Visitor Check-In lady even said sympathetically, "Y'all must've been at that party with Doctor Dowling . . ." The patient's son, she informed them, had arrived already and was in a special standby room. They should make themselves comfortable over yonder (she indicated a couch-and-chair area across the fluorescent-lighted room, which they were relieved to see was unoccupied); she would keep them posted, she promised.

And so they sat, side by side on one of the dark gray plastic-cushioned couches, Sue's left hand clasped in Dick's right; too shocked to do more than murmur how sad it all was. On end tables beside them were back issues of *Time, Fortune, People, Chesapeake Living, Sports Illustrated, Field & Stream.* The sight of their covers, attention-grabbing reminders of the busy World, made Dick Felton wince: Never had he felt more keenly that All That was behind them. If Dr. Dowling's wife, per instructions, came to fetch her husband half an hour or so after he left the toga party, Sue presently speculated, then there must be a special entrance as well as a special standby room, as more time than that had passed since their own arrival at Avon Health Center without their seeing any sign of her or him. Eventually, however, the receptionist's telephone warbled; she attended the message, made some reply, and then called "Mister and Miz Felton?" There being no one else to hear, without waiting for them to come to her station she announced Dr. Dowling's opinion that there was no reason for them to stay longer: Mr. Bailey, his condition stabilized, had been moved to Intensive Care in serious but no longer critical condition. He had lost a great deal of blood, injured some internal organs, and would need further surgery down the line, but was expected to survive. His son was with him.

"Poor bastard," Dick said — meaning either or both of the pair, he supposed: the father doomed to an even more radically reduced existence than the one he had tried unsuccessfully to exit; the dutifully attentive but already busy son now saddled with the extra burdens of arranging the care of an invalid parent and the management of that parent's house until he could unload it and install the old fellow in Bayview Manor (another Tidewater Communities project, across and downriver from Heron Bay Estates) or some other assisted living facility.

"Loving children *do* those things," Sue reminded him. "Sure, it's a major headache, but close families accept it."

Lucky them, they both were thinking as they drove back to HBE, through the main entrance gate (which opened automatically when its electronic scanner read the bar-coded Resident sticker on their Toyota's left rear window), and on to their Rockfish Reach neighborhood, Sue having cell-phoned her promised report to the Hardisons as they left the AHC parking lot. How would either of themselves manage, alone, in some similar situation, with their far-flung and not all that filially bonded son and daughter?

"We wouldn't," in Dick's opinion, and his wife couldn't disagree.

All the partygoers' cars were gone from Loblolly Court, they observed as they passed it, but lights were still on in #12, where cleanup no doubt continued. By the time they reached their own house's pleasantly night-lighted driveway and entranceway, the car's dashboard clock read the same as their Shoreside Drive house number: 1020. Noting the coincidence, "Now *that* means something," Susan said: a Felton family joke, echoing Dick's late mother (who'd fortunately had a devoted or anyhow dutiful unmarried middle-aged daughter to attend her senile last years over in western Maryland). But her effort at humor was made through suddenly welling tears: tears for herself, she explained when her husband remarked at them as he turned into their driveway; tears for them both, as much as for poor Sam Bailey.

Dick pressed the garage door opener button over the rearview mirror, turned their convertible expertly into the slot beside their station wagon, shifted into park, clicked off the headlights, and pressed the remote-control button again to roll the door back down. Instead of then shutting off the engine and unlatching his seat belt, however, after a moment he pushed the buttons to lower all of the car's windows, closed his eyes, and leaned his head back wearily against the driver's headrest.

"What are you doing?" There was some alarm in Susan's voice, but she too left her seat belt fastened, and made no move to open her door. "Why'd you do that?"

Without turning his head or even opening his eyes, her husband took her hand in his as he'd done back in the hospital waiting room, squeezing it now even more tightly. "Shit, hon: Why not? We've had a good life together, but it's done with except for the crappy last lap, and neither of us wants that."

"*I* sure don't," his wife acknowledged, and with a sigh backrested her head, too. Already they could smell exhaust fumes. "I love you, Dick."

"I love *you.* And okay, so we're dumping on the kids, leaving them to take the hit and clean up the mess. So what?"

"They'll never forgive us. But you're right: So what?"

"We'll each be presumed to have survived the other, as the saying goes, and neither of us'll be around to know it."

The car engine quietly idled on.

"Shouldn't we at least leave them a note, send them an e-mail, something? . . ."

"So go do that, if you want to. Me, I'm staying put."

He heard her exhale. "Me too, I guess." Then inhale, deeply.

If "Doc Sam" Bailey were this story's teller, he'd probably end it right here with a bit of toga-party Latin: *Consummatum est; requiescat in pacem* — something in that vein. But he's not.

The overhead garage light timed out.

ANN BEATTIE

Solid Wood

FROM BOULEVARD

THE YEAR WRIGHT KEMZELL published his book about my former colleague, friend, and mentor, Jacob Foxx Greer, I found myself with my sister in Key West. At first we thought we'd take a cruise that boarded in Ft. Lauderdale and continued to St. John's and Tortola. But instead we decided to do something simpler and flew to Miami and rented a car and called the tourist information center, who put us in contact with the Key West Hilton, where two rooms were available. My sister was secretly glad of this: she'd rather be on land than on a ship. In the last two years she's had a hysterectomy and been diagnosed with diabetes; she hadn't felt particularly well and lacked her usual energy. She'd have to resist the endless buffets; shuffleboard wasn't exhausting, but it wasn't her thing, either. Neither was sitting in a deck chair, which she said would make her feel old. She'd just turned sixty-two, and looked like she was in her late forties; her neighbor in Arlington had proposed one week after his wife died. She had not only expressed dismay to the man, she had phoned to ask if I felt like a vacation.

If we'd only been there for an afternoon, I don't think I would have called Jacob Foxx Greer's widow, Clemmie. I'd have gone to Fort Taylor to see the Australian pines again — especially since their existence was threatened. (They're opportunistic, not indigenous. There was a lot of support for getting rid of them.) Instead of coming along, my sister Doris decided to take a boat ride from the hotel to a tiny island across from it, where she could have lunch with a woman she'd met at the airport, who'd belonged to a branch of her old college sorority. I was always happy if Doris was happy, and she hadn't been smiling much during the past year.

I walked to the wall of the Greers' compound, remembering where to find the recessed doorbell for their unit. A plaque had been hung, noting that this had been Jacob Foxx Greer's residence from 1979 until 1989 — the year he died. I rang the bell and waited. It was two o'clock on a sunny Wednesday, so there was every reason to fear no one would be home. But I was wrong; instead of the crackly voice over the intercom I'd heard before, I heard someone calling, "Who's there?" I gave my name and a woman raised the latch of the heavy white gate with its peephole surrounded by a painted circle of flowers that harmonized nicely with the bougainvillea dripping over the wall. Someone who was not Clemmie stood looking at me. "Would Clementine be home?" I said, removing my cap. "I'm an old friend."

She looked at me flatly. "An old friend," she repeated. "From where?"

"From New York. I've visited them here several times," I added.

I realized, then, that I was looking at Penny, quite a bit heavier, without any makeup and with uncombed hair. She stepped back to allow me entrance. A cat darted behind her. Just inside the gate there was a blue recycling box filled with empty bottles of water and wine. Somewhere deep down, I could see the colorful label of a juice bottle.

"Penny? Jake Stiles. I remember that pretty red hair. I sometimes drove you to the pediatrician for allergy shots. Do you remember?"

"I do, I think," she said slowly. Perhaps the memory of being taken to and from the appointments wasn't a pleasant one.

"I've stopped by for old time's sake," I said, embarrassed the moment I spoke for uttering such a cliché. "Is your mother here?"

"Here, there, and everywhere, as the Beatles say."

She led the way to their house and preceded me up the stairs, pushed open the front door, and crossed the room to open the door of the refrigerator. "Coffee, tea, orange juice, water," she said.

I nodded. "Delightful."

She smiled slightly. "Should I mix it in a punch bowl?"

"Orange juice. No ice, please."

She took the carton from the refrigerator, poured some in a glass, and handed it to me. Her hand shook as she held out the glass. She replaced the carton.

"Do you live in Key West, Penny?"

"That would require that I be a famous writer like my father. No,

I don't. I live in Ohio where the real estate is affordable. I'm here to look after Mother and get out of the snow for a week. Clem's gone to get me a fleece jacket. She'll get the right size and pick a nicer color than I would." She'd poured herself a drink that looked like ginger ale. "Wheatgrass juice," she said. "I assumed you wouldn't want any."

I shook my head no. She had poured a tall glass.

She sat on the sofa. She had turned into a chunky woman, wearing a T-shirt with a deep V that showed cleavage and pastel green pants cropped at the knee. She, or someone — someone else, with a steadier hand — had done a henna painting of flowers around one thick ankle.

She said, "Susan Sontag went to Sarajevo and helped them put on *Waiting for Godot.* I'm sure Father would have approved — especially from the vantage point of his favorite chair. I think it's a good idea when artists get involved in politics. Are you active, yourself?"

"I'm afraid not, except for casting my vote," I said.

"Well, I'm certainly not saving the world. I'm not a musician anymore, either. I sold the cello to put on a garage." She lit a candle on the tray table beside her and fanned out the match.

"Did you know Jacob's body is being moved to a mausoleum in Cincinnati near me? Clem got upset when she heard about the way they churn the graves."

"I didn't know that," I said.

"We often go to the graveyard here in the afternoon. Have you made the pilgrimage? There's quite a plastic flower collection. When the Conch Tram goes past, there's a canned voice telling the tourists about the tombstone engraved, 'I told you I was sick.'"

"And how have you been?" I said, as earnest as I could be without becoming solicitous. "I saw a picture of you in the *Times,* at a charity ball. At the Cloisters, I think it was. You looked lovely."

She smiled. The candle smelled like an apple pie baking. "From time to time I represent the family," she said. "Good you took me to my doctor appointments and kept me alive." I waited for her to continue, but she stopped talking. She sipped from the glass. Finally, she said: "I do volunteer work in Ohio, explaining what people can and can't eat when they have various allergies. They're shocked to hear how many things they wouldn't expect contain vinegar."

"Nothing fermented because you're allergic to mold. Do I remember correctly?"

"Perfectly," she said. "When she comes in, will you make small talk, or talk about the book?"

I looked at her. "Do you have some advice about that?" I said.

She shrugged. "Let's put it this way: I don't think middle America cares."

The Kemzell biography gave information about her father's addiction to amphetamine, to treat what his colleagues politely pretended was "narcolepsy." It mentioned a man by name, now in Alaska, who'd lived in Stonington with Jacob during the time he was separated from Clemmie. My sister Doris was not mentioned.

I made one more attempt to turn the discussion to Penny. "You must have been seven or eight when I met you," I said. "You had an Eloise doll, and we used to make up stories about things Eloise had done at the Plaza."

"I don't remember that," she said. "Did Eloise steal her daddy's drugs and sleep around?"

I shook my head no.

"Then Eloise must have been too young. Was Eloise a drudge, fucking up her fingers practicing the cello? Running down the hallways of the Plaza with her fingers spouting blood?" She leaned forward and scratched behind the cat's ear. Another cat poked its head into the room, wearing a wide silver-studded collar. "That's bondage kitty," she said, nodding in the direction of the French doors. "The estimable Jacob Foxx Greer's converted garage is rented out to two gay guys from Toronto."

The cat pawed something in the doorway, then darted off.

"It's not right of me to take any more of your time, Penny. My sister and I are at the Hilton for two more days. Will you ask Clemmie to call? We'd love to take you both to dinner, if you have the time."

"If she'll call," Penny said. "I can't remember; how do you figure in the book?"

"Pretty much as a footnote. As someone on board for his famous Monday night reading of the classics. As the younger faculty member who was privileged to share his office and as the white knight who transported his daughter on many occasions, because he didn't drive. As a sometimes babysitter. You may remember that I was also the person who saved your life when you fell through the ice."

She looked up, surprised. "I read the book," she said. "That wasn't in there."

"Ah, but at least we remember," I said.

No phone call came that night, or the next morning. Doris, in the room next to mine, had hung a DO NOT DISTURB sign on the door and did not come out when the late morning vacuuming of the hallway began. I finished reading the paper, then tried to push a note under her door asking her to join me at the pool, which was impossible. I ended up tearing the paper and pushing it over the doorknob. I put on my swim trunks and shirt, my flip-flops, and waited by the elevator, where a red-nosed brat made nonsense noises and tried to pull his mother's arm off. I took the stairs, but found a sign on the door at the bottom saying that an alarm would sound if the door was opened. I walked back upstairs, peeved, but it was just as well: Doris was coming out of her room, her big unicorn tapestry purse slung over her shoulder, wearing a sundress and sandals. "I've got a hangover," she said. "With this goddamn diabetes, I can't have even one drink and still take my melatonin. Waking up is like coming out of anesthesia."

"Would coffee help? Did you take some aspirin?"

"Maybe coffee," she said.

"We can order it poolside. Would you mind?" I said.

No answer, but then, Doris was never big on small talk.

The elevator stopped on the fourth floor, and the woman, minus her son, got on the elevator. Her eyes were red — from crying, I supposed. I nodded, but she gave no sign that she'd seen me before. I saw that her arm was scratched.

I showed my room key at the poolside cabana, signed for two towels, and followed Doris to a shady lounge as far back from the pool as possible. Even as a child, she'd loved water but hated to be splashed. I summoned the tan girl in white shorts and top who worked for the hotel. "Two coffees, please," I said. She wrote down my room number from the key on top of the towels. "We have some delicious Danish," she said. "That'll be all," Doris said. She took a hat out of her bag and pulled it onto her head with finality. She said, "So. Did you see the widow?"

"Not yet. Penny was there, though. She apparently lives in Cincinnati. I couldn't tell much from what she said, but I gather Clemmie was as unhappy about the book as everyone thought she'd be."

"I am so lucky I escaped that boy reporter academic jackass," Doris said.

"Mr. Kemzell didn't seem so interested in stories about women as he was in stories about men."

"Man, singular. At least, until the next biography. I might also point out that I never lived with him in Stonington, either. You don't move to Stonington unless you want to make a statement." She looked at me. "He would have done anything to get closer to James Merrill," she said. "He plunked a piano down in that tiny living room, so *Jimmy* could come over and play."

"This is the green-eyed monster, Doris," I said. "You were through with him, remember."

The waitress did not alter her expression of benign oblivion as she placed the tray with two coffee mugs and its little pitcher and packets of sugar on the table between us. "Enjoy," she said.

Instead of sipping, I adjusted the lounge to recline. Beneath my sunglasses, I squinted to see what Doris would do. She reached for her cup, blew on the coffee as I knew she would, as if three seconds of blowing could effectively cool something, then took a sip and jerked the cup away with the other hand cupped beneath it, as I also knew she would. She replaced it on the tray, poured in a bit of milk. My sister had had a son by Jacob when she was nineteen whom she'd given up for adoption. With our parents dead, as well as our Aunt Rachel, I was the only one who still knew. At least, we assumed that, because Clemmie never gave any indication she was aware of it. She sent the same Christmas greetings to me each year, with a personal message including Doris — whom she knew not only as my sister, but as one of her husband's former students — in her Palmer Method handwriting. There had never been a second of hesitation when she embraced us, on the rare occasions she'd seen Doris through the years. Yet I'd always wondered if she knew. And if she did, didn't she wonder how things had turned out? For years after the birth, until Doris returned to Columbia to finish her degree, even Jacob hadn't known what had become of the child. For close to ten years after the birth of the child she had not returned to New York; she had first lived with a friend from high school in Ann Arbor. I'd told Jacob it was not a subject I would ever discuss with him, and to my surprise, he'd only asked once. It was such a different time: Hollywood actresses bore children who they pretended were adopted; Ingrid Bergman had been shamed. Such a very different time, with the scandal of Eddie Fisher, married to perky little Debbie Reynolds, falling in love with Mike Todd's widow and leaving his family to marry Elizabeth Taylor. Rock Hudson hiding his homosexuality — even marrying. Now, unconventional behavior was flaunted. Doris would have rushed to tell her story to this newest biographer. But if you missed the first moment of revealing your transgression, it was difficult to confess later, with dignity. I never mentioned the child, either. I'd only asked once, been told that our aunt arranged for a private adoption, and that what Doris then intended to do was to marry the man she'd loved all along — the captain of the football team in high school, if you can believe it, with a name even the old Hollywood couldn't invent — Troy Brilliant. He died of friendly fire in Vietnam.

Many times each day I stop and consider the world around me: here I am strapped into an airplane seat, going somewhere that could be most anywhere, yet I have decided on a particular place; here I am driving down a familiar street, yet suddenly there are red tennis shoes dangling from the power wires. Here I am retired at seventy, identifying with a little boy I see out the car window, riding his bike, perhaps ten years old. Lately I've also thought *there I go:* there I go, swerving to avoid the bicyclist, avoiding years of guilt and days in court; there are the red shoes that may tantalize the imaginations of many would-be writers, not just me. ("Would-be" is not quite correct; as a young man, I published one enthusiastically received book, but have never completed another.) I still don't know whether I should have intervened, if I should have urged Doris not to have the child (which was her initial inclination), if I should have ended my friendship with Jacob — who was no more to blame than my sister, after all. I saw the child once, the day after his birth. I most certainly do not go around imagining random children to be my nephew, but I do wonder whether my dislike of children resides in that traumatic moment when I laid eyes on him (never named). Others see children as bright and original, with an inspirational energy; I see them as willful, repetitive in their boring demands, exhausting.

"May I invite you to a special performance tonight?" the girl who brought our coffee intones, speaking as if she knows us, holding out flyers to people on the lounges. "A special performance," she whispers almost intimately in some people's ears, when she sees she has their attention. "The Key West Hilton invites you to a special performance this very night!" when she's tired of trying to establish personal contact. "Tonight there is a special performance," she says, hand extended, voice fading. I reach up and take Doris's flyer. It says: TONIGHT AT 6:30, ON OUR FAMOUS SUNSET PIER, PLEASE JOIN THE GUESTS AND CREW OF THE DISNEY SHIP AS WE CELEBRATE THE ANNUAL PERFORMANCE OF MAURICE THE MAGNIFICENT WHO IS HERE FOR ONE NIGHT ONLY. PREPARE TO BE AWED AND AMAZED BY THE SPECTACULAR TALENT OF THIS VERY SPECIAL ARTIST IN HIS MOST SPECTACULAR PERFORMANCE YET.

"I'm sure we wouldn't miss it," Doris mutters.

But do you know, we go. We go because I receive a call from Clemmie late in the afternoon, saying that a friend's son will be performing on "our" sunset pier, and that she would most certainly like to accept our dinner invitation after seeing the performance. She hopes we will join her to see Martin. She corrects herself and says, "Dear me, I mean *Maurice.*"

"Why don't you go and phone my room afterward?" Doris says.

But at 6:10, when I go down to the lobby to meet them, Doris is sitting in a chair, wearing her sundress and sandals, a cashmere stole around her shoulders, her hair neatly styled, smiling her enigmatic smile as I approach.

There is a large crowd, but then, there is always a large crowd to celebrate sunset in Key West. Clemmie looks frail, much shorter than when I last saw her, and she clasps Penny's arm and does not talk at the same time she is walking. I ask a question that is met by silence. Clemmie has on a shapeless dress to disguise her thinness, but her shoes are amusing: rhinestone-trimmed sneakers. She, too, wears a stole, though hers is held in place with a pin. Doris trails a bit behind us, either distracted by the scenery or pretending to be distracted by the scenery: boats cruising by; tourists sipping tropical drinks. I walk next to Penny, chatting, as she guides her mother to the place where the crowd has gathered. "A special performance," the girl in white says. She is still at it, passing out flyers. This time, she wears Mickey Mouse ears.

"Just like life. A special performance," Clemmie says, smiling faintly at Doris. She does not relinquish her daughter's arm, though she's standing still. We manage to keep a little space around us as people move forward; a few people step back, noticing the age of the lady holding the woman's arm.

"Did you make a reservation for dinner?" Penny says to me. "I should have thought to."

"I made a reservation at the hotel for 7:30. I hope that's all right."

"Anything's fine, as long as I don't have to cook," Penny says.

A man in a silver bomber jacket rides onto the dock, pedaling a unicycle. This is not Maurice the Magnificent, but someone who jumps down, catching the handlebars with one hand, and removing a harmonica from a backpack. He is barefoot, wearing a silver visor and wraparound sunglasses. He lowers the cycle to its side, shakes out the visor so that it becomes a hat, then upends it, placing something heavy in the bottom to weigh down the collection plate. He begins to play "Mr. Tambourine Man." Some people move closer; others move away. "I'm not sleepy, and there ain't no place I'm going to," a drunk sings loudly, raising his beer bottle to the sky. He removes a toy horn from his pocket and blows into it. The look the man in silver gives him insures that we will not have any more of his drunken antics.

"Mother and I have been thinking about selling while real estate prices are still going through the ceiling," Penny says. "We're thinking about moving to Andros. All this" — she gestures — "isn't happening there. Yet."

A three-wheel vehicle appears: Maurice, who is dropped off by a young man driving a Hilton hotel golf cart, also wearing Mickey Mouse ears. Maurice does not look at the crowd, but lifts a hoop from the cart, and a duffel bag. From the bag he removes his own mouse ears, which he puts on, looking slightly abashed, and what look like bowling pins, with Mickey and Minnie's curved faces filling the lower part of the pins. He juggles them for a minute, then puts some things from his bag into his pocket. "Oh, no, let's not disturb his concentration," I hear Clemmie saying to Penny, who must have asked if she wanted to say hello to Maurice. Slowly, backing up to inspect them, Maurice sets the pins first on one part of the pavement, then another. He scans the sky, then says, in a booming voice: "Ladies and gentlemen, in only a few moments tonight's special performance, sponsored by the Hilton Hotel and Walt Disney's cruise line, will begin. May I ask for a volunteer from the crowd? Step up, please. Don't be shy. Is there a volunteer? Step forward. Thank you for joining me on what will be an amazing journey. I ask you to inspect these and to inform the crowd that they are ordinary juggling pins, with no special adaptations . . . won't you step forward?" If this is the son of one of her mother's friends, has Penny met the man? He is appealing to her, but she blushes — blushes! — and declines. Doris, though, standing behind her, suddenly brushes past Penny and appears in front of him. She throws one end of her scarf over her shoulder, so both hands are free. The man inclines his head toward her and says something the crowd can't hear. She picks up one of the pins. She examines it carefully, running her hands over it. She replaces it and examines the other. "Completely smooth," she says, taking a silent cue from Maurice and quickly turning to face the crowd. I look to my side, as if the real Doris might still be there. Doris is a shy woman. Doris disdains things like this. For a second the breeze lifts a corner of her wrap, but the ruffle of breeze subsides; her cashmere scarf remains in place. "All right, ladies and gentlemen. Our time together on what will be an amazing adventure in belief is about to begin. During the time I juggle, I ask you to be as quiet as possible, and not to move further forward, to avoid injury. Once again, will you please check the pins and attest to the fact that they are solid carved wood?" Maurice had picked them up; he holds them by their necks, as if he's had a successful moment hunting. Doris moves forward and strokes them, as they dangle. "Solid wood," she says.

Suddenly a white dove rises out of one of the pins Maurice holds and flies away. It is followed by a streak of flame that rises and quickly burns out. As this amazing sight focuses our attention, a second white dove rises from the other pin and flaps after the first. Both birds fly out over the water, past the huge white ship docked there, and become smaller and smaller until they can no longer be seen. The second pin, also, erupts briefly in flame. The crowd exclaims. People near the front step back. A child in its father's arms shrieks, "Daddy, where they come from?" As if summoned by the noise, the birds appear and land on the pins, sucked into them in some way I cannot imagine. With a flourish, Maurice places the juggling pins on the dock: Minnie and Mickey with their gleeful, unchangeable expressions. He steps aside and picks up the hoop — it looks no different than a plastic Hula-Hoop — and tosses it in the air. As he catches it, many white doves fly out and rise to circle in the sky, then disappear — as the expression goes — into thin air. How can this happen? Doris's head is tipped back; I cannot see her expression as the birds simply vanish. There is a hushed silence as people wait for what will come next. Taking off his hat, Maurice bows deeply. Above him is the darkening sky. When the birds do not return — and when Maurice, himself, does not say anything — people begin to talk quietly, nervously. "Ladies and gentlemen, I ask you to contribute nothing unless this performance has revealed to you the extraordinary power of magic. The deepest concentration is required for this act, which I work to perfect continually. I now perform only once a year, out of respect for the birds, currently endangered. Thank you, on behalf of myself, Maurice the Magnificent, and the Hilton Hotel and Walt Disney. I hope you may see me in 2006, when I perform outside the pyramid of the great Louvre, in Paris, France." He bows deeply. Then he turns to Doris, reaches out thumb and finger, moves close to her, and asks, "I may borrow this for one minute, madam?" He does not touch the cashmere shawl, and neither does she; it seems to rise of its own accord, then flaps in the air until he reaches up and it is transformed into a delicate, spherical bowl, which he then presents her with, to pass among the crowd. All around me, too amazed even to leave before having to pay, people discuss what they've seen and wonder aloud how it was done. I am equally amazed that Doris has been part of the act, and that her stepping forward must have been agreed upon beforehand. But how that was done — how any of it happened — perplexes me entirely. Gradually, as the crowd disperses, I realize that Clemmie and Penny no longer stand beside me. They are nowhere to be seen. Had she needed to sit down? I search the crowd. Perhaps, while I'd been lost in thought, they'd returned to the lobby to rest until dinner — rest being its own kind of magic, at a certain age. Doris seems energized by the performance; she seems almost girlish. As Doris circulates with the big bowl made from her fabric, and mystified but pleased tourists reach into their pockets and handbags to contribute, I try to catch her eye, though she willfully avoids mine as she turns from person to person, smiling but saying nothing. Her familiar face lovely, but expressionless — so absolutely devoid of emotion . . . how had she managed not to gasp in disbelief?

Doris's face was not entirely unreadable. She had begun to frown, holding out the white leather folder stamped with the golden logo "H," my gold AmEx card protruding like a feather from a cap. "Shall I add the tip?" Doris said gently. And, to the others: "We both have trouble seeing in dim light."

We are sitting at a table covered with a white linen cloth in the hotel dining room. The candle has been pushed close to me to illuminate the bill. When, with a sudden sizzle, the flame leaps a bit too high, a hand appears and silently removes the candle, placing another, with a tiny flame already lit, in its place. The windows are almost, but not quite, opaque with darkness. A shimmer of color narrows in the sky above the enormous shape of a cruise ship turning into mere outline against the night sky.

"May I offer my reading glasses?" Clemmie says. Dessert plates are lifted from the table in synchronized movement by two waiters in silver vests, who stack our plates and disappear.

"How many evenings do we have like this one?" Clemmie says, settling her glance on her daughter.

"We appreciate your taking us out. I'm especially glad I didn't have to cook," Penny says. "People come to visit, and you'd think that just because you offer, they really think it's your pleasure —"

"It used to be my pleasure to provide some refreshment for tired travelers," Clemmie says. "Of course, that was what everyone did in those days. I could do it when my eyes were better."

The waiter, with studied consideration, is aiming his penlight onto the receipt and pretending to look elsewhere. I wince, suddenly reminded of a doctor, aiming a light into my eye. The restaurant has become teeth-chatteringly cold. Except for us, everyone has left, the tablecloths are being folded, the music has stopped playing.

"It's a sad moment when such pleasure ends," Clemmie says.

"Don't turn into a gray cloud, now, Mother," Penny says, pushing back her chair.

"After such pleasure, sadness," Clemmie says vaguely. "I think your father married me because he could count on me to remark on the obvious. Or not, I suppose. To not remark on the obvious." I hear in the way she speaks a bit of my false cheer from the day before — the way I'd said to Penny, "I'm just stopping by for old time's sake." "I couldn't have attained this great age without realizing everything changes," Clemmie says. Her voice sounds tired.

Penny is standing. This is our cue to leave, but I falter, remembering the night she and I went skating: little Penny, preceding me, then my rushing forward to sink into the water in the same spot where she vanished. We had been on the pond, just a few of us, it was so late, and then she had fallen in as ice popped and cracked. Then I, too, was in, intent upon sinking as deep as I needed to reach her, my eyes frantically scanning the watery darkness, finally seeing the shape of her. If I hadn't made my comment the day before, would she even have referred to that night? Or was it expected that a man would save a child? Had we both accepted that tragedy had been averted and put it out of our minds? I'd grabbed her arm — not upon leaving the house, but years before, in the water. Someone had tossed me a lifesaving ring. Before I knew what happened, Penny was streaming wet, standing above me: a thin little child with a dislocated shoulder. A blanket covered me, or was it someone's coat? Penny crawled under, crying, shaking me, or just shaking against me, I couldn't tell. And then we were in the ambulance, going toward something. I could remember a pinpoint of light that zigged and zagged like Tinkerbell, illuminating first one place, then another, but too briefly to allow me to see. Words, too, shot away like shooting stars. Everything became silent, and then I understood that a doctor was shining a light in my eye.

At the moment, the waiter's penlight is aimed down, as my hand draws a diagonal line from the tail of the *S* to the top, closing the numeral *8*. It is neatly drawn. Everyone seems pleased, including the waiter who is young, and has not quite mastered feigning disinterest in his tip.

"I thank you for a lovely evening," Clemmie says, grasping the edge of the table. "I have a confession to make, though."

Doris looks at me.

"I'm not good company late at night," Clemmie says, her voice wavering. "My mind drifts. I think better early in the day."

"You've done fine, Mother, but we'd better leave now," Penny says.

Her mother looks at her. "That's a beautiful jacket," she says. "Bright pink is one of my favorite colors."

"Well, I guess that would explain why you picked this out for me, then!" Penny says loudly, as if her mother has trouble hearing.

The last person has paid and is leaving the bar, a bit unsteady on his feet. I place my hand on the back of my sister's chair. She rises, clutching the edge of her shawl, pulled tightly across her chest. It has become chilly in the restaurant. Then suddenly we are outside, on the curb at the rim of the circular driveway, and my head is inclined; I brush Clemmie's cool cheek with a tiny kiss. She is an old lady I might not see again. Her hand is as delicate as if bird bones stretched inside. Penny — she has become such a big girl; firm legs that could do damage kicking; shoulders she could hunch on any football field — extends her hand quickly when the valet appears with the car. Doris places her hand lightly in the crook of Clemmie's arm, moving her forward ever so gently. "Thank you for everything," Clemmie says. Doris nods, but — perhaps out of her own exhaustion — stands silently now by the car door. Doris is all stomach, carved like a primitive figure, narrow except for the swelling. I say, "Is it too late to rethink things?"

"Things?" Doris says, reaching for my arm. "What things need to be rethought so late at night?"

T. C. BOYLE

Balto

FROM THE PARIS REVIEW

THERE ARE TWO KINDS of truths, good truths and hurtful ones. That was what her father's attorney was telling her, and she was listening, doing her best, her face a small glazed crescent of light where the sun glanced off the yellow kitchen wall to illuminate her, but it was hard. Hard because it was a weekday, after school, and this was her free time, her chance to breeze into the 7-Eleven or instant message her friends before dinner and homework closed the day down. Hard too because her father was there, sitting on a stool at the kitchen counter, sipping something out of a mug, not coffee, definitely not coffee. His face was soft, the lines at the corners of his eyes nearly erased in the gentle spill of light — his *crow's-feet,* and how she loved that word, as if the bird's scaly claws had taken hold there like something out of a horror story, Edgar Allan Poe, the raven, nevermore, but wasn't a raven different from a crow and why not call them raven's-feet? Or hawk's-feet? People could have a hawk's nose — they always did in stories — but they had crow's-feet, and that didn't make any sense at all.

"Angelle," the attorney said — *Mr. Apodaca* — and the sound of her own name startled her, "are you listening to me?"

She nodded her head. And because that didn't seem enough, she spoke up too. "Yes," she said, but her voice sounded strange in her ears, as if somebody else were speaking for her.

"Good," he said, "good," leaning into the table so that his big moist dog's eyes settled on her with a baleful look. "Because this is very important, I don't have to stress that —"

He waited for her to nod again before going on.

"There are two kinds of truths," he repeated, "just like lies.

There are bad lies, we all know that, lies meant to cheat and deceive, and then there are white lies, little fibs that don't really hurt anybody" — he blew out a soft puff of air, as if he were just stepping into a hot tub — "and might actually do good. Do you understand what I'm saying?"

She held herself perfectly still. Of course she understood — he was treating her like a nine-year-old, like her sister, and she was twelve, almost thirteen, and this was an act of rebellion, to hold herself there, not answering, not nodding, not even blinking her eyes.

"Like in this case," he went on, "your father's case, I mean. You've seen TV, the movies. The judge asks you for the truth, the whole truth, and nothing but the truth, and you'll swear to it, everybody does — your father, me, anybody before the court." He had a mug too, one she recognized from her mother's college days — BU, it said in thick red letters, *Boston University* — but there was coffee in his, or there had been. Now he just pushed it around the table as if it were a chess piece and he couldn't decide where to play it. "All I want you to remember — and your father wants this too, or no, he needs it, and needs you to pay attention — is that there are good truths and bad truths, that's all. And your memory only serves to a point; I mean, who's to say what really happened, because everybody has their own version, that woman jogger, the boy on the bike — and the DA, the district attorney, he's the one who might ask you what happened that day, just him and me, that's all. Don't you worry about anything."

But she was worried, because Mr. Apodaca was there in the first place, with his perfect suit and perfect tie and his doggy eyes, and because her father had been handcuffed along the side of the road and taken to jail and the car had been impounded, which meant nobody could use it, not her father or her mother when she came back from France or Dolores the maid or Allie the au pair. There was all that, but there was something else too, something in her father's look and the attorney's sugary tones that hardened her: they were talking down to her. Talking down to her as if she had no more sense than her little sister. And she did. She did.

That day, the day of the incident — or accident, he'd have to call it an accident now — he'd met Marcy for lunch at a restaurant down by the marina where you could sit outside and watch the way the sun struck the masts of the ships as they rocked on the tide and the light shattered and regrouped and shattered again. It was one of his favorite spots in town — one of his favorite spots, period. No matter how overburdened he felt, no matter how life beat him down and every task and deadline seemed to swell up out of all proportion so that twenty people couldn't have dealt with it all — a team, an army — this place, this table in the far corner of the deck overlooking the jungle of masts, the bleached wooden catwalks, the glowing arc of the harbor and the mountains that framed it, always had a calming effect on him. That and the just-this-side-of-too-cold local sauvignon blanc they served by the glass. He was working on his second when Marcy came up the stairs, swaying over her heels like a model on the runway, and glided down the length of the deck to join him. She gave him an uncomplicated smile that lit her eyes and acknowledged everything — the day, the locale, the sun and the breeze and the clean pounded smell of the ocean and him perched there in the middle of it all — and bent to kiss him before easing herself into the chair beside him. "That looks nice," she said, referring to the wine dense as struck gold in the glass before him, and held up a finger for the waiter.

And what did they talk about? Little things. Her work, the pair of shoes she'd bought and returned and then bought all over again, the movie they'd seen two nights ago — the last time they'd been together — and how she still couldn't believe he liked that ending. "It's not that it was cheesy," she said, and here was her wine and should they get a bottle, yeah, sure, a bottle, why not, "and it was, but just that I didn't believe it."

"Didn't believe what — that the husband would take her back?"

"No," she said. "Or yes. It's idiotic. But what do you expect from a French movie? They always have these slinky-looking heroines in their thirties —"

"Or forties."

"— with great legs and mascara out of, I don't know, a Kiss revival, and then even though they're married to the greatest guy in the world they feel unfulfilled and they go out and fuck the whole village, starting with the butcher."

"Juliette Binoche," he said. He was feeling the wine. Feeling good.

"Yeah, right. Even though it wasn't her, it could have been. Should have been. Has been in every French movie but this one for the past what, twenty years?" She put down her glass and let out a short two-note laugh that was like birdsong, a laugh that entranced him, and he wasn't worried about work now, not work or anything else, and here was the bottle in the bucket, the wine cold as the cellar it came from. "And then the whole village comes out and applauds her at the end for staying true to her romantic ideals — and the *husband,* Jesus."

Nothing could irritate him. Nothing could touch him. He was in love, the pelicans were gliding over the belly of the bay and her eyes were lewd and beautiful and pleased with themselves, but he had to pull the stopper here for just a minute. "Martine's not like that," he said. "I'm not like that."

She looked over her shoulder before digging out a cigarette — this was California, after all — and when she bent to light it her hair fell across her face. She came up smiling, the smoke snatched away from her lips and neutralized on the breeze the moment she exhaled. Discussion over.

Marcy was twenty-eight, educated at Berkeley, and she and her sister had opened an artists' supply shop on a side street downtown. She'd been a double major in art and film. She rode a bike to work. She was Asian. Or Chinese, she corrected him. Of Chinese descent anyway. Her family, as she'd informed him on the first date with enough irony in her voice to foreground and bury the topic at the same time, went back four generations to the honorable great-grandfather who'd smuggled himself across the Pacific inside a clichéd flour barrel hidden in the clichéd hold of a clichéd merchant ship. She'd grown up in Syracuse, in a suburban development, and her accent — the *a*'s flattened so that his name came out *Eelan* rather than Alan — just killed him, so incongruous coming from someone, as, well — the words out of his mouth before he knew what he was saying — as *exotic*-looking as her. And then, because he couldn't read her expression — had he gone too far? — he told her he was impressed because he only went back three generations, his grandfather having come over from Cork, but if it was in a barrel it would have been full of whiskey. "And Martine's from Paris," he'd added. "But you knew that already, didn't you?"

The bottle was half gone by the time they ordered — and there was no hurry, no hurry at all, because they were both taking the afternoon off, and no argument — and when the food came they looked at each other for just the briefest fleeting particle of a moment before he ordered a second bottle. And then they were eating and everything slowed down until all of creation seemed to come into focus in a new way. He sipped the wine, chewed, looked into her unparalleled eyes, and felt the sun lay a hand across his shoulders, and in a sudden blaze of apprehension he glanced up at the gull that appeared on the railing behind her and saw the way the breeze touched its feathers and the sun whitened its breast till there was nothing brighter and more perfect in the world — this creature, his fellow creature, and he was here to see it. He wanted to tell Marcy about it, about the miracle of the moment, the layers peeled back, revelatory, joyous, but instead he reached over to top off her glass and said, "So tell me about the shoes."

Later, after Mr. Apodaca had backed out of the driveway in his little white convertible with the Mercedes sign emblazoned on the front of it and the afternoon melted away in a slurry of phone calls and messages — *OMG! Chilty likes Alex Turtie!, can you believe it?* — Dolores made them chile rellenos with carrot and jicama sticks and ice cream for dessert. Then Allie quizzed her and Lisette over their homework until the house fell quiet and all she could hear was the faint pulse of her father's music from the family room. She'd done her math and was working on a report about Aaron Burr for her history teacher, Mr. Compson, when she got up and went to the kitchen for a glass of juice or maybe hot chocolate in the microwave — and she wouldn't know which till she was standing there in the kitchen with the recessed lights glowing over the stone countertops and the refrigerator door open wide. She wasn't thinking about anything in particular — Aaron Burr was behind her now, upstairs, on her desk — and when she passed the archway to the family room the flash of the TV screen caught her eye and she paused a moment. Her father was there still, stretched out on the couch with a book, the TV muted and some game on, football, baseball, and the low snarl of his music in the background. His face had that blank absorbed look he got while reading and sometimes when he was just sitting there staring across the room or out the window at nothing, and he had the mug cradled in one hand, balanced on his chest beside the book.

He'd sat with them over dinner, but he hadn't eaten — he was going out later, he told her. For dinner. A late dinner. He didn't say who with, but she knew it was the Asian woman. Marcy. She'd seen her exactly twice, from behind the window of her car, and Marcy had waved at her both times, a little curl of the fingers and a flash of the palm. There was an Asian girl in her class — she was Chinese — and her name was Xuan. That seemed right for an Asian girl, Xuan. Different. A name that said who she was and where she was from, far away, a whole ocean away. But Marcy? She didn't think so.

"Hey," her father said, lifting his head to peer over the butt of the couch, and she realized she'd been standing there watching him, "what's up? Homework done? Need any help? How about that essay — want me to proof that essay for you? What's it on, Madison? Or Burr. Burr, right?"

"That's okay."

"You sure?" His voice was slow and compacted, as if it wasn't composed of vibrations of the vocal cords, the air passing through the larynx like in her science book, but made of something heavier, denser. He would be taking a taxi tonight, she could see that, and then maybe she — *Marcy* — would drive him back home. "Because I could do it, no problem. I've got" — and she watched him lift his watch to his face and rotate his wrist — "half an hour or so, forty-five minutes."

"That's okay," she said.

She was sipping her hot chocolate and reading a story for English by William Faulkner, the author's picture in her textbook a freeze-frame of furious eyes and conquered hair, when she heard her father's voice riding a current down the hall, now murmurous, now pinched and electric, then dense and sluggish all over again. It took her a minute: he was reading Lisette her bedtime story. The house was utterly still and she held her breath, listening, till all of a sudden she could make out the words. He was reading *Balto,* a story she'd loved when she was Lisette's age, and as his voice came to her down the hall she could picture the illustrations: Balto, the lead dog of the sled team, radiating light from a sunburst on his chest and the snowstorm like a monstrous hand closing over him, the team fighting through the Alaskan wind and ice and temperatures of forty below zero to deliver serum to the sick children in Nome — and those children would die if Balto didn't get through. Diphtheria. It was a diphtheria epidemic and the only plane available was broken down — or no, it couldn't fly in winter. *What's diphtheria?* she'd asked her father, and he'd gone to the shelf and pulled down the encyclopedia to give her the answer, and that was heroic in itself, because as he settled back onto her bed, Lisette snuggled up beside her and rain at the windows and the bedside lamp the only thing between them and darkness absolute, he'd said, *You see, there's everything in books, everything you could ever want.*

Balto's paws were bleeding. The ice froze between his toes. The other dogs kept holding back, but he was the lead dog and he turned on them and snarled, fought them just to keep them in their traces, to keep them going. *Balto.* With his harnessed shoulders and shaggy head and the furious unconquerable will that drove him all through that day and into the night that was so black there was no way of telling if they were on the trail or not.

Now, as she sat poised at the edge of her bed, listening to Lisette's silence and her father's limping voice, she waited for her sister to pipe up in her breathy little baby squeak and frame the inevitable questions: *Dad, Dad, how cold is forty below?* And: *Dad, what's diphtheria?*

The sun had crept imperceptibly across the deck, fingering the cracks in the varnished floorboards and easing up the low brass rail Marcy was using as a backrest. She was leaning into it, the rail, her chair tipped back, her elbows splayed behind her and her legs stretched out to catch the sun, shapely legs, stunning legs, legs long and burnished and firm, legs that made him think of the rest of her and the way she was in bed. There was a scar just under the swell of her left kneecap, the flesh annealed in an irregular oval as if it had been burned or scarified, and he'd never noticed that before. Well, he was in a new place, half a glass each left of the second bottle and the world sprung to life in the fullness of its detail, everything sharpened, in focus, as if he'd needed glasses all these years and just clapped them on. The gull was gone but it had been special, a very special gull, and there were sparrows now, or wrens, hopping along the floor in little streaks of color, snatching up a crumb of this or that and then hurtling away over the rail as if they'd been launched. He was thinking he didn't want any more wine — two bottles was plenty — but maybe something to cap off the afternoon, a cognac maybe, just one.

She'd been talking about one of the girls who worked for her, a girl he'd seen a couple of times, nineteen, soft-faced and pretty, and how she — her name was Bettina — was living the party life, every night at the clubs, and how thin she was.

"Cocaine?" he wondered, and she shrugged. "Has it affected her work?"

"No," she said, "not yet, anyway." And then she went on to qualify that with a litany of lateness in the morning, hyper behavior after lunch, and too many doctor's appointments. He waited a moment, watching her mouth and tongue, the beautiful unspooling way the words dropped from her lips, before he reached down and ran a finger over the blemish below her kneecap. "You have a scar," he said.

She looked at her knee as if she wasn't aware it was attached to her, then withdrew her leg momentarily to scrutinize it before giving it back to the sun and the deck and the waiting touch of his hand. "Oh, that?" she said. "That's from when I was a kid."

"A burn or what?"

"Bicycle." She teased the syllables out, slow and sure.

His hand was on her knee, the warmth of the contact, and he rubbed the spot a moment before straightening up in the chair and draining his glass. "Looks like a burn," he said.

"Nope. Just fell in the street." She let out that laugh again and he drank it in. "You should've seen my training wheels — or the one of them. It was as flat" — *flaat* — "as if a truck had run me over."

Her eyes flickered with the lingering seep of the memory and they both took a moment to picture it, the little girl with the wheel collapsed under her and the scraped knee — or it had to have been worse than that, punctured, shredded — and he didn't think of Lisette or Angelle, not yet, because he was deep into the drift of the day, so deep there was nothing else but this deck and this slow sweet sun and the gull that was gone now. "You want something else?" he heard himself say. "Maybe a Rémy, just to cap it off? I mean, I'm wined out, but just, I don't know, a taste of cognac?"

"Sure," she said, "why not?" and she didn't look at her watch and he didn't look at his either.

And then the waiter was there with two snifters and a little square of dark chocolate for each of them, compliments of the house. *Snifter,* he was thinking as he revolved the glass in his hand, what a perfect designation for the thing, a name that spoke to function, and he said it aloud, "Isn't it great that they have things like snifters, so you can stick your nose in it and sniff? And plus, it's named for what it is, unlike, say, a napkin or a fork. You don't nap napkins or fork forks, right?"

"Yeah," she said, and the sun had leveled on her hair now, picking out the highlights and illuminating the lobe of one ear, "I guess. But I was telling you about Bettina? Did you know that guy she picked up I told you about — not the boyfriend, but the one-night stand? He got her pregnant."

The waiter drifted by then, college kid, hair in his eyes, and asked if there'd be anything else. It was then that he thought to check his watch and the first little pulse of alarm began to make itself felt somewhere deep in the quiet lagoon of his brain: *Angelle,* the alarm said. *Lisette.* They had to be picked up at school after soccer practice every Wednesday because Wednesday was Allie's day off and Martine wasn't there to do it. Martine was in Paris, doing whatever she pleased. That much was clear. And today — today was Wednesday.

Angelle remembered waiting for him longer than usual that day. He'd been late before — he was almost always late, because of work, because he had such a hectic schedule — but this time she'd already got through half her homework, the blue backpack canted away from her and her notebook spread open across her knees as she sat at the curb, and still he wasn't there. The sun had sunk into the trees across the street and she felt a chill where she'd sweated through her shorts and T-shirt at soccer. Lisette's team had finished before hers and for a while her sister had sat beside her, drawing big *X*'s and *O*'s in two different colors on a sheet of loose-leaf paper, but she'd got bored and run off to play on the swings with two other kids whose parents were late.

Every few minutes a car would round the turn at the top of the street, and her eyes would jump to it, but it wasn't theirs. She watched a black SUV pull up in front of the school and saw Dani Mead and Sarah Schuster burst through the doors, laughing, their backpacks riding up off their shoulders and their hair swaying back and forth as they slid into the cavernous back seat and the door slammed shut. The car's brake lights flashed and then it rolled slowly out of the parking lot and into the street, and she watched it till it disappeared round the corner. He was always working, she knew that, trying to dig himself out from under all the work he had piled up — that was his phrase, *dig himself out,* and she pictured him in his office surrounded by towering stacks of papers, papers like the Leaning Tower of Pisa, and a shovel in his hands as if he were one of those men in the orange jackets bent over a hole in the road — but still, she felt impatient. Felt cold. Hungry. And where was he?

Finally, after the last two kids had been picked up by their mothers and the sun reduced to a streak that ran across the tile roof of the school and up into the crowns of the palms behind it, after Lisette had come back to sit on the curb and whine and pout and complain like the baby she was *(He's just drunk, I bet that's it, just drunk like Mom said)* and she had to tell her she didn't know what she was talking about, there he was. Lisette saw the car first. It appeared at the top of the street like a mirage, coming so slowly round the turn it might have been rolling under its own power, with nobody in it, and Angelle remembered what her father had told her about always setting the handbrake, always, no matter what. She hadn't really wanted a lesson — she'd have to be sixteen for that — but they were up in the mountains, at the summer cabin, just after her mother had left for France, and there was nobody around. "You're a big girl," he'd told her, and she was, tall for her age — people always mistook her for an eighth-grader or even a freshman. "Go ahead, it's easy," he told her. "Like bumper cars. Only you don't bump anything." And she'd laughed and he laughed and she got behind the wheel with him guiding her and her heart was pounding till she thought she was going to lift right out of the seat. Everything looked different through the windshield, yellow spots and dirt, the world wrapped in a bubble. The sun was in her eyes. The road was a black river oozing through the dried-out weeds, the trees looming and receding as if a wave had passed through them. And the car crept down the road the way it was creeping now. Too slow. Much too slow.

When her father pulled up to the curb, she saw right away that something was wrong. He was smiling at them, or trying to smile, but his face was too heavy, his face weighed a thousand tons, carved of rock like the faces of the presidents on Mount Rushmore, and it distorted the smile till it was more like a grimace. A flare of anger rose in her — Lisette was right — and then it died away and she was scared. Just scared.

"Sorry," he murmured, "sorry I'm late, I —" and he didn't finish the thought or excuse or whatever it was because he was pushing open the door now, the driver's door, and pulling himself out onto the pavement. He took a minute to remove his sunglasses and polish them on the tail of his shirt before leaning heavily against the side of the car. He gave her a weak smile — half a smile, not even half — and carefully fitted them back over his ears, though it was too dark for sunglasses, anybody could see that. Plus, these were his old sunglasses — two shining blue disks in wire frames that made his eyes disappear — which meant that he must have lost his good ones, the ones that had cost him two hundred and fifty dollars on sale at the Sunglass Hut. "Listen," he said, as Lisette pulled open the rear door and flung her backpack across the seat, "I just — I forgot the time, is all. I'm sorry. I am. I really am."

She gave him a look that was meant to burn into him, to make him feel what she was feeling, but she couldn't tell if he was looking at her or not. "We've been sitting here since four," she said, and she heard the hurt and accusation in her own voice. She pulled open the other door, the one right beside him, because she was going to sit in back as a demonstration of her disapproval — they'd both sit in back, she and Lisette, and nobody up front — when he stopped her with a gesture, reaching out suddenly to brush the hair away from her face.

"You've got to help me out here," he said, and a pleading tone had come into his voice. "Because" — the words were stalling, congealing, sticking in his throat — "because, hey, why lie, huh? I wouldn't lie to you."

The sun faded. A car went up the street. There was a boy on a bicycle, a boy she knew, and he gave her a look as he cruised past, the wheels a blur.

"I was, I had lunch with Marcy, because, well, you know how hard I've been — and I just needed to kick back, you know? Everybody does. It's no sin." A pause, his hand going to his pocket and then back to her hair again. "And we had some wine. Some wine with lunch." He gazed off down the street then, as if he were looking for the tapering long-necked green bottles the wine had come in, as if he were going to produce them for evidence.

She just stood there staring at him, her jaw set, but she let his hand fall to her shoulder and give her a squeeze, the sort of squeeze he gave her when he was proud of her, when she got an A on a test or cleaned up the dishes all by herself without anybody asking.

"I know this is terrible," he was saying, "I mean I hate to do this, I hate to . . . but Angelle, I'm asking you just this once, because the thing is?" — and here he tugged down the little blue disks so that she could see the dull sheen of his eyes focused on her — "I don't think I can drive."

When the valet brought the car round, the strangest thing happened, a little lapse, and it was because he wasn't paying attention. He was distracted by Marcy in her low-slung Miata with the top down, the redness of it, a sleek thing, pin your ears back and fly, Marcy wheeling out of the lot with a wave and two fingers kissed to her lips, her hair lifting on the breeze. And there was the attendant, another college kid, shorter and darker than the one upstairs frowning over the tip but with the same haircut, as if they'd both been to the same barber or stylist or whatever, and the attendant had said something to him — *Your car, sir; here's your car, sir* — and the strange thing was that for a second there he didn't recognize it. Thought the kid was trying to put something over on him. Was this his car? Was this the sort of thing he'd own? This mud-splattered charcoal-gray SUV with the seriously depleted tires? And that dent in the front fender, the knee-high scrape that ran the length of the body as if some metallic claw had caught hold of it? Was this some kind of trick?

"Sir?"

"Yeah," he'd said, staring up into the sky now, and where were his shades? "Yeah, what? What do you want?"

The smallest beat. "Your car. Sir."

And then it all came clear to him the way these things do, and he flipped open his wallet to extract two singles — finger-softened money, as soft and pliable as felt — and the valet accepted them and he was in the car, looking to connect the male end of the seat belt to the female, and where was the damned thing? There was still a sliver of sun cutting in low over the ocean and he dug into the glove compartment for his old sunglasses, the emergency pair, because the new ones were someplace else altogether, apparently, and not in his pocket and not on the cord round his neck, and then he had them fitted over his ears and the radio was playing something with some real thump to it and he was rolling on out of the lot, looking to merge with the traffic on the boulevard.

That was when everything turned hard-edged and he knew he was drunk. He waited too long to merge — too cautious, too tentative — and the driver behind him laid on the horn and he had no choice but to give him the finger and he might have leaned his head out the window and barked something too, but the car came to life beneath him and somebody swerved wide and he was out in traffic. If he was thinking anything at all it probably had to do with his last DUI, which had come out of nowhere when he wasn't even that drunk, or maybe not drunk at all. He'd been coming back from Johnny's Rib Shack after working late, gnawing at a rib, a beer open between his legs, and he came down the slope beneath the underpass where you make a left to turn onto the freeway ramp and he was watching the light and didn't see the mustard-colored Volvo stopped there in front of him until it was too late. And he was so upset with himself — and not just himself, but the world at large and the way it presented these problems to him, these impediments, the unforeseen and the unexpected just laid out there in front of him as if it were some kind of conspiracy — that he got out of the car, the radiator crushed and hissing and beer pissed all over his lap, and shouted, "All right, so sue me!" at the dazed woman behind the wheel of the other car. But that wasn't going to happen now. Nothing was going to happen now.

The trees rolled by, people crossed at the crosswalk, lights turned yellow and then red and then green, and he was doing fine, just sailing, thinking he'd take the girls out for burritos or In-N-Out burgers on the way home, when a cop passed him going in the other direction and his heart froze like a block of ice and then thawed instantaneously, hammering so hard he thought it would punch right through his chest. *Signal, signal,* he told himself, keeping his eyes on the rearview, and he did, he signaled and made the first turn, a road he'd never been on before, and then he made the next turn after that, and the next, and when he looked up again he had no idea where he was.

Which was another reason why he was late, and there was Angelle giving him that hard cold judgmental look — her mother's look exactly — because she was perfect, she was dutiful and put-upon and the single best kid in the world, in the history of the world, and he was a fuckup, pure and simple. It was wrong, what he asked her to do, but it happened nonetheless, and he guided her through each step, a straight shot on the way home, two and a half miles, that was all, and forget stopping at In-N-Out, they'd just go home and have a pizza delivered. He remembered going on in that vein, "Don't you girls want pizza tonight? Huh, Lisette? Peppers and onions? And those little roasted artichokes? Or maybe you'd prefer worm heads, mashed worm heads?" — leaning over the seat to cajole her, make it all right and take the tightness out of her face, and he didn't see the boy on the bicycle, didn't know anything about him until Angelle let out a choked little cry and there was the heart-stopping thump of something glancing off the fender.

The courtroom smelled of wax, the same kind of wax they used on the floors at school, sweet and acrid at the same time, a smell that was almost comforting in its familiarity. But she wasn't at school — she'd been excused for the morning — and she wasn't here to be comforted or to feel comfortable either. She was here to listen to Mr. Apodaca and the judge and the DA and the members of the jury decide her father's case and to testify on his behalf, tell what she knew, tell a kind of truth that wasn't maybe whole and pure but necessary, a necessary truth. That was what Mr. Apodaca was calling it now, *necessary,* and she'd sat with him and her father in one of the unused rooms off the main corridor — another courtroom — while he went over the whole business one more time for her, just to be sure she understood.

Her father had held her hand on the way in and he sat beside her on one of the wooden benches as his attorney went over the details of that day after school, because he wanted to make sure they were all on the same page. Those were his words exactly — "I want to make sure we're all on the same page on this" — as he loomed over her and her father, bracing himself on the gleaming wooden rail, his shoes competing with the floor for the brilliance of their shine, and she couldn't help picturing some Mexican boy, some dropout from the high school, laboring over those shoes while Mr. Apodaca sat high in a leather-backed chair, his feet in the stainless-steel stirrups. She pictured him behind his newspaper, looking stern, or going over his brief, the details, *these* details. When he'd gone through everything, minute by minute, gesture by gesture, coaching her, quizzing her — "And what did he say? What did you say?" — he asked her father if he could have a minute alone with her.

That was when her father gave her hand a final squeeze and then dropped it and got up from the bench. He was wearing a new suit, a navy so dark and severe it made his skin look like raw dough, and he'd had his hair cut so tight round the ears it was as if a machine had been at work there, an edger or a riding mower like the one they used on the soccer field at school, only in miniature, and for an instant she imagined tiny people like in *Gulliver's Travels* buzzing round her father's ears with their mowers and clippers and edgers. The tie he was wearing was the most boring one he owned, a blue fading to black, with no design, not even a stripe. His face was heavy, his crow's-feet right there for all the world to see — gouges, tears, slits, a butcher's shop of carved and abused skin — and for the first time she noticed the small gray dollop of loose flesh under his chin. It made him look old, worn-out, past his prime, as if he weren't the hero anymore but playing the hero's best friend, the one who never gets the girl and never gets the job. And what role was she playing? The star. She was the star here, and the more the attorney talked on and the heavier her father's face got, the more it came home to her.

Mr. Apodaca said nothing, just let the silence hang in the room till the memory of her father's footsteps had faded. Then he leaned over the back of the bench directly in front of her, the Great Seal of the State of California framed over the dais behind him, and he squeezed his eyes shut a moment so that when he opened them and fixed her with his gaze, there were tears there. Or the appearance of tears. His eyelashes were moist, and the moistness picked each of them out individually until all she could think of was the stalks of cane against the fence in the back corner of the yard. "I want you to listen very carefully to what I'm about to say, Angelle," he breathed, his voice so soft and constricted it was like the sound of the air being let out of a tire. "Because this concerns you and your sister. It could affect your whole life."

Another pause. Her stomach was crawling. She didn't want to say anything but he held the pause so long she had to bow her head and say, "Yeah. Yeah, I know."

And then suddenly, without warning, his voice was lashing out at her: "But you don't know it. Do you know what's at stake here? Do you really?"

"No," she said, and it was a whisper.

"Your father is going to plead no contest to the charge of driving under the influence. He was wrong, he admits it. And they'll take away his driving privileges and he'll have to go to counseling and find someone to drive you and your sister to school, and I don't mean to minimize that, that's very serious, but here's the thing you may not know." He held her eyes, though she wanted to look away. "The second charge is child endangerment, not for the boy on the bike, who barely even scraped a knee, luckily, luckily, and whose parents have already agreed to a settlement, but for you, for allowing you to do what you did. And do you know what will happen if the jury finds him guilty?"

She didn't know what was coming, not exactly, but the tone of what he was conveying — dark, ominous, fulminating with anger and the threat about to be revealed in the very next breath — made her feel small. And scared. Definitely scared. She shook her head.

"They'll take you and Lisette away from him." He clenched both hands, pushed himself up from the rail, and turned as if to pace off down the aisle in front of her, as if he was disgusted with the whole thing and had no more to say. But then, suddenly, he swung round on her with a furious twist of his shoulders and a hard accusatory stab of his balled-up right hand and a single rigid forefinger. "And no," he said, barely contained, barely able to keep his voice level, "in answer to your unasked question or objection or whatever you want to call it, your mother's not coming back for you, not now, maybe not ever."

Was he ashamed? Was he humiliated? Did he have to stop drinking and get his life in order? Yes, yes, and yes. But as he sat there in the courtroom beside Jerry Apodaca at eleven-thirty in the morning, the high arched windows pregnant with light and his daughter, Marcy, Dolores, and the solemn-faced au pair sitting shoulder to shoulder on the gleaming wooden bench behind him, there was a flask in his inside pocket, and the faint burning pulse of single-malt scotch rode his veins. He'd taken a pull from it in the men's room not ten minutes ago, just to steady himself, and then he'd rinsed out his mouth and ground half a dozen Tic Tacs between his teeth to knock down any trace of alcohol on his breath. Jerry would have been furious with him if he so much as suspected . . . and it was a weak and cowardly thing to do, no excuse, no excuse at all, but he felt adrift, felt scared, and he needed an anchor to hold on to. Just for now. Just for today. And then he'd throw the thing away, because what was a flask for anyway except to provide a twenty-four-hour teat for the kind of drunk who wore a suit and brushed his teeth.

He began to jiggle one foot and tap his knees together beneath the table, a nervous twitch no amount of scotch would cure. The judge was taking his time, the assistant DA smirking over a sheaf of papers at her own table off to the right. She wore a permanent self-congratulatory look, this woman, as if she were queen of the court and the county too, and she'd really laid into him before the recess, and that was nasty, purely nasty. She was the prosecution's attack dog, that was what Jerry called her, her voice tuned to a perpetual note of sarcasm, disbelief, and petulance, but he held to his story and never wavered. He was just glad Angelle hadn't had to see it.

She was here now, though, sitting right behind him, missing school — missing school because of him. And that was one more strike against him, he supposed, *because what kind of father would* . . . ? but the thought was too depressing and he let it die. He resisted the urge to turn round and give her a look, a smile, a wink, the least gesture, anything. It was too painful to see her there, under constraint, his daughter dragged out of school for this, and then he didn't want anybody to think he was coaching her or coercing her in any way. Jerry had no such scruples, though. He'd drilled her over and over and he'd even gone to the extreme of asking her — or no, *instructing* her — to wear something that might conform to the court's idea of what a good, honest, straightforward child was like, something that would make her look younger than she was, too young to bend the truth and far too young even to think about getting behind the wheel of a car.

Three times Jerry had sent her back to change outfits until finally, with a little persuasion from the au pair (*Allie,* and he'd have to remember to slip her a twenty, a twenty at least, because she was gold, pure gold), she put on a lacy white high-collared dress she'd worn for some kind of pageant at school, with matching white tights and patent-leather shoes. There was something wrong there in the living room, he could see that, something in the way she held her shoulders and stamped up the stairs to her room, her face clenched and her eyes burning into him, and he should have recognized it, should have given her just a hair more of his attention, but Marcy was there and she had her opinion and Jerry was being an autocrat and he himself had his hands full — he couldn't eat or think or do anything other than maybe slip into the pantry and tip the bottle of Macallan over the flask. By the time he thought of it, they were in the car, and he tried, he did, leaning across the seat to ply her with little jokes about getting a free day off and what her teachers were going to think and what Aaron Burr might have done — he would've just shot somebody, right? — but Jerry was drilling her one last time and she was sunk into the seat beside Marcy, already clamped up.

The courtroom, this courtroom, the one she was in now, was a duplicate of the one in which her father's attorney had quizzed her an hour and a half ago, except that it was filled with people. They were all old, or older, anyway, except for one woman in a form-fitting plaid jacket Angelle had seen in the window at Nordstrom's who must have been in her twenties. She was in the jury box, looking bored. The other jurors were mostly men, businessmen, she supposed, with balding heads and recessed eyes and big meaty hands clasped in their laps or grasping the rail in front of them. One of them looked like the principal of her school, Dr. Damon, but he wasn't.

The judge sat up at his desk in the front of the room, which they called a bench but wasn't a bench at all, the flag of the State of California on one side of him and the American flag on the other. She was seated in the front row, between Dolores and Allie, and her father and Mr. Apodaca sat at a desk in front of her, the shoulders of their suits puffed up as if they were wearing football pads. Her father's suit was so dark she could see the dandruff there, a little spray of it like dust on the collar of his jacket, and she felt embarrassed for him. And sorry for him too — and for herself. And Lisette. She looked up at the judge and then at the district attorney with his grim gray tight-shaven face and the scowling woman beside him, and couldn't help thinking about what Mr. Apodaca had told her, and it made her shrink into herself when Mr. Apodaca called her name and the judge, reading the look on her face, tried to give her a smile of encouragement.

She wasn't aware of walking across the floor or of the hush that fell over the courtroom or even of the bailiff who asked her to hold up her right hand and swear to tell the truth — all this, as if she were recalling a fragmented dream, would come to her later. But then she was seated in the witness chair and everything was bright and loud suddenly, as if she'd just switched channels on the TV. Mr. Apodaca was right there before her, his voice rising sweetly, almost as if he were singing, and he was leading her through the questions they'd rehearsed over and over again. Yes, she told him, her father was late, and yes, it was getting dark, and no, she didn't notice anything strange about him. He was her father and he always picked her sister and her up on Wednesdays, she volunteered, because Wednesdays were when Allie and Dolores both had their day off and there was no one else to do it because her mother was in France.

They were all watching her now, the court gone absolutely silent, so silent you would have thought everyone had tiptoed out the door, but there they all were, hanging on her every word. She wanted to say more about her mother, about how her mother was coming home soon — had promised as much the last time she'd called long distance from her apartment in Saint Germain des Prés — but Mr. Apodaca wouldn't let her. He kept leading her along, using his sugary voice now, talking down to her, and she wanted to speak up and tell him he didn't have to treat her like that, tell him about her mother, Lisette, the school and the lawn and the trees and the way the interior of the car smelled and the heat of the liquor on her father's breath — anything that would forestall the inevitable, the question that was tucked in just behind this last one, the question on the point of which everything turned, because now she heard it, murmurous and soft and sweet, on her father's attorney's lips: "Who was driving?"

"I just wanted to say one thing," she said, lifting her eyes now to look at Mr. Apodaca and only Mr. Apodaca, his dog's eyes, his pleading soft baby-talking face, "just because, well, I wanted to say you're wrong about my mother, because she *is* coming home — she told me so herself, on, on the phone —" She couldn't help herself. Her voice was cracking.

"Yes," he said, too quickly, a hiss of breath, "yes, I understand that, Angelle, but we need to establish . . . you need to answer the question."

Oh, and now the silence went even deeper, the silence of the deep sea, of outer space, of the Arctic night when you couldn't hear the runners of the sled or the feet of the dogs bleeding into the snow, and her eyes jumped to her father's then, the look on his face of hopefulness and fear and confusion, and she loved him in that moment more than she ever had.

"Angelle," Mr. Apodaca was saying, murmuring. "Angelle?"

She turned her face back to him, blotting out the judge, the DA, the woman in the plaid jacket who was probably a college student, probably cool, and waited for the question to drop.

"Who," Mr. Apodaca repeated, slowing it down now, "was" — slower, slower still — "driving?"

She lifted her chin then to look at the judge and heard the words coming out of her mouth as if they'd been planted there, telling the truth, the hurtful truth, the truth no one would have guessed because she was almost thirteen now, almost a teenager, and she let them know it. "*I* was," she said, and the courtroom roared to life with so many people buzzing at once she thought at first they hadn't heard her. So she said it again, said it louder, much louder, so loud she might have been shouting it to the man with the camera at the back of the long churchy room with its sweat-burnished pews and the flags and emblems and all the rest. And then she looked away from the judge, away from the spectators and the man with the camera and the court recorder and the bank of windows so brilliant with light you would have thought a bomb had gone off there, and looked directly at her father.

RANDY DEVITA

Riding the Doghouse

FROM WEST BRANCH

A STORM OUTSIDE. Beside me the soft breath of my wife shifts the covers that we share. I am dozing, trapped between midnight and dawn, and in my half-sleep, I listen as rain sleets against our bedroom window; oak branches, stripped by autumn, scrape at the back of the house. A surge of electrons excites the air; my ears hum. There is a violent crash, like a shattered windshield, and thunder drums past like traffic on the interstate. The windows rattle in their frames.

My eyes snap open.

A voice, a gentle murmur, is coming from my son's room next door. I look at the clock — 3 A.M. — then fold the covers back and climb out from the bed. The carpet feels soft beneath my bare feet, and my toes curl reflexively. I cross the room and rest my head against the wall. The wallpaper is slick, like sweating skin. I hear my son speaking, but the wall dulls his words.

Who is he talking to?

I leave the bedroom and walk down the hallway. Dim light from a small lamp on a table at the end of the hall spills onto the floor. A beam of light extends into his bedroom through the narrow gap between the open door and frame. In the darkness my son's features are grainy and imperfect, but I see his eyes are closed. I whisper his name. Thunder rolls in the distance; rain washes down the roof, drains from the gutters. Soft but distinct from the storm, I hear his breath, a tender pattern that lacks the stain of worry. Today is his birthday — twelve years old — and he's sleeping now.

I stand outside his door. Lightning flares. I flinch and close my eyes.

When I was twelve, my best friend was Doug Middleton, who lived in the new development outside of town. We collected comic books together and traded the science fiction paperbacks that we read. But my father drove a truck, so we were different, too. His father carried a briefcase filled with neatly typed reports and thin manila folders into the office where he worked; my father came off the road with his briefcase crowded with logbooks, chaotic bundles of receipts, and music cassettes. And once a year, Doug visited his father's office for a corporate father-son day; each summer I went out on the road with my father for a week in his truck.

"One rule," he said after we climbed into the cab of the Kenworth and packed our bags into the bunk. My father pretended to be busy — inspecting odd gauges, throwing unknown switches — while he waited for me to ask. At the start of each trip it was always the same rule, but my father was that way, repeating himself like a comedian with the same tired routine.

"What?" I said.

And my father smiled, pleased because he was fond of scripted things. "No touching anything when I'm not in the truck." Then he lowered his voice and announced: "It's your captain speaking. Fasten your seat belts and prepare for takeoff." The Kenworth rumbled to life, and our laughter was lost beneath the diesel rattle of the engine.

Day and we drove west through the mountains of central Pennsylvania, following the interstate from the Delaware Water Gap toward Grand Rapids. I sat on the doghouse — the padded cover between the driver and passenger seats, directly over the engine — where I watched as the traffic and the road signs and the exit ramps we passed were recycled over and again. My father smoked as he drove, holding the cigarette below his open window; now and then the wind sent ashes spinning inside the cab. Each time we came to the base of another mountain, he lifted the cigarette to his mouth, double-clutched, and downshifted. Exhaust whined through the smokestacks, and the engine vibrated under the doghouse as the Kenworth strained to pull our loaded trailer up the incline. By late afternoon I was tied into a sullen knot and crawled off the doghouse into the Kenworth's sleeper, where it was dim and quiet and humid with the odor of bedding. I opened an air vent and as the Kenworth raced to the west, the vent captured the dead summer air and transformed it into a thin, gentle breeze. The flow of warm air brushed my hair, and in the narrow moment between consciousness and sleep, I thought of my mother, who stroked my hair on summer nights when my father was away and I could not sleep. Lying beneath the vent, I slept as her fingers combed through my hair and tickled my scalp.

Night and the darkness flooded past, washing clean the monotony of day and bruising the spinelike cirrus clouds, which extended toward the horizon. I returned to the doghouse, where I sat balanced on my knees. Because the Kenworth was a cab-over — with the engine under the cab rather than extended out front — I could see over the ledge of the dashboard and down to the road below. Each time my father changed lanes, the painted lines rushed through an illuminated patch of highway and were swallowed beneath the Kenworth.

We spoke infrequently. Perhaps a quarter of an hour elapsed before we responded to something the other had said. I was fascinated by the rare and minor sights at night: the faint lemon glow that backlit the gauges inside the cab, the sudden wash of our headlamps against the automobiles we passed, the skeletal outlines of a radio tower braced against the distant horizon, crowned by red beacon lights.

At night the transmissions on the CB were like frantic sparks lifted from a midnight campfire. The CB was mounted on the ceiling, beside the windshield at the center of the cab, and had a simple layout: a small knob that powered it on, then served as the volume control; a square UHV display with a red needle that twitched as the CB received a signal; an oversized dial for changing the channel; and beside that, the channel's crisp digital display of lime-colored numerals. My father always kept the CB set to nineteen. Like schools of fish in a dark sea, the eighteen-wheelers streamed along the interstate, and while chatter crowded the channel with voices that leaped and growled — often with white blades of feedback between them — I knelt on the doghouse and watched the red UHV needle bounce.

"How many channels are there?" I asked, reaching up to turn the dial.

"Don't," my father said. "Leave it." He exhaled cigarette smoke, then tapped his cigarette on the edge of the dashboard ashtray. "Forty. But nineteen is for truckers, the rest for jerks."

I took my hand away just as we drummed beneath an overpass. Wind punched at his open window and lifted a flurry of ashes; the ashtray was filled with bent filters, the ends pinched flat. On the road my father smoked with a grim devotion, using one cigarette to light the next; at home, he couldn't smoke inside the house, so he sat alone on the front porch, watching the traffic on the highway while he smoked with a soft, guilty expression.

I waved my hands. "Dad, you're getting ashes on me."

He smiled and stubbed out his cigarette in the ashtray.

"Sorry," he said, and reached over to tousle my hair. "All right?" His hand bumped my head, and I felt the calluses on the bottoms of his fingers against my forehead.

"You shouldn't smoke," I said.

"You're right."

"Doug's father doesn't."

I felt him look at me. "Doesn't what?"

"Smoke," I said.

"Yeah?" He picked out his cigarette, then ground it again in the ashtray. "Well, Doug's father ain't out here working."

I crossed my arms. "He works."

"Hey." He stabbed his finger at the windshield and I saw his reflection pointing at mine. "Sitting in air conditioning ain't work," he said, reaching down beside his seat. His eyes fixed on the interstate, my father pulled out his logbook, slapped it down on the doghouse, and fanned the pages with his thumb. "Here," he said. "At the end of the day, I know every mile I've logged. Can his father say that? What's he do?"

"I don't know," I said. "I'm just saying he doesn't smoke."

"No, that's not what you said." He dropped the logbook on the floor. "Here," he said, fumbling as he lifted his cigarettes from the breast pocket of his T-shirt and whipped the pack out the open window. They bounced off the mirror frame and spun away into the darkness.

"So I won't smoke," he said. "Now I'm like Doug's father."

I climbed off the doghouse to the passenger seat and stared through the window.

"No, you're not," I said.

When he slowed for the exit ramp, there'd been twenty minutes of silence between us. I listened to the neat clicks of the transmission as he switched the splitter and cycled down through the gears. My father looked over at me.

"We need fuel," he said, and I shrugged.

He pulled into the truck stop and swung the trailer in a long wide arc, parking beside the diesel pumps. When the engine stopped, the silence seemed to have been there waiting for us.

Typically, I would scramble down from the cab the instant the parking brakes hissed, and while my father pulled on his diesel-stained gloves to fuel the truck, I would check the air in the trailer tires, thumping each with a short, heavy rubber mallet. Then, I would circle behind the trailer and rattle the door locks, making certain they were secure. Last, I would push a rolling metal ladder of stairs in front of the Kenworth and climb up to the steps to clean the windshield, dragging a broad squeegee across the glass with both hands and ignoring the line of oily truck-stop water that always ran back down the handle and onto my arms. Silent and smiling, his gloved hand resting on the handle of the fuel pump, my father would watch me, pleased, I think, more by my company than my help.

But I stayed in the cab that night, listening as my father did his work and mine. When he was finished, he climbed back up into the truck, the cab rocking slightly as he did so.

"You coming in?" he asked, sweeping ashes off the doghouse.

When I shook my head, he climbed down and walked with small, reluctant steps across the parking lot, his shoes making crisp echoes in that distinctive silence. I waited until he crossed inside the truck stop to pay for the fuel. Then I climbed on the doghouse, reached up, and lifted the CB mike off its cradle, and broke his only rule.

The mike felt like a forest stone in my hand. Feedback squawked from the CB, and I turned the volume down. It burped static again, softly.

Through the windshield, the interior of the truck stop gleamed as bright as an operating room. My father, framed by the glare of the oversized front window, stood at the fuel counter, paying for the diesel. A wall clock behind the counter read ten minutes to three. As he left the counter, I saw the *Open Road* magazine tucked under his arm, and I knew he was headed for the men's room.

I lifted the mike to my mouth, cocked it sideways as I'd seen him do, and depressed the mike key.

"Breaker one-nine," I said. My voice sounded small and awkward, distant from the collection of sandpaper and hammers that filled the channel at night. The response came at once.

"Go ahead break one-nine."

On the CB, truckers identified themselves with "handles," invented and often boastful appellations — Lead Foot or Six-Pack or Alabama Slammer. Mine was Scooter; he called himself Midnight. He had a Southern accent, a common currency on the CB, but his inflection seemed counterfeit and forced.

"How are you tonight, Scooter? Good?"

I held the microphone against my lips, trying to disguise my age.

"Ten-four."

The channel was busy with chatter, and I heard two or three other conversations; their transmissions were weak and distant.

"No smokies out tonight," said Midnight. "A good night for riding."

"Copy that," I said.

The speakers whined and a thin voice interrupted, ". . . channel, kid."

I heard footsteps on the pavement outside and straightened up on the doghouse. A trucker with sharp-toed cowboy boots, dark blue jeans, and a heavy-looking silver belt buckle crossed in front of the Kenworth, heading toward the truck stop. He was lean, with slick gray hair combed back from his temples, and the heels of his cowboy boots tapped as he crossed the parking lot.

"What's your ten-twenty?" said Midnight.

"We're going to Grand Rap —" A surge of static on the channel cut me off.

"Get off the channel, kid."

"Roger that," echoed another voice.

Midnight seemed irritated. "Never mind them," he said. "Switch over to thirty-one, Scooter, and holler."

Then he was gone.

Outside, the parking lot was still and dark. The interior of the truck stop was empty. Balancing on my knees, I reached up and twisted the dial to thirty-one, where it was as silent as a closed room. I adjusted the volume.

"Break thirty-one for Scooter."

The sudden transmission was loud, and his words arrived like pale forks of summer lightning.

"Break for Scooter. Come back."

I thumbed the mike key closed, but then froze. Looking across the dim expanse of the parking lot into the bright interior of the truck stop, I read the wall clock and my throat closed. I released the key, and a small metallic click broke the silence on the channel.

"That you I hear, Scooter?"

The sound of his voice inside the cab of my father's truck seemed a blind appendage searching for me; I imagined Midnight huddled close to his CB, listening for the whisper of my breath.

He barked — once, twice — and I flinched.

"Scooooo-ter," he sang, as if calling a dog.

Then he laughed, a low chuckle that sounded like a bag full of broken glass.

I looked at the wall clock again.

Three o'clock. It was three o'clock.

On other summer trips, my father parked in rest areas beside the interstate, and when he climbed into the bunk to sleep, I sat on the doghouse watching the traffic, listening to the CB as a stream of excited voices surged into range, then dissolved like ribbons of exhaust. Those grainy and fleeting voices possessed the characteristics of ghosts — here, then gone. Because the CB had a range of only three or four miles, the conversations I heard were abbreviated things, small patches of sound that arrived and fled.

Three o'clock.

Ten minutes had passed, but Midnight's voice remained dangerously clear. I was stationary. So, then, was he.

Turn it off, I thought, staring at the black, pinholed face of the mike. Static leaked from the speakers at the corners of the cab, sounding like the insistent rustle of wasps inside a paper nest.

"That you riding the doghouse, Scooter?"

I dropped the mike onto the doghouse as if stung, then leaned over the dashboard and looked out the passenger window. Two islands down, an old, faded blue Peterbilt was parked beside the fuel pumps. Inside its dark cab the orange point of a cigarette flared, then dimmed.

"That your daddy's name and address on the side of the KW?"

He chuckled softly, his laughter joining the shadows inside the cab.

"Maybe we can have a correspondence?" he said, drumming out each syllable. I glanced up at the CB; the red needle in the UHV display was motionless, undisturbed by Midnight's transmissions.

I looked out the windshield as a red Freightliner, its trailer lights glistening in the darkness, rumbled past, briefly obscuring the truck stop. A foil wrapper from a cigarette pack twisted and scraped along the petroleum-stained pavement, captured in the dirty wake of the Freightliner.

"Want a truth, Scooter?"

I stared down at the mike on the doghouse.

"When you close your eyes, what do you see? Nothing, yet. But the dark stares back. Every time you close your eyes, it sees you."

Midnight's voice filled the cab, a venom poisoning my senses.

"I watch your daddy, Scooter. We're out working the same highway, clocking and recycling the same miles. But one of these trips I'll find him. He'll close his eyes and see me. He has only so many miles before —"

Quickly, I snatched the mike off the doghouse, rattled it back onto its cradle, and switched off the CB. My ragged breath was the only sound left inside the abrupt stillness of the cab. I squeezed my eyes shut.

"No," I whispered.

I repeated the word as if it were a talisman, over and again, until I heard a sudden scrape of footsteps outside the Kenworth. I darted back into the boxed shadows of the sleeper as the cab swayed left, and then rebounded to the right. I heard a thin metal scrape at the driver's door.

The door lock popped up, and the handle unlatched. Then the driver's door pulled open, and my father climbed inside.

"Touch anything?" he asked, the same question he always asked. He reviewed the miscellany of gauges and dials and switches, expecting the same routine answer.

"No," I said.

My father started the Kenworth and the Detroit Diesel engine rumbled beneath the doghouse. The truck began to shake and the mirrors buzzed in their aluminum frames.

Slap.

Slap.

Slap.

He punched in the air brakes — blue, red, yellow — then released the trailer brake. The Kenworth lurched and started forward. I leaned out over the doghouse and looked through the passenger glass toward the old blue Peterbilt. As we pulled away, I saw the point of a cigarette flare to life; I saw the slow movement behind the driver's window; I saw a flash of teeth, the shade of tar-stained chrome.

Then Midnight was gone.

The Kenworth climbed through the gears, and we were up to speed and into the center lane before my father turned the CB on. He switched the channel back to nineteen, but said nothing. I heard the soft chatter on the channel. Then my father opened his window and the voices were gone. A lighter scraped and I smelled cigarette smoke tangled with the warm summer air. And I said nothing.

I curled under a closed vent in the bunk, holding my eyes open against sleep. Occasionally, my father coughed or reached his hand inside a plastic bag of licorice balanced on the dashboard. Somewhere in the darkness behind us, I imagined a blue Peterbilt raced above the interstate, chasing the faded white bath of its headlights, and I strained to hear the interruption of Midnight's voice on the CB. But I never heard it again. Helpless with exhaustion, I soon fell into a dreamless sleep, feeling the regular bump of the Kenworth cycling over the seams in the highway.

My father drove through the entire night without me. The next morning I woke to the distinctive growl of the Detroit Diesel as it strained to pull us and twenty tons of freight up a steep incline. Though his eyes were trained on the road, my father affectionately scratched at the top of my head when I climbed from the bunk and onto the doghouse.

"Sleep good?" he asked, and because I didn't want to talk, only sit with him, I nodded.

I sat then, riding the doghouse throughout the morning and into the afternoon, watching the scenery pass, as if my sitting beside him could help my father push through all the miles left ahead.

Two weeks later, the day before summer ended and school began, I received a note in the mail, folded inside an anonymous envelope, with a black-and-white photograph attached.

> Dear Scooter,
> I took this one while your Daddy slept outside of Grand Rapids. It was a hot day and he was snoring. He looked bad. Remember, each engine has only so many miles in it.

I burned the photograph, but I have continued to trace the blurred, indistinct outlines of that grainy exposure with the invisible finger of my memory. My father lay in the bunk on his back, shirtless, his belly distended. Dark, curled hairs covered his pale skin like the crawl and brush of spiders. And though my father died seven years later, during my first year away at college, clutching at his chest and collapsing inside the torpid heat of a freshly unloaded trailer, he looked dead in that photo.

The storm passes and dawn bleaches the night sky. I return to bed and find the sheets have grown cool. I lie down with the experienced care of an insomniac, careful not to disturb my wife. I close my eyes, my breath grows shallow, and I descend toward sleep. Today we will celebrate my son's birthday. I hear a gentle roll of thunder, distant and impotent.

Where is it my father has gone?

JOSEPH EPSTEIN

My Brother Eli

FROM THE HUDSON REVIEW

NEVER LET IT BE SAID that my kid brother Eli failed to give me anything: he gave me five ex-sisters-in-law and seven (I think I have the number right) nephews and nieces, three of whom I met for the first time at his funeral. (My wife and I are childless.) At a memorial service I attended a few months afterward, a number of professors and writers and, yes, even the mayor of the city of Chicago talked about the struggles, sensitivity, and soulfulness of a man bearing Eli's name but who, tell you the truth, I wasn't able to recognize in any of these tributes.

My brother Eli is, make that was, the famous novelist, winner of all the literary prizes, national and international, a guy who scooped up most of the world's rewards (by which I mean money, women eager to sleep with him, praise from every quarter, international celebrity) without ever seeming particularly happy about any of them.

Eli took his life at the age of seventy-nine. You read about it, I'm sure. The official word was that he killed himself because he was diagnosed with Alzheimer's, but I'm not so sure something else wasn't behind my brother's putting a Beretta in his mouth and pulling the trigger. All the obituaries mentioned the Beretta, a nice detail that my brother himself would have appreciated. Eli always wore Borsolino hats; I wonder if he bought the Beretta in the same neighborhood in Rome where he bought his expensive hats, which, befitting the rake he became, he always wore at a rakish angle.

There were three of us: I was the firstborn, our sister Arlene came two years later, and then Eli (whose real name was Eliezer Schwartz) four years after that. Our old man worked for a man named Schinberg in the produce market on Fulton Street. An immigrant, unable to read English, he came to this country at sixteen from Bialystok, and, contrary to the standard American success story, never really made it. I don't think he ever felt at home here. He was stubborn, argumentative, a difficult character in almost every way, the old man. I call him "the old man" because I can't remember him young. He left for work at 3 A.M., took two different streetcars to Fulton Street, returned at 4 P.M., ate, and went to bed early. None of his children was sorry not to have seen more of him. He died at work, our father, outdoors, unloading cases of Texas apples from the back of a truck on a blustery February morning when he was forty-nine years old. Unlike the case with Eli, at the old man's funeral no one knew what to say on his behalf.

Our mother was the hero of the family. She was from Kiev. I don't ever remember her other than without makeup, gray hair pulled back in a bun. She worked a sixteen-hour day: cooking and washing and cleaning for her family, then after supper taking out her Singer sewing machine, which she set up on the kitchen table, doing piecework for Hart, Shaffner & Marx, the men's clothier, then on Franklin Street. In the few minutes she had for herself, she read novels in Yiddish. She died, worn-out, at fifty-four. Eli once told me that he thought our mother never loved him. I told him I didn't know when she would have found time, which wasn't the answer he wanted to hear.

The six years' difference in Eli's and my age was enough to keep us from ever establishing any real closeness. And then we led such different lives. I went to work in high school for Ben Belinsky, the used auto-parts king, on Western Avenue, near Augusta Boulevard, and never left. I worked for a few years out in the yard, with the Polacks and the colored guys, and then Mr. Belinsky, who was childless, took a shine to me. He was tough but straight, no crap about him, and he gave me a sense of what was honorable conduct, even in a competitive business like auto parts. If you worked hard for him — and I did — he took care of you.

He must have seen something in me. He had me to his home for dinner on Jewish holidays. When I was eighteen, he brought me inside, into the office, and began to teach me the business.

"Where you make your dough is in buying," he used to tell me. "Any *schmageggi* can move the goods if the price is right."

When I graduated from Marshall High School, I thought about going to college, maybe studying accounting.

"What do you need to study accounting?" Mr. Belinsky said. "You don't become an accountant, Louis. You hire an accountant. Forget about accounting. Stick with me. You won't be sorry."

And I wasn't. At twenty I was making more money than my old man. In my middle twenties, Mr. Belinsky told me that, if I wanted it, really wanted it, someday his business would be mine. I wanted it, all right. None of this was ever put on paper, you understand. It didn't have to be. He was solid, Ben, though I never called him that. I always called him Mr. Belinsky, even when I was in my thirties and he was in his early eighties, still coming down five days a week, working half a day on Saturday. Not long before he died, I arrived one morning and saw a new neon sign across the front of the place reading BELINSKY & SON, AUTO PARTS.

"That *Son* on the sign, Louis," he said, "that's you." I excused myself, went into the bathroom, and wept.

When Eli was in high school, I arranged for him to work in the yard at Belinsky Auto Parts. You could see right off his heart wasn't in it. Heavy lifting wasn't in my kid brother's line. He didn't like to get dirty. He was dreamy. He'd bring a book to work, which he read on breaks and which didn't at all please Mr. Belinsky.

What Eli didn't get in affection from our mother, he got from our sister Arlene. Eli was what you might call a sister's boy. Everything a person could do for another person without money, Arlene did for Eli: ironed his shirts, helped him buy his clothes, cooked special treats for him, slipped him an extra buck or two when she had it. Arlene and Eli looked a little alike. They both had our mother's fine features. I resembled more the old man; I have his large feet, thick wrists, big chest, black hair.

Arlene didn't have an easy life. Something in her eyes, in the way she carried herself, suggested vulnerability. She had two bad marriages, no children. Her second husband, a car salesman named Ralph Singer, used to beat her up. I didn't know about it until one day she turns up at our house for Passover with a black eye. I called Singer, asked him to come to my office the following Monday. When he showed up, I handed him an envelope with five grand in it, told him I wanted him to return home and get his things out of my sister's apartment, and that I never wanted him to bother my sister again. To show him I was sincere, right there in my office I broke his fuckin' nose.

Eli probably had no bigger fan than Arlene, who, later in life, used to keep scrapbooks filled with the reviews of his novels and the interviews he gave and everything else she found in the papers about him, which was quite a lot. I may not be the most careful reader of my brother's novels, but I did try my best to follow his career and his life, even if always from a distance. And I noticed a pattern over the decades, which was that Eli seemed to betray everyone who ever loved him. He never betrayed me, not really, but then maybe that was because I got off the love train for my brother fairly early.

What I sensed from the beginning was that Eli was in business for himself, and in a way that didn't make family love any easier. Maybe our father was unfeeling and our mother was certainly preoccupied. But in my mother's case at least we all knew that she would do everything she could for us, that as best she was able she was in our corner. Of course it wasn't like today, when if you don't tell your kid you love him every twenty minutes you could go to jail for child abuse. I always felt close to my sister, close to her and sorry for her both. But for Eli, as I say, I ran out of love fairly soon. I suppose I sensed that he didn't have much feeling for me, either.

When he graduated from Marshall, Eli came to tell me that he had a partial scholarship to Columbia University in New York, but he would need my help to pay his way. If I told you how little he needed, you'd laugh, because the sum today would sound trifling. Yet in those days, it wasn't; it seemed like a fairly big ticket. Still, a brother is a brother, and I said sure, why not, and every month I sent him a check to cover part of his tuition and his living expenses. I never expected a regular thank-you note. But I did make a small mental note in later years, when Eli was making big money, that it never occurred to him to offer to pay me any of that money back, or to say thanks for helping him out when he needed it. Maybe I was supposed to feel privileged to have contributed to the education of the great novelist, though I note that none of Eli's three biographers ever mentioned how this poor kid from the West Side of Chicago found the money to go off to school in New York.

Because so much is known about my brother's life, I don't have to connect all the dots about how he fell in with the New York writers he met when he lived there, how he met his first wife, his trips to Europe, things of that nature. But I first knew something was up when Eli published his second novel — I was still reading everything he wrote in those days — the book called *The Packard's Running Board.* I'm the so-called hero of that book, in which I'm called Eugene Siegel, and to Mr. Belinsky he gave the name Fred Armitage and made him a Gentile.

I don't read a lot of fiction. I tried, especially when my kid brother was gaining a reputation for turning the stuff out, but I never found the payoff was there, if you know what I mean. I like to read books about Franklin Delano Roosevelt and Harry Truman, and about the periods in history I've lived through myself, like the Depression and World War II. Eli's first novel, about a young guy growing up in a neighborhood where no one understood his sensitivity, was tough for me to get through at all. I had to drag my eyes across every page, thinking who could possibly give a damn about all this. So the hero of the book is sensitive and the people he's forced to live among aren't. I didn't see the big deal.

In *The Packard's Running Board,* the character Eugene — me, that is — is on fire with ambition and wanting to impress his boss, who runs a large auto-parts store. (Eli, far as I can see, never did invent a hell of a lot.) So his boss, Mr. Armitage, who is an anti-Semite amused at his employee's eagerness to get ahead, assigns him the job of finding a running board, driver's side, for a 1942 Packard. Eugene goes scurrying all over the city, trying every scrap yard in the county, but no luck. Then one day he spots a '42 Packard parked on the street in Oak Park and waits outside to see who owns it. The owner turns out to be one of those old dames with blue-rinse white hair. Eugene follows her home to a mansion in River Forest. He hangs around the neighborhood. He finds out that the old broad's name is Emily Thornborough, and that she's the widow of a successful architect. Although the car is old — the novel is set sometime in the late 1950s — the woman loves it, treats it like a baby, or so Eugene discovers by asking the mechanic at a nearby garage where she takes it in for servicing.

To make a long story short, Eugene realizes that he is going to have to steal the goddamn running board. And the rest of the book is about the complications of his finally doing it. A lot of comic high jinks follow: he nearly gets caught, he has the problem of how to get the unwieldy running board back into Chicago on public transportation. When he finally brings it to his boss, the man is unimpressed and says something like "You boys will do anything to get ahead" — "you boys," we are meant to understand, are Jews — and he fires Eugene on the spot, calling him a thief. End of story.

I took this book to represent Eli's opinion of me, his older brother, who was dedicated to the idea of getting ahead and willing to do anything to do so. Eugene is me, down to the gap between my front teeth, the hair covering the knuckles on my large hands, the way my face sweats when I'm under pressure. In the novel, I'm resourceful but also a major schmuck — and, when you get right down to it, a crook, too. For me the book wasn't exactly what you'd call easy reading.

I don't know why, but I never confronted Eli with his portrait of his older brother. I wonder if I wouldn't have done better to call him on it right then and there. I suppose I could have said, "Eli, where do you get off making me out to be such an obnoxious putz in your book? Is this what you really think of me? Explain this — and now." I was young enough in those days to put the hint — and maybe more than a hint — of menace in my voice. Maybe if I had done this I might have saved a number of other people Eli later put into his books a lot of grief.

Eli's first marriage was at City Hall in Jersey City, New Jersey. My sister and I heard of it after the fact. He married a girl named Elise Lensky, whose family were big in the socialist movement. Jews went in for this left-wing stuff more in New York than in Chicago. Here we're happy just to make a living and get some kind of fix on reality. Our hands are full trying to cope with the world as it is. We don't waste a lot of time on the world as it ought to be.

Around this time, Eli himself turned socialist, with a big interest in Leon Trotsky. I learned this from his wife, who called me one day to tell me that she was pregnant, in her sixth month, and that Eli and a pal had gone off to tour all the Communist countries of Eastern Europe to view at firsthand how Trotsky's teachings had been perverted under Stalin. She had medical and other expenses, and Eli had told her to get in touch with me if she ran out of the money he had left with her. The money was gone, and now she had nowhere else to turn. I sent her a grand, by Western Union.

I have no idea why Eli needed to leave a pregnant wife the way he did, but when he returned two months later, he called to thank me for coming through with the money. He said that he had a new book in the works that his publisher thought might make some serious dough, and that he would repay me as soon as he could. I can't remember how I found out that he and his wife had had a son named David; probably through Arlene, who kept in better touch with Eli than I did. But less than a year later, he broke up his marriage to the Lensky girl.

Five or so years must have passed before I next saw my brother. The book his publishers had thought would make some money for him apparently did well, and it also evidently increased his reputation, putting him, as Arlene said, in the front rank of contemporary writers. He had a new wife, a painter of abstract art whose name was Felicia, and he had taken to wearing expensive, somewhat gaudy clothes: suits with tight trousers, shirts with bold stripes, loud ties, pointy shoes. He was losing his hair, which may have explained why he was increasingly being photographed wearing a hat. He was in town to pick up a literary prize and give a talk at Roosevelt University.

I went with Arlene to hear the talk. The auditorium was filled. Eli was introduced as a writer who had changed the nature of modern writing. The talk was about an Irishman named James Joyce, who was evidently a great man for my brother. I couldn't make out a lot of it, but I did get that Eli admired this Joyce because he let nothing stand in the way of his writing, not the welfare of his family, nothing, even, I couldn't help note, continually borrowing from a brother, Stanislaus, I think the guy's name was, whom he never repaid.

Eli came up to Arlene and me at the reception after the talk. He embraced Arlene, put out his hand to me.

"How goes it, Lou?"

"Not too bad, Eli," I said, "but not so good as it seems to be going for you. This is a nice crowd you drew tonight."

"I provide artificial pearls for real swine," he said, looking around the room. He was wearing some sort of sharkskin suit, light gray, with high pockets in the trousers, a belt of matching material, and a silky green tie with a thick knot under a spread collar. I couldn't remember if he always had this drugstore wise-guy air about him. Or had it come with his success?

"How's auto parts?" he asked me.

"It's a living," I said, adding, "and a hell of a lot easier now that no one's asking for old running boards."

"Who'd have thought my big brother read my books?" he said with a smile. "Lou, you please me more than you can know. You astonish me, in fact."

I was about to tell him my opinion about that particular book but then thought better of it. He was my brother, after all, and I'm not good at telling people off. I tend to go too far, and I really didn't want to break things off with Eli, not yet anyhow.

The young woman who had introduced Eli, a Professor Shansky —Jewish, zaftig, in her midthirties — came up, excused herself for taking Eli off, but the president of the university and some of its larger donors were expecting him for a small dinner party. Eli smiled at her in a way that implied if not possible past intimacies then certainly future ones to come. He was then married to his second wife.

"I better run," he said. He kissed Arlene on both cheeks and gripped my upper right arm. "Stay well, both of you. I'll be in touch."

"You know, Lou," Arlene said to me on the way home, "he's not really our brother anymore. He belongs to the world now. He's a famous man, our little Eli."

"I suppose that's so," I said. "But I wish I liked him a little more."

"What's not to like?" Arlene said. "He's our brother."

"My guess is that he doesn't harbor many brotherly feelings about either of us, though probably more toward you than me. Eli's going to take what he wants and do what he wants, with very little obligation felt on his side. Eli's one of life's takers."

"I wonder, Lou, if you aren't being too hard on him. He's not like the rest of us, you know. Eli's an artist."

"I see where your brother's got his ass in a sling," Al Hirsch said, smiling the kind of smile lawyers do when they discover fresh news of greed or other human depravity of the kind off which they make their living.

"What for?" I asked.

"As you probably know, he's going through his third divorce, and it seems that he left falsified tax documents around the marital apartment, to make it look as if he's been earning a lot less money than he's actually been earning. It's an old trick, and an extremely dumb one, if I may say so."

As a matter of fact, I didn't know that Eli was going through another divorce. I'd met his third wife twice. Her name was Sharon Lefkowitz, and she was a striking-looking woman, dark good looks, terrific figure, all-year-round suntan. Formidable, a tiger of a woman, is how I'd describe her. Unlike Eli's first two wives, she was no socialist or artist, but the daughter of a Chicago dentist known for his cleverness at real estate deals. She didn't figure to be a girl who would take divorce lightly. She must have scared Eli good with her demands for him to hoke up fake tax documents. But now that he's done it, my poor schmuck little brother had apparently really put his head in the tiger's mouth.

"Who's my brother's attorney?"

"A moron named Morty Silverman. He has an office on Washington off LaSalle. A flamboyant guy who's known to bang his female clients and who's never really made his nut."

I remember Morty Silverman from the old neighborhood. His father had a dry cleaner's on Roosevelt Road. Morty was a little guy, dressed flashy, wore porkpie hats. Funny that Eli would use Morty Silverman when serious things were at stake. It showed a kind of loyalty, I guess.

"I thought your kid brother's supposed to be a genius," Al said.

"A limited genius," I said. "He's mostly a genius at telling other people what's wrong with the way they live. Not so smart, though, when it comes to his own life."

Eli had moved back to Chicago a few years before. In an interview he gave to the *New York Times,* which Arlene had sent to me, he said that he no longer needed to live in New York, its rhythms weren't his, he needed Chicago where the grit of reality was in the air. Well, from what Al Hirsch said, Eli must by now have had a mouth full of this grit.

Arlene, always the family peacemaker, gave a dinner to which she invited me, my wife Gerry, and Eli and a new lady friend of his, a professor of some kind at the University of Chicago. She also invited another couple, named Wertheimer, who lived in her building. They were both shrinks, Arlene said, foreign-born, a little nutty, but nice. They were fans of Eli's novels and wanted to meet him.

Eli arrived after the rest of us. His lady friend, he explained, couldn't make it. "Illness in the family" is all he offered in the way of an excuse. We sat in Arlene's living room, the six of us. Eli seemed harried, tired; his face was pouchier than I remembered. He had dark circles under his eyes. He was wearing a tan suit with an emphatic Gleneagle plaid. He had a silk handkerchief in his jacket pocket, purple to match his wide necktie.

Before Eli had arrived, the Wertheimers asked me a number of questions about my brother. The Wertheimers were Jews who had escaped Germany and spoke with strong accents, Henrietta Wertheimer's stronger than her husband Karl's. Henrietta said that one of her special interests was in the childhood of artists, and she wanted to know what I could tell her about my brother's upbringing, particularly anything that might have contributed to his impressive career. The truth was, I couldn't think of a damn thing. A shame our father wasn't in the room, I thought; his gruff presence would have given the Wertheimers a lot to think about in connection with what Karl Wertheimer called "the developmental aspect of the artist's early years." I could have told them that Eli's father never gave him or any of his children the time of day, and he thought his mother didn't love him. Let them chew on that for a while. But I said very little, except that my brother's talent had not shown up early, at least that I was aware. He just seemed a very bright kid.

"You were an adherent of the doctrines of Wilhelm Reich, no?" Henrietta Wertheimer asked Eli. "Are you still?"

Eli laughed. "That was a long while ago," he said. "My brother Lou here, who is in used auto parts, probably never heard of an orgone box, but I had my very own such appliance. Kept it in a large closet in an apartment I lived in on West 106th Street in the late 1940s. Spent hours in it brooding in the hope of increasing my sexual energy, but mostly I sat there thinking of ways to advance the plots in my novels."

"Reich was of course a fascist," said Karl Wertheimer.

"I gather he was," Eli said, "but not so great a totalitarian as your man Sigmundo the Freud." I didn't know what the hell Eli was talking about, but you had to be a dope not to recognize that he didn't like the Wertheimers.

"Well, totalitarian, I don't know," Karl Wertheimer said. "Freud was in possession of the most powerful ideas of the age, and I think it unfair to consider him more than judicious in guarding them from those who might dilute or otherwise corrupt them."

"*Powerful ideas?* You mean like the unrelenting desire of children to sleep with their parents? Lou," Eli said, turning to me, "funny but I can't ever recall your mentioning your ardent desire to mount up on Ma. Or am I wrong about this?" I didn't answer.

Things didn't get better at dinner, for which Arlene had obviously gone to a lot of trouble. Between the vegetable soup and the salad, Karl Wertheimer asked if anyone at the table had read Shakespeare in German. I felt like saying that I couldn't make him out so easy in English — except the play *Julius Caesar,* which they made us read in high school — but I clammed up. Dr. Wertheimer then went on to say that there is a school of thought that held that Shakespeare, in the Schiller or Schlegel or some other kraut's translation, was even better in German. I was watching Eli, who, up till now, I thought was trying, if not very hard, not to wreck his sister's dinner party completely.

"You know," Eli said, "I think I've had just about enough of this German-Jewish bullshit."

You'd think that after making a remark like that he'd toss his napkin on the table, get out of his chair, and ask for his hat and coat. But Eli did nothing of the kind. He just sat there. Which meant that the Wertheimers had to get up and leave. They did so without much fuss, I'll give them that.

"Perhaps this meeting was a mistake, Arlene," Karl Wertheimer said. "I hope you will forgive us if we depart early." On the way out, Henrietta Wertheimer mumbled something about how nice it was to meet my wife Gerry and me. I shook Karl Wertheimer's small soft hand.

Eli sat there, finishing his soup. When they left the room, Arlene followed them to the door, offering God knows what excuse for her brother's behavior.

"I've heard it said," Eli noted, "that if you dislike a person, it always helps to imagine that person as German. And if you really dislike him, it's best of all to imagine him as a German woman. I'll say this for Henrietta Wertheimer: under this arrangement she doesn't force the imagination into a lot of extra exercise."

"You were pretty tough on those people," I said.

"Lou," he said, "I've come to an age and stage in life where I no longer feel it incumbent upon me to listen to crap, and if there are greater purveyors of crap than intellectuals, then it is people with pretensions to knowledge of the soul, like Arlene's good German neighbors."

"A little hard on Arlene, though, wouldn't you say, Eli?" my wife said. "I mean these people were her guests."

"I don't worry about Arlene," he said. "Arlene'll understand."

When Arlene returned, I was a little surprised to discover that she didn't say a word to Eli about his treatment of the Wertheimers. She just served the rest of the meal as if nothing unusual had happened, and we talked about the old days on the West Side and, of course, about Eli.

"Is your new lady friend all right?" Arlene asked him.

"She's fine," Eli said. "We had an argument. She wants me to marry her. Her name's Karen Wilkinson, by the way. She's an astronomer at the University of Chicago. Not having had very good luck with wives in the humanities — and in the case of Sharon, my last wife, in the inhumanities — I thought I'd shop the sciences for a while."

"And you're not interested in remarrying?" Gerry asked him, with an unmistaken note of wonder in her voice.

"God, no. I'm already a three-time loser. And besides, it's 1974, and, as I'm sure you've noticed, it isn't such a hot time for marrying. Sex is hanging everywhere, like salamis in a delicatessen. The country's gone nuts. Everything's up for grabs. A man would have to be insane to marry today."

On the drive home, my wife said that she didn't understand why any woman would want to marry her brother-in-law, since he was so obviously a bad risk, certain to bring unhappiness to any wife, not to mention his being a certifiably lousy father.

"And I would have killed your brother if he ever did anything like what he did to the Wertheimers to any guests of mine," Gerry said. "I don't get Arlene's being so calm about it."

"Arlene is devoted to Eli. She's sure he's a genius. She accepts his own idea of himself as a great man."

"And you, what do you think?"

"I think something's wrong with him. He may be talented, like everyone says, but I think he's got a screw loose. Something's missing in him."

"Maybe he's beginning to believe all the things that are written about him," Gerry said.

"Maybe, except I think Eli believed them even before they were written."

Three weeks later we learned through Arlene, our usual source, that, despite all his talk about society and sex and salami and the rest of it, Eli had married his astronomer. I had another sister-in-law, my fourth.

As I said earlier, I didn't have much luck reading my brother's novels. I tried, but it was no-go. They weren't about a world I knew, nor did I find myself caring very much about how things worked out in them. Near as I could make out, they seemed to be mostly about Jewish intellectuals who thought that life had dealt them a bad hand and that reality was hard for them to locate. Gerry read them, and while she wasn't crazy about them either, she felt forcing her eyes across the pages to finish them was part of her duty as a sister-in-law. Occasionally, she would call my attention to a passage or section where she thought I might know if Eli was writing about something or someone from the old neighborhood. She was usually right about this.

In the most recent book of my brother's, called *Kaiserman's Kiss of Death,* Gerry pointed out some rough passages about a character he called Leo Kaiserman, a failed lawyer, a little guy in a porkpie hat. He's unethical in every way possible. This Kaiserman is also sex-crazed, not to be trusted around any skirt. He uses the same methods of seducing every woman he confronts. He quotes poetry to them and also a Russian named Berdaev. When Kaiserman at one point goes into the hospital, Eli has him flash himself in front of nurses. Kaiserman is Morty Silverman, there can't be any doubt about it, and my brother has made his old pal out to be a real creep.

Why would Eli do this? Maybe he was paying Morty back for the stupid advice he gave him about faking his tax forms. This seemed a pretty stiff payback. I wondered if Morty himself would read it — I was fairly sure he would — and how he would react?

Gerry told me that Eli had done much worse with Elise, his first wife. In a novel with the title *Skolnik,* which I never got around to reading, he painted her as betraying him with another man and running off with him and their three-year-old son. This isn't the way I heard the story. I was told that Eli had left Elise because he said that an artist can't be tied down to a family, with a baby carriage in the hallway and the rest of it. I don't know the real story. What is true is that Eli made his first wife out to be a real *nafke.* What must she have thought of it? What would be the effect on their child in real life, who by now must be in his twenties? I recall being pissed off when my brother had written about me, and I felt all the more strongly that I should've kicked his ass and put a stop to this kind of thing right then and there.

What amazed me is that no one seemed much to mind Eli's behavior. His fame spread. Gerry was always calling my attention to some item about him in the Chicago papers. He gave a lot of interviews, Eli did, but he always seemed to do so reluctantly, almost as if he were being forced into it. I noticed, too, that whenever he won a prize, many of them involving fairly heavy cash, he would accept it with a slight grudgingness. "I am very pleased to have been awarded this prize, if only . . ." "I'm grateful to be the recipient of this prize, though I have to say that while it pleases me greatly it also makes me dubious of . . ." There was something phony about the whole deal, but it seemed to be working. I can't speak about the importance of my brother's writing, but he was a real public-relations genius.

Maybe Eli thought I was insufficiently impressed by him, or thought that, unlike the rest of the world, I didn't praise him enough, tell him how proud I was of him every other day, but then Gerry and I didn't see much of him, even though we were now living in the same city, we on Lake Shore Drive, Eli and his new wife in Hyde Park.

One day we get an invitation from the mayor's office for an event at which Eli was going to be presented with a medal from the city of Chicago. There was a dinner involved and an award ceremony at Navy Pier. It was black tie. What the hell, I said to Gerry, let's see how the other half lives.

"Which half is that?" she said.

This turned out to be not so dumb a question. At the reception before the dinner, every *tuchas lecher* in town was on display. One of the first sights I saw after entering the hall was the gossip columnist Irv Kupcinet hug a small guy named Walter Jacobson, used to be a batboy for the Cubs, who now does the local evening news. While hugging each other, I notice each of them is looking over the shoulder of the other to see if there isn't someone more important in the room. A strange little guy named Studs Terkel, who has a radio interview show on the classical music station, is racing around pressing the flesh of everyone in the place. I don't know much about him, but I remember Eli once calling him "a cracker-barrel Stalinist" and his laughing at the pleasure the phrase gave him. Gerry once asked me if I ever noticed that Eli seemed to laugh a lot but rarely smiled.

Lots of women from the Gold Coast, the high-maintenance kind, were there with their tired-looking husbands, who'd probably be happier if left to stay home to watch the Bulls-Lakers game. I recognized a number of aldermen who, they don't steal enough as it is, can always be counted on to show up for a free meal. Mike Ditka, the former coach of the Bears with his thick features, was talking to the mayor. Gerry spotted Jesse Jackson leaning in close to talk to a striking black woman who does the evening news on Channel 9.

Then Eli walked in with his wife, who, after four years of marriage to my brother, already looked exhausted. There was something dark and haunted in her eyes. She seemed thinner than I remembered when I first met her. In her red gown and high heels, she was a few inches taller than Eli. Eli was wearing a tux with an especially wide sateen collar, a shirt with lots of big ruffles, and a red cummerbund and an enormous red bow tie, of the kind which, if, when you shook his hand, it flashed "Kiss Me," you wouldn't be in the least surprised. He looked like a Jewish trombone player in the old Xavier Cougat orchestra. His wispy, now completely white hair was combed over and patted down to cover his baldness. He got the family talent, wherever in the hell it came from originally, but I got our old man's thick hair, which maybe was the better deal.

The dinner was first class: large platters of seafood to start, choice of prime rib or salmon, lots of wine, cherries jubilee to end. When the dishes were cleared, the mayor, who wasn't known for fancy language, rose to say that culture has always been important to the city of Chicago, and then he reeled off a number of names of writers who had lived here, and he said that Eli was continuing in their line. In honoring Eli, he said, a man who had been born and grew up in Chicago and was now its greatest writer, the city was honoring one of its own, and he was proud to bestow the city's medal for literature on him, which he then did.

Eli stood at the podium, the heavy medal dangling from his neck on a red-white-and-blue ribbon, the large red bow tie just above it. He looked clownish. He waited for the applause to end. He grinned. I looked over at Karen, his wife, who was sitting across from me. She was staring down at the tablecloth.

"Well," Eli began, "this is quite an honor. I want to thank the mayor for his kind words. I want to thank Lois Weisberg and others in the city's office of culture. My big brother's here tonight, so I have to be careful what I say. He's a tough guy, and, should I step out of line, he's sure to let me have it. Isn't that so, Lou?

"The relation of writers to power is a subject with a long and often squalid history," he continued. "I can't help wondering if, in accepting this handsome medal and eating this luscious food, I've not become part of that history. Literature is supposed to represent truth, and, as such, to tell truth to power, if only because everyone else is frightened to do so." Here Eli looked over to the mayor. "How're you doing, kiddo?" he said.

"Yes," he went on, "truth speaks to power, but the question is, does power ever really listen? Or does it instead merely pretend to listen and honor it with occasions such as this evening's gala? In Communist countries they take writers very seriously — so seriously that they often kill them. Here in the United States, in the city of Chicago specifically, they offer them a choice of roast beef or salmon. Don't get me wrong — I'll take the salmon over a firing squad any day. Still, it would be nice to be taken seriously, too."

And then Eli just stopped. That was it. Done. Finished. At first people didn't know what to do. Everyone looked at the mayor, who, after an interval of maybe ten seconds, began to applaud, which allowed everyone else in the room to do so, though the clapping was polite at best. I looked over at Eli's wife, who, returning my look, rolled her eyes back in her head, as if to say, "Here's your brother, you figure him out."

"So," Eli, now back at our table, leaned over and said to me, "how did I do?"

"I'd have to say that you didn't exactly knock 'em dead, kid."

"That's okay," he said. "The main thing is that I knocked 'em."

Gerry took a cab home; she had an early morning appointment the next day, and I stuck around a little longer. When I was getting ready to leave, Eli asked me if I would mind taking his wife home. He had some business to attend to after the party. I said of course, why not?

I had been around my sister-in-law maybe four times, and never alone. I wasn't sure what we'd have to talk about, but it turned out that it didn't matter much because she did most of the talking.

"You know, Louis," she said, as I pulled out of the garage at Navy Pier, "Eli and I are splitting up. He's an impossible person, which you must already know."

"I've had some strong hints," I said.

"He needs to flirt with all kinds of women. His fame as a writer gives him some strange aphrodisiac quality for them, or so I suppose. They like to sleep with a famous writer. What I find hard to understand is that he, Eli, doesn't seem to have all that much interest in what really, you know, goes on in bed. He's a very impatient lover, Eli. Forgive my not saying this more politely, but your brother doesn't know a clitoris from a kneecap."

I nearly drove over the median into onrushing Outer Drive traffic.

"It was a serious mistake on my part ever to start up with your brother. He humiliates me in public. He ignores me in private. I'm sure that someday he'll put me in one of his novels as a witch and whore and add a few bad hygienic habits at no extra charge. I don't care. I don't need money from him. To be free from him is gift enough. I'll be very happy no longer to be Mrs. Eli Black, the fourth. I'm sure there'll be a few more Mrs. Eli Blacks, all with numbers after their names, like ennobling suffixes."

When I let her out of the car in front of her and Eli's apartment at the Cloisters, before opening the door, she said, "Your brother thinks that because he's an artist he can do what he wants, hurt people whenever he likes. Everything is justified by his books. As an astronomer, I don't think Eli knows how small, how truly insignificant, he really is. Maybe someday he'll find out. Goodbye, Louis." She shook my hand as she left the car, and I never saw her again.

Maybe it was a year after this that Gerry and I went to a United Jewish Fund dinner and found ourselves seated at the same table with a young guy named Rick Feldrow. He was a lawyer who also wrote novels; all of them were made into movies, and damn good movies, too. He was a small guy, bald, but he looked firm, like he must've spent some time on treadmills. When we were introduced, he said he'd heard that I was Eli Black's brother. When I told him I was, he opened up to me in a way that took me a little by surprise.

"I can't tell you how much I admire your brother's writing," he said. "He's my personal hero, make that my household god."

"Why's that?" I asked.

"Because he writes like an angel. Because he understands what is really going on in the country. Because his novels will live forever."

"How's it you're so sure of all this?"

"Well," he said, "I can't of course be sure. But right now, of everyone who's scribbling away, he looks like the top contender to be read fifty or a hundred years from now."

"Have you met my brother?"

"Never," he said. "I'd still be daunted to meet him. When I was young, I used to imagine that Eli Black was my father, that I had inherited his talent, that he would guide me through the rocky places in life. My own father, who was a physician, never had much time for me, and when he did, he was hypercritical."

"Sorry to hear that," I said. "But I don't think you'd have had much luck with my brother Eli as a father either."

"Really?" he said. "Why's that?"

I felt a light kick under the table from Gerry. "It's complicated," I said, and turned to the woman sitting on my left.

Eli and I were never in anything like regular touch. Six, eight months might go by without either of us calling the other. Sometimes we'd meet at the funeral of a cousin — Eli had a touch of family sentimentality — though not that often. But one day he calls and says that he has to meet me on urgent business. How's tomorrow for lunch? he wants to know.

We met at the Standard Club. Eli was waiting in the foyer, dressed in one of his racy suits, this one black-and-white checks, wearing a shirt with thick red stripes, white collar and cuffs, and a yellow necktie. As we walked to our table in the main dining room, I sensed people staring at us — at my brother, for Eli's picture was fairly often in the papers and he qualified around town as a celebrity.

After the waiter took our order, Eli, looking around the room, smiled and said, "Wouldn't the old man be amused to see us having lunch in this joint? We've both come a long way from Roosevelt Road and Kedzie."

"You a lot way farther than me," I said. "But what's on your mind?"

"I need a loan of a quarter of a million dollars," he said.

"That's a pretty serious number. For what, may I ask?"

"You may. I'm in deep water with a man named Sid Gusio on a bad deal I made in an investment in nursing homes."

"Where do you come to know a thug like Gusio?" I asked.

"I met him at the Riviera Club, where I play racketball," Eli said. "A very amiable fellow, or so he at first seems."

Sid Gusio was the Chicago Syndicate's man in charge of gambling and prostitution, and, as that job description implies, not a man to fool with. Eli had no more business with a man like Gusio than a mouse walking into the den of a lion.

"He's a dangerous character, Eli."

"Tell me about it," Eli said. "He was, he said, putting me onto a good thing. For a hundred grand investment in a nursing-home complex being built in Oak Lawn, I'd get triple my investment back within two years, or so he claimed. Only now he tells me that they vastly underestimated costs. I need to come up with another two-hundred-and-fifty grand to protect my original investment. Except that Gusio made it evident that I didn't have much choice in the matter. It wasn't, he made it fairly plain, an entirely voluntary matter. I couldn't just walk away and lose my original investment of a hundred thousand, though at this point this is what I wouldn't so much mind doing. But walking away, I strongly suspect, isn't really an option."

I couldn't help thinking, Eli, my schmuck brother, gets his pecker in a wringer every time he ventures away from his desk, Eli, who wouldn't know reality if it bit him in the ass, the man who writes books telling everyone else they're living badly, Eli going up against Sid Gusio was no contest.

"What makes you sure he won't come back to you for still more money?"

"Nothing," Eli said. I could sense his fear. Also his embarrassment. Always so goddamn knowing about everything, Eli was reduced to coming to his big brother for help.

"You don't have any of this money yourself?" I asked.

"I have a high nut, Lou, lots of ex-wives, kids, school bills, you don't know the half of it."

"Christ, Eli, every time I open the paper someone's giving you a new prize. You must get ten or twenty grand a shot for talks. And what about the dough your books bring in? How broke can you be?"

"Look, Lou, without going into details, all I can tell you is that I don't have the money and no prospects of getting it except from you."

I had already made up my mind to lend Eli the money, but, for some reason, I didn't want to make it easy for him. I hate to admit it, but I found myself enjoying this.

"Suppose I loan you the money," I said. "What're you offering in collateral? The Pulitzer Prize?"

"How about I give you the continuing royalties for my first three novels?" he said, quite serious.

"An I.O.U. will do, with a schedule of repayment," I said. "But Eli, maybe you'll take a little free literary advice. Don't ever put Sid Gusio into one of your novels. Unless you want a couple of knee-replacement operations."

One day at the office, my secretary tells me that David Black is on the phone. I don't recall knowing any David Black, but I pick up the phone anyway.

"Hello, Uncle Lou," a voice says, "I'm your brother Eli's son, and I'm in Chicago for a couple of days and I wonder if we could maybe meet."

Then it clicked in. David was Eli's son by his first marriage. I remember him only as a child. He must be in his thirties by now. He lived in northern California, Santa Rosa, if I remembered correctly.

"Where are you?" I asked. "Staying with your dad?"

"No," he said, "it turns out that my father's out of town. I'm here on business, staying at the Continental Hotel on Michigan Avenue. I don't really know Chicago at all. But is it possible we could meet for lunch or a drink?"

"Sure, kid," I said. "It'd be fine."

We arranged to meet the next day at a bar in the Drake Hotel called the Coq d'Or, which served good sandwiches and which, if you arrived after the lunch rush, provided a certain amount of privacy, though I wasn't sure what this boy and I had to talk about.

The first thing I discovered was that my nephew was no kid. He was balding, slightly paunchy, with his father's nose and slightly flared nostrils. He was taller than Eli and darker. Something a little soft about him, vulnerable, but something, too, that made my heart go out to him. It was probably his having grown up without a father.

"Thanks for meeting me," he said, putting out his hand.

We took a table against the far wall, ordered beers and hamburgers, and I asked him what brought him to Chicago.

"I'm here for a conference," he said. "I'm a civil engineer and work for the California highway system. The conference is about state highway funding. Dull stuff to most people, I suppose, but important in my line of work."

"Have you seen your father recently?"

"I called him before coming to town, but he told me that he was going to be in London."

"Are you in regular touch with him?"

"Irregular touch would be closer to it. Sometimes a year or two will go by without our meeting. Usually I call him on his birthday."

Eli had divorced David's mother when he was three years old. She took him to California and remarried a few years later. Eli hadn't much money in those days and saw his son probably no more than once a year, if that. When he remarried and had other children, he saw him even less.

"I learned to get on without my father," David said. "When I was a teenager, I sort of followed his career in the newspapers. At school nobody knew that my father was the famous writer, which was fine by me. My stepfather, who died two years ago, was a decent man. My mother had two other children with him, but he always treated me fairly. I have no complaints."

David told me that he had three children of his own. Eli had not yet seen the youngest, a boy who was four years old. I thought how much my own wife missed having grandchildren.

"I suppose the one grudge I hold against my father is the way he portrayed my mother in one of his novels, where he makes her out to be so vengeful and little more than an obstacle to his own career. I've always wanted to say something to him about the meanness of that but I've never had the guts. When it comes to his writing, he can be very touchy, my father."

"I haven't had much luck reading your dad's novels," I said.

"Maybe it's because they don't have plots. I'm just an engineer, what do I know, but my father's books seem to be mostly about men like him, Jewish intellectuals who feel the world has screwed them in some deep yet not entirely clear way. His main points, near as I can make out, are that nobody understands the modern artist and just about everyone is an anti-Semite. But his books seem to charm lots of people. I don't think there's a prize left he hasn't won. And he's been translated in all kinds of languages."

David went on to talk about his wife, who is a graphic artist, and his children and how he came to study engineering. When he asked me about my own family and business, he listened carefully as I told him about my life. He seemed a solid kid, my nephew, and I wished I could do something for him, something to make up for all the things that my brother didn't do. Eli's and Arlene's and my father wasn't much, but at least he was on the premises, and he sure as hell didn't attack our mother in public. Thank God for small blessings.

Out on the street in front of the Drake, David and I exchanged business cards, and he said he hoped I would visit him and my grandnephews and niece if I should ever find myself in Santa Rosa. "It's the wine country, you know, Sonoma Valley," he said. I told him I'd try to stay in touch, but life being what it is, I was fairly sure that we probably wouldn't meet again.

A few weeks later, I called my brother to tell him about my meeting with his son and what a fine young man I thought he is. "You're lucky to have such a kid," I said. "It's none of my business, but you probably ought to see him more than you do."

"You're right, Lou," Eli said. "It isn't any of your business. Look, I don't expect you to understand this, but all the energy I have goes into my books — all of it. There isn't anything left for anything else."

"Whaddaya writing, the Bible?" I said. "They're only novels, Eli. We're talking about human beings here, a son and grandchildren."

"What the hell do you know about the life of an artist?" he said, and hung up on me.

My sister Arlene had had a bout with breast cancer, and now, four years later, she called one night in tears to tell us that the cancer had returned, metastasized to the brain. It was inoperable. Arlene's two marriages, like my own marriage, produced no children. She hadn't gone to college and worked for many years as the bookkeeper at Zimmerman's Liquors in the Loop. I helped her out a bit financially when her building went condo and she wanted to buy her apartment; I also gave her some investment advice that worked out well. But she had no one in the world except Gerry and me, who loved her, and Eli. She was given between six to eight months to live.

Arlene was the most generous-spirited person I ever knew. She had no meanness, no anger, no envy — at least none that I ever saw. When I went with her to see Al Hirsch to discuss her will, she decided to divide everything she had between Eli's grandchildren. I learned then that she had a list of their birthdays and every year sent each one of them a card with a $50 bill in it. She made me promise not to tell Eli about the return of her cancer. "He hates death," she said. "He can't stand hearing about it. I'll tell him when the time gets nearer."

Arlene had also arranged another dinner with her neighbors the Wertheimers. She had a bad conscience about the way the previous one had turned out, and she hoped that we would come again. Of course we said yes. She told us, too, that she hadn't told the Wertheimers about the return of her cancer, and we were instructed not to mention it.

The going was much easier without Eli there. We talked about the Wertheimers' and Arlene's neighbors, about the American infatuation with sports, about their foreigners' view of American politics. "Too much virtue in American politics," Karl Wertheimer said. "I prefer a straighter kind of political engagement. I mean one in which one votes one's interests and beliefs and doesn't think people who vote otherwise are monsters or idiots."

Arlene is a good cook, and the dinner was excellent. It was only at dessert — a pineapple upside-down cake — and coffee that Henrietta Wertheimer asked if we minded talking about Eli. No one seemed to object.

"Your brother, you know, is a peculiar but not entirely unknown type," she said. "Nothing, it seems, makes him happy. Not his successes, not his wives and children, not all the world's lavish praise of his work. Psychotherapy doesn't really have a label for such a condition. He isn't a depressive, nothing so simple as that. Yet, one could tell from a single meeting with him, and from the many seemingly grudging interviews he has given to the press, that the world — how to say this? — the world disappoints him. It isn't, somehow, good enough for him."

"I note from a recent interview," Karl Wertheimer joined in, "that your brother has begun a dalliance with the doctrines of Rudolf Steiner. Perhaps you know of this man Steiner?"

None of us did.

"A quack not even of the first order," he continued. "In his doctrine, spirits are aloft, souls join in the empyrean, all sorts of other — how do you Americans say? — fun and games. But what I find interesting in all this is your brother's need for a higher doctrine, for a system of ideas, no matter how foolish. He was a Trotskyist, I understand, as a young man, then there is the Wilhelm Reich period, which we talked about earlier, now there is Rudolf Steiner. Perhaps, who knows, in the end he will die, your brother, as a Catholic."

I didn't know how to respond. The Wertheimers knew a lot more about the intellectual side of Eli than I did. But what I took from their account of my brother's adventures among the quacks was his basic unreality. He grew up on the same streets I did. We had the same parents. How could two people be so different?

"What do you make of all my brother-in-law's marriages?" Gerry asked.

"A number of possible ways of viewing this," Henrietta Wertheimer said. "Perhaps they express a yearning for the settled life that he thinks he wants but does not really want. Perhaps he operates, your brother-in-law, under a theory of muses, like the painter Picasso or the choreographer Balanchine, who had different wives and mistresses for different phases of their respective careers. This, too, is possible."

"What seems clear to me," Karl Wertheimer joined in, "is that Eli Black believes in the myth of the artist. This is a myth that holds that everything must be sacrificed for art. It may not be a foolish myth if one is, say, Michelangelo or Beethoven. But if one is less than that then the myth of the artist is very destructive, sadly so for the people who become too closely involved with him."

When it finally came time to tell Eli about the return of Arlene's cancer, he did come to visit. He had by this time moved to Washington, planning, he said, to write a political novel, though he never did. (Instead, Gerry tells me, he wrote a novel attacking his fourth wife for not understanding the condition of the artist and for her unconscious anti-Semitism.) He stayed at Arlene's apartment over a long weekend. I never found out what they spent their time talking about, but I'd bet it wasn't about death. When I tried to talk to Eli about hospice and other arrangements for Arlene, he seemed very uncomfortable. Nobody likes death, but Eli seemed to take death personally. He didn't quite see why death should one day have to happen to him, too. He seemed to feel there was something unfair about it, at least in his case.

Now that he was near seventy, he did what he could to fight it. When he came over for dinner at our apartment, he told Gerry beforehand that he no longer ate meat. He spent a lot of time in gyms. He took up yoga. He became thin, which only made him look older. A picture of him published in the *Chicago Tribune Magazine* shows his skin sagging, his hooded eyes looking wrinkled like a lizard's, his nose larger, wearing one of his crazy suits (blue-gray with red stripes outlined faintly in yellow), a pink shirt, a bandanna around what appeared to be his goiterish neck. He looked, Gerry said, like an ancient Jewish parrot.

I also noted a strong strain of sentimentality in my brother. Although Eli didn't come to Arlene's funeral — he said it would have been too much for him — once she was dead he spoke of her as if she were a saint. "She was the only person who ever truly loved me," he told me, "who took me exactly as I am, no questions asked." He even had kind words for our father. He was supercritical of other writers, but if one of them died, he spoke more kindly about him. To earn Eli's respect, apparently you have to die first. That seemed to me a very steep price to have to pay.

Eli had repaid my quarter-of-a-million loan, right on schedule. His life seemed, at least as far as I could tell, on a firmer basis. He was married to the same woman, the dean of a university in Washington, where he now lived, for eight or so years. He published a new novel. As a writer, he was respected more than ever, or so Gerry reported from reading the reviews of this latest book. I was headed toward eighty; my brother was seventy-three.

And then I hear that Eli had left his wife to marry a graduate student at Georgetown University, a woman not yet thirty. Which means she was more than forty years younger than he was. Something in my brother evidently can't stand peace and quiet. I knew nothing about the girl, but I could imagine what her parents must have felt when she told them she was going to marry a man older than they were. I shouldn't be surprised if Eli, in his vanity, felt his sexual attraction was still there, he was still in the game, still a player. Gerry jokingly wondered if her brother-in-law and his new bride were registered at Marshall Fields. I felt sorry for the girl.

I felt even sorrier when, a year or so later, Eli's son David called to tell me that his father and his young wife had had a Down syndrome child, a boy they named Frederick. What the hell was Eli thinking! No doubt jacked up on Viagra, was he going to show the world he was still virile? Hadn't he already proved he was a misery as a father? Why prove it again? Gerry thought that a child probably wasn't Eli's idea but his young wife's. She said that it sounded like the notion of a young woman to want the child of the much older husband, something to have after he had gone. A part of me felt sorry for Eli. I found it hard to imagine the life he led with a young wife, with whom he couldn't have all that much in common, and now a retarded son.

Eli never called to tell me that he had remarried or that he had had a child, and this time the lapse in our relations ran four or so years. I sold my business. Gerry and I now lived half the year in a condo we purchased in Boca Raton. Our health had held up fairly well, though I had begun to have arthritis in my elbows and ankles, about which there isn't much to be done but grin and bear it. I try to find pleasure in each day. The truth is that I feel myself damn lucky: I'd always made a good living, I wasn't dependent on anyone my whole life, and I still enjoy my wife's company.

I'd pretty much lost touch with Eli's son David — his other kids I can't say I really ever knew to begin with — when one day I decided to call David to see how things were going with him.

"Things aren't too bad, Uncle Lou," he said. "I've had a promotion. My kids are in good shape. We bought a larger house. Can't complain."

"How's your father?"

And then David told me that his father was suffering from dementia.

"How bad?" I asked.

"I guess it tends to be day to day — that is, some days he's better than others. I went out to visit him in Washington. He sleeps a lot. He knows who everyone is, but his sense of time is way out of whack. He sometimes thinks people who died years ago are still alive. Maybe you ought to try to see him before things get a lot worse."

The next day I called Eli's young wife and asked when it might be convenient to see my brother. Anytime I wished, she said. When I asked how he was, she said, "Some days he's pretty good. Today happens to be one of his bad days."

I took a cab from Reagan Airport to Eli's house, on Hoban Road. His wife greeted me at the door, saying that her husband was sleeping. She was not a beautiful woman, my new sister-in-law, but she had an intelligent face. When I addressed her as Mrs. Black, she said, "Call me Sandy, please."

She made coffee, which we drank sitting in the large kitchen. Her son, she said, was off at something called Playschool. She wanted to know if I knew anything about Down syndrome kids.

"They have their own charms, you know," she said. "Frederick is very dear."

"How is my brother with him?"

"Before his illness, he was marvelous with him, though at first he was shocked, and blamed himself, his being so old, for the child's not being normal."

Eli now entered the kitchen. He was in slippers, pajama bottoms, an undershirt with a V neck. He looked tired; his skin sagged badly; his left eye was almost closed. If you hadn't known him and someone told you he was ninety, you'd have believed it.

"Lou," he said. "What a nice surprise! Did Arlene come along? Arlene always loved me, you know. She was my first and best friend."

I thought to tell him that Arlene had died more than a decade ago, but then figured that it would only agitate him to do so and so said nothing.

"No, Eli," I said. "Arlene couldn't make it this trip. Why don't you join us for some coffee?"

"A good idea, Louie, sure, why not?" He never called me Louie before; nobody ever called me Louie.

"We have a son, Louie. Frederick the Great, I call him. Cute kid. You'll like him. So tell me, Louie, how's the old man? Still working for Schinberg on Fulton Street?"

"He's fine, Eli. He still doesn't say much. What do you suppose he's thinking? You're the novelist. You probably know."

"He's thinking, what am I doing in this damn country? He's thinking, who needs this goddamn English language? He's thinking life is full of dirty tricks. It really is full of dirty tricks, Louie, an endless variety of them, I'm here to tell you. But then you probably noticed on your own."

"Hard not to notice, Eli."

"Take me," he said. "Take me, Louie. Somewhere along the way I slipped off the track. Could never get back on. Not good. Wrote the books, though. That must stand for something with someone or other. Only one life to live, I'm afraid, and it's getting obvious that I'm not going to be allowed to live mine as a blond." He put a hand to the few fluffy white hairs that remained on his head.

"Think I'll take a pass on that coffee," he said. "Wake me when Frederick gets home, Sandy. There's lots of things I have to tell him. Next time bring Arlene, Louie. She's my true friend, always was, always will be." And then he shuffled out of the room, my kid brother, and I never saw him again.

I don't know how Eli got the gun, the Beretta he killed himself with. And of course I don't know what the exact motives for his suicide were. It may be that he was terrified of slipping any further down into the dark hole of his dementia. Maybe he found he lived his life so badly that he wanted to end it. When I remember how much he feared death, I shudder at the picture of him getting up the courage to put the gun in his mouth and then pulling the trigger. He slipped off the track and couldn't get back on, he told me that morning in his house on Hoban Road. What in the hell did he mean? I'll never understand him, my kid brother, Eli.

WILLIAM GAY

Where Will You Go When Your Skin Cannot Contain You?

FROM TIN HOUSE

THE JEEPSTER COULDN'T KEEP STILL. For forty-eight hours he'd been steady on the move and no place worked for long. He'd think of somewhere to be and go there and almost immediately suck the life from it, he could feel it charring around him. He felt he was on fire and running with upraised arms into a stiff cold wind, but instead of cooling him the wind just fanned the flames. His last so-called friend had faded on him and demanded to be left by the roadside with his thumb in the air.

The Jeepster drove westward into a sun that had gone down the sky so fast it left a fiery wake like a comet. Light pooled above the horizon like blood and red light hammered off the hood of the SUV he was driving. He put on his sunglasses. In the failing day the light was falling almost horizontally and the highway glittered like some virtual highway in a fairy tale or nightmare.

His so-called friend had faded because The Jeepster was armed and dangerous. He was armed and dangerous and running on adrenaline and fury and grief and honed to such a fine edge that alcohol and drugs no longer affected him. Nothing worked on him. He had a pocket full of money and a nine-millimeter automatic shoved into the waistband of his jeans and his T-shirt pulled down over it. He had his ticket punched for the graveyard or the penitentiary and one foot on the platform and the other foot on the train. He had everything he needed to get himself killed, to push the borders back and alter the very geography of reality itself.

On the outskirts of Ackerman's Field the neon of a Texaco station bled into the dusk like a virulent stain. Night was falling like some disease he was in the act of catching. At the pumps he filled the SUV up and watched the traffic accomplish itself in a kind of wonder. Everyone should have been frozen in whatever attitude they'd held when the hammer fell on Aimee and they should hold that attitude forever. He felt like a plague set upon the world to cauterize and cleanse it.

He went through the pneumatic door. He had his Ray-Bans shoved onto the top of his shaven head and he was grinning his gap-toothed grin. Such patrons as were about regarded him warily. He looked like bad news. He looked like the letter edged in black, the telegram shoved under your door at three o'clock in the morning.

You seen that Coors man? The Jeepster asked the man at the register.

Seen what? the man asked. Somewhere behind them a cue stick tipped a ball and it went down the felt in a near-silent hush and a ball rattled into a pocket and spiraled down and then there was just silence.

The Jeepster laid money on the counter. I know all about that Coors man, he said. I know Escue was broke and he borrowed ten bucks off the Coors man for the gas to get to where Aimee was working. Where's he at?

The counterman made careful change. He don't run today, he said. Wednesday was the last day he's been here. And what if he did run, what if he was here? How could he know? He was just a guy doing Escue a favor. He didn't know.

He didn't know, he didn't know, The Jeepster said. You reckon that'll keep the dirt out of his face? I don't.

They regarded each other in silence. The Jeepster picked up his change and slid it into his pocket. He leaned toward the counterman until their faces were very close together. Could be you chipped in a few bucks yourself, he finally said.

Just so you know, the counterman said, I've got me a sawed-off here under the counter. And I got my hand right on the stock. You don't look just right to me. You look crazy. You look like you escaped from prison or the crazy house.

I didn't escape, The Jeepster said. They let me out and was glad to see me go. They said I was too far gone, they couldn't do anything for me. They said I was a bad influence.

The Jeepster in Emile's living room. Emile was thinking this must be the end-time, the end of days. The rapture with graves bursting open and folk sailing skyward like superheroes. There was no precedent for this. The Jeepster was crying. His shaven head was bowed. His fingers were knotted at the base of his skull. A letter to each finger, LOVE and HATE inscribed there by some drunk or stoned tattooist in blurred jailhouse blue. The fingers were interlocked illegibly and so spelled nothing. The Jeepster's shoulders jerked with his sobbing, there was more news to read on his left arm: HEAVEN WON'T HAVE ME AND HELL'S AFRAID I'M TAKING OVER.

Emile himself had fallen on hard times. Once the scion of a prosperous farm family, now he could only look back on long-lost days that were bathed in an amber haze of nostalgia. He'd inherited all this and for a while there were wonders. Enormous John Deere cultivators and hay balers and tractors more dear than Rolls-Royces. For a while there was coke and crack and wild parties. Friends unnumbered and naked women rampant in their willingness to be sent so high you couldn't have tracked them on radar, sports cars that did not hold up so well against trees and bridge abutments.

Little by little Emile had sold things off for pennies on the dollar and day by day the money rolled through his veins and into his lungs, and the greasy coins trickled down his throat. The cattle were sold away or wandered off. Hogs starved and the strong ate the weak. It amazed him how easily a small fortune could be pissed away. Money don't go nowhere these days, Emile said when he was down to selling off stepladders and drop cords.

Finally he was down to rolling his own, becoming an entrepreneur, slaving over his meth lab like some crazed alchemist at his test tubes and brazier on the brink of some breakthrough that would cleanse the world of sanity forever.

The appalled ghost of Emile's mother haunted these rooms, hovered fretfully in the darker corners. Wringing her spectral hands over doilies beset with beer cans and spilled ashtrays. Rats tunneling in secret trespass through the upholstery. There were man-shaped indentations in the Sheetrock walls, palimpsest cavities with outflung arms where miscreants had gone in drunken rage. JESUS IS THE UNSEEN LISTENER TO EVERY CONVERSATION, an embroidered sampler warned from the wall. There were those of Emile's customers who wanted it taken down or turned to the wall. Emile left it as it was. He needs an education, Emile would say. He needs to know what it's like out here in the world. There's no secrets here.

The Jeepster looked up. He took off his Ray-Bans and shook his head as if to clear it of whatever visions beset it. Reorder everything as you might shake a kaleidoscope into a different pattern.

You got to have something, he said.

I ain't got jack shit.

Pills or something. Dilaudid.

I ain't got jack shit. I'm out on bond, and I done told you they're watchin this place. A sheriff's car parks right up there in them trees. Takin pictures. I seen some son of a bitch with a video camera. It's like bein a fuckin movie star. Man can't step outside to take a leak without windin up on videotape or asked for an autograph.

What happened?

I sent Qualls to Columbia after a bunch of medicine for my lab. He kept tryin to buy it all at the same drugstore. Like I specifically told him not to do. He'd get turned down and go on to the next drugstore. Druggists kept callin the law and callin the law. By the time they pulled him over it looked like a fuckin parade. Cops was fightin over who had priorities. He had the whole back seat and trunk full of Sudafed and shit. He rolled over on me and here they come with a search warrant. I'm out on bond.

I can't stand this.

I guess you'll have to, Emile said. Look, for what it's worth I'm sorry for you. And damn sorry for her. But I can't help you. Nobody can. You want to run time back and change the way things happened. But time won't run but one way.

I can't stand it. I keep seeing her face.

Well.

Maybe I'll go back out there to the funeral home and see her.

Maybe you ought to keep your crazy ass away from her daddy. You'll remember he's a cop.

I have to keep moving. I never felt like this. I never knew you could feel like this. I can't be still. It's like I can't stand it in my own skin.

Emile didn't say anything. He looked away. To the window where the night-mirrored glass turned back their images like sepia desperadoes in some old daguerreotype.

You still got that tow bar or did you sell it?

What?

I'm fixing to get that car. Aimee's car. Pull it off down by the river somewhere.

This is not makin a whole lot of sense to me.

They wouldn't let me in out there, they won't even let me in to see her body. I went and looked at her car. Her blood's all in the seat. On the windshield. It's all there is of her left in the world I can see or touch. I aim to have it.

Get away from me, Emile said.

Aimee had turned up at his place at eight o'clock in the morning. The Jeepster still slept, it took the horn's insistent blowing to bring him in the jeans he'd slept in out onto the porch and into a day where a soft summer rain fell.

Her battered green Plymouth idled in the yard. He stood on the porch a moment studying it. In the night a spider had strung a triangular web from the porch beam and in its ornate center a single drop of water clung gleaming like a stone a jeweler had set. The Jeepster went barefoot down the doorsteps into the muddy yard.

He was studying the car. Trying to get a count on the passengers. He couldn't tell until she cranked down the glass that it was just Aimee. He stood with his hands in his pockets listening to the rhythmic swish of the windshield wipers. The dragging stutter of a faulty wiper blade.

I need a favor, she said.

It had been a while and he just watched her face. She had always had a sly, secretive look that said, I'll bet you wish you had what I have, know what I know, could share the dreams that come for me alone when the day winds down and the light dims and it is finally quiet. She was still darkly pretty but there was something different about her. The grain of her skin, but especially the eyes. Something desperate hiding there in the dark shadows and trying to peer out. She already looked like somebody sliding off the face of the world.

I don't have a thing. I'm trying to get off that shit.

Really?

I've had the dry heaves and the shakes. Fever. Cramps and the shits. Is that real enough for you? Oh yeah, and hallucinations. I've had them. I may be having one now. I may be back in the house with baby monkeys running up and down the window curtains.

She made a dismissive gesture, a slight curling of her upper lip. Will you do me a favor or not?

Is Escue all out of favors?

I've left him, I'm not going back. He's crazy.

No shit. Did a light just go on somewhere?

He stays on that pipe and it's fucked him up or something. His head. You can't talk to him.

I wouldn't even attempt it.

I don't understand goddamn men. Live with them and they think they own you. Want to marry you. Eat you alive. Jimmy was older and he'd been around and I thought he wouldn't be so obsessive. Sleep with him a few times and it's the same thing over again. Men.

The Jeepster looked away. Blackbirds rose from the field in a fury of wings and their pattern shifted and shifted again as if they sought some design they couldn't quite attain. He thought about Aimee and men. He knew she'd slept with at least one man for money. He knew it for a fact. The Jeepster himself had brokered the deal.

What you get for taking up with a son of a bitch old enough to be your daddy.

I see you're still the same. The hot-shit macho man. The man with the platinum balls. You'd die before you'd ask me to come back, wouldn't you?

You made your bed. Might as well spoon up and get comfortable.

Then I want to borrow a gun.

What for?

I'm afraid he'll be there tonight when I get off work. He said he was going to kill me and he will. He slapped me around some this morning. I just want him to see it. If he knows I've got it there in my purse he'll leave me alone.

I'm not loaning you a gun.

Leonard.

You'd shoot yourself. Or some old lady crossing the street. Is he following you?

He's broke, I don't think he's got the gas.

I hope he does turn up here and tries to slap me around some.

I'll drop him where he stands and drag his sorry, woman-beating ass inside the house and call the law.

Loan me the pistol. You don't know how scared I am of him. You don't know what it's like.

The loop tape of some old blues song played in his head: *You don't know my, you don't know my, you don't know my mind.*

No. I'll pick you up from work. I'll be there early and check out the parking lot and if he's there I'll come in and tell you. You can call the cops. You still working at that Quik Mart?

Yes. But you won't come.

I'll be there.

Can I stay here tonight?

You come back you'll have to stay away from Escue. I won't have him on the place. Somebody will die.

I'm done with him.

The Jeepster looked across the field. Water was standing in the low places and the broken sky lay there reflected. Rain crows called from tree to tree. A woven-wire fence drowning in honeysuckle went tripping toward the horizon where it vanished in mist like the palest of smoke.

Then you can stay all the nights there are, he said.

The murmur of conversation died. Folks in the General Café looked up when The Jeepster slid into a booth but when he stared defiantly around they went back to studying their plates and shoveling up their food. There was only the click of forks and knives, the quickstep rubber-soled waitresses sliding china across Formica.

He ordered chicken-fried steak and chunky mashed potatoes and string beans and jalapeño cornbread. He sliced himself a bite of steak and began to chew. Then he didn't know what to do with it. Panic seized him. The meat grew in his mouth, a gristly, glutinous mass that forced his jaws apart, distorted his face. He'd forgotten how to eat. He sat in wonder. The bite was supposed to go somewhere but he didn't know where. What came next, forgetting to breathe? Breathing out when he should be breathing in, expelling the oxygen and hanging onto the carbon dioxide until the little lights flickered dim and dimmer and died.

He leaned and spat the mess onto his plate and rose. Beneath his T-shirt the outlined gun was plainly visible. He looked about the room. Their switchblade eyes flickered away. He stood for an awkward moment surveying them as if he might address the room. Then he put too much money on the table and crossed the enormity of the tile floor and went out the door into the trembling dusk.

So here he was again, The Jeepster back at the same old stand. On his first attempt he'd almost made it to the chapel where she lay in state before a restraining hand fell on his shoulder, but this time they were prepared. Two uniformed deputies unfolded themselves from their chairs and approached him one on either side. They turned him gently, one with an arm about his shoulders.

Leonard, he said. It's time to go outside. Go on home now. You can't come in here.

The deputy was keeping his voice down but the father had been waiting for just this visitor. The father in his khakis rose up like some sentry posted to keep the living from crossing the border into the paler world beyond. A chair fell behind him. He had to be restrained by his brothers in arms, the sorriest and saddest of spectacles. His voice was a rusty croak. Crying accusations of ruin and defilement and loss. All true. He called curses down upon The Jeepster, proclaiming his utter worthlessness, asking, no, demanding, that God's lightning burn him incandescent in his very footsteps.

As if superstitious, or at any rate cautious, the cops released him and stepped one step away. One of them opened the door and held it. Doors were always opening, doors were always closing. The Jeepster went numbly through this opening into the hot volatile night and this door fell to behind him like a thunderclap.

In these latter days The Jeepster had discovered an affinity for the night side of human nature. Places where horrific events had happened drew him with a gently perverse gravity. These desecrated places of murder and suicide had the almost-nostalgic tug of his childhood home. The faces of the perpetrators looked vaguely familiar, like long-lost kin he could but barely remember. These were places where the things that had happened were so terrible that they had imprinted themselves onto an atmosphere that still trembled faintly with the unspeakable.

The rutted road wound down and down. Other roads branched

off this one and others yet, like capillaries bleeding off civilization into the wilderness, and finally he was deep in the Harrikin.

Enormous trees rampant with summer greenery reared out of the night and loomed upon the windshield and slipstreamed away. All day the air had been hot and humid and to the west a storm was forming. Soundless lightning flickered the horizon to a fierce rose, then trembled and vanished. The headlights froze a deer at the height of its arc over a strand of barbed wire like a holographic deer imaged out of The Jeepster's mind or the free-floating ectoplasm of the night.

He parked before the dark bulk of a ruined farmhouse. Such windows as remained refracted the staccato lightning. Attendant outbuildings stood like hesitant, tree-shadowed familiars.

He got out. There was the sound of water running somewhere. Off in the darkness fireflies arced like sparks thrown off by the heat. He had a liter of vodka in one hand and a quart of orange juice in the other. He drank and then sat for a time on a crumbling stone wall and studied the house. He had a momentary thought for copperheads in the rocks but he figured whatever ran in his veins was deadlier than any venom and any snake that bit him would do so at its peril. He listened to the brook muttering to itself. Night birds called from the bowered darkness of summer trees. He drank again and past the gleaming ellipse of the upraised bottle the sky bloomed with blood-red fire and after a moment thunder rumbled like voices in a dream and a wind was at the trees.

He set aside the orange juice and went back to the SUV and took a flashlight from the glove box. Its beam showed him a fallen barn, wind-writhed trees, the stone springhouse. Beneath the springhouse a stream trilled away over tumbled rocks and vanished at the edge of the flashlight's beam. You had to stoop to enter the stone door, it was a door for gnomes or little folk. The interior had the profound stillness of a cathedral, the waiting silence of a church where you'd go to pray.

This was where they'd found the farmer after he'd turned the gun on himself. Why here? What had he thought about while he'd waited for the courage to eat the barrel of the shotgun? The Jeepster turned involuntarily and spat. There was a cold metallic taste of oil in his mouth.

Light slid around the walls. Leached plaster, water beading and dripping on the concrete, the air damp and fetid. A black-spotted salamander crouched on its delicate toy feet and watched him with eyes like bits of obsidian. Its leathery orange skin looked alien to this world.

Against the far wall stood a crypt-shaped stone spring box adorned with curling moss like coarse, virid maidenhair. He trailed a hand in the icy water. In years long past, here was where they'd kept their jugged milk. Their butter. He'd have bet there was milk and butter cooling here the day it all went down. When the farmer walked in on his wife and brother in bed together. The Jeepster could see it. Overalls hung carefully on a bedpost. Worn gingham dress folded just so. Did he kill them then or watch a while? But The Jeepster knew, he was in the zone. He killed them then. And lastly himself, a story in itself.

When The Jeepster came back out, the storm was closer and the thunder constant and the leaves of the clashing trees ran like quicksilver. He drank from the vodka and climbed high steep steps to the farmhouse porch and crossed it and hesitated before the open front door. The wind stirred drifted leaves of winters past. The oblong darkness of the doorway seemed less an absence of light than a tangible object, a smooth glass rectangle so solid you could lay a hand on it. Yet he passed through it into the house. There was a floral scent of ancient funerals. The moving light showed him dangling sheaves of paper collapsed from the ceiling, wallpaper of dead, faded roses. A curled and petrified work shoe like a piece of proletarian sculpture.

The revenants had eased up now to show The Jeepster about. A spectral hand to the elbow, solicitously guiding him to the bedroom. Hinges grated metal on metal. A hand, pointing. There. Do you see? He nodded. The ruined bed, the hasty, tangled covers, the shot-riddled headboard. Turning him, the hand again pointing. There. Do you see? Yes, he said. The empty window opening on nothing save darkness. The Jeepster imagined the mad scramble over the sill and out the window, the naked man fleeing toward the hollow, pistoned legs pumping, buckshot shrieking after him like angry bees, feets don't fail me now.

The Jeepster clicked out the light. He thought of the bloodstained upholstery strewn with pebbled glass and it did not seem enough. Nothing seemed enough. He stood for a time in the darkness, gathering strength from these lost souls for what he had to do.

He lay in the back seat of the SUV and tried to sleep. Rain pounded on the roof, wind-whipped rain rendered the glass opaque and everything beyond these windows a matter of conjecture. The vodka slept on his chest like a stuffed bear from childhood. It hadn't worked anyway, it might as well have been tap water. Things would not leave him alone, old unheeded voices plagued his ears. Brightly colored images tumbled through his mind. An enormous, stained-glass serpent had shattered inside him and was moving around blindly reassembling itself.

He'd concentrate on more pleasant times. His senior year in high school, he saw his leaping body turning in the air, the football impossibly caught as if by legerdemain, he heard the crowd calling his name. But a scant few years later he was seated alone in the empty stands with a bottle between his feet. A winter wind blew scraps of paper and turned paper cups against the frozen ground and the lush green playing field had turned brittle and bare. He wondered if there was a connection between these two images and, further, what that connection might be.

A picture of himself and Aimee the first time, try to hold on to this one. Fooling around on her bed. Her giggling against his chest. A new urgency to her lips and tongue. Leonard, quit. Quit. Oh quit. Oh. Then he was inside her and her gasp was muffled by applause from the living room and her father chuckling at the Letterman show. Other nights, other beds. The Jeepster and Aimee shared a joint history, tangled and inseparable, like two trees that have grown together, a single trunk faulted at the heart.

Drink this, smoke this, take these. Hell, take his money, you won't even remember it in the morning. You'll never see him again. Ruin, defilement, loss. One pill makes you larger, one pill makes you small, one pill puts you on the road to Clifton with a Ford truck riding your bumper.

For here's what happened, or what happened on the surface, here's what imprinted itself on the very ether and went everywhere at once, the news the summer wind whispered in The Jeepster's sleeping ear.

The truck pulled up on Aimee past Centre. Escue blew the truck horn, pounded on the steering wheel. She rolled down the glass and gave him the finger. She sped up. He sped up. She could see his twisted face in the rearview mirror. The round O of his mouth seemed to be screaming soundlessly.

When she parked on the lot before the Quik Mart he pulled in beside her. He was out of the Ford before it quit rocking on its springs. He had a .357 magnum in his hand. As he ran around the hood of his truck she was trying to get out of her car on the passenger's side. Just as he shot out the driver's-side window the passenger door on the Plymouth flew open and she half-fell onto the pavement. She was on her back with her right elbow on the pavement and a hand to her forehead.

She looked as if she might be raking the hair out of her eyes. He shot her twice in the face. Somebody somewhere began to scream.

Hey. Hey goddamn it.

A man came running out of the Quik Mart with a pistol of his own. His feet went slap slap slap on the pavement. Escue turned and leveled the pistol and fired. The running man dropped to his palms and behind him the plate-glass window of the Quik Mart dissolved in a shimmering waterfall.

The man was on his hands and knees feeling about for his dropped weapon when Escue put the barrel of the revolver in his own mouth with the sight hard against his palate and pulled the trigger.

Now The Jeepster opened the door of the SUV and climbed out into the rain. He raised his arms to the windy heavens. All about him turmoil and disorder. Rain came in torrents and the thunder cracked like gunfire and lightning walked among the vibratory trees. His shaven head gleamed like a rain-washed stone. He seemed to be conducting the storm with his upraised arms. He demanded the lightning take him but it would not.

Mouse-quiet and solemn, The Jeepster crossed the rich mauve carpet. Who knew what hour, the clock didn't exist that could measure times like these. This time there were no laws stationed to intercept him and he passed unimpeded into another chamber. Soft, indirect lighting fell on purple velvet curtains tied back with golden rope. He moved like an agent provocateur through the profoundest of silences.

This chamber was furnished with a steel gray casket, wherein an old man with a caved face and a great blade of a nose lay in state. Two middle-aged female mourners sat in folding chairs and watched The Jeepster's passage with fearful, tremulous eyes.

He parted another set of purple curtains. Here the room was empty save for a pale pink casket resting on a catafalque. He crossed the room and stood before it. Water dripped from his clothing onto the carpet. A fan whirred somewhere.

After a while he knew someone was standing behind him. He'd heard no footsteps but he turned to face an old man in worn, dusty black hunched in the back like a vulture, maroon tie at his throat. His thin hair was worn long on the side and combed over his bald pate. The Jeepster could smell his brilliantined hair, the talcum that paled his cheeks.

The Jeepster could tell the old man wanted to order him to leave but was afraid to. The old man didn't want to be here. He wanted to be ten thousand miles away, in some world so far away even the constellations were unknowable and the language some unintelligible gobbledygook no human ear could decipher. He wished he'd retired yesterday.

For The Jeepster looked bad. He was waterlogged and crazed and the pistol was outside his shirt now and his eyes were just the smoking black holes you'd burn in flesh with a red-hot poker.

He laid a hand on the pink metal casket. Above where the face might be. He thought he could detect a faint, humming vibration.

I can't see her, The Jeepster said.

The undertaker cleared his throat. It sounded loud after the utter silence. No, he said. She was injured severely in the face. It's a closed-casket service.

The Jeepster realized he was on the tilted edge of things, where the footing was bad and his grip tenuous at best. He felt the frayed mooring lines that held him part silently and tail away into the dark and he felt a sickening lurch in his very being. There are some places you can't come back from.

He took the pistol out of his waistband. No it's not, he said.

When the three deputies came they came down the embankment past the springhouse through the scrub brush, parting the undergrowth with their heavy, hand-cut snake-sticks, and they were the very embodiment of outrage, the bereft father at their fore goading them forward. Righteous anger tricked out in khaki and boots and Sam Browne belts like fate's gestapo set upon him.

In parodic domesticity he was going up the steps to the abandoned farmhouse with an armful of wood to build a fire for morning coffee. He'd leaned the girl against the wall, where she took her ease with her ruined face turned to the dripping trees and the dark fall of her hair drawing off the morning light. The deputies crossed the stream and quickened their pace and came on.

The leaning girl, The Jeepster, the approaching law. These scenes had the sere, charred quality of images unspooling from ancient papyrus or the broken figures crazed on shards of stone pottery.

The Jeepster rose up before them like a wild man, like a beast hounded to its lair. The father struck him in the face and a stick caught him at the base of the neck just above the shoulders and he went down the steps sprawled amid his spilled wood and struggled to his knees. A second blow drove him to his hands, and his palms seemed to be steadying the trembling of the earth itself.

He studied the ground beneath his spread hands. Ants moved among the grass stems like shadowy figures moving between the boles of trees and he saw with unimpeachable clarity that there were other worlds than this one. Worlds layered like the sections of an onion or the pages of a book. He thought he might ease into one of them and be gone, vanish like dew in a hot morning sun.

Then blood gathered on the tip of his nose and dripped and in this heightened reality he could watch the drop descend with infinitesimal slowness and when it finally struck the earth it rang like a hammer on an anvil. The ants tracked it away and abruptly he could see the connections between the worlds, strands of gossamer sheer and strong as silk.

There are events so terrible in this world their echoes roll world on distant world like ripples on water. Tug a thread and the entire tapestry alters. Pound the walls in one world and in another a portrait falls and shatters.

Goddamn, Cleave, a voice said. Hold up a minute, I believe you're about to kill him.

When the father's voice came it came from somewhere far above The Jeepster, like the voice of some Old Testament god.

I would kill him if he was worth it but he ain't. A son of a bitch like this just goes through life tearin up stuff, and somebody else has always got to sweep up the glass. He don't know what it is to hurt, he might as well be blind and deaf. He don't feel things the way the rest of us does.

MARY GORDON

Eleanor's Music

FROM PLOUGHSHARES

"DO BE SURE, DEARIE, that you get the plain yogurt for your father. I brought home vanilla by mistake last week, and he was ready to call out the constabulary."

"Entendu," Eleanor called back, straightening her collar in front of the spotted mirror in the hall. How like her mother to use the phrase "call out the constabulary." It was the kind of charming phrase that was all too rare in this overwhelmingly crude world; soon that kind of charm, that kind of light playfulness, would be lost entirely.

How she loved her mother! Still perfectly beautiful at eighty-six. The only concession she'd made to her age was a pair of hearing aids. "My ears," she called them. Everything her mother touched she touched carefully, and left a little smoother, a little finer for her touch. Everything about her mother reminded her of walking through a glade, from the chestnut rinse that tinted what would be bright white hair, to the shadings of her clothes. Each garment some variety of leaf tone: the light green of spring with an underhint of yellow, the dark of full summer, occasionally a detail of bright autumn — an orange scarf, a red enamel brooch. Wool in winter, cotton in summer; never an artificial fiber next to her skin. What she didn't understand, she often said, was a kind of laziness, which in the name of convenience in the end made more work and deprived one of the small but real joys. The smell of a warm iron against damp cloth, the comfort of something that was once alive against your body. She was a great believer in not removing yourself from the kind of labor she considered natural. She wouldn't own a Cuisinart or have a credit card. She liked, she said, chopping vegetables, and when she paid for something, she wanted to feel, on the tips of her fingers, on the palms of her hands, the cost.

Some people might have considered these things crotchets or affectations, but Eleanor considered them an entirely admirable assertion of her mother's individuality. As she considered her father's refusal to step outside their Park Avenue apartment without a jacket and tie, regardless of the heat of the day or the informality of occasion. And she supposed it might be said that his continuing to smoke a pipe, when there was clear evidence that it was hazardous to his health, could be interpreted as a stubborn self-indulgence. But she always liked hearing him say to a born-again nonsmoker, "At my age I have the right to not listen to a bunch of damn fools who want to tell me I can live forever."

No, they were marvelous, her parents. She adored them, as she adored the apartment on Park Avenue where the three of them had lived since Eleanor was three. Except for the years she'd been married to Billy. Then she had lived downtown.

She had been shattered when Billy had told her he was leaving, but it had just seemed natural to let him keep the apartment and for her to move back in with her parents, "until you're back on your beam," as her father said. It was eighteen years later, and she'd never moved out.

She knew that many people thought it odd, to say nothing of unhealthy, for her to be living with her parents at the age of fifty-one. "Health," said her father, "is the new orthodoxy. The new criterion by which we are judged of the fold or outside it. In the old days, they just tested people by trying to drown them, and if they survived they were allowed back in the community. But that's too good for the health nags."

So she didn't listen any longer to the whispers she might once have overheard: that there was something wrong with her going on living with her parents. She had long ago given up that last residue of her embarrassment, which at one time, like a pile of dried leaves, could be set adrift by the slightest wind, and would flutter inside her, cause her to put her hand, splayed out and flat, against her chest. Something had damped the pile; she liked to think of it as a gentle, constant, nourishing rain: the rain of time. The pile of leaves never flared up now. No, she never thought of it at all.

She enjoyed her life. She liked her job, teaching music at the Watson School, directing the chorus and the a cappella singers.

She knew that the girls found her a little old-fashioned, a little stiff, but she believed that they were secretly pleased to have in her a sign of unchangeable standards; she allowed them to tease her, occasionally, but would not give in to their demands to include one rock-and-roll song at the Christmas concert, and she refused to disband the bell ringers, although it was, each year, increasingly difficult to find candidates. She deliberately stopped the repertory of the chorus at Victor Herbert, although one year she had allowed a Johnny Mercer song, *"Dream, when you're feeling blue, dream and they might come true."* She'd been surprised that, to the girls, that song was from the same out-of-memory basket as Purcell or Liszt — it had happened before they were born and was therefore apart from them. But that was her job: to instill in them, gracefully, she hoped, a sense of the value of tradition, of the beauty of the past. If that meant she wasn't one of the most popular teachers, well, she had long ago learned to live with that. She had her votaries: one or two a year, never the most popular girls, and, increasingly, not the most talented.

But she had something that the other teachers didn't have: she had a professional life. She was a member of the chorus of the Knickerbocker Opera Company, a small company that had three performances a year: *Amahl and the Night Visitors* at Christmas, their bread and butter, a Gilbert and Sullivan in late February, and, in early May, one of the operas in the common repertory, *Carmen, Lucia di Lammermoor.* She wasn't paid much, but she was paid. She felt this distinguished her, and she thought of the words "distinguished" and "distinction." Being in the company allowed her to attach both words to herself. She was not an amateur, like many of her friends whose relationship to the arts was a species of volunteerism.

Her friends were dear to her, essential, old friends, some from when she was a student at Watson herself, some from Bryn Mawr, newer friends, one young colleague who was struggling with the fledgling string quartet, others from her book group. She was proud that her friends ranged in age from her parents' compatriots to a twenty-five-year-old ex-student, now an investment banker who sang in a Renaissance quintet and traced her devotion to music straight to Eleanor.

And of course there was Billy. People thought it was peculiar that she should be such close friends with her ex-husband, as they thought it was peculiar that she lived with her parents. But she was proud of that as well; she considered the shape of her life not peculiar, but original; she lived as she liked; real courage, she believed, was doing what you believed in, however it appeared.

Of course, if it had been up to her, she and Billy would never have split. And some people might have found that peculiar, too, that she would have been willing to go on with a marriage that had no physical side to it, or no, that wasn't right, because many of the pleasures she and Billy enjoyed were physical, winter skiing in Colorado, swimming in Maine in summer, ballroom dancing in their class on the West Side. She thought it was such a narrow understanding, to think that in a relationship between man and woman, "physical" and "sexual" were precise synonyms. She firmly believed that they were not.

And she didn't believe that her relationship with Billy, even now, was devoid of a sexual component. She knew he appreciated her as a woman, and that his appreciation was that of a man. He had come to her, weeping, confessing that his problems in bed with her had nothing to do with her, or with him, for that matter: it was just the way he was; he had fallen in love with Paul, and realized for the first time the way he had always been, the way he had always been made, what he had been afraid of, had repressed, but could no longer. Because love had come his way.

"Love," she had said, as if she'd just picked up, between two fingers, an iridescent, slightly putrefying thing. "And what do you call what we have for each other, devotion, loyalty, shared interests, shared values, joy in each other's company, what do you call that if not love?"

She didn't say, "Don't you know that I would die for you," because although she meant it, she didn't want to mean it, and certainly, she would never say it. It sounded too operatic. Opera was the center of both their lives, she as a singer, he as an accompanist, but she had no interest in living at the intense, excessive temperatures opera suggested.

He had knelt before her (a gesture that was far too operatic for her tastes) and taken her hands. "Of course I love you, Eleanor. I will always love you. You are my dearest friend, and always will be. But this is of another order."

"Get up, Billy," she said. "You must do what you think you must. I'll stay with Ma and Pa until you come to a decision."

She was sure he'd come around, come to his senses, show up with flowers, take her to an expensive dinner, where they would eat luxuriously, drink an extravagant wine, and not mention what she thought of as "his little lapse." But no, it didn't happen, he moved in with Paul, or rather, Paul moved in with him, and she moved in with her parents. It seemed sensible; she had the option of moving in with her parents, and he had no other way of staying in New York. He taught music at St. Anselm's, a boys' school that was a brother school to Watson. And Paul was a conductor; he survived by doing legal proofreading; he'd never, as far as Eleanor could see, been able to support himself in any reasonable way. So it was better that Billy kept the apartment; anything else would have been vindictive. And above all, she didn't want a vindictive parting.

That had been eighteen years ago; she had been thirty-three. She and Billy had been married for nine years. A *mariage blanc*. That was a nicer way of putting it than using the word "unconsummated." On their wedding night, he'd said he just wasn't ready, and he had never been ready, and she had never felt free to bring it up. She'd thought they were happy, and she didn't miss what she'd never known. He was affectionate; they shared a bed, and held each other, sometimes, in the mornings. She found him beautiful; sometimes she was moved to weep at the sight of his back when he was shaving. But she would never tell anyone the truth of her marriage, and she would never speak to Billy about it: she couldn't see the good.

They still had lunch together every sixth Sunday, and, of course, they saw each other at the Knickerbocker Opera, the small company where she was in the chorus and he was rehearsal pianist. They had never, officially, divorced.

The chive-colored scarf that she tied around her neck was a present from him on her last birthday. Really, Billy was wonderful at knowing what would suit her; his gifts were always exactly right; if she bought a new pair of shoes, he noticed, and was complimentary; he would take her hand and tell her that she still had the alabaster hands of a Canova statue; if she changed the shade of her lipstick, he'd comment, disappointed. He'd said, "Eleanor, my love, you must promise me that no matter what, you will be the one I can count on not to change in the slightest bit."

She had been glad to promise. And, looking in the mirror, she could be satisfied with her looks. With her *look*.

"Eleanor Harkness has a kind of timeless elegance." She had never actually heard anyone saying that about her, but she imagined it was the kind of thing that people thought.

She believed — she hoped it wasn't vanity — that she was fortunate in her looks, that she still had the right to think of herself as a good-looking woman. Good-looking in a way that brought with it neither danger nor corrupting adulation. "Neither Madonna nor whore," she'd said to herself once, of herself, feeling a thrill in the harshness of the sharp words, uttered in silence, resonant only to her own ears. She believed she had the kind of features she would have chosen for herself: small, neatly made, her eyes gray-green, a modest, well-cut nose, a moderate mouth with a generous enough underlip. "A witty mouth," Billy had said once, and she had treasured that.

She patted her hair one last time in front of the mirror. She was particularly fond of her hair — beginning to gray now, but still arranging itself, when she took it out of its pins, in vibrant, abundant waves. But she never let it down in public: she clasped it to the back of her head with bone or tortoise shell or amber clips and pins. No one saw her hair as she saw it when she sat in front of the dressing table that had been her grandmother's: carved cherry, with clusters of oak leaves and acorns forming an arch across the top. It was a secret thrill: to pull the last bone pin out of her hair and watch it fall down her back. Occasionally, she might have wished to do that for a man — that set piece of ancient feminine allure — but she had come to understand that what she would really have liked would be to do it not in a bedroom, but on a stage.

If she had any disappointment in her life it was that her music had not come to more. But she had refused to dwell on it. As her mother always said, "It does no good to sit in the damp dark smelly places of the mind. It only leads to rot." But sometimes she allowed herself to wish she had performed more, that she could give recitals of lieder and songs of the French composers she so loved, Debussy, Fauré, Ravel. It had been ten years since she'd had a recital. When her beloved teacher had died, she took it as a sign and didn't look for a replacement. She could never have borne the kind of singer's life that required so much pushing and striving. She was pleased to think of herself walking lightly, gratefully, into a space that seemed provided for her. Not the star of the company, but a member of the chorus. That was pleasing, that was satisfying. She was a fortunate woman. She knew it wasn't vanity that shaped this self-assessment. It was, rather, a habit of mind she had inherited from her parents. She was certain that acknowledging such heritance could never be thought a form of pride.

It was a perfect autumn morning, and she took pleasure not only in the weather but also in her being perfectly dressed for it. She knew that her pantyhose were not silk, but they felt silky, nearly the color of her flesh, but a shade or so lighter. And riding lightly over them, the satin lining, a lighter shade of chive than the fine wool of her skirt itself, or the scarf Billy had given her. Her blouse, of course, was silk; at first glance it seemed gray, but looked at more closely, examined for a while, it was obvious that it had been dipped in a bath of bluish green. A shade to complement both her eyes and the loden of her cape, in its turn set off by Billy's scarf. The sun made the mica flecks in the pavement sparkle, she wanted to say, like diamonds; she was pleased by the sounds the heels of her Ferragamo oxfords made — so comfortable for walking, but Italian, not earnest-looking. The sky was slate blue, and the yellow maples flashed against it as if they'd been scooped out of a plane of light the slate concealed and shielded. A perfect day to walk across Central Park, this Saturday, October 17. Children played with large balls in bright primary colors; rash boys skated dangerously; girls, their dress another kind of danger, sauntered, smoking, tipping back their soda cans for the last sweet drops.

She knew that Fairway would be crowded, but even the crowding was, today, enjoyable. She imagined assignations at the cheese counter — surely the blond thirty-year-old and the bearded ginger-haired fellow holding a green bicycle helmet would meet up once again for drinks, for dinner, maybe — who knew? — for life. The cheese man gave out samples, try this, try this, this Brie is from Belgians, don't be prejudiced, it's cheap but good, and this Asiago — he kissed his fingers to his reddish lips — I envy you if you're trying it for the first time.

She bowed her head when he offered her a piece, as if she were a knight taking upon herself the tribute of a king. Yes, half a pound, she said, and half a pound of Port Salut. She bought three kinds of dried bean — pinto, fava, cannellini, modest and sensible as old jewels in their barrels. Her mother was planning today to make a hearty soup. She bagged two pounds of McIntosh with the smell of autumn on them. Where, she wondered, did they grow? Into her cart she carefully placed endive, arugula, free-range eggs. The yogurt, plain, that her mother had told her to be sure of. She would take a cab home. What she had bought would be too much to carry through the park.

She put all the food away, keeping out for her lunch and her mother's the Port Salut and two of the largest apples.

"Mustn't linger. Rehearsal," she said, wiping her lips with the flax-colored napkin her mother had laid out. She brushed her teeth, put on some lipstick, and made her way downtown.

The Knickerbocker Opera Company rehearsed in the basement of Holy Paraclete Episcopal Church on 32nd Street and Madison Avenue. Eleanor took the Lexington Avenue bus downtown, glad to find one of the single seats vacant; she preferred not having to share a seat, which so often meant either having to shift to let the inside person out or stepping over that person. She was looking forward to having a cup of tea with Billy before rehearsal; tea with lemon to keep her voice clear. He would order, as he always did, a Coke, a habit she found boyishly endearing and so sophisticated and cultivated in a man.

She was the first to arrive. She saw him frown, as he always did, when he walked into a restaurant, as if he were at once displeased to be in the room at all and concerned that the person he was meant to meet might never arrive.

She hadn't seen him since the tenth of June, their wedding anniversary; he hadn't, of course, forgotten. He and Paul had spent the summer at the house in Maine that had been his parents', where he and Eleanor had spent their summers when they were married. She had often wished that Paul would betake himself to an artists' colony — preferably in Europe — one summer and that Billy would invite her to Maine once again. It had never happened; each year she would listen to Billy's groans about what had fallen off or broken down at "the old manse." It was a rare instance of insensitivity on his part not to imagine that such a recitation might be painful for her. She spent her summers, as she had as a child, in her parents' cottage on Cape Cod.

He looked young and fit and tan in gray wool trousers, oxford shirt, blue blazer. There were lines around his eyes, but they suited him, made him look less provisional, less the eternal boy. She thought how much better looking a couple she and he made than he and Paul. Paul had put on weight, and a look that was, in his youth, romantic and bohemian had become, in middle age, merely slovenly. She was sure that this change must be a grief to Billy, who cared so very much about the look of things.

"How's every little thing, old girl?" he said, kissing her cheek.

"Right as rain, old boy."

"I see you kept yourself out of the Wellfleet sun. No chance of your marring your alabaster perfection to catch a few rays."

"I think we all need to be careful about skin cancer with the ozone layer thin as it is. Not that Pa would think of sunblock."

"How are the terrible two?"

"Very well, indeed. They send their love."

As they finished their tea, Billy said to her, "Dearest, I want you to be the first to know. Paul will make the announcement. Instead of doing *Iolanthe* this spring, we've commissioned a new work."

Eleanor's heart sank. She had little taste for contemporary music, and Billy knew it. She wiped the corner of her mouth.

"It's a very fine piece by a young composer, a protégé of Paul's. The commission is a great thing for him."

She didn't want to ask where the money came from, to pay this protégé. Instead she said, "What a fine thing for Paul to have done."

"Yes," Billy said, "I think it is. He's quite young, this fellow, twenty-four, but he has an extraordinary gift, he can write lyrically and satirically at the same time. A bite, but an aftertaste of sweetness. This piece is called *The Dream of Andy Warhol.* Andy Warhol relives the highlights of his life in the moments before his death."

"Andy Warhol?" she said, not even trying to conceal her shock. "An opera about Andy Warhol? Hardly a suitable subject, I'd have thought."

Billy's face reddened. He wiped his mouth, very much as she had just done, with the white cloth napkin.

"Try and keep an open mind, there's a good girl. We'll be passing out the score today. Must dash."

He left her to pay the check, which was, she thought, most unlike him.

She was never sure how many of the Knickerbockers knew that she and Billy had been married. She never wanted to bring it up herself, because she wasn't certain if she wanted it known or not. Billy was universally loved by all the singers for his kindness and admired for the suppleness and flexibility of his accompaniment, so luster would attach to her if it were known that she had been his wife. On the other hand, everyone knew that he and Paul were partners, so humiliation would attach to her, inevitably, as a woman who had been left. But to be left for a man was not the same, by a long chalk, she had always told herself, as being left for another woman. She found it hard to determine which would attach to her more securely: luster or humiliation. And so, she had held herself back from the other people in the chorus; after twenty-five years of being a member, there was not one of them she could call a friend. Even those she would have thought of as close acquaintances had left the chorus, because they had reached a certain age, the age at which their voices weren't up to certain musical demands. She was one of the older members now — but that was all right, she liked to think that she maintained a nice balance: she kept her reserve, but she was friendly to everyone. If occasionally she picked up a whiff of resentment, she reminded herself that musical people were temperamental and self-centered, and that it had nothing to do with her.

She was asking Lily Streicher, who had been to Tuscany, how her summer was, when Paul arrived, dressed in navy pants, a yellow shirt (untucked, Eleanor noted, to hide his belly), and black loafers that made his feet look like thick fish, steaming in pans that were too narrow for them, straining against the sides.

He was carrying a stack of scores, and he laid them dramatically on the top of the piano.

"Something exciting, boys and girls. Papa has quite a special treat."

There was a stir among the singers; Eleanor felt complacent in her secret knowledge.

"I've commissioned an opera for us. By the next genius among us; we've stolen a march on the MacArthurs. I'll pass out the score, and Billy will play some bits for you. It's called *The Dream of Andy Warhol.* I'll allow the composer to fill you in. It's my honor to introduce him. Ladies and gentlemen: Desmond Marx."

Certainly, there wasn't a gasp when the young man walked through the door, but there was something like it in the feeling that spread through the air. It was as if a Bronzino had walked in, Eleanor thought, one of those arrogant courtiers in velvet and satin with the full lower lip and dissolute, commanding stare. Desmond Marx was beautiful, there was power in his beauty, and he knew it. His black jeans were creased perfectly, as if they'd just been pressed; his shirt, a bluish violet open at the neck, spread itself lightly, easily, over his muscular torso; he wore loafers — the same loafers Paul was wearing, but without socks, and his feet were thin and shapely in the loafers, whereas Paul's looked overstuffed.

"Hi," he said, looking challengingly at the chorus. "Well, as Paul told you, my opera is called *The Dream of Andy Warhol,* and I know perfectly well it's a lot different from the kind of thing you do. Maybe a little bit shocking for you. But I think Warhol was a great visionary, the person who had the clearest vision of his time and ours, its violence, its strangeness, and this is my vision of his vision. I like to think it brings out the pathos and the grandeur of this artist. And I look forward to your responses."

"Billy, if you would," said Paul.

Billy and Paul looked at each other, Eleanor thought, like a pair of cats that had swallowed the cream. She wondered where this Desmond Marx was living; Billy had said he was staying with them. It was, as she very well knew, a one-bedroom apartment. She wondered if they had recently got around to buying a foldout couch.

Eleanor didn't know if everyone feared, as she did, the harsh, atonal sound so typical of contemporary music. But Billy was right, Desmond Marx had a lyric touch, and the melodies were sweet and haunting.

"Turn to the first scene in the Factory, the second place where the chorus comes in," Paul said.

There was the sound of turning pages. Someone giggled. Eleanor didn't know why at first, and then her eye fell on the second page of the section that the chorus was meant to sing. She took her glasses off and put them on again. Surely she couldn't be reading what she thought she saw.

"Fuck me, suck me fuck me suck me." The words were peppered all over the page like a noxious mildew.

Someone else giggled. One of the tenors coughed.

"Anyone have a problem?" Paul said.

Did she imagine it or was everyone looking at her? She'd been in the chorus longer than any of the others, except Randy Brixton, the tenor who had coughed. And nothing would make Randy Brixton speak up; he was pathologically disinclined to conflict. He would give way if anyone so much as asked him anything, so much as indicated he might have to assert himself. Randy would be no help. She looked around at everybody in the chorus, trying, in her teacherly way, to make eye contact. But now, no one would look up from the score.

"I don't know whether I have a problem, which would suggest something stemming from a personal set of circumstances," she said, "but I believe there's a problem with the Knickerbocker chorus, taking into consideration our history and the nature of our audience, singing words like these."

"Anyone else like to respond to this outburst?" Paul said. She had always known he disliked her, but he had made a point of being coldly correct with her. She tried to get Billy's eye. Surely Billy would back her up. But Billy had his eye on the score; he was turning pages, as though he were looking for something real.

"I'd hardly call it an outburst, Paul. You asked for a response. I'd assumed it was a question asked in good faith."

It was as if a knife had been thrown down on the ground between them. Mumbledy peg, she thought, remembering a game she'd played in her childhood. One of those words that didn't sound like what it was. Which was certainly not the case with the ones on the page she was holding.

Silence shimmered in the air like an iron ring. Paul was indicating by his particular silence — a silence that was separate from the others as if it had been traced with a chalk line — that what she had just said wasn't worthy of a reply. And that was, she felt, the most insulting thing that he could do. The pusillanimity of her fellow choristers appalled her. She felt it was time to take a dramatic stand; that, she believed, would put some spine into some of them, at least.

"I cannot bring myself to use such language," Eleanor said.

"You can't bring yourself. Then I suppose we'll have to do without you. But let me make this clear, you will sing in this opera, or you will not sing with us at all. This season or any other."

"You can't do that."

"Oh yes, my dear, I'm the director, and I can. And many, I'm sure, would support me in saying that it's a bit overdue. You might have made a graceful exit, as many of your cohorts have, but you've outstayed your welcome. Your taste is as tired as your voice. It's time to leave now, Eleanor. Pick up your toys and go."

She waited a few seconds, certain that someone would come to her defense. But no one raised eyes from the score or the ground at their feet. And Billy was looking into space, as if she had already left the room and he was waiting for the next thing that would happen.

She understood that there were no words that would do anything but weaken her position. She made her way to the front of the chorus — she was, unfortunately, in the third row — and heard her heels making a sharp *clack clack* on the gray linoleum floor.

She closed the door and flung her cape around her shoulders, pleased at the military suggestions of the gesture. She was afraid her face must be bright red; heat climbed up it as she thought of Paul's crude words, his vulgar insults. She was certain that Billy would be behind her in a moment; certainly, even if he didn't stand up to Paul, he wouldn't allow her to make her way home like this, entirely unsupported.

But as she climbed the last stair, opened the heavy door, and found herself outside, shocked at the brightness of the day, she began to realize that Billy was not going to follow. Why had it been so difficult for her to admit, always, that he had always been a coward? And why had she tried for so long to deny what Paul was, what he had always been, an insignificant and stinking little turd? She banished the word from her mind; she would not sink to his level. Or to the level of the little Bronzino, the Bronzinetto, she called him to herself. Desmond Marx. Composer of that preposterous atrocity, *The Dream of Andy Warhol.* She'd have liked to call it instead *The Nightmare of the Modern Age.*

She must have been walking very fast, propelled by her rage, her shock; before she knew it, she was in front of her building. Had she really walked forty blocks in half an hour? She could smell her sweat underneath the wool of her cape, the silk of her blouse, and it shocked her with its robust meatiness. She had never before associated such a smell with her own body.

She couldn't bear to wait for the elevator. She burst into the apartment, hardly able to get her key into the lock. "Anybody home?" she called. Her mother's bedroom door was closed. Well, she would open it; she felt, today, she had a right. It was something she never did, but now she couldn't help herself. She had to tell her mother.

She knocked three times, but didn't wait for a response. At first, she couldn't tell whether or not her mother was there; the heavy velvet drapes were closed, and she could barely make out her mother's shape under the satin coverlet. But then her eyes got used to the light, and she saw her mother, lying on her back, her mouth open. On the night table beside her bed were her hearing aids, and in a glass, one on top of the other, the two halves of her dentures. Her mother's open, toothless mouth made her head look like a skull.

Had she known, had she ever considered, that her mother was toothless, that her mother wore false teeth? When had that happened? How was it that in all the years that they had lived together it was something she never knew? The rage that had consumed her body spilled now over to her mother. Why had her mother kept this from her? And how could she allow herself to be like this? It was against everything her mother stood for, to be lying here, in the middle of the afternoon, the drapes closed against the brilliant autumn sun, impervious to every sound, impervious to her shocking appearance.

She knew that she must leave the room. But she allowed herself to look at her mother for a few more seconds. Her mother was very old. Her mother's life was almost over. She was, lying on her back, cut off from light and sound, her countenance a corpse's, trying out the position she would, quite soon now, Eleanor realized, be permanently taking up. "It's over, it's finished," she said in her heart, but she would not allow herself to say anything aloud, and anyway, there was no one to say it to. Her mother was deaf; her mother was asleep — she supposed it was peacefully — and her father was nowhere around.

Something had been taken from her: something definite and solid and her own — as if a thief had broken in and stolen her purse containing all the documents and proof of who she was. And now how could she prove her worth — and to whom would she think she had to prove it? Who would even be interested enough?

She had been stolen from; the thief had been not only thief but assailant. She resisted the impulse to go to the mirror and see whether, as a result of the assault, her looks had changed. That would be ridiculous, that would be — her mother's word, always used mockingly — "dramatic." This was her life, it was not an opera, and she would live as she always had, as her parents always had: with dignity, on her own terms. And yet there had been this theft — must she think of herself now as impoverished, as her parents had never had to do? Would she wear the badge of poverty now, would she give off the stink of it, like those women you gave a wide berth to in the park, on street corners — those women whom you could only turn your eyes from, because to look at them in their humiliation was another kind of theft, something else taken from them? "I have been stolen from," she wanted to say. But to whom? And how could she name the thing whose absence made her feel so utterly bereft? It wasn't something with one name — and if it was impossible to name, it must be irreplaceable. She couldn't resist the impulse anymore: she must look at herself in the mirror to see if the loss was visible.

She patted her hair. Of course it looked the same, of course her face was identical to the one she had seen only a few hours before. She need not feel humiliated; humiliation was a trick of the eye, and she would be sure, always, that when eyes fell on her they would see something admirable, something fine. She could do that. It might not even be so difficult. She might even make it into something of the game she played with herself: this covering up, this patching over.

She made her way into the living room, the room her mother had made so delightful, had made her own, so high and airy and refined, and yet so simple, so easy to be one's self in. One's best self.

In a little while, her mother would walk in, fresh, rested from her nap; together they would set the table for an early dinner, beginning with the soup her mother had made, for which Eleanor had bought the ingredients. Things would go on; life would go on.

Above all, she must not let her mother know what had happened, that she was suffering. It was beautiful, her mother's world, and Eleanor knew now that the most important thing she could do would be to play her part, so that her mother wouldn't know that the world she still believed she was inhabiting had disappeared. Had been stolen.

There would be no need to tell her mother what had happened to her today. There would be no need to tell anyone. No one in the chorus knew anyone she knew — and Billy would never say anything. It suddenly occurred to her that there might be a difficult moment the next time she and Billy met. Perhaps it would be better to say nothing of what had happened. As for the other people, her friends, her colleagues, she would simply say that she had decided to resign from the company. And when people asked her why, she'd say, "The time has come, the walrus said." Something light, something amusing. The kind of thing her mother would have said.

LAUREN GROFF

L. DeBard and Aliette: A Love Story

FROM THE ATLANTIC MONTHLY

HE IS AT FIRST A DISTANT WAVE, the wake-wedge of a loon as it surfaces. The day is cold and gray as a stone. In the mid-distance the swimmer splits into parts, smoothly angled arms and a matte-black head. Twenty feet from the dock he dips below the water; a moment later he comes up at the ladder, blowing like a whale.

She sees him step onto the dock: the pronounced ribs heaving, the puckered nipples, the mustache limp with seawater. She feels herself flush, and, trembling, she smiles.

It is March 1918, and hundreds of dead jellyfish litter the beach. The newspapers this morning include a story, buried under the accounts of battles at the Western Front, about a mysterious illness striking down hale soldiers in Kansas.

The swimmer lifts his towel to gain time, wondering about the strange, expectant trio that watches him. The man in the clump is fat and bald, his chin deeply lined from mouth to jowl. His shave is close, his clothes expensive. A brunette stands beside him, the wind chucking her silk collar under her chin: the fat man's young wife, the swimmer thinks, mistakenly.

Before them sits a girl in a wheelchair. The swimmer's glance brushes over her, and veers away when he sees her wizened child's face, the diluted blond of her hair, her eyes sunken in the sickly white complexion. A nothing, he thinks. That he looks past her is not his fault. He doesn't know. And so, instead of the lightning strike and fluttering heart that should attend the moment of their meeting, all the swimmer feels is the cold whip of the wind, and the shame at his old suit, holey and stretched out, worn only on the dark days when he needs nostalgia and old glory to bring him to the water.

The swimmer is a famous man. He is an Olympian: gold medalist in the 1908 London Olympics in the 100-meter freestyle, anchor on the 4 × 200 relay. Triple gold in the 1912 Stockholm Olympics: 100-meter freestyle, 100-meter backstroke, anchor again on the 4 × 200. He was on the American Swim Association's champion water polo team from 1898 through 1911. He is, quite simply, the World's Best Swimmer.

His name is L. DeBard, though this was not always his name. He was born Lodovico DeBartolo, but was taken from Rome at the age of six and transplanted to New York, where the Ukrainians, the Poles, the Chinese couldn't pronounce Lodovico. He reworked his last name when he discovered in himself literary agility and a love of Shakespeare.

He is a swimmer, but he is other things, too: a forty-three-year-old with a mighty set of pectorals, one chipped front tooth, and a rakish smile; a rumored Bolshevik; a poet, filler of notebooks, absinthe drinker, cavorter of the literary type. He knows a number of whores by name, though in the wider world he is thought to be a bit queer, his friendships a mite too close with the city's more effeminate novelists and poets. He has been alone in the company of Tad Perkins, C. T. Dane, Arnold Effingham. Something is suspect about a man-poet anyway, and many of his critics ask each other, pursing their lips lewdly, why he is not in France, fighting for the Allies. The reason is that his flat feet make him unfit for battle.

And today he is one last thing: starving. Poets and swimmers are the last to be fed in these final few months of the Great War.

The fat man steps forward. "L. DeBard?" he says.

L. wraps the towel under the straps of his suit. "Yes," he says, at last.

Then the girl in the wheelchair speaks. "We have a proposition for you," she says. Her voice reminds the swimmer of river rock: gravelly, smooth.

*

The girl's name is Aliette Huber. She is sixteen, and she is a schoolgirl, or was before her illness. She won her school's honors for French, Composition, Rhetoric, and Recitation for three years in a row. She can read a poem once and recite it perfectly from memory years later. Before the polio, she was a fine horsewoman, a beautiful archer, the lightest dancer of any of the girls at the Children's Balls society had delighted in staging in the heady days before the war. Her mother died when she was three, and her father is distantly doting.

She knows L. from his book of poetry, which she read when she was recuperating from her illness. She feels she knows him so intimately that now, freezing on the dock, she is startled and near tears: she has just realized that, to him, she is a stranger.

And so, Aliette does something drastic: she unveils her legs. They are small, wrinkled sticks, nearly useless. She wears a Scottish wool blanket over her lap, sinfully thick. L. thinks of his thin sheet and the dirty greatcoat he sleeps under, and envies her the blanket. Her skirt is short and her stockings silk. L. doesn't gasp when he sees her legs, her kneecaps like dinner rolls skewered with willow switches. He just looks up at Aliette's face, and suddenly sees that her lips are set in a perfect heart, purple with cold.

After that, the swim lessons are easily arranged. When they leave — the brunette pushing the wheelchair over the boards of the docks, her trim hips swishing — their departure thrums in L.'s heels. The wind picks up even more, and the waves make impatient sounds on the dock. L. dresses. His last nickel rolls from the pocket of his jacket as he slides it on over his yellowed shirt. The coin flashes in the water and glints, falling.

At night Aliette lies in her white starched sheets in her room on Park Avenue and listens to the Red Cross trucks grinding their gears in the streets below. She puts the thin book of poetry under the sheets when she hears footsteps coming down the hall to her door. But the book slides from her stomach and between her almost useless legs, and she gasps with sudden pleasure.

Her nurse, the brunette from the dock, enters with a glass of buttermilk. Rosalind is only a few years older than Aliette, but looks as hearty and innocent as Little Bo Peep, corn-fed, pink with indolence. Aliette tries not to hate her as she stands there, cross-armed, until Aliette drains the glass. The nurse's lipstick has smeared beyond the boundaries of her lips. From the front hall, Mr. Huber's trilling whistle resounds, then the butler says, "Good afternoon, sir," and the door closes, and Aliette's father returns to Wall Street. The girl hands the glass back to Rosalind, who smiles a bit too hard.

"Do you need a trip to the water closet, miss?" the nurse asks.

Aliette tells her no, she is reading, and that will be all. The nurse goes. When her footsteps have faded, Aliette retrieves the book of poetry from under the covers where it had nestled so pleasingly. *Ambivalence,* the title says. *By L. DeBard.*

While L. and Aliette wait to begin their first lesson the next day, the mysterious illness is creeping from the sleepy Spanish tourist town of San Sebastián. It will make its way into the farthest corners of the realm, until even King Alfonso XIII will lie suffering in his royal bed. French, English, and American troops scattered in France are just now becoming deathly ill, and the disease will skulk with them to England. Eventually even King George V will be afflicted.

In New York, they know nothing of this. L. eats his last can of potted meat. Aliette picks the raisins from her scones and tries to read fortunes in the dregs of her teacup.

They will use the natatorium at the Amsterdam Hotel for the lessons. It is a lovely pool of green tile, gold-leaf tendrils growing down the sides, and a bold heliotrope of yellow tile covering the bottom. The walls and ceiling are sky blue. They cannot use it during the guest hours and must swim either in the early morning or at night.

Both, insists L., hating to take so much money from Mr. Huber for so little work. He comes early for the first lesson, marveling at the beautiful warmth and crystal water. He leaps from the sauna to the pool, laughing to himself. His mustache wilts in the heat.

When Aliette comes in, steaming from the showers, her hair in a black cloth cap with a strap under the chin, L. lifts her from her chair and carries her into the water. Rosalind sits in the corner by the potted palm, takes out her knitting, and falls asleep.

*

In the beginning, they don't speak. He asks her to kick as he holds her in the water. She tries, making one tiny splash, then another. Around the shallow end they go, three, four times. Rosalind's gentle snores echo in the room. At last, Aliette slides one thin arm around L.'s neck. "Stop," she says, panting with pain.

He brings her to the steps and sets her there. He stands before her in the waist-deep water, trying not to look at her.

"What is wrong with Rosalind?" he asks. "Why is she sleeping?"

"Nothing is wrong," Aliette says. "Poor thing has been up all night."

"I trust that she was not caring for you? I assumed you were healthy," L. says.

Aliette hesitates and looks down. "She was caring for me, yes — and others," she says. Her face is tight and forbidding. But then she looks at him with one cocked eyebrow and whispers, "L., I must admit that I like your other suit better."

He is wearing a new indigo bathing costume with suspenders, and he looks down at himself, then at her, puzzled. His new suit cost him a week's wages. "Why is that?" he asks.

She glances at the sleeping nurse, then touches him where a muscle bulges over one hip. "I liked the hole here," she says. Then her hand is under the water, where it looms, suddenly immense. She touches his thigh. "And here," she says. Her fingertip lingers, then falls away.

When he has steadied himself to look at her face, she is smiling innocently. She does not, however, look like a little girl anymore.

"They were only small holes," he says. "I am surprised you noticed."

"I notice everything," she says. But her face grows a little frightened; her eyes slide toward Rosalind, and she gives a great roar, as if he'd told a stunner of a joke. This awakens the nurse, who resumes her knitting, blinking and looking sternly at the pair. "Let's swim," cries Aliette, and slaps both of her hands on the water like a child.

During the late lesson that night, as Rosalind again succumbs to the heat and damp of the room, Aliette watches with amusement as L. tries to hide his chipped tooth from her by turning his face. He has waxed his mustache mightily, and the musky fragrance of the wax fills her head and makes it swim. She laughs, her face in the water. He thinks she is only blowing bubbles.

By the end of the first week, Aliette has gained ten pounds. When she is not swimming, she is forcing herself to eat cheese and bread with butter, even when she is not hungry. She loosens her corset, then throws it away. At night, though exhausted from swimming, she climbs out of bed and tries to stand. She succeeds for one minute one night, and five minutes the next. She has a tremendous tolerance for pain. At the end of the week, she can stand for thirty minutes and take two steps before falling. When she does fall, it is into bed, and she sleeps immediately, L.'s poetry beating around in her brain like so many trapped sparrows.

All that week, L. paces. On the cloudy Friday, he kicks the notebooks full of weightless little words, and they skitter across his floor. He decides that he must quit, tell that Wall Street Huber that he has another obligation and can no longer teach Aliette to swim. Blast her pathetic little legs to hell, he thinks. L. stands at his window and looks down into the dark street, where urchins pick through boxes of rotting vegetables discarded from the greengrocer's downstairs. A leaf of cabbage blows free in the wind and attaches itself to the brick wall opposite L.'s window, where it flutters like a small green pennant.

"Porca madonna," he says. Then, as if correcting himself, he says in English, "Pig Madonna." It doesn't sound right, and in the wake of its dissonance he finds that he is completely unable to walk to Park Avenue and quit.

Late that evening he sits by the pool. He touches the place on his thigh where Aliette's finger touched him a week earlier. He does not look up until he hears a throat clearing, then startles and finds himself staring up into Mr. Huber's face, the fat man's hand on his daughter's capped head.

"Papa is going to chaperone us the nights that Rosalind is off," Aliette says, her eyes bright with merriment. L. tries to smile, then stands, extending his hand for a shake. But Aliette's father doesn't shake L.'s hand, just nods and rolls the cuffs of his pants over his calves. He takes off his shoes and socks and sticks his legs, white and hairy, into the warm water. "Go on," he says, "don't let me get in the way of your lesson." He takes a newspaper from his pocket and watches them over the headlines as L. carries Aliette into the shallow end.

L. is teaching her the frog kick, and she holds onto the gutter as he bends both of her knees and helps them swing out and back. When her father's attention is fixed on an article, Aliette takes L.'s hand and slides it up and over her small breast. By the time her father has read to the bottom of the page, L. has moved his hand to her neck, and he is trembling.

As Rosalind sleeps under the palm the next morning, Aliette tells L. that her father didn't say one word to her in the cab home. But when they were coming up in the elevator, he asked her if something wasn't a little funny about L., something a little girlish. And she laughed, and related to her father the gossip about her swim coach's *bosom* friends.

"Very subtly, of course," she says. "I am not supposed to know of those things."

She tells L. that later, as she was drinking her last glass of buttermilk before bed, she left out his book, open to a poem titled "And into the Fields the Sweet Boys Go" —

L., face dark, interrupts her. "That poem is about innocence; my Lord, I'm not —"

She puts a hand on his mouth. "Let me finish," she says.

He shuts his mouth, but his face is set angrily. She continues that she heard her father and Rosalind talking about L. in the morning, and her father called him "that nance."

L. is so offended he drops Aliette unceremoniously into the water. She swims, though, and reaches the wall in three strong strokes, her legs dragging behind her.

She says, grinning, "You didn't know I was a nixie, did you?"

"No," he says, darkly. "I am amazed. And for your information, I am *not* a —"

"L.," Aliette says, sighing. "I know. But you *are* a fool." Then, very deliberately, she says, "The nances of the world have many uses, my dear coach."

When he says nothing, trying to understand, she droops. "I'm tired," she says. "This lesson is over." She calls for Rosalind, and will not look at L. as the nurse wheels her away.

*

Only later does he realize she has read his book. He cannot look at her that evening, he is so flattered and fearful of her opinion.

Sunday, his day off, L. goes to Little Italy for supper with his family. His mother holds him to her wren's chest; his father touches his new linen suit with admiration. In Rome, Amadeo was a tailor; here he is a hearse driver. He mutters, "Beautiful, beautiful," and nods at his son, fingering the lapels, checking the seams. L.'s older sister is blind and cannot remark upon the visible change in him.

But in the trolley home, his stomach filled with saltimbocca, L. thinks of his sister when she touched his face in farewell. "You have met a girl," she whispered. Lucrezia has never seen her own face, and cannot know its expressions — how, at that moment, her smile was an explosion.

In late April, the newspapers are full of news of a strange illness. The journalists try to blunt their alarm by exoticizing it, naming it Spanish Influenza, La Grippe. In Switzerland, it is called La Coquette, as if it were a courtesan. In Ceylon it's the Bombay Fever, and in Britain the Flanders Grippe. The Germans, whom the Allies blame for this disease, call it Blitzkatarrh. The disease is as deadly as that name sounds.

Americans do not pay attention. They watch Charlie Chaplin and laugh until they cry. They read the sports pages and make bets on when the war will be over. And if a few healthy soldiers suddenly fall ill and die, the Americans blame it on exposure to tear gas.

L. has gone tomcatting with his writer friends only twice by the time spring rolls into summer. The second time, he has only had one martini when he pushes one very familiar redhead from his lap so roughly that she hits her head on the table and bursts into tears. C. T. Dane comforts her. When Dane is leaving, the indignant redhead on his arm, he raises an eyebrow and frowns at the steadily drinking L.

From that night on, his friends talk about him. "What's eating old fishface L.?" Tad Perkins will ask anyone who will listen.

Finally, someone says, "He's writing a novel. It's like having a mistress. Once he's through with her, leaves her on the floor, weeping for more, he'll be back."

The friends laugh at this. They raise their glasses. "To the mistress," they cry.

Aliette's cheeks grow plump, and her legs regain many of their muscles. By May, L. is being driven crazy by the touches, leg sliding against leg, arm to knee, foot sliding silky across his shoulder. He immerses himself in a cold-water tub, like a racehorse, before coming out to greet her.

Their flirtation slips. Dawn is pinkening in the clerestory window, and L. is lifting Aliette's arm above the water to show her the angle of the most efficient stroke, when his torso brushes against hers, and stays. He looks at the dozing Rosalind. Then he lifts Aliette from the water and carries her to the men's room.

As she stands, leaning against the smooth tile wall and shivering slightly, he slides her suit from her shoulders and slips it down. To anyone else, she would be a skinny, slightly feral-looking little girl, but he sees the heart-shaped lips, the pulse thrumming in her neck, the way she bares her body bravely, arms down, palms turned out, watching him. He bends to kiss her. She smells of chlorine, lilacs, warm milk. He lifts her and leans her against the wall.

When they reemerge, Rosalind still sleeps, and the pool is pure, glossy, as if nobody has ever set foot in it.

Who, in the midst of passion, is vigilant against illness? Who listens to the reports of recently decimated populations in Spain, India, Bora Bora, when new lips, tongues, and poems fill the world?

And now, when they don't touch, they share the splash and the churn, the rhythm of the stroke, the gulps of water in the gutter, the powerful shock of the dive, and a wake like smoke, trailing them.

Aliette leaves her wheelchair behind and begins to walk, even though the pain seems unbearable when she is tired. She loves the food she loathed before, for the flesh it gives her. She eats marbled steaks, half-inch layers of butter on her bread. She walks to the stores on Madison, leaning against a wall when she needs to, and returns, victorious, with bags. On one of her outings, she meets her father coming home for lunch. As she calls to him, and runs clumsily the last five steps, his eyes fill. His fleshy face grows pink, and the lines under his mouth deepen.

"Oh," he says, holding out his arms and nearly weeping. "My little girl is back."

In the hot days of the summer, the pool sessions are too short and the day that stretches between them too long. In his anxiety to see Aliette, L. writes poetry. Those short hours of relief aren't enough, so he walks. But on the streets everything sparkles too brightly: the men selling war bonds smile too much, the wounded soldiers seem limp with relief, their wives too radiant and pregnant. He hates it; he is drawn to it.

To forget her need to be with him, Aliette keeps herself busy. She takes tea with school friends at the Plaza, goes to museums and parties, accepts all dates to the theater that she can. But when her dates lean in to kiss her, she pushes them away.

Five times in the Amsterdam before July: that first time in the men's room; in the lifeguard's chair; in the chaise longue storage closet; in the shallow end; in the deep end, in the corner, braced by the gutter.

All this time, Rosalind sleeps. The days that Aliette suspects she won't, she fills her nurse's head with glorious evocations of the cream puffs that are the specialty of the hotel's pastry chef. Rosalind, she feels certain, will slip out at some point during the lesson and return a half an hour later with a cream puff on a plate for her ward, licking foam from her lip like a cat.

The second wave of the illness hits America in July. People begin to fall in Boston, mostly strong young adults. In a matter of hours, mahogany spots appear on cheekbones, spreading quickly until one cannot tell dark-skinned people from white. And then, the suffocation, the pneumonia. Fathers of young families turn as blue as huckleberries, and spit a foamy red fluid. Autopsies reveal lungs that look like firm blue slabs of liver.

Aliette slips away on a day that Rosalind is off, visiting a cousin in Poughkeepsie. She takes a cab to the dark and seedy streets where L. lives, but is so thrilled she doesn't see the dirt or smell the stench. She gets out of the cab, throwing the driver a bill, and runs as quickly to the door of L.'s close, hot bedroom as her awkward legs will allow.

She comes in. He stands, furious to suddenly see her in this hovel. She closes the door.

It is only later, sitting naked on the mattress, dripping with sweat and trying to cool off in what breeze will come from the window, that she notices the bachelor's funk of his apartment, the towers of books and notebooks lining the walls like wainscoting, and hears the scrabble of something sinister in the wall behind her head. That is when she tells L. her plan.

That night Mr. Huber is chaperoning. L. pays his friend W. Sebald Shandling, starving poet, to sit by the pool. Shandling is foppish, flings his hands about immoderately, has a natural lisp.

"Watch me like a jealous wife," L. instructs him.

And his friend does watch him, growing grimmer and grimmer, until, by the end of the session, when Aliette comes to the wall and touches L. on the shoulder, he is pacing like a tiger and glaring at the pair. Mr. Huber looks on with an expression of jolly interest.

In the cab home that evening, as the horse's hoofs clop like a metronome through the park, Aliette asks her father if L. can come live with them, in one of the guest bedrooms.

"Daddy," she says, "he told me how disgusting his room is. But he cannot afford to live elsewhere. And I've decided to train for the New York girls' swimming championships in September, and need to add another session in the afternoon, at the Fourteenth Street YMCA. It will just be easier if he lives with us."

"You have become friends?" he says.

"Oh, we get along swimmingly," she laughs. When he doesn't smile, she adds, "Daddy, he is like a brother to me."

And her father says, without much hesitation, "Well, I don't see why not."

On the July day he leaves his hovel, L. stands in his room, looking around at the empty expanse. He hears children playing in the alley below. He goes to the window and watches. Two girls skip rope, chanting.

> *I had a little bird,* they sing, rope clapping to the words.
> *Its name was Enza.*
> *I opened the window.*
> *And In-Flu-Enza.*

Then they shriek and fall to the ground, clutching their chests, giggling.

L.'s world is spun on its head. Now he deals with servants, people calling him "sir," any food he likes at any time of the day, the palatial apartment filled with light. And, of course, midnight creeping, and free midafternoon siestas in the cavernous cool apartment, as the servants sit in the kitchen and gossip about the war. In mid-August, L. is deemed chaperone enough, and Rosalind stays home when they go to the Amsterdam or the Y. If Aliette's father leaves for work a bit later than usual on those mornings, the servants' bland faces reveal nothing. Rosalind begins wearing a long strand of pearls, and French perfume. She takes to sitting on Aliette's bed, combing her hair and asking the girl about her dates with the Ivy League boys. Her voice is rich and almost maternal.

Aliette tells her father that she no longer needs Rosalind, that she is healthy, and he can let the nurse go. Rosalind becomes *his* nurse, for he has discovered gout in his toes.

One golden night at the end of September, they are all listening gravely to the radio's reports of war dead, eating petits fours in Aliette's father's study. Mr. Huber and Rosalind go into his bedchamber to treat his gout. Through the walls, L. and Aliette can hear their murmuring voices.

L. takes the cake from Aliette's hand, and lifts her skirt on the morocco leather couch. She bites his shoulder to keep from screaming. Throughout, they can hear her father moving about behind the wall, Rosalind's heels tapping, the maid dusting in another room.

When Rosalind and Mr. Huber return, Aliette is reading a novel and L. is still in his wing chair, listening intently to the radio. Nobody notices the pearls of sweat on his forehead, or, when Aliette stands for bed, the damp patch on her skirt.

The marvel is, with all she and L. do together, that Aliette has the time to train. But she does, growing muscles like knots in her back, adapting her kick from the standard three-beat to a lightning-quick eight-beat flutter, better suited for her weak legs.

At the competition in September in the 200-meter freestyle, she is already ahead after her dive, and draws so far away from the other girls that she is out on the diving platform, wearing her green cloak, when the other girls come in. She also takes the 100-meter freestyle.

The captions below her picture in the *Times* and the *Sports News* say: "Heiress NY's Best Lady Swimmer." In the photo, Aliette stands radiant, medals gleaming in the sunlight on her chest. If one were to look closely, however, one would see a bulge around Aliette's waist.

The slow rumble of influenza becomes a roar. September drips into deadliest October. In Philadelphia, gymnasiums are crowded with cots of sailors healthy just hours before. America does not have enough doctors, and first-year medical students, boys of twenty, treat the men. Then they too fall sick, and their bodies are stacked like kindling with the rest in the insufficient morgues. More than a quarter of the pregnant women who survive the flu miscarry or give birth to stillborn babies.

Aliette's stomach grows, but she does not tell L., hoping he'll notice and remark upon it first. He is in a fever, though, and sees nothing but his passion for her. She begins wearing corsets again, and she makes a great show of eating inordinately, so that her father and Rosalind think she is simply getting fat.

The plague hits New York like a tight fist. Trains rolling into the boroughs stop in their tracks when engineers die at the controls. After 851 New Yorkers die in one day, a man is attacked for spitting on the street.

Mr. Huber sends his six servants away, and they are forbidden to return until the end of the plague. Three of them won't return at all. Mr. Huber, Aliette, Rosalind, and L. remain. They seal the windows, and Mr. Huber uses his new telephone to order the groceries. They buy their food in cans, which they boil before opening, and their mail is baked piping hot in the oven before they read it.

After the second week of quarantine, Rosalind becomes hysterical and makes them drink violet-leaf tea and inhale saltwater. She paces the apartment wildly and forgets to brush her hair. They cannot persuade her to make up the fourth for bridge, so they play Chinese checkers, backgammon, and gin. Mr. Huber suddenly unveils his collection of expensive liquors, and dips gladly into them. When he has had too much, he and Rosalind go into the servants' quarters and hiss at one another. At those times Aliette sits on L.'s lap and presses her cheek against his, until the shape of his mustache is embossed on her skin.

When her father and Rosalind return, Aliette is always balanced on the arm of a couch, air-swimming, as L. critiques her form. He makes her air-swim and do jumping jacks for hours every day. The cloistered life suits her. She is radiant.

After a month, Rosalind watches from a window as a coffin falls from a stack on a hearse, the inhabitant spilling out when it hits the ground. She goes nearly mad. She breathes into a paper bag until calm and makes them wear masks inside. She forces them to carry hot coals sprinkled with sulfur. The apartment stinks like Satan.

When Aliette and L. kiss through their masks, they laugh. And when Aliette comes to L. in the night, she swings her coals like a priestess swinging a censer.

On a lazy day of snoozing and reading, L. gets a letter from his mother. He doesn't bother to bake it. He tears it open, Aliette watching, hand over her mouth.

In three sentences, in her shaking hand, his mother tells him that his father, hearse driver, was one of the rare lightning deaths. Amadeo toppled from his horse and was dead before he hit the ground. Two hours later, Lucrezia fell ill, her knees wobbling, joints stiffening, the fever, the viscous phlegm, the cyanosis, the lungs filling.

L. understands only years later that when his sister died, she died of drowning.

He stays in bed for one week and does not weep. He lets Aliette hold his head for hours. Then he rises, and shaves his mustache off. Its outline is white on his tan face, and looks exceptionally tender.

In the first week of November the crisis slackens. People emerge into the street, mole-eyed and blinking, searching for food. In some apartments, whole families are found dead when their mail can no longer fit through their slots. Rosalind, however, will not let the Huber household leave the apartment. L. reads the baked newspapers, saddened. In addition to his family, he has lost his novelist friend, C. T. Dane; his fellow swimmer Harry Elionsky, the long-distance champion; the actress Suzette Alda, with whom he once danced for an entire night.

Life picks up again, though some new cases are still reported, and the horror is not completely over. More than nineteen thousand New Yorkers have died.

Early in the morning of November 11, the streets burst into triumphant rejoicing in victory. Sirens blare, churchbells ring, New Yorkers pour into the streets, shouting. Newspaper boys run through the sleeping parts of town, shouting, "The war is ovah!" An effigy of the kaiser is washed down Wall Street with a fire hose; confetti pours down; eight hundred Barnard girls snake-dance on Morningside Heights; and a coffin made of soapboxes is paraded down Madison, with the kaiser symbolically resting in pieces within.

Many people still wear masks.

A mutiny occurs in the Huber apartment, and Rosalind wrings her hands as the other three rush into the street to join the celebration. They are all in their nightclothes. Mr. Huber dances a jolly foxtrot with a dour-faced spinster. When a blazing straw dummy is kicked down the street, L. turns to look for Aliette. She is standing on a curb, clapping her hands and laughing. As the dummy passes, the wind picks up and billows out Aliette's nightgown. Through the suddenly sheer garment, he sees how her belly is extended above her thin legs.

When Aliette sees him swaying there on the sidewalk, his face pale, she puts a hand on her belly. A soldier and his girl pass between them, but they don't notice. When she turns, L. is beside her, gripping her arm too tightly.

He drags her into the building and to the doorman's empty room. A thin wedge of light falls across her flushed cheek.

"You didn't tell me," he says. "How long?"

She stares at him, defiant. "Since May," she says. "That first time, I think."

"My God," he says, then leans his forehead against the door, above her shoulder. She is pinned. He rests his stomach against hers, and feels a pronounced thump, and another. "My God," he repeats, but this time with awe.

"A good swimmer, I'll bet," she says, daring to smile a little. But he doesn't smile back. He just stands, leaning against her, until he feels another kick.

They wait until December, a day when Mr. Huber has returned to Wall Street and Rosalind has gone shopping.

Once the house is empty, they pack only what she needs. In the cab to Little Italy she squeezes his hand until it goes numb. The driver is singing boisterously to himself.

"You're kidnapping, you know," she whispers to L., trying to make him laugh.

He looks away from her, out the window. "Only until we can figure out what to do. Until you have him and we can be married."

"L.," she says, ten blocks later, "I don't want to be married."

He looks at her.

"I mean," she says, "I would rather be your mistress than your wife. I don't need a ring and a ceremony to know what this is."

He is silent at first. Then L. says, "Oh, Aliette. Your father does. And that is enough."

His mother, aged with recent grief, meets them at the door. She looks at her son, and touches his lip where his mustache had been. Then she looks at Aliette, and holds open her arms to embrace her.

The detectives don't come looking for Aliette for a week, unable to find out where L.'s mother lives. When at last they do, she hides the couple in her bedroom, and opens the door, already talking. In her quick jumble of Italian, the detective who knows the language passably becomes confused, then tongue-tied, then shamefaced when he tries to tell her why he is there. "L. DeBard," he says. "*Noi cerciamo L. DeBard.*"

She looks at him as if he were the greatest fool the world had seen. DeBartolo, she cries, hitting her fist on her chest. She points to the card in the door. DeBartolo. She throws her hands to the skies, and sighs. The detectives look at one another, bow, and leave.

In the bedroom, L. and Aliette listen to this barrage, and press tightly together.

The next day, Aliette goes into labor. Though the baby is more than a month early, Aliette is very small, and it takes a long time. From morning until late at night, L. paces down the street, finally going into a bar. There, he discovers Tad Perkins drinking himself into a stupor, alone.

"Isn't that old fishface L.?" Tad cries. "My God, I thought you damn well died."

"You're not that lucky," L. says, laughing with great relief. "You still owe me thirteen dollars." He sits down and buys Tad and himself four quick martinis.

Later, staggering slightly, he goes out into the street. The moon is fat above. When he reaches the apartment, all is still. His mother sits beaming by the side of the bed, where Aliette sleeps. In his mother's arms, he sees a tiny sleeping baby. A boy, he knows, without being told.

When Aliette awakens, she finds L. sitting where his mother was. She smiles tiredly.

"I am thinking of names," L. says, hushed. "I like Franklin and Karl."

"I have already named him," Aliette says.

"Yes? What's my son's name?"

"Compass," she says. And though he presses, she won't tell him why. At last, grinning, he accepts the name, vowing to nickname him something more conventional. He never does. After the child is a few months old, L. will find the name suits his son to perfection.

They have a month together in that tiny flat. L.'s mother bustles and looks after them, feeding them elaborate meals and rocking the baby while L. reads Aliette his new poems.

"You are growing into the best poet in America," she says.

"Growing?" he jokes. "I thought I already was."

"No," she says. "But now you might be." And she lies back, letting the words from his poems sift into her memory. She looks a little ill, and doesn't complain, but L. can see that something is not right with her. He worries. At night, he hears a soft rasp as Aliette grinds her teeth in pain.

Soon, the detectives return. L.'s mother does not let them in this time, but their voices grow loud in the hallway. They shout and rage at her. At last they leave. L.'s mother is shaky and collapses into a chair, and puts a cloth over her face, and weeps into it, unable to look at the couple for fear.

L. looks at Aliette. "I am taking you back," he says. "I'll keep Compass with my mother."

Aliette says, very quietly, "No."

"Yes," L. says. He tells her that he knows she is ill and her father can afford physicians that he cannot. If she returns without Compass, her reputation will not be tarnished, and no one will know about her pregnancy. Later, when they marry, they can adopt him. Their argument is quiet, but goes on for many hours, until Aliette finally succumbs to her illness and the pain and his arguments. She has been afraid that she is growing worse: she feels herself weakening, and allows herself to be convinced about something that, if she were stronger and less frightened, she never would have countenanced.

At last she clutches Compass to her chest and smells her fill of him. Weeping, feverish, longing for him already, she agrees to go.

L. stops the cab a half a block from Aliette's father's house, and leans close to her. Their kiss is long and hungry. If they knew how often they would remember it, for how many years it would be their dearest memory, this kiss would last for hours. But it ends, and she climbs out, wincing with pain, and he watches her walk away, so lovely, the feather of her hat bouncing.

When Aliette walks back into the house, her father is sitting in the parlor, head buried in his hands. When he looks up, he clearly does not recognize her. She looks at the mirror above the mantle, and sees herself: pale and skinny again, hair dun-colored, her face above her fur looking a decade older than her age. When she looks back, Rosalind is in the doorway, and the tray she is holding is chattering. Her face is pinched with unhappiness, while a broad, bright smile spreads across her father's red face.

*

After the doctor visits Aliette, she is forced into bed rest. She sleeps while, across town, L. holds Compass and sees Aliette in his son's small face.

Only years later does Aliette trace the pieces of her loss in the evidence scattered through her fever. Her father's expression when he looks at her as she first walks in, a mixture of hurt and relief. How the doctor asks probing questions about her delicate parts until she admits to the pain, and allows him to examine her. How her father's expression changes after conferring with the doctor, how he looks at her angrily. And a year later, she will hear him shouting at Rosalind one night when drunk. "Nobody, *nobody* abandons a Huber," he'll say. "We were right to do what we did."

Two nights after L. has returned Aliette to her father's house he is feeling a little restless, anxious to hear of Aliette's health. He decides to take a walk in the wintry streets, to kick through the snow and work off his anxiety. He leaves Compass in his mother's lap, and hurries down the dank stairwell and into the night.

He does not see the shadows detaching from the alleyway, or how they steal close to him. He feels the sudden grip on his arms, then the handkerchief with the sour stink of chloroform pressed over his nose and mouth. The gas lamps flicker and darken, the street becomes wobbly, and a snowbank catches him as he falls.

Much later, L. can see a golden light growing between his lids. His head is bound with pain. His eyes open slightly. He is on the hard wooden floor of what appears to be an office, a vast mahogany-paneled room, bookshelves, paintings of ships. His fingertips lie on what feels like rubber.

Two unfamiliar faces loom over him. "He's waking up," one says. The men back away, and in their place stands Mr. Huber, transformed and dangerous with rage. Beside him is Rosalind's brunette head, in her mask, eyes filling with tears. Suddenly, L. feels cold. He is naked, he realizes, a window is open, and snow is pouring in and powdering the rug.

"You deserve this, and more," says Mr. Huber.

L.'s lips move, but he can't say anything. He closes his eyes.

"Rosalind," says the fat man, "give it to me."

When L. looks again, Rosalind's eyebrows have come together

above her mask in a frown. But she hands Mr. Huber what he wants, something that appears to be a blade, glinting. Aliette's father stoops closer. Through his numbness, L. can feel hands grasping his legs roughly and pulling them apart.

"Bastard," Aliette's father breathes in his face. L. has only a moment to smell his sour breath before he goes out of L.'s line of vision.

He hears a thunk. Then such pain, and so impossible, that L. blanks out again.

Time runs fluidly through the rest: the discovery of the fiercely bleeding L. in the snowbank by a police officer on patrol. The rescue and delivery to the hospital, the doctors unveiling his wound, vomiting, the cauterizing of the hole between his legs. And, at last, the fever that makes him delirious, and lasts for months.

His literary friends come to visit him, and out of kindness they do not bring the newspapers lurid with the story of his gelding. When L. seems unlikely to survive, W. Sebald Shandling visits L.'s mother. He finds her holding Compass. The baby is chewing on his father's most recent poems. In an act of uncharacteristic selflessness, Shandling persuades a publisher to take the collection, to provide something for the baby in case his father dies. And L. rages while the world shifts into treaties and recovery, while President Wilson is struck by influenza but recovers in time to sign at Versailles.

Just when his fever begins to dissipate, L. catches one of the last strands of the flu.

For three days the only thing he can hear is the gurgle of water in his lungs. He doesn't think he'll live. When the worst is over and he can sit up again, a young doctor whose face is prematurely lined comes to see him. He looks as if he might begin to cry.

"Mr. DeBard," he says. "I am afraid your lungs are so damaged you will never swim again. They're so bad, you won't be able to walk far unaided. You will wheeze for the rest of your life." Then he gives a curious half sob, and says, "I followed your swimming, sir. When I was a boy, I admired you greatly."

L. looks at the doctor for some time before closing his eyes and sighing.

"Frankly, doctor," he says, at last. "Of all the many things I do extraordinarily well, it is not the loss of swimming that upsets me."

The doctor frowns and is about to say something. Then, remembering, he flees.

By the summer, L. is still recovering, walking around weakly. His mother leaves Compass with a neighbor when she visits, but brings a photograph of the boy that L. stares at for hours, and keeps in the breast pocket of his pajamas when he sleeps.

In all the time L. is in the hospital, Aliette does not come to see him. She is paying dearly for her transgressions, supervised day and night, only allowed to go to the pool with her female coach. She is not allowed to see Compass, though two or three times she tries to slip out at night, only to be collared each time by her coach or her father. She is not allowed to keep the baby blanket she had taken with her, and is not allowed to send money for his care. Rosalind and another nurse follow her everywhere, even to the bathroom. She spends her rage in the water, holding her breath until she almost drowns.

L. comes home from the hospital on the day his new book sells out in one hour. Though his enemies claim it is the shock of his story, the scandalous tale, they cannot explain why it continues to sell long after the story is forgotten. Compass cries when he sees this strange man, but slowly grows used to him, and in a fortnight he tugs on L.'s reinstated mustache and touches his cheek in wonder.

At last, after its third time around the globe, the pandemic burns itself out. By the end, whole villages have been wiped clean from history; in a single year, more Americans have died from it than from all of the battles of the Great War. In one small part of its aftermath, the plague will be linked to an encephalitic state in which patients can walk, answer questions, and be aware of their surroundings, but with such vagueness that they are described as somnambulists, or sleeping volcanoes.

L. and Aliette never meet again. She will hold her breath every time she sees a man walking a little boy down the street, and go home so agitated she will be unable to speak. She will begin letters that she will never send, and with every new one she tears into confetti she will hope fervently that L. and Compass understand.

But at first L. doesn't understand. Her absence is an ache. He knows that if they were to meet, they wouldn't be able to look at each other, hot with shame and loss, but he doesn't understand how Aliette could give up her own son; it seems a horror. Then, Compass begins to speak and to develop his own little grave personality, and on the boy's fifth birthday, as they sit on the glowing grass of the park and eat cake together, L. looks at his son, who is kicking his legs at the sky, and in the fullness of the boy's presence and his delicious joy, L. finally knows what Aliette has done. She has released Compass to him, an exculpatory gesture, a self-sundering. He imagines her in the city somewhere, staring out the window on her son's birthday, and knows she is dreaming of their child.

By then, though, no other life is imaginable, and Compass will never tell L. he missed having a mother, for the older he becomes, the more his father will depend upon him. And L. will still be drenched with sweat every time he smells lilacs or sees a tiny blonde from afar.

L. reads about Aliette's few, small rebellions in the newspapers. How she is arrested for nude bathing at Manhattan Beach after removing her stockings before swimming, and how through this act and its subsequent uproar, women are liberated from having to wear stockings when they swim. He reads of how she goes, with an escort of four strong matrons, to bombed-out Antwerp for the 1920 Olympics, and wins every gold medal in women's swimming, breaking world records in that estuary, more mud than water. He saves the papers for Compass, for when he is older. And L. is there on the opening night of her water performance in the Royal Theatres, but leaves when he sees the falseness of the smile pasted on her face. When he wakes up the next morning, his heart still hurts.

And in the papers he notices her one last rebellion: she is arrested for swimming at night in the pond in Central Park. But the mayor intervenes, and from this incident comes a good thing: New York's first public swimming pool. She sinks quietly back into her life, coaches a few women swimmers to the Olympics, and has no more children, as far as he can tell. He hopes, from his spacious apartment on the East Side as he watches Compass grow, that she is happy.

*

Aliette watches him, too. She follows him as he grows famous, and reads every one of his new books. She leaves them strewn so conspicuously in her home on nights when she holds soirées that her high-society guests, most of whom have never read a line of poetry, cite him in interviews as their favorite poet. She reads the profiles of him in the papers and watches Compass grow and become his father's amanuensis, his nurse, his friend. Compass goes to Harvard when his father is offered a lectureship there, and lives with him during his college years. He graduates with a degree in English, and holds three school records on the pool's walls. Later, when the interviewers can induce the boy to speak, he smiles his serious smile, and says, "I can't imagine a better life than the one I live with my father." Aliette snips this quote and carries it in a locket that hangs from her neck.

One night she turns on the radio and hears L.'s dear voice reciting some of his oldest poems, the ones from *Ambivalence.* He gasps slightly with his troubled lungs as he reads the lines, "I have dreamed a dream of repentance / I have known the world eternal." She listens, rapt, and when she switches off the radio, her face is wet.

She sees him only once, in all this time. They are both old, and he has just published his twelfth book of poems. He stands on a stage, behind a lectern. His hair is white, and he is stooped. He reads deliberately and well, stopping after each poem to catch his breath.

He does not notice the plump woman in the gray cloche and chinchilla coat in the back of the auditorium. He doesn't see how she mouths with him each word he reads, how her face is bright with joy. Later, after he has shaken the hands of his admirers, and is alone with Compass in the theater, she is long gone, in bed with a hot-water bottle. But though she is nowhere around, he has felt all evening the change her very presence makes in the air.

He walks on the arm of his handsome son onto the cool New York street glistening with rain. Out on the sidewalk he tells Compass to halt. L. lifts his face to the drizzle and closes his eyes, breathing deeply once, twice. When he brings his face back down, he is grinning.

Then he tells his son, "This feels like that breath you take after coming up from a long swim underwater. The most gorgeous feeling, that sip of air you feared you'd never have again." He looks at Compass, and touches his cheek, gently. "Surfacing," he says.

BEVERLY JENSEN

Wake

FROM NEW ENGLAND REVIEW

Boston, January 1956

"Good God Almighty. We've lost the damned body." Avis stood on the North Station train platform, her small leather suitcase pressed between her knees as though it, too, might be whisked away. "Dalton, we've lost Dad. What the hell are we going to do?"

"Call Stan, I guess. He'll know."

Avis kept going through the motions of stamping snow from her feet, though it had all melted down into her boots an hour ago. They'd gotten off the train from Connecticut late last night, thinking Dad, in his coffin, had been rolling along behind them in the baggage car. The train up to Canada didn't leave till this morning, so they'd gone and got themselves an excuse for a room in that excuse for a hotel Dalton knew about, to try to get some sleep. But when they'd come staggering back into the station this morning, thinking to crawl up to Bathurst with Dad in tow for his own funeral, and they'd gone to make sure that the body was on board with the other baggage, there was no body to be had anywhere for love nor money.

Dalton strode helplessly back and forth in front of Avis, as though trying to determine which of the trains on either side of the platform might offer escape. His legs were so long and wiry that he could not pace without seeming to lope. He needed a wide open field before him, not the crowded confines of this train platform filled with heavy-coated strangers who all knew exactly where they were headed and how they were going to get there. None of them was missing a body all laid out in its casket.

"What exactly did the baggage man say?" Avis asked.

"There's no casket anywhere in this station. Hasn't been one since a week ago Saturday, and that one went to Toledo, and he believes it was a woman. He's going to call the Connecticut station, but it'll be a while 'cause of the snow, and schedules are off, and if we don't get on this train to Canada we won't be going to Canada anytime soon, 'cause this is the only train to New Brunswick today, and he has his doubts about tomorrow 'cause he's heard the storm's supposed to get worse before it gets better. He says they'll be calling this the 'Storm of '56,' like as not. One for the books, he says. He says it's an odd thing to lose a casket like that, as they don't get that many coming through and they usually take note of it, and did we have a receipt or a claim check?" Dalton stopped pacing and stood in front of Avis. "I thought maybe you had one."

"Christ, he was ready to chat. Hadn't anyone asked him a question in the last ten years?" Avis searched through her purse for some sort of ticket or receipt or piece of paper with a number on it. "Nothing."

"Check inside your gloves. Maybe it's in a finger."

"Check inside your own damn gloves."

"I don't have any."

"I have no memory of anyone handing me anything." Avis turned her wet gloves inside out. "I never had it. It was you that talked to the man in the uniform before we got on in Cohasset, wasn't it? Didn't you talk with some official? I know I never did."

"Well, if I did, I don't recall. I was awful tired."

"You were shitfaced, is what you were." Avis stuck her hands down into her coat pockets. Nothing but cigarettes in one pocket and a hole in the lining of the other. She stuck her finger down through it and opened her coat to show Dalton. "There. Maybe that's what happened to it."

"Hell, I got one of them too." Dalton stuck his whole fist through his pocket lining and waggled his fingers at Avis. "We may have solved the problem."

"We haven't solved anything. There was no receipt. I think we got the casket with us to the station and neither one of us made sure it was on the train. That damned hearse unloaded and drove off. What did he care?"

"Do you have to buy a ticket for a dead man?"

"You've got to do something. You can't drag bodies around like it was regular luggage."

Dalton stopped pacing and flicked his fingers under his chin. "Christ, I forgot to shave."

"I guess Roger thought we would take care of it, seeing as it's our father, not his." Avis sighed.

"He should've known better." Dalton shook his head. "Course, he married you. That shows lack of judgment."

"Shut your damn mouth."

"He should have gotten us all three onto the train." Dalton resumed his pacing.

"He was glad to get us out of the car. Poor old Roger. He'd had his fill of Hillocks."

Dalton turned just short of an open train door. "I know one thing for damned sure."

"What might that be?" Avis reached into her coat pocket and pinched a cigarette from her pack. There were only about three more in there, by the feel of things.

"I need a drink." Dalton reached over and took the cigarette.

"You had a drink."

"It wasn't tall enough, nor wide. Not by a couple of long shots."

She slipped her fingers back into her pocket for another cigarette. Two left. "Smoke your own damned cigarettes."

"I did already."

"And quit your roaming! It's like talking to a fly in a manure pile. Stand still. We have to figure out what to do."

Dalton stopped and looked down at her. "I'm not getting on any train going up to Dad's funeral if we don't have Dad's body with us."

Avis lit her cigarette and took a long drag, blowing the smoke up past Dalton's ear. "It must not have made the switch. It must still be waiting on some platform in Connecticut."

"The man said to check back with him in fifteen minutes." Dalton lit his cigarette from hers.

"How long has it been?"

Dalton looked up at the big round station clock. "Twenty. What if someone took it?"

"Who's going to walk off with a coffin, you damned fool?"

"Who'd walk off and leave one?" Their eyes met as they exhaled smoke into each other's faces.

"Go on," Avis said, brushing him away like a gnat. "Go find the baggage man."

Avis watched Dalton stride off through the crowds. Even slouching like he was now, with that hang-dog look of his, he was a head taller than everyone else.

"Last call, last call for the Canadian to Halifax, Nova Scotia, leaving from Track 9. Making stops at Portland, Lewiston, Augusta, Bangor, Houlton, and St. John's. Final destination, Halifax. Last call."

Avis stood smoking. That was the train they were supposed to be on. She watched as the conductor strode up and down the platform, helping people into the cars. She looked in the windows and saw passengers clogging the aisles, stowing bags onto the overhead racks. Already some were taking off gloves and scarves and settling their coats around them, slipping into their seats, and snuggling in for the long ride north. Soon they would be leafing through magazines and spreading newspapers across their laps. Some would head to the club car as soon as the train was moving, for hot coffee. Cigarettes would flicker to life, their owners leaning back into the seats, looking out at the storm.

Avis longed to be on the train with them. She wanted to be in a window seat with her toes tucked under her. Her feet were cold, her leather boots soaked through. She was beyond tired. She needed to curl up into herself and blot out everything while the world swirled around her.

It had been snowing all night — a full out nor'easter. She and Dalton hadn't slept much. Christ, every time either one moved on that rickety bed the springs sang the "Hallelujah Chorus." And the wind roared in under the window as if it had been wide open, it was so damn cold. Then with Dalton turning on the light to go relieve himself, and banging into the bed on the way back — and taking up all the space with his long Hillock legs once he got there — it was one ungodly night. They both finally said, "The hell with it," and got up and smoked almost all the cigarettes till they were out of matches, and drank all they had left of Roger's whiskey.

Dad'd get a laugh out of this now, seeing his two "damned fools" wondering where they'd put his dead body. Avis didn't find it so funny. Her head pounded like someone was going at it with a sledgehammer. She couldn't absorb the shock of Dad's being gone, never again to drive into town unexpected, mad or drunk or both. She'd heard his voice commenting, making jokes at someone else's expense, throughout the whole day of people coming in to view him. His voice in her was so strong, it kept on going without him.

Dad's real voice had been altered for over three years, since he'd had that first stroke that left him all flaccid on the one side. He'd get so frustrated at not being able to move one whole half of himself, or talk right, or drink without dribbling all over his shirt front, that he'd kick at anything within range of his good leg. He'd kicked Avis a few times as hard as he'd kicked the furniture.

His second stroke, three months ago, left him completely mute. She'd moved in with him then. Poor old Roger just watched her pack and drove her over. She'd been living with Dad, nursing him, those last three months. He could talk with his eyes. Avis could make out his needs. She'd had him to take care of like a baby. She'd read to him by the hour the way she'd always heard Mother had read to him. Wife, mother, daughter. She'd been all three for him at the end.

"Well, sister, he's lying on the platform in Connecticut. They'll send him on here to Boston. Should be here a little before noon, no guarantee 'cause of the weather." Dalton shook a pack of Lucky Strikes at her. He'd restocked. "They can't have his funeral without him, so we're not going to miss it." He ground the stub of his current cigarette flat out on the platform with a twist of his foot. "Just like that ornery bastard, to miss his own burying."

"We'd best call Stan up in Maine," Avis said. "He'll know what to do."

"Yeap. We'd best let the cat out of the bag."

"They'll blame us." Avis buttoned her coat as though preparing for battle. "Everyone will lay the blame right on us. You're prepared to start hearing about it?"

"Yeap."

"We'll never hear the end of it."

"Nope."

"I'll call Stan." Avis marched down the platform and up the stairs.

She had been relying on her cousin Stanley Hillock to get her out of trouble since she was five years old. They'd emptied the well when they made him. Here she was now, forty-five years old and married even, to poor meek Roger, but Stan was the man to call.

"I hope he'll accept the charges," Dalton called after her.

*

Bathurst, New Brunswick

Idella stood staring uselessly down the tracks. She held her squirrel fur coat tightly together to keep out the cold wetness. Tiny pellets of ice were biting at her eyes and hitting the tip of her nose. There weren't going to be any more trains coming down them tracks anytime soon. The one that had just pulled out was three hours late as it was, and — most important — it didn't have Dad in his casket, or Avis, or Dalton on board, as planned, as they said they'd be, as they had promised. The goddamned fools.

Frozen rain pinged and bounced off the metal rails, the wooden gates, the shingled roof of the Bathurst station. You could hear the crunch underfoot as people milled about on the platform, most of them Hillocks or former Hillocks or married to a Hillock. They were all here waiting for Dad — Wild Bill Hillock as he was known to them and liked to call himself. The whole family lined the edge of the platform, looking futilely down the darkened stretch of track into an empty black hole, ringed with sleet.

"No guest of honor. No hallowed attendants." Her sister Emma came and stood next to Idella. She was her baby sister, but she was the biggest and tallest of the three Hillock girls.

"Now what?"

"I don't know what to do," Idella said. "I'm at a loss."

"Won't be no more trains tonight, Miss Hillock. You'd best go on inside." John Farley, stationmaster here since Christ was born, still called her Miss Hillock, even though she'd come to know herself as Mrs. Jensen, married to Edward now for over twenty-five years. "Sorry for the loss," he said, wiping frozen pellets from off the top of his hat.

"Oh, we'll find him, surely," Idella said, suddenly alarmed. "They've got to be some place."

"We never should have left it to those two." Emma sighed.

"The blind leading the blind." Idella sighed.

"They're probably waiting for the storm to blow itself out," Emma said. "Probably holed up somewheres. I'm going back in the station."

"I'm going to stand here for a bit to get some air."

"Don't stay out too long." Emma patted Idella's fur shoulder. "Oh, you're so puffy, like a bear cub."

Idella took a deep breath of the cold, sharp Canada air. Good God, what a week. What a time. And it wasn't finished yet. Eddie'd gone back home to Maine with the kids, thank God. Everyone had had enough of him. Especially after that ear incident — following Avis into her cellar and falling down the whole flight of stairs, drunk, and landing with a caterwaul that would wake the dead. Everyone said it was a wonder Dad didn't jump out of the casket. And the way Eddie's glasses landed so perfectly on the little shelf at the top of the stairs, as if they'd been laid there on purpose, while Edward himself hurtled all the way to the bottom. Everyone remarked on the placement of those glasses.

Eddie's ear bled like a stuck pig. There were quite a few stitches. And his being so squeamish at the sight of blood. Thank goodness the emergency room was nearby. And that bandage! Idella laughed at the thought of it, wrapped up all around his head at that queer angle. He insisted on wearing his hat, perched on top of that bandage like a bird's nest. God Almighty, though, they did tease him — Avis and Dalton. Once they got going on something, they wouldn't drop it. They each tried to top the other. Eddie couldn't stand it. The more he fumed, the funnier he looked. Everyone was so giddy and there'd been so much drinking and it was such an odd occasion — Dad laid out in Avis's parlor like that with the chairs all around the edges of the room. People were going a little stir crazy. If Dad had been there, he would have had a field day with Edward — it was so easy to give Eddie a hard time.

What in God's name Edward thought he was going to do to help fix Avis's furnace she'd never know. He couldn't change a light bulb without having a fit. There was always something to get in his way. The bulbs were too delicate, breaking in his hand, or the screwing mechanism didn't work right, or something. He acted like the bulbs were purposely designed to make it hard for him, Edward Jensen.

He hadn't wanted to let her come up here, even. But there was no way he was keeping her from coming. After Dad's services in Connecticut she was bound and determined to proceed up to Canada and see Dad get laid to rest next to Mother, all these many years later. "I'm going all the way," she'd said. "All the way!" Edward had finally closed his trap.

Idella looked around her. She was the only one left on the platform. It was miserable out. She turned her coat collar up and walked into the small wooden station. "I got my air," she said as she closed the door behind her.

People were huddled in clumps with their coats and boots and hats still on. She could hear conversations hissing around her like steam from a room full of kettles, everyone pondering what to do next.

Idella stamped the slush from her feet, adding to the dark puddles on the old wooden floor. She started to brush the pellets off her coat before they melted and got the fur wet.

"Jesus, Della," said Uncle Sam, "I never seen so much fur except on a bear — have you, Guy?"

"No, I ain't." Uncle Guy stretched out his long legs and winked at Idella. "Unless it was on your backside, Sam." They'd get on this bone together and gnaw it clean to help pass the time.

Uncle Sam and Guy had been teasing Idella about her fur coat ever since she got out of the car. Everyone had taken note of it and made little comments. You couldn't have anything really nice without people acting like you didn't deserve it, or had betrayed them, or were putting on airs. It was only squirrel, for God's sake, and Idella had earned it, working in that airplane factory all during the war, standing in that line assembling parts. She'd earned it.

"Looks mighty wet, Idella," Uncle Sam continued. "Give yourself a good shake."

"Well, don't shake that thing over here," Guy said, his head rising up from the group and looking over.

Idella shook her coat off by the door and then joined Emma, huddled in front of the wood stove. The Hillock girls were given the best seats. She fluttered her hands in front of the fire.

"The way I see it . . ." Uncle Sam's voice rose up from behind Idella. He was speaking to the whole roomful of people and everyone turned to listen. "Bill's just taking his own sweet time to get here, following his own route. That's his way. I say we wait over at the church and be ready to receive him. Let's make the best of it for Bill."

Idella looked over at Sam's familiar face, so like Dad's. There weren't too many teeth left in his mouth now, but the sweetness came through when he smiled. He'd been a handsome man. People down here didn't know much about caring for teeth. If you happened to get dealt a poor set, you just lived with them or pulled them out.

Mr. Farley, the stationmaster, shuffled over to the wood stove and stoked the fire. He moved from group to group, nodding and smiling. There were more people crowded into his little station today than since the war started and men headed out to go shoot the Germans. "You folks stay here as long as you want." Mr. Farley was being a real host. He was a gentleman, in his way. "I won't close till the last one's out. It's an unusual time."

Mr. Farley had helped Idella onto the train the day she left here to go down to the States, to get the hell out of here, more than thirty years ago. He'd shaken her hand, as if he knew something big was taking place, and wished her well on her journey. He'd used that word, "journey." She'd been so scared and so determined, with no more than twenty dollars tucked in her shoe. Dad had gotten it from someone, Uncle Sam probably, and given it to her right here at this station, just before she'd boarded. "Tell them you've got two hundred," he'd told her. "When you get to the border. Two hundred." Dad knew. He knew she had to go.

Now she was back, maybe for the last time. The farm would stand empty for a while. Then someone would see a good thing and move on in. To people up here, that old house would look like a good thing. She wouldn't be surprised if some of these relatives were feeling each other out right now as to who might be taking up residence.

'Course it'd all go to Dalton, legally. He was the oldest and the male. Nothing left for the sisters but what they might scrounge from the house, which was another way of saying "nothing."

"Let's head over to the church then." Emma stood up. "No use waiting for a train that won't come."

Idella joined her. "I could call down to Maine, see if Edward has heard anything."

They stood side by side, staring into the flickering wood stove.

"Where in hell are they?" Emma asked.

Idella sighed. "The fools."

"The goddamned fools."

They pulled their coats tight about them, shaking their heads in unconscious unison.

"Where in hell are we?" Avis was squeezed into the middle of the front seat between Dalton and Stanley.

"There's the one road and we're on it," Stan answered. "We're nearly to Bangor."

"Did I fall asleep?"

"Yeap. You could call it that."

"Christ. How long we been driving?"

"Going on eight hours." Stan drove steadily through the darkness, the wipers of the hearse thumping back and forth like a steadily rocked chair.

"Storming the whole time?"

"Yeap."

"I feel like a puckered-up pea wedged between two stalks of corn. There's no room for my legs." Avis shifted herself around on the seat. "I'm numb. My 'dairy-aire' isn't there."

"Well, don't put it here." Dalton was slowly emerging from sleep. "Christ. My elbows is down behind my knees somewhere." He stared dully out his window. "Jesus, Mother of God. What's it doing out there?"

"Some of everything. Snowed from Boston to Portland. Rained near the coast. Few times it freezed and come down like pellets."

"What a mess." Avis stared out the windshield.

"Been that the whole time."

"I don't just mean the weather," Avis said.

"Me neither," Stan replied.

Dalton scraped his fingernail down his side window. "It's all blurry."

"Be blurred to you with the sun shining, the shape you two were in." Stan's long body was folded at sharp angles behind the wheel of the hearse. His neck was hunched over like a vulture's, trying to see through the windshield.

"I assume we got Dad in the back?" Avis tried to turn her head and peer through the little window.

"Yeap. We got Bill for ballast. Took four grown men to get him in there."

"Was I one of 'em?" Dalton rubbed his eyes.

"Nope."

"He said grown men, Dalton."

"I'm grown."

"I didn't know which port you two were holed up in when I got to North Station. I thought I'd best get Bill in back so we wouldn't drive off without him."

"Were you waiting on us long?" Avis asked, looking over at Stan. The collar of his familiar flannel shirt was poking out around his neck. Avis knew he'd have suspenders on under his coat.

"Long enough to notice."

"I'm sorry, Stan. We lost track of the time."

"You lost track of everything. Do either of you remember me pulling you out of that bar at the station?"

"Not really." Avis sighed.

Dalton shook his head, slowly taking stock of his position. "Can you drive this thing all the way up? You want I should take the wheel?"

"No use showing up with four bodies." Stan glanced over at Dalton.

"Hell, they could bury us all and be done with it." Avis laughed. "Emma and Della will be ready to string us up in the barn."

Stan leaned even closer to the windshield. "I can't see but what's two inches in front of me."

"That'd be your nose." Avis snickered.

Stan laughed. "It's good to have some company. Even the likes of you two."

"Who but you, Stan, could come up with a hearse in the middle of a goddamned nor'easter?" Avis ran her hand over the front of the dashboard. SUTTON'S FUNERAL HOME — GORHAM, MAINE was printed in gold letters across the leather.

"Promised Sutton a well dug out back of his place come spring," Stan said. "We're counting on the Gorham population to remain steady for the next few days."

"Here's to the population of Gorham!" Avis rummaged into her purse to unearth a flask. "You want to drink to Gorham, Dalton?"

"I never liked Gorham." Dalton reached for Avis's bottle and took a drink.

"I promised Sutton that every Hillock this side of the North Pole, and there's a lot of them, would be obliged. Said we'd all throw our business his way when the time comes."

"I'll try to remember," Dalton said, taking another drink. "When my time comes."

They rode along without talking for a long time. The sounds of the storm filled up the car — splatters and taps and whining winds. Stan kept his attention riveted to the road. Avis and Dalton stared ahead, the wipers screeching to and fro in front of them.

"The old goat is dead." Dalton's voice was clear and unexpected.

Avis looked over at him. "You sound glad."

"I can breathe. Never did when he was living."

"You get the farm, you bastard."

"That'll change my life. Lording over that pile of wind and rock."

"You inherit it all," Avis said, "being the only male."

"The only male we know about."

"What's that supposed to mean?"

"There's more than one Hillock walking that goes by the name of bastard. And I wouldn't be surprised if some of them had French accents or Indian braids."

"You don't know that."

"Hell, he probably didn't know the half of them. Why do you think there was so many French girls come and gone so quick as housemaids?"

"They were dumb cows is why."

"Hell, if he'd kept his hands off Mother some of the time, instead of filling her with his stinking seed, maybe she wouldn't have died birthing one."

"That's a fine way to refer to us. If they'd stopped with just you things'd be a lot better, is that what you're saying, Dalton?"

"Before that, even," Dalton said softly.

"Seems like I was having more fun when you two were asleep. Maybe you'd best say nothing."

"Any word yet, Idella?" Uncle Sam stood up in the pew as she walked into the church.

"Nothing. Roger don't answer. Edward don't either. Just keeps ringing." Idella had been trying to get through for almost an hour.

"The lines must be down," Uncle Guy offered.

"It's awful crackly, that's true," Idella said. "I don't know what's become of them."

"Move over." Avis elbowed Dalton.

"The only way I can move over is to open the door and fall out."

"Well go on, then. I can't sit like this much longer."

"If you're so cramped why don't you go lay down in the back next to Dad?"

"Maybe I will."

"I understand it wouldn't be the first time."

"What the hell is that supposed to mean?"

"You know damn well what I mean."

"I know what you think you mean, you half-assed son of a bitch, and it's not true."

"Quit yammering, the both of you. We're coming into Houlton. We'll get some coffee and try to call up there again and tell 'em we've got Bill."

"I need to piddle," Avis said.

"There's a diner up ahead, by the look of it. Don't look quite open or quite closed." Stan slowly pulled the hearse up in front of the dimly lit restaurant. "One of them signs is lit, anyway, and I see someone in there behind the counter." He opened his door and climbed out. "Jesus God Almighty, that's a tight fit."

"It's pissing down like a horse," Dalton said as he stuck one long leg and then the other out of the car.

"Don't let's talk about pissing till I've done it," Avis said from inside the car. "One of you is going to have to peel me out of here."

"I preferred the snow," Stan said, tugging Avis out of the car. "At least you can see it."

"It's all ice out there," Idella said. "It's just terrible. I'm dripping icicles."

"Any luck, Idella?" Emma came up to her as she walked back into the church, stomping the wet off her boots.

"The lines are definitely down in Connecticut. The operator can't get through at all."

"And Edward?"

"Still no answer. But it appears to be ringing."

"The scrape of them wipers is vibrating my whole head," Avis said. They were riding on into the night with only the greeny lights of the dashboard to outline their three huddled shapes. Avis sighed and closed her eyes. She was exhausted from staring past the smeared windshield, trying to follow the wavering headlight beams as they reached out, feebly, for the road.

Dalton was pressed against her, snoring. "Nothing like bacon and eggs to set the world right," had been his last and only words after they'd left the diner. He'd been asleep since they'd pulled back onto the road.

"Don't worry, Stan," Avis whispered, "I'm not going to sleep."

"I'm into my third wind here. That coffee helped. I just wish we'd been able to get through up there. No one up at the house. They must all be waiting at the church, God love 'em."

Avis kept her eyes shut. She folded her hands and listened to the sounds around her — the steady *bump thump* of the wipers, the *slooshing* of the tires as they spewed rain and snow out from under them, Dalton's raspy, smoke-heavy breath as he slept with his head pressed against the side window, his long body all curled on itself like a fiddlehead.

As cold and cramped and tired as they all were, she didn't quite want this ride ever to end. She had all three men that she'd ever really loved, and who she knew for a fact loved her, all to herself. Della and Emma loved her, like sisters. But they weren't as forgiving. She supposed Roger loved her, poor old soul that he was, but she couldn't return it. She was grateful to him for his kindness, for marrying her in spite of who she was instead of because of it, for putting a roof over her head. But she was beholden to him, and that brought out the worst in her.

Dalton twisted in his sleep, pushing his knee into her legs. She pushed it back. Just enough flesh on it to cover the bone. She and Dalton had never been too good at doing what they were supposed to, or what was expected of them — except now that they were expected by everyone to drink and screw things up, they did manage to do that pretty good.

Even when they bickered, which was plenty, they were still fighting a war alone against the others. They'd always been in cahoots. There was that scheme when they were about ten and fourteen — they'd worked a way to sell lobsters to the passengers on the trains going through Uncle Sam's property. The train would stop for water, and the two of them would climb aboard and sell whatever catch Dalton had managed from taking out that little boat he'd built. Avis did the talking, knowing even then that the way you asked for things, and how you looked doing it, mattered. They sold the lobsters for six cents apiece and lorded their mounting proceeds over the others at every opportunity. Dalton finally spent his getting more traps and then lost interest in the whole enterprise.

Avis had kept her money — it wasn't even five dollars total — in a variety of hiding places, each more elaborate than the last, till one day Dad ran across it when he went to empty out a seed bag in the barn. It was drunk and gone by the time Avis discovered it missing. "That's what you get for being so secretive," Idella'd said. No sympathy from her. "If you'd put it in the bedroom and left it there, this wouldn't have happened." Hiding it from Idella had been half the fun.

Avis knew she was Dad's favorite. They had found comfort in each other. She closed her eyes tighter. There were times when she'd be overcome by the need to be alone in the world with Dad, holed up in some room lying next to him, the two of them giving each other a bodily comfort that went right through them. It was like being home when she could just lie there quiet in his arms. Even Stan, dear Stan, probably thinks the worst, thinks they were being dirty. But they weren't. They were both so lonely, she and Dad, standing on earth like that godforsaken house they lived in, spindly and forlorn atop that great cliff, exposed to every wind that blew from any direction. That's how Avis had felt, as a little girl, after Mother had died and there was no one to talk to about her secrets or fears. Della was, what? Too distrustful? Too scared herself to offer any real comfort.

No one who saw Dad bluster and bang, who heard him drink and yell and carry on, would ever know the agony that man went through, for years, after Mother died. He didn't let on, after the funeral and all, after that first stretch of time passed and people thought he'd got over it enough to keep going. But Avis knew.

It was Avis that first went down, unbidden, when she knew that Della was sleeping. She slipped out from next to her and tiptoed down the stairs and into his bedroom. Without a word she crawled in beside him, and he turned and scooped up her puny little nothing of a body and wrapped his arms around her and they went off to sleep. Dad must've woken up some time and brought her upstairs, because she woke up the next morning curled beside her sister. That was how it began, their special closeness, that lasted right on through.

Avis knew people wondered about her and Dad. She could feel their eyes trying to look through her. The old biddies up in Canada would make judgments about her. "She's been to prison," their eyes said when they looked at her. They'd got themselves through many a long afternoon discussing Avis. She could just hear them — Maisey Moore and Mrs. Doncaster — clinking their teacups and crunching their dry toast, hardly waiting to get the words out before they swallowed. "Sent away, you know, for luring men up to her room down in Boston." "Got took up with a gangster of some kind." "He was handsome, I hear. He got her to do all sorts of things till they finally got caught." Avis sighed. Tommy was handsome, there was no denying.

It was Dad who drove down to Boston and got her out of that hellhole after two years of being locked up. No one knew but Dad. She'd told him. Neither of her sisters knew the half of what she put up with, of what got done to her. All they knew is she learned to be a beautician. Like she was in some kind of finishing school. The "hotel," Idella called it.

At least Idella didn't say anything to that damn fool Edward. Poor Idella would never know the number of times he'd tried getting his big, clumsy hands up inside her skirt. Even at the wake, with Dad laid out in her parlor and the house all full of people, Edward had come lumbering after her down into the cellar to "help her fix the furnace." Damn fool. He wanted to start a fire, all right, but not in the furnace. Put more than two drinks in him and he was nothing but trouble. Avis started to laugh.

"What are you finding so funny? I sure as hell could use a laugh right about now."

Avis looked over at Stan's familiar shape, all angles and points, as Hillock as they come. He was leaned over staring hard at what little bits of road he could see. He was getting tired. The storm, by the look of it, was getting worse.

"Oh, I was laughing about Edward. He tumbled head over heels down the cellar stairs and looked so funny with that bandage all around his head. When he put that damned brimmed hat on he's always wearing, perched up on top of all that gauze, I about peed my pants."

"Poor Eddie," Stan chuckled. "If you act like a damn fool, then damn fool things are going to happen to you."

"He brought it on himself," Avis said.

"What are you two finding to laugh about?" Dalton was coming to. "Damned if something don't ache, it hurts; if it don't hurt, it's wet. I feel like throwing Dad out of that damned box. I need it more than he does." He peered forward. "My God, it's ice now, ain't it?"

"Been more ice than rain this last half hour. I'd like to pull over to scrape some off the windshield," Stan said, "but I'm afraid if we stop we won't get going again. The defroster in this hearse isn't up to this."

"I guess they don't want too much getting defrosted, if you know what I mean," Dalton suggested.

"Yeap. Maybe that's it," Stan agreed.

"Let's change the subject," Avis said.

"What have you heard, Idella? Any news? Could you get through?" The pews were filled up. People had turned askew so as to talk better. Voices were coming at her from all directions.

She stood at the front of the little English church where the casket was supposed to be and talked loud so that everyone could hear. "I can't get through to Roger. Those lines are down. But I *did* finally get ahold of Donna, down in Maine. She's my second oldest. She was there babysitting Beverly and Paulette. I don't know where Edward is. Donna said, 'They lost the box. Stanley has gone to get it. He's got the box.'" Idella repeated that exact quote from Donna slowly and deliberately. "That's the message she had to give us from Katherine — Stan's wife. Evidently Avis, or Dalton, or both, lost the box — the casket — with Dad in it — evidently they lost it somewhere between here and there, closer to there, and Stan's got himself a hearse and he's gone to get them. They're on the road somewheres is my understanding."

A cheer went up through the church with shouts of "Good old Stan" and "You can count on Stan."

"Now I know" — Idella put up her hands to calm things and raised her voice a little — "I know that if Stanley is involved he'll get them here." She nodded her head, to give her speech a little ending. She'd never spoken like this before a crowd. "Thank you all for coming." She continued standing there and raised her head up. "Now I don't know what to do."

"Well, we're not leaving!" Everyone started shouting that they were sticking it out.

"Come have a drink, Idella." Uncle Sam was beckoning to her.

"We can't drink in the church!" Idella said, knowing full well that bottles were being passed up and down the pews like collection plates on Sunday morning.

"Goddamn, it's pure ice out there now." Uncle Guy was at the window. "It's sticking like a new coat of paint."

Sam was on his feet now, leaning over the front of a pew. "I want to drink to Bill, to my big brother, Bill Hillock. May he rest in peace, wherever the hell he is."

Bottles were raised all up and down. Seems more had one than didn't. "To Bill," went murmuring through the little church, some voices together, some out of sync.

Then the lights went. There was a loud crack, and total darkness came down over them as if a black velvet curtain had dropped.

"Holy Mother of God," a lone voice rose up.

"Goddamn," another answered from the blackness.

"Damn it all to hell," muttered Dalton, staring down at the back wheel of the hearse as it spun in response to Avis's foot on the gas pedal.

"Take your foot off it, Avis," Stan called in to her. "Just that back wheel we got to get up onto the road."

"Never seen ice like this." Dalton looked at the lunging shapes on either side of the road. The trees were stooped down low by the weight of ice that had been steadily falling.

"We got to get something in there for traction," Stan said.

"Where's Edward with his bag of sand when you need him?" Avis joined the two men at the end of the car. They were so tired and cold and miserable that being soaked through didn't seem to add or detract.

"Sometimes a branch'll do it, but there's nothing along here that ain't stuck to the ground or ice coated." Stan was scooching down and feeling around the wheel.

"Would a belt do? I got a leather belt."

Stan considered. "Maybe."

"How 'bout my hat?" Avis offered. "It's all shot to hell anyway. Being run over by a hearse could only improve it."

"If that's the case," Dalton said, "why don't I lie down there in front of the wheel. There's one thing I ought to be good for."

A sudden crack ricocheted from out of the woods behind them.

"What the hell!" Avis yelled.

"They got me," Dalton whispered, without moving.

"Tree snapped," Stan said. "That ice'll snap whole trees."

Dalton pulled his leather belt out from under his overcoat and handed it to Stan, who bent over and crammed it, folded once, up under the edge of the tire. "Give me that hat, Avis. It'll give it something more to go on for them few inches."

A second and third crack shot out from dark woods. Dalton joined Stan behind the rear of the car and prepared to help push. Avis crawled in behind the wheel.

"Go on, Avis," Stan said. "Slow and steady. If we get her up on the road, we're not stopping." Dalton and Stanley leaned into the car with their shoulders, their fingers grabbing under the fender. The wheel came up against the wedged leather. "A little more!" Stan called. "Push like hell!" he said to Dalton, and the two of them heaved the hearse forward, over the belt and the hat and up onto the road. It lurched forward, swerved its long behind to the left, and came to a tentative, cockeyed halt.

"There's a God in heaven!" Dalton called out into the darkness. "Get my hat!"

Stan bent himself back down behind the wheel. "I reckon it's three more hours of slow and steady. It'll be well after midnight."

"I'm sorry we got you into this pickle." Avis pushed Stan's glasses back up his long nose.

"I'd swear them trees cracking back there was Dad firing off his last shots." Dalton pulled his door to and locked it.

"It's well after midnight," Idella said.

"The time don't matter no more," Emma said. "We're in it."

Idella settled down onto a pew. Some of the men had got lanterns from the back of the church and hung them all about from the rafters. Long gray shadows lurched up the walls to the ceiling. It was spooky, but it was beautiful. Everyone looked so tall, looming like giants. She pulled her squirrel coat tighter. It was cold in here, and damp. The softness of the fur was comforting and luxurious. She felt like a squirrel curling up in its hole, waiting for the storm to pass. The wind was still wrapping around and around the little church, making an eerie sound up in the bell tower. It whumped the bell back and forth, and sometimes the bell would ring out, though no one was pulling the rope. "That's Bill, now, up in heaven, ringing for room service," is what they all started saying every time it rang. "He's ordering more whiskey."

And the frozen rain kept coming. It'd let up a bit, and the tapping sound, like thousands of little chickens pecking on the floor and walls and windows trying to get in, would get so gentle you could barely hear it, and then it'd start right up again.

"Them's the ghosts of all the lobsters he took out of season," Uncle Ernest said, after a quiet spell. "Them little ones he should've thrown back are walking all over the building."

"Go on!" Maisey said. "Don't scare us."

"Then there ought to be a big deer come loping through here any time," Uncle Guy said. "Remember that time Bill went to flush that buck out of the woods and one of you damn fools shot him. Them's Bill's words now, not mine."

Idella didn't want to be reminded of that time, taking care of Dad after the accident.

"We had him strapped down on an old door to get him out of the woods," Uncle Sam said.

"I used my good sheets to do it. Not that I minded." Dear old Mrs. Doncaster, Idella thought, hearing her voice.

"Bill used to say he broke down your bedroom door, Elsie, and was lying between your sheets." Everyone laughed.

"It wasn't my bedroom door," Mrs. Doncaster laughed. "But it was my good sheets."

"Bill would always fatten up a story in the telling," Uncle Sam laughed.

Idella fuzzed out the noise around her. She tried to think of something good Dad did for them, something kind. Oranges at Christmas. Where did he get them? He always came up with an orange for each of them at Christmas, and maybe a washcloth. And there was the time he got her a new hairbrush when she promised to let her hair grow back long. Aunt Francie had bobbed her and Avis's hair, in an effort to make them stylish. Dad hated it. He liked long hair — like Mother's had been. Dad had been at such a loss when Mother died. For all his faults. That poor man. Left alone with four children and no idea even how to do a wash.

"Best story Bill ever told was the time he got hauled into court for putting a potato in some little country girl's oven." That fool Willy Smythe had to go boom that across the church. He had to go bring that story up.

"What was it Bill said to the judge?" Uncle Guy asked.

"It was the trapdoor that got him off, the one going up into the hayloft." Will Smythe was such a loudmouth, Idella thought. "She said he carried her up there, see, against her will."

"Bill stood up in court, as tall as I've ever seen 'im . . . ," Uncle Ernest jumped in, ". . . and he looked right in the judge's eye, you know . . ."

"I'm telling this here, Ernest," Will Smythe cut him off. They were all over themselves to tell it. "Damned if he don't stand up and say, 'Your honor, you see what a tall man I am. You understand what kind of small trapdoor she's referring to. Do you think that I could carry that young woman up a ladder against her will and through a trapdoor and into a hayloft with a goddamned hard-on?'"

"Had the judge laughing, right up there on the bench," Uncle Sam said. "He threw the case out then and there."

Idella hated that story. Many's the time she'd had to sit through Dad regaling everyone with it and hear him get whoops and hollers and free drinks, for God's sake, in the face of that poor girl's plight — some poor French girl who used to work at the lobster factory. Idella never knew what became of that girl and her baby.

Things went on when Dad was living alone on the farm. She leaned her head back. Every piece of her was tired. The tumble of raucous familiar voices surrounded her as if she were in a dream. She imagined the quiet flickers from the candles on the coffin stand gently pressing on her closed lids like warm pats of butter.

"It's a damn shame Bill's missing this," Uncle Sam said quietly, when the laughing had petered out.

That brought things to a standstill. People listened to the ice coming down.

Idella sighed. Everybody had at least one story about Dad. She had a few of her own that she would not be telling. Some stories were for keeping, hurtful ones, that she would probably never tell a soul, certainly not Edward. Good God. And there were stories Avis was keeping, but she'd never know the extent of it. She guessed she didn't want to.

Bill Hillock was no saint, that's for sure. He was a complicated man. He'd been so hard on Dalton. Beat the bejesus right out of him sometimes, like he was taking his anger at the whole world out on poor Dalton's shoulders. It affected Dalton. He didn't make much of himself. So much drinking and wandering. Him and Avis both got that from Dad. They'd drink to please him. Everyone always wanted to please him one way or another, and take care of him. He needed more taking care of than he'd ever let on. After

Mother died Idella had tried as best she could — cooking and cleaning and sewing. Christ, she was just a kid. And he'd taken it for granted. He'd never really thanked her, or given her any affection to speak of. He'd saved that for Avis.

Who knew the extent of it? Idella burrowed her hands down into her coat pockets and rubbed the silky lining around and around between her thumb and forefinger.

"We're closing in on it now, Avis. Less than ten miles to Tetagouch," Stan said.

"I'm ready to be declared dead this minute," Dalton said.

"Wait till Della gets her hands on us," Avis said. "You won't know what dead is till then."

"Good thing Eddie isn't here, eh?" Emma said with her little smile, sliding in next to Idella. "He's none too good at waiting, now is he?"

"Oh, I'm used to putting up with him," Idella said. "He's no worse than the rest. At least he don't drink to speak of."

"We've all had to put up with people," Emma said.

"And Edward's a long sight more reliable than Dad ever was. More considerate. We had to put up with an awful lot on that farm. No life at all fit for young girls, growing up with that kind of man, and no mother. You don't know the half of it. All I had was Avis, and that wasn't much."

"Well, then. I had less than no one, now didn't I?" Emma's voice was steady and deliberate. "I was totally on my own. No mother, no father, no sisters nor brother to live with, to fight with, even. I only got to visit you all on the farm every now and again. You know, Dad scared me. I was scared of him. He was so gruff. I never got to see the soft side much, you see."

"Why, Emma," Idella whispered, taken by surprise. Emma had tears running down her cheeks. Emma never cried. She always had a little joke or a comment to make light of things.

"I always felt, you know, that he hated the sight of me — that you all did. He never said as much, mind, but I felt it. My being there reminded him, you know. Of her dying. I always felt like it was my doing. By being born. And he couldn't get over it."

"Why, Emma." Idella reached over and took her hand. "We all

thought you were lucky being taken in like you were by Aunt Beth and Uncle Paul. They wanted a baby so, we were told. You had a real home with two parents. Adopted, you know."

"There are dirty, dirty secrets." Emma wiped her cheek, not looking at Idella. "God knows we all have dirty secrets. Let's say I was glad to leave there. Let's say Dad will never know, whether he cared or not, he won't know. He wasn't so much better, himself, from what I understand."

"Lord God Almighty." Idella stared into the flickering candles as she spoke. "What poor waifs we were. At the mercy of shameless men."

"Sometime, someday, when we're all drunk or sober, I don't know which, we'll ask Avis what she knows on the subject," Emma said.

"I don't think so," Idella said. "I don't believe I will. Some things are best left unsaid. I don't want to know any more than I know already."

"It's all part of growing up is what I was told," Emma said. "If ever I was to protest or try to question. Anything anyone takes or wants from you without asking is all 'part of growing up.'"

"What's that noise, now?" Uncle Sam rose up and hushed the congregation of waiting mourners.

Idella lifted her head. She heard it too.

"That's a car horn!" Uncle Sam said.

Everyone rushed to a window, some climbing onto pews to see. Men opened the doors and went right out into the storm. Way up ahead, Idella could see headlights winding around the turns in the road, heading toward the long stretch of Main Street. The horn was blowing without letup.

Everyone was talking at once.

"By God, it's Bill!"

"It's Bill Hillock! He's riding down Main Street at midnight! Ain't that like him? Ain't that just the way he'd choose it?"

"By God, it's past midnight. It's two o'clock in the morning."

"It's three."

The horn got louder. Everybody scrambled together and buttoned their coats and went running out to line the street. They were making as if for a parade in the dead of night, in an ice storm, with but one vehicle in the procession. People were shouting and cheering and clapping like it was a whole troop of soldiers returning home from the war. Someone found his way to the bell rope and started clanging in earnest. That sent roars and cheers all up and down.

Idella pulled her coat around her and stepped out onto the church steps. The storm was letting up some. Emma came and stood next to her. "The damn fools made it," she whispered.

And here came the hearse. People slapped it and pounded on the roof as it passed by. The horn never stopped blowing the whole time. It was Avis, Idella could now see; Avis was leaned over practically on top of poor Stan, laying on that horn as if she was stuck there.

The two sisters stood watching from the church steps as the hearse pulled up in front of them and came to a halt. Everyone gathered around it as if movie stars were arriving at a premiere. First Stan's door opened. "Somebody get me a drink."

The other door opened and Dalton emerged, unwinding himself with difficulty. When he got to full standing he called out, "Bring me *two* drinks — and a cigarette!" The crowd loved it.

Finally, Avis wriggled out, looking like a drowned rat. She turned to the crowd. "Bring me a whole damn *bottle* of whiskey and a *pack* of cigarettes!"

Idella watched as that Willy Smythe came and picked Avis up like she was nothing and put her up on his shoulders! Someone handed Avis a flask. Someone else passed her a lit cigarette.

"Let the funeral begin!" Uncle Sam called out.

"Hey, what about Bill? We got to get him in on this!"

Idella watched as the back of the hearse was opened, and Avis got put down, thank heaven. In this ice someone was apt to fall and break a neck. Avis would not look either sister straight in the eye.

Stan and Dalton went around to the back of the hearse. "I carried Bill this far," Stan said, "I'll get him into the church."

"He ain't been to church for a while," Dalton said, finishing his cigarette. He threw back the drink he'd been given, and leaned into the hearse to take hold of the coffin. "Neither have I."

Men lined up in two rows, hauled out the coffin, and hoisted it onto their ready shoulders.

"Watch the ice!" the women called, parting on the church steps to let them through. "Step careful!"

Idella and Emma stood silent on the top step and watched the coffin pass into the church and down the aisle. It was all black shapes moving toward the gold flicker of the candles that lit the front of the church. Avis tentatively joined her sisters.

"Look what the cat dragged in." Emma smiled and held out her hand. "Jesus, Lord Almighty, you took your sweet time getting here." She started to laugh.

"Come on, you damned fool," Idella said. "Let's proceed." The sisters stepped together into the church and down the aisle. Sandwich wrappers and bags and paper cups with drops of whiskey still at the bottom were cleared away before the coffin could be put down proper. After much fiddling and prying with pocketknives, Stan got the lid open and propped up. Lanterns and candles were brought in close.

The four Hillock children were the first to gather round the coffin, now resting on its pedestal. The congregation lined up behind them, waiting to get a good look at Bill before the service began.

The four stood silently, looking down at their father as candlelight flickered eerily across his sunken features. Then Idella led them away in a dutiful line, to take their proper seats in the front row and wait for the ceremony to begin.

The lantern light and candles made the ceremony mysterious, Idella thought. Once there was a body in a casket laid out in the front, the solemnity of the occasion returned. Bill Hillock was dead and needed burying.

Joe Major, the minister, had gone home when he'd heard the coffin was lost. Now he'd come back from his bed, with a nice speech all prepared. And the choir, those dear old women who had waited all night long, like soldiers, sang so pure and sweet that everyone cried. Their shadows lurched around the walls when they came forward and sang. Mrs. Foster played the organ enough to get by and fill things out a little, and it was just thrilling. People Idella never would have suspected of singing knew most of the words and sang along. Uncle Ernest and Uncle Sam, especially, sang out, deep and throaty but beautiful.

Idella closed the hymnbook she'd held absently throughout the funeral and put it on the pew beside her. She'd done more watching than singing, absorbing the look of all the faces around her. They were simple faces with hard edges and lines like cracked cement across their foreheads and around their mouths and eyes.

The lantern light made these crevices seem even deeper. These faces, tilted forward in song or bent down in prayer, had met storms and winds of one kind or another, head-on, all their lives. They worked fields that were best suited to brambles and wild grasses, struggling, Dad and Uncle Sam included, to unearth potatoes and carrots and turnips along with the rocks that seemed to multiply with every turn of a spade. These were the people she'd known as a little girl living up here so long ago. They hunted and fished and lived off the land and by their wits, which were more considerable and deep-rooted than their plantings, and hardier than an outsider might suspect.

Idella had left this Canada far behind and gone to find a better life. It was just being a maid, after all, and a household cook, but it had led to meeting Edward and marrying and having the children and the store and a house in Westbrook. She felt rich by comparison, wrapped in her squirrel coat, knowing she had a nice house to go home to down in Maine and a grocery to run. She'd set out, launched herself forward as best she could, and felt both relieved and saddened to have done so.

When the last "amen" rang all up and down the rows, Idella stood with everyone else, giving the whole ceremony an ending. She looked out the window. It wasn't quite light yet, but it was going to be soon. The storm had finally stopped. Now it was time to get Dad to the gravesite. Two of Uncle Sam's sons had gone on ahead to prepare it. The hole had been dug sometime yesterday morning, and covered over with canvas.

Idella watched as Dad's brothers and Dalton and Stanley all lifted the casket to their shoulders and started for the door.

"All aboard that's going aboard," Dalton muttered as he passed Idella. He looked terrible, just terrible, but Idella figured she couldn't blame him.

"I've never seen anything close to it," Idella said as she sat in the back of Sam's car with Avis and Emma, gazing at the landscape that was revealed with the gradual coming of light. They were taking Dad on to New Bandon to be put in the ground with Mother. The sky had gone from a foggy gray shroud to yellow and pink, and then the sun showed up and brought out a morning of cold, crystal glaze that shone blindingly in every direction, the light bounced off the ice so. It was remarkable, like an entire new world had moved in overnight. Nothing seemed familiar. Every inch of anything was coated thick with ice. Little nothing shrubs and bushes and roadside weeds were transformed into delicate ice sculptures. Everything drooped, as if in prayer, or was snapped off completely, sticking up at odd angles, like farm implements — rakes and scythes and spades — tossed into the air to fall where they might when the farmers abandoned their duties.

"What'll the little birds do?" Idella asked suddenly.

"Fall on their little asses, I suppose," Avis said, laughing. "Like us."

"Jesus, Idella," Emma laughed from up front, wedged between Dalton and Uncle Sam. "Leave it to you to worry about the birds."

"I was just wondering," Idella said. "Just making conversation."

"Well, don't," Avis said.

They sat in silence, each looking out her own window, all the way to the cemetery.

Everyone stood huddled around the gravesite and watched, quietly, as the men baled out the water. They baled and baled. The steady slosh filled the air. There was no getting it all out.

"We're just going to have to lower him in," Uncle Sam finally said. "This here's a spigot to the bowels of the earth."

"Let's have a last drink with Dad," Dalton said, taking a new fifth of whiskey from his coat pocket with ceremony. Idella didn't know where he'd come by that.

"Hell, yes," Avis said.

It did seem appropriate, Idella thought. Even it being morning would suit Dad.

"Gather round, Bill's children," Dalton called out, like he was a preacher. "Let's open him up and do it proper."

Stanley and Dalton unscrewed the clasps of the coffin and pulled back the lid. Idella looked in. Dad didn't look so good in the clear light of morning. His face was more sunken than ever and the bits of makeup they'd used on him at the funeral parlor — he would have kicked and screamed if he'd seen that coming — well, it had got to looking waxy and garish.

"It doesn't look like him anymore," Avis said, staring down.

"Those are his hands," Idella said. "Those long fingers. The hands are his."

"Yeap." Emma nodded.

The four of them — Avis, Idella, Emma, and Dalton — pressed

up against the side of the coffin. Stan kept a hand on the open lid from down at the feet end. People stepped away a bit and let Bill's children say their last farewell.

"It still don't seem right," Emma said, "to see him in a suit. One of them red flannel shirts he wore would have been more like him."

"He could spruce himself pretty well when he wanted," Avis said. "He was a handsome man."

"I'll start the toast," Dalton said. "Let's do it in birth order." He lifted the whiskey bottle. "To Dad!" He swallowed a mouthful. "To the old bastard!" He handed the bottle to Idella.

"To Dad," Idella said, taking a swallow. "To Dad."

The bottle went to Avis and Emma in turn, each raising it up to toast Dad before taking a swig. Dalton took the bottle from Emma and capped it.

Avis stood pressed up against the coffin, staring down into it. Then she stepped away. "I hate sticking him in the cold water."

"Put this whiskey in with him." Dalton handed the bottle down to Stan. "Under his feet there. That way, he can have a drink if he needs one when that water starts seeping in."

"There's room." Stan placed the whiskey bottle in the coffin. "Let's seal him up and set him down."

Everyone watched as the coffin was slowly lowered. There was an unmistakable splash when it hit bottom. No one commented. Uncle Sam's boys and some of the Smythes grabbed their shovels and started breaking off lumps from the mound of displaced dirt beside the grave. They had to crack down through the ice that lay on top like a hard candy coating. It'd be quite a job, but there were enough of them, they said, and they'd take turns. Everyone else should go on back to their homes.

"Well," Dalton said, helping Emma down the hill to the car. "That's that."

"Mother and Dad are together." Idella looked back once more as the men chipped and shoveled. She turned to her brother and sisters. "We're orphans now — all alone in the world."

"Oh, we've been that for a long time," Avis said.

"Christ, yes," Dalton said.

"We've been orphans all along." Avis was already lighting a cigarette.

They climbed into Uncle Sam's car and drove the two miles to the little ramshackle house on the cliff where they'd all got born.

ROY KESEY

Wait

FROM THE KENYON REVIEW

WAITING LOUNGE 19A in Wing D of Terminal 4 is precisely full. The airline personnel smile. The loudspeaker voice says that the flight will begin boarding shortly; the announcement is in English, the woman's accent a mix of Portuguese, Dutch, and Malay.

A Canadian accountant snaps his briefcase shut and stares out at the fog that is settling on the tarmac. The fog is dense and gray and certain. He glances at the passengers seated to either side of him — an old Bulgarian man working a crossword puzzle, an older Honduran woman fast asleep — then at the statue in the center of the lounge, a naked boy holding a cell phone and some sort of globular tropical fruit.

The plane is now invisible, but the smiles of the airline personnel do not wane. The accountant wonders if his futures market holdings back home are headed for contango or backwardation. He shivers, walks from his seat to the windows, presses his fingertips to the pane.

The pilot and crew stride into the lounge, consult with the airline personnel, stride back out. The scheduled boarding time comes and goes. The loudspeaker voice announces that the fog will be lifting momentarily.

The accountant returns to his seat, removes a pad of paper from his briefcase, commences doodling. Children take out coloring books. Other passengers unfold newspapers and magazines. Airline personnel daydream of islands, and speak urgently into handheld radios though this is only for show: the batteries have been on back order for years.

Aircraft scheduled to land circle invisibly overhead. The fog flares against the glass. The Bulgarian clutches at his forehead, and the accountant asks if he needs medical assistance.

"No, thank you."

"You're sure?"

"Do I look as though I need it?"

"A little."

"Yes. I am attempting to think of something for which the flaring of this fog might be metonymically appropriate."

The Canadian squints.

"I am a poet," says the Bulgarian.

"Ah."

"Yes."

The Bulgarian also squints, then shrugs and returns to his crossword. The televisions buzz and mumble, news about a war that is beginning or ending in a country nearby, not the neighboring country to the west but the next one over. All but one of the children close their coloring books and take out their jacks; a small Mongolian boy takes out his checkerboard instead, and worries that this will make him unlikable.

The accountant pulls a scarf from his carry-on, winds it around his neck. Across the lounge sits a girl from Ghana, and she is unthinkably beautiful; he stares at her until he realizes that she is staring back. He looks down, pretends to find a doodle that needs improving, and the girl from Ghana smiles.

The loudspeaker voice announces that there will be a brief delay as the plane's instruments are recalibrated. The Mongolian boy plays himself to a draw; the airline personnel hand out dense cassava crackers and bright purple tea, assure everyone that it will be only a few minutes more, and the air thickens with discontent.

The fog shifts to the left, and back to the right. The televisions brim and burble about soccer. The poet asks the accountant if he knows the name of the Norse goddess who keeps the Apples of Eternal Youth in a box. The accountant apologizes for not knowing. The poet asks if he knows the capital of Bahrain. Again the accountant says that he is sorry. The poet asks if he knows the smell of *kyufte* as it fries on the stove; the accountant asks how a smell could be a crossword clue, and the poet says it has nothing to do with the puzzle — he hasn't been back to Bulgaria in forty years, and the smell of *kyufte* is his favorite childhood memory.

The accountant nods and shakes his head. The poet throws the newspaper in a garbage can and goes to sleep. The accountant turns to the old Honduran woman, now awake. She gums a smile at him. He stares out the window again.

The Mongolian boy plays himself to another draw as the other children put away their jacks and take out their comic books. The aircraft circling invisibly overhead are sent to alternate airports. The airline personnel report that the boarding of the flight will be delayed for another hour to allow the fog to lift. The bookstore manager laments not having raised his prices this morning.

Passengers now crowd the gate. Urgencies are explained — pregnant wife, dying father, sick cat, ex-husband in pursuit — and the airline personnel communicate their understanding and deep regret. There is shrieking with spittle in regard to eggplant rotting on a dock in Stockholm, and the poet wakes, scratches his face, shouts "Iduna!" The accountant leans slightly away. The poet roots through the garbage can, pulls out the crossword puzzle, fills in the word.

A bar that has run short of ice negotiates with another that has run short of napkins. The televisions shudder and flash: there has been a chemical spill of some sort just outside the airport. The driver missed his exit because of the fog, says the reporter; a taxi skidded and a bus swerved, the truck jackknifed, and for the moment no one is allowed in or out the main entrance.

Groups form: impatient passengers versus patient passengers. The accountant and the poet are neither patient nor impatient, and pretend to read as the yelling begins.

The loudspeaker voice says that anyone wishing to leave the airport will be escorted out the cargo bay entrance located in Terminal F. The other passengers discuss options. The fog flexes. The old Honduran woman gums a smile to no one in particular. The accountant asks the poet if he knows why some of the terminals have numbers and some have letters.

"Manama," says the poet.

"I beg your pardon?"

"Manama. Six letters, begins with an *M*. Yes, it can only be Manama."

The girl from Ghana stretches, and the air around her hums. Night closes in, and the airline personnel report that they are unfortunately unable to offer proper lodging for the evening, as all the hotels in the city are full. None of the passengers believe this.

More shouting ensues, and an exodus, all of the locals and a number of hopeful nonlocals.

A café runs short of creamer; a restaurant runs short of cheese. The airline personnel announce that each passenger still present will receive free cassava crackers and purple tea for the remainder of his or her stay in the airport. The children are very pleased. The poet asks the airline personnel if all traces of cyanide were removed from the cassava roots before they were ground into flour, is assured that in fact they were.

Pillows and blankets are brought from the invisible plane on the tarmac. Children stretch out on the floor. Parents drape themselves with coats. The girl from Ghana stares at the fog, wondering how many days it will take her ex-husband to track her from Berekum. Bars run short of bitters and the cleaning staff cleans, threading themselves between sleepers and sacks in silence.

The poet elbows the accountant, points to the checkerboard protruding from the Mongolian boy's carry-on. Four hours later, with the score 9–7 in favor of the accountant, the old Honduran woman asks if she might play as well. She wins the next twelve matches, falls asleep midmove at dawn.

The accountant slides the board back into the child's bag. Other passengers stir and scratch. The members of last night's exodus come traipsing back, the locals smiling, satisfied at having chosen wisely, the nonlocals exhausted, mumbling anecdotes of numberless cab rides and the infinite walk back from the cargo bay entrance.

Children whine. Airline personnel bring thin coffee and bad rolls, promise that today is the day, that it is only a question of minutes. The fog appears still denser, still grayer, still more certain. The televisions say that the chemical spill is nearly cleaned up and vehicular traffic will soon be permitted on the access road once again.

And the passengers wait. All the bars have run short of cognac and celery sticks. The accountant follows the girl from Ghana into Duty Free, observes her observing ceremonial daggers, buys a key chain bearing an animal that looks part monkey, part ferret, part partridge — a favored local pet.

The loudspeaker voice whistles briefly. The televisions flip and flap, a cholera epidemic spreading toward the city, and the airline personnel assure everyone that their best bet now is staying put.

Groups are reconfigured: locals versus foreigners. There are hygiene-based accusations, a few punches thrown but none landed.

The children ignore this, chase one another through the wing, and one kicks at a carry-on. Both the child and the carry-on belong to locals, but from different parts of the city, and now the groups split into subgroups, the foreigners based on nationality, the locals based on neighborhood and therefore class. Each subgroup retreats into itself, then expands slightly, seeking more terrain; neither the Canadian nor the Bulgarian fit into any subgroup, and they keep their eyes down, their elbows firmly on their armrests.

More shrieking occurs, and some kickboxing, and a small amount of tae kwon do. It is the Belgians who have the first idea for a way to diminish the tension and pass the time: a congress followed by a pageant. Eyes are rolled, but all subsequent ideas are worse. Delegates are nominated, gather in the bookstore and hammer out agreements, square yardage assigned per capita, dotted borders drawn in masking tape. Magazines are shoplifted, and the bookstore manager flutters.

The pageant: middle-class locals drag the statue to one side, and each subgroup pools its makeup and clothes and advice. The women dress in the restrooms, fight for mirror space, angles, and light. Improvised sashes, Swiss judges, an Italian emcee; the vast gifts of the girl from Ghana deafen the crowd, swing each decision, and even so the Venezuelans protest.

Lunch is worrisome: restaurant prices have trebled and there is no ham to be found. Afterwards, children remove toys from bags. The boys have plastic soldiers, the girls have Barbie dolls, and they all play together at war. The dolls wear stiletto heels, are ten times the size of the soldiers, leave death and destruction in their wakes.

There is a new phenomenon, light seeming to sift through the fog that now appears thinner, striped, not entirely sure. The loudspeaker voice announces that the flight will be departing momentarily. The pilot and crew stride again into the lounge, they nod and wave, and applause floods the air.

Magazines are stowed and carry-ons are hefted, hands are shaken, and a line forms. The line lengthens, and yet there is no cutting in. The line arcs and straightens. The boarding-gate door is opened, then closed.

An upper-middle-class local child points out the window. The fog has thickened, darkened, grown more assured.

The pilot and crew stride again out of the lounge, and they do not nod, and they do not wave. The loudspeaker voice announces that the flight will be delayed momentarily. The subgroups sulk back to their territories. Children poke each other and cry.

An hour passes this way, and another hour, and another. The bookstore manager aligns his paperbacks. The fog surges, stalls, surges. The Mongolian boy comes to the accountant, asks what is in his briefcase, says that he hopes to be an accountant when he grows up, or else a matador, and then his mother calls and he runs away.

The old woman from Honduras champs and sighs and dreams of a pageant she once won, a pageant that never occurred, but it was wonderful, wonderful; she waved to the throng, thanked her father for his unwavering support, and the poet turns to the accountant.

"Would you happen to know —"

"No."

"I was only wondering —"

"It doesn't matter. The answer is no."

The Bulgarian shrugs, Afghanistan's longest river goes unnamed, and there is an explosion not far away; children fall and parents stumble, the lounge windows crack, ceiling tiles pinwheel through the air and dust pours into the wing, the lights go out and the televisions fall dark, there is shouting and screaming and hands clawing at necks and eyes.

Then there is the hum and grind of generators, and the electricity returns, and the passengers go still.

The loudspeaker voice requests that all available security guards and cleaning staff report immediately to their respective central workstations. Airline personnel run in medium-size circles. The passengers gather around the televisions that clatter and spark. They wait and wait and at last the answer comes: a small meteor has hit the main lobby.

It is not easy to believe, but the images are undeniable. Delegates meet at the boarding gate and reach no conclusions. Children kick one another. Restaurants run short of lettuce.

And now the airline personnel assure the passengers that there is no reason to panic, that while the number of dead and wounded is not yet known, there is no structural damage to Wing D, and the plane and runway and control tower are wholly intact, and it is therefore only a question of the fog lifting and then the flight will be on its way.

Passengers wander out to see the meteor and the damage, are met by armed guards and partitioning, wander back. The Honduran woman finds a large fuchsia bug crawling up her pant leg; it has nine eyes and twenty-two legs, reminds her of her mother's flower garden, and she squashes it with her fist. Bars run short of swizzle sticks, and then, improbably, gin.

The fog scurls. Toilets clog and garbage cans overflow. Darkness drops, the generators growl and fail, and the airline personnel regret that no additional blankets are available. The subgroups gather into themselves. The girl from Ghana dreams the roar of a thousand fontomfrom drums while across the lounge the accountant fights through a nightmare involving misconstrued negative amortization schedules.

In the morning there is still no electricity, and the subgroups curse and pace. There are accusations of theft — missing magazines, missing mints. The fog slackens, then stiffens, and at the masking-tape borders there are dark suggestions, darker looks.

The local delegates gather in a sloppy oval, announce that they have had enough, that they are going home, that they will break down the door if necessary, will walk across the tarmac and scale any fence and be free. The airline personnel insist that the flight will be departing at any moment. The locals gather their things. The airline personnel take a stand at the boarding gate. The locals push them aside, then hesitate: lined outside the door are a dozen armed soldiers standing shadowed and gray in the fog.

The locals look at the airline personnel. The airline personnel shrug and say that they have no idea either. The locals set down their things, gather again. The soldiers grimace and strut. The airline personnel wave the unit captain up to the glass, and words are passed, and the words are diffuse, something about a quarantine, but its cause is unclear: the word "virus" is heard, but what came before? AIDS? Space?

The locals froth. An hour passes angrily. The fog lifts eight inches, drops back down. The Bulgarian rereads an old poem in his notebook, contemplates adding an adverb, and the Belgians have another idea: an Olympiad.

Enough already, say the Dutch. And yet no better idea is brought forward. Judges are appointed, and passengers who belong to no subgroup are assigned to one now created: Other. A program is drawn up on stationery bought by the Saudis; the Americans want baseball, the Russians want volleyball, the Chinese want table tennis, and all are disappointed. The upper-lower-middle-class locals suggest that children ride their parents for the equestrian events. Synchronized swimming is exchanged for synchronized walking; water polo becomes carpet polo, and archery is replaced with Throw the Ball of Paper into the Garbage Can from Increasingly Great Distances. Winter events are ignored until the Norwegians threaten to boycott; then babies in strollers are called bobsledders, and curling is given pride of place and time.

Hog lines are drawn in chalk, brooms are taken from closets, wheeled carry-on bags replace rocks, and the Scottish skip's hammer is a double takeout draw for the gold. Next comes fencing, a question of umbrellas; then rowing occurs with baggage carts and mops, and the Australian coxless four is untouchable.

Dressage is won by a Chilean toddler when the Mongolian boy's father hashes a last-minute piaffe. Kenyans of course sweep the marathon, hours of quick circling; Cubans of course sweep the boxing. A Turk and a Greek meet in judo, half-middleweight the only division: the Greek has mastered the body drop, the naked strangle, and the inner thigh, but the Turk has mastered the sweeping hip, the scarf hold, and both the major inner and major outer reaps, thereby carrying the day and declaring the Cyprus question settled.

The Latvians are accused of doping, the Nigerians of bribery. A tenor from Surinam sings so that rhythmic gymnastics might flourish. Again there is a small amount of tae kwon do, the lower-upper-upper-class locals upsetting the Koreans to everyone's moderate surprise.

The members of Other are the Canadian, the Bulgarian, five stout young women who are not willing to say where they are from, an Orthodox priest from Ukraine, and a lawyer from Pakistan. They consistently come in fourth. The Canadian apologizes for his failure to hurdle more deftly, and his teammates tell him not to worry as long as he did his best, which they are sure he did.

The girl from Ghana blows him a kiss from the long jump pit, and the fog brindles and shies. The competition lasts until nightfall the following day. The medal ceremony is lighthearted yet dignified, and the medals donated by Duty Free are foil-wrapped chocolate coins that gleam in the low, gray light.

The members of Other admire their Participant ribbons. The

airline personnel announce that 19A is surely the greatest intact lounge in the entire airport. Free purple tea for everyone!

But in the morning: post-Olympic malaise. The five women announce that they will no longer be known as Other, that such marginalization will not be tolerated in this day, and this age. No one is listening. The restaurants and bars and cafés have run short of most things; what were meant to be in-flight meals are defrosted in the plane on the tarmac, brought and handed out. Spouses bitch to and at one another. Parents smack children, generally their own but not always. The Honduran woman snorts. Still there is no electricity; still the fog hangs.

The accountant gets up, walks past the girl from Ghana, stands looking out the window. The girl from Ghana smiles. The accountant sees the smile reflected in the cracked glass, turns, attempts conversation.

They discuss the man from New Guinea and the woman from Guinea-Bissau, unknown to each other until this wait, and the Ukrainian priest who now weds them; they discuss the man from Madrid and the woman from Warsaw, eight years of marriage, of bickering and contempt, and the Pakistani lawyer who draws up the papers for their divorce. They discuss the soldiers and the statue, the meteor and the fog. They do not, however, discuss their respective ex-spouses: warlord currently closing in, librarian currently dating a podiatrist.

A young Bolivian woman gives birth in the bookstore, the manager himself delivering, while in a restroom an old Kazakh man is bitten by a tiny blue snake — a species of viper says one local, a species of adder says another. The viper or adder escapes through a crack in the tile; the Kazakh dies and is buried in a planter. Then night swells. The priest agrees to swap seats with the accountant in exchange for a fountain pen. The accountant puts his arm around the girl, feels the thick, chaotic scars on her far shoulder, wonders; they slump together, sleep, snore not quite silently.

The next morning, again there are things to discuss: Cubans, for example. The Cubans are up to something. They have been gathered since well before dawn, whispering, and now are approaching each of the other subgroups, and whispering again. Finally one comes to where the accountant and the girl from Ghana sit.

"It is time," whispers their Cuban, a thin boy perhaps nine years old.

"Time for what?" says the accountant.

"Time to go."

"Go where?"

"To the plane."

"What for?"

"My uncle is a trained pilot. My cousin is a trained stewardess. We will fly the plane ourselves."

"But how do we know if the plane even has fuel? And what if mechanical difficulties occur? Have you considered the possibility of in-flight mechanical difficulties?"

"All possibilities have been considered. My aunt is a trained aircraft technician. My brother is a trained philosopher but has worked at a gas station."

"What about the quarantine?"

"It does not interest us."

"And the soldiers?"

"We do not think they will try to stop us once they see our determination."

"But if they do?"

"That will be unfortunate. Very, very unfortunate. It is the price that must be paid, however. You do not have to join us. We are not asking you to join us. You are welcome to join us if you wish, but you are also free not to join us, if that is your desire."

The girl from Ghana stands; the accountant catches her arm, shakes his head. She sits back down, watches as the Cubans are joined by a number of other passengers, all of them childless, all of them medalists: an ululating rhombus of discontent. The locals, too, have formed a rhombus, a separate and smaller rhombus; it appears that they intend to take advantage of the Cuban commotion, to escape across the tarmac and climb any fence as planned.

The soldiers' expressions are not clearly visible in the fog. The larger rhombus slides toward the boarding-gate door. The airline personnel attempt dissuasion, promising limitless purple tea, and also mauve tea, and even the rare chartreuse tea, if the Cubans and childless medalists will just have a little patience.

The larger rhombus shouts and charges, the smaller rhombus slips in behind, the boarding-gate door is broken down; shouts and flashes fill the fog, and it can only be imagined, some soldiers beaten to the ground, others crouched and firing, the running and falling, the gurgle of death, the scrambling and standing and running once again.

Another sound now, the sound of jet engines, and some of them have made it, a few Cubans, a few childless medalists must have made it! The accountant and the girl from Ghana hug each other and cry, ashamed of their cowardice, though thrilled for those who have triumphed. The scream of the engines dissipates, and surely the plane is trundling out to the runway; the scream returns, louder and louder and the plane must now be going airborne and then an explosion as loud as that of the meteor, and the brightest of muffled flashes, and in the light of that flash is a moment when all can just be seen: the plane has hit the control tower.

The accountant and the girl from Ghana hug each other again, and cry again, no longer thrilled or ashamed. They hold each other through the numb silence, and the shrieks, and the wailing, and the Mongolian boy stares from where he hides beneath his seat.

All eyes close for a time. When they open again, airline personnel are repairing the door, and soldiers are once more visible out the windows, though fewer of them and in some disarray. The remaining subgroups return to their territories, extend their boundaries, claim two seats per passenger.

There is no food or drink to be had in any bar, café, or restaurant; the remaining delegates gather, discuss, and ransack Duty Free. The spoils are distributed equitably, chocolate and champagne and cigarettes for all. Again the fog flares. The poet takes out his notebook, scribbles at length, hides the scribbling with his hand when the Honduran woman leans close, and now the airline personnel announce that they have good news: the Cubans and childless medalists took the wrong plane, and the remaining passengers' flight will be departing momentarily, just as soon as the fog lifts and the electricity is restored and the quarantine is ended and the control tower is rebuilt.

All of the women in the lounge begin menstruating simultaneously; a tampon is worth a bottle of champagne, then two bottles, then a case. The men of each subgroup huddle, discuss suicide. The cold has gone treacherous, and as darkness at last descends, all extra seats are destroyed for fuel. The bookstore is dismembered for kindling, the manager at first resisting, then remembering his insurance and standing aside. Each fire is tended gently, but in the morning there are new claims of theft — missing Marlboros, missing Kents.

The delegates meet desperately; the Belgian suggests a spelling bee and is beaten senseless. The girl from Ghana tells the Canadian that things will soon go bad, that she has been in similar situations, and always things go bad. She asks if he has any skills that might be useful.

"I'm a whiz at analyzing debenture impact on leverage."

"Anything else?"

"I've been known to make adequate preparations for balloon maturity."

Just then, on the far side of the wing, the Greek defeats the Turk at ticktacktoe, announces that the Cyprus question has been reopened. The Turk pushes the Greek. The Greek pushes the Turk. Sides are drawn up, only two of them now, and there is punching and kickboxing and tae kwon do, there is pinching and biting and scratching, the soldiers kick down the boarding-gate door, are attacked by passengers bearing burning armrests and broken bottles of Moët et Chandon, the girl from Ghana drags the accountant into a corner and lays herself across him, there is automatic weapons fire and the jolt of grenades, shouting and screams and then silence.

The girl from Ghana lifts her head. She asks the accountant if he is all right, and he says that he thinks he is. Together they stand. There is a gash in the girl's right forearm, and the accountant binds it with his scarf. Nothing else moves but dust. They walk through the lounge, and the statue of the boy with his cell phone and globular fruit is perfectly intact against the far wall, but all else is shattered glass, strangled soldiers, torn carpet, impaled passengers, broken brooms, disemboweled airline personnel.

The accountant stumbles over the Honduran woman, her neck bent obliquely. He closes her eyes and mouth, hears a slight moan to his left, and finds the poet bleeding from the chest, his bare feet burned black, tendrils of smoke extending from each toe.

"That is it," says the poet.

"What is what?"

"The smell of *kyufte* as it fries on the stove."

"But there is no *kyufte* here."

"There is. There must be. It can only be *kyufte*."

The accountant takes the poet in his arms, shakes his head, but then he knows: it is the smell of the poet's own charred flesh. He tells the Bulgarian that he is right, that it is *kyufte,* the finest *kyufte* ever fried, and the waiter will be arriving at any moment to serve them. The Bulgarian nods and dies. The accountant lays him down.

There is light and sputtering from many directions: the electricity has returned. The televisions declare that the national cricket team has finally gotten its new uniforms. The girl from Ghana finds another survivor, the Mongolian boy, and she brushes the glass from his hair and picks him up.

The loudspeaker voice clears its throat, announces that the departure of their flight will be delayed momentarily. There is a thump, and another, and the Mongolian boy points. The accountant and the girl from Ghana look. Something large and brown is smacking against the window frame.

They step to the boarding-gate door. Before them is a massive rattan basket hanging half a foot off the ground. Loose tethers writhe to either side. The balloon itself can barely be seen, a vast round dense yellow presence above them, and the basket slumps and settles as they watch.

"You told me that you are an expert with balloons," says the girl from Ghana.

"I — not balloon-balloons. Balloon maturity. It's —"

"Balloons are balloons. It is not a difficult thing."

"Right, but —"

"Owuraku."

"Well, be that as it may —"

"My ex-husband."

The accountant follows her eyes. Working toward them is a very tall, very black, heavily armed man whose expression oscillates between rage and despair. He searches from body to statue to bookstore. He glances at the boarding-gate door.

Now the girl from Ghana climbs into the basket, sets the Mongolian boy down, flips switches at random. The pilot light ignites. The girl from Ghana reads labeling, fires the burner, looks at the accountant. From deep in the fog comes a voice shouting about the difference between hands on and light hands on. The warlord is now pacing toward the door.

The accountant climbs in, and the Mongolian boy comes to stand beside him. The girl from Ghana tosses ballast. The basket begins to lift. The accountant tells the boy that there is nothing to be afraid of, taps at the gauges for the pyrometer, the altimeter, and the variometer, wonders what they signify and hopes they are not important.

The warlord appears at the door. The accountant reels in the tethers. The warlord screams and falls and begs. The air smells of *kyufte.* The basket rises into the cold, wet gray, and the warlord weeps, aims, fires, misses, beautifully.

STELLAR KIM

Findings & Impressions

FROM THE IOWA REVIEW

MY FIRST GLIMPSE of her was of a single small breast. Flashed on the x-ray screen. Lit in contrast. A hint, just a bump of fatty tissue against the chest cavity. Next to it, its close twin. Asymmetrical like most women's breasts. A far cry from spectacular.

Straninsky, Alicia: the way her name first appeared to me, across a computerized label on her medical chart. A name that brought back memories of my Polish grandmother stuffing pierogis with thick fingers, the faint smells of the Baltic Sea that wafted from her sweaters, the way she swayed her hips as she sang, "*Hej, górale, nie bijcie siÿ. Ma góralka dwa warkocze podzielicie siÿ!*"

Other information I learned: Age 32; Single; No history of breast irregularities; No children; Allergies to penicillin.

What I saw: The usual striations indicating a buildup of calcium.

What I also saw: Just past the spiculated masses of microcalcification, something that fanned out to form a white mass. An uneven density in the left quadrant of the right breast.

About cancer: Mention this word, and people talk about randomness, about mystery. But the guesswork is mostly in why it forms. Once it hits you, charting the course of the disease is pretty much a matter of exact science, despite the runaround health professionals will give, despite the stories of miraculous recoveries. Even as a radiologist, I can predict who'll make it and who'll be a goner and it is of little surprise when the condemned grow weaker with each visit and then simply stop showing up.

Where I've been wrong: It still stuns me to see the eighty-two-year-old World War II vet who shuffles in every six months, his steps made small by the humongous growth on his hipbone the doctors left him to carry to his grave three years ago. Then there was the soccer player, a sixteen-year-old with more muscles in her calves than most men could flex in the length of their legs. She should've fallen into the category of healthy children who recover largely unscathed from acute lymphoblastic leukemia. She came in every few months with a flock of friends, their heads shaven in solidarity. They practically sprinted into the office, death for them a thing too distant even in a hospital basement. But in less than a year, the slippery thing in her bones had burrowed its way into her head and her brain began to swell and then she wobbled in, first on a cane, and then a walker, even its four legs not proving sturdy enough for her trembling hands. Her mother stopped calling for appointments and then, when a year passed, I had the intern call her doctor and move her files to one of the cabinets marked DECEASED.

What a radiologist does: Nick, my seven-year-old, periodically asks me to explain. I look at pictures of sick people, I tell him. There are the one-timers: fractures, sprains, chest x-rays for pneumonia. But mostly, I search for benign tumors, lesions, and cancer. I suggest biopsies to seal diagnoses. I look for patterns of tissue density. The skill of a radiologist is in determining what's harmless and what'll have to be cut out or irradiated.

For years, I haven't been able to sleep with a woman without subjecting her to thorough analysis. I poke in the usual spots and work three fingers in circular motion. My onetime wife, good Lillian with her sense of humor, would offer me her breasts, cupping them while I searched for sinister growth under her soft skin.

What I failed to diagnose: The slickness of the roads in an intense April rain, the impatience of Baltimore drivers after a 17–20 loss by the Ravens against the Titans in overtime, the sudden, illogical curvature of I-95 near the Russell Street ramp, Lillian's eyes fatigued after filing another late-night report for the WXIP eleven o'clock news. How easy it must've been for her to sink into the plush leather seat, to let her eyes glaze over the sea of red brake lights, to let her mind settle onto the party for Nick's third birthday, how effortlessly the impact would've crushed her beautiful skull.

I should've been prepared for: The cruelty of grief.

For months, Nick looked for Lillian on the evening news. When he saw Lillian's replacement — an eerily close copy of my wife with shoulder-length blond hair, he yelled, *Mommy!* pointing to the TV. *Mommy!* he demanded several times a day, often just as I'd gathered enough focus to vacuum or wash a load of laundry. I took the boy through the talk, telling him of the changing seasons, of molting snakes, of butterflies and cocoons, of how everything that lives must die. I took him down to the river where we'd said goodbye to what could be salvaged of Mommy, and finally when the boy couldn't be made to understand, I turned on the TV night after night, putting him to sleep with his digital mom. *Say goodbye to Mommy,* I'd say when he struggled to keep his eyes open until the end of the newscast, and he'd wave a chunky, sleepy hand to Linda Jones of WXIP. When he kissed his surrogate mother good night, his thin hair turned all static.

Maybe I took the easy way out. *Tell Mommy you love her,* I encouraged. And he'd babble incomprehensible reviews of his day and declare all kinds of love and ask for promises impossible to keep.

After a few months, he asked with a tired voice one Saturday morning, *When is Mommy coming home?* And I said, doing my best to look him straight in his eyes, *She can't leave the TV, my little man.* I called him what Lillian would when he'd done something exceptionally good for her, like pouring milk into her cereal long before she'd sat down at the table or offering half-melted M&M's from his palm.

Nick began to look for Lillian inside the TV. He clawed at it with pink fingers.

What friends suggested: Get out there again. Married friends, especially, said with feigned enthusiasm, "One of us has to keep this interesting." They flattered me, called me Sean the Man. Lady Killer Miller. They envied my brief relationship with a part-time lingerie model. But after the accident, they held their wives closer.

Transition into relationships: It sounded doable, almost. But there seemed no clear end to grief and the beginning of happiness. I expected the fluttering of the heart on first dates. I allowed myself to turn into a romantic. I put on freshly ironed shirts. I spritzed cologne and felt for butterflies in my stomach. But even with Tanya, even after sex with a model, the kind of sex that made me shudder with force, something would creep up — an image, a recollection of a graze, the way Lillian and I giggled like teenagers after making loud love into the pillow to keep Nick from waking — and, always, it would make me turn my back in a heavy way while Tanya stroked my back and said she understood, that I should talk to somebody about loss, about starting anew.

When Alicia Straninsky appears: She surprises me by coming in person to pick up the CT report. Normally, I send these off directly to the doctors. I'm surprised to see that Alicia's shockingly short — only about five feet tall. But more than that, I'm unprepared to see so much vitality. Her cheeks are ruddy in a way that must make her seem permanently embarrassed. She looks like she might never have stretched out properly from a child's portly body. She has substantial arms and legs, like those of hefty old women who can chop wood and move a refrigerator. Something about her smells vaguely like cinnamon. All I can think is, I've never seen a chubby woman with small breasts.

"Did you have a question, miss?"

"Yes. I'd like this explained."

No patient has questioned me on my reports. The normal course of things involves a statement of my findings and impressions. I make recommendations, suggest checkups. I make no promises and no advisements. So-and-so has been diagnosed with terminal brain cancer, I write in my reports. It's the oncologists who'll talk to newly retired couples about debilitating therapies. It is they who are left to explain to teary-eyed parents why modern medicine could not save their children.

But Alicia reads over my report, right in front of me. Although I forget my brother's birthday and seldom call the parents of Nick's playmates by their correct names, I can mouth along with every word Alicia reads.

Findings: Malignant tumor with diameter measuring 5 cm in the lower left quadrant of right breast. Infiltrating ductal carcinoma, grade 3. Metastatic carcinoma involving two of thirteen axillary lymph nodes. No nipple involvement noted. No indication of abnormal growth in the contralateral breast.

Impressions: Stage III invasive carcinoma of the breast.

"So what does this mean?" Alicia asks, her cheeks impossibly pinker than before.

"You'll have to talk to your doctor."

"You're an MD, right?" she asks, and I tell her this is true.

"It's Friday. You're going to make me wait all weekend? Monday's a holiday."

I agree with her again. There's something about that face, a certain helplessness that inexplicably reminds me of Nick after he's dropped his ice cream cone. I'm not sure why I give in, but I explain the major thrust of the pathology report and wait a minute for her to digest this. Nothing changes in her expression. All she says is, "How can you be so sure? Just from pictures?"

"And from your biopsy."

"I see. The little needle can tell all this?"

"That's right."

"In my ducts?"

"That's where it often starts."

"I guess I'm never breastfeeding."

"Do you have children?"

"No. But I guess this rules that out."

"Not necessarily. You should talk to your doctor."

After a while, she says, "So what does this mean, though? I mean, what are my prospects here?"

"You have to talk to your doctor. He can tell you better what to do from here."

"Right. I don't suppose I can ask that of you. Thanks. It was kind of you to explain this."

A week passes. I don't think about Alicia, but I do pull into work each morning with some vague anticipation.

When she next appears: "Hey," Alicia says to me, a woman with a yellow parka pulled over her head. I'm returning from lunch and had broken into a jog because I've forgotten my umbrella at the restaurant. "You're the radiologist."

"Hi," I reply before I recognize her. She has the same ruddiness in the cheeks, but dressed in yellow, she looks like one of the plastic ducks I use to lure Nick into the bath.

"About to go in for my first radiation," she says. "You were right, I guess. I got something in there that's not good news."

"Good luck to you," I say, and then wonder what more appropriate, reassuring things might be expected from someone with years of medical training.

"What's the deal with these hospitals? They have a different person doing every part of your treatment. I thought I'd be seeing you, but I see a radiologist who just does radiation oncology?"

"That's right. We're all one-trick ponies, I guess."

She doesn't laugh. I catch a glimpse of a cigarette between her fingers.

"You know, you should give those up."

She offers me one and says, "It's only ex-smokers who say things like that. You born-agains."

There's nothing for me to say. We let the soft patter of the rain do our work. I try to keep my lungs from burning as I inhale hard on the damp Camels.

When I pull out of the parking lot at the end of the day, the rain has died down, leaving a general mist. I recognize Alicia right away. Her yellow parka is bright even through the haze. She's sitting at the bus stop, a newspaper folded under her to absorb the rainwater.

"Alicia," I call out. It takes her a minute to realize where the voice is coming from. She spots my open window and stares hard, squints. She walks over and ducks her head toward me, keeping herself well within running distance. "It's Sean, the radiologist." It's odd to identify myself this way.

"Hi," she says, not moving.

"It's raining. Where're you headed?"

"Home. Morrell Park," she adds.

"I'm driving that way," I offer, but she gives no response. "Well, jump in if you want."

Alicia enters slowly, planting herself squarely in the seat before swinging her legs in. We drive out of the lot and into traffic in silence until it occurs to me to ask about her treatment.

"You feeling okay?"

"It wasn't as bad as they say. Although your first time's supposed to be the easiest."

"That's what they say."

I follow her sparse directions, and when I pull up to a block of row houses, she says, "This is good" in front of a fading tan unit. We sit in silence, staring ahead.

"Nice house."

"There's not that much inside. I just moved down here. I'd planned on fixing it up a bit."

"Looks fine to me as is," I say. She catches me watching a torrent of water bypass a gutter that hangs broken off the roof. She presses her lips, trying to suppress a laugh.

"Feel better," I manage to mutter.

"Thanks," she says, and I'm not sure if she means this for the ride or the failed compliment.

The second time she comes in: Alicia takes me by surprise because it's been only weeks since her last exam. On the form, I see she's scrawled, next to CHANGES SINCE LAST EXAM, "subcutaneous mastectomy." And indeed, her breast has been scooped out, sparing her nipple but leaving her with even less tissue than before. Still, this is enough flesh to require routine monitoring.

"How've you been?" I ask, unable to make the moment less awkward, this attempt at exchanging pleasantries before I crush the remainder of her breasts between glass plates. She's clutching the back of the thin hospital gown, making laborious efforts to keep its ends together.

I help Alicia position one breast at a time onto the bottom plate. "Sorry. It'll be cold," I warn her. I switch on the machine and let the compressor do its work. In the end, I have to manually squeeze the plates to spread the meager amount of fat across the glass. She takes it heroically, wincing briefly. Other women, big-busted women for whom this is a less painful process, yell and curse.

"You know, it might be easier, it'd hurt less if you came in when you're not so tender. The week after your menstruation," I say as I help her retie her gown.

"Thank you."

"You might be sore today. If it gets really bad, take a Tylenol." I prepare my patients for everything. Everything except how the disease itself will ravage them.

There were no ways to prep Nick for the mourning. Lillian simply didn't come home one night; there was no process to his mother's dying. Each year, on Nick's birthday, we go to the Patapsco to visit Lillian on the anniversary of her river burial. Afterwards, we go for cheeseburgers and I buy Nick the works, everything off the menu. Last year, he asked between bites, "So she's just swimming around?"

This took me by surprise, and I had to sip my soda for a while before I could formulate an answer. "Mom never wanted to be boxed in."

"Dad." He didn't say anything until he had my full attention again. "Can I have my ashes spread?"

"Hey, that's no way for a boy to talk," I said sternly. When the waitress came around, I ordered us banana splits. I even insisted on brownies — Nick's favorite.

When Nick asks *Why did Mommy have to go away?* I have no reasons to give him. I command him to take a bath and go to sleep. I watch his pajama legs disappear down the hall and wonder how even his walk could be like that of the mother he couldn't possibly remember in physical detail. I can hardly look at him when he stands with the sun slanting onto his head, his hair a shade like Lillian's.

After I buried Lillian, I found I couldn't get rid of even the things I'd sworn I hated. The dog that pissed on the couch reminded me of Lillian showing up one day with the terrier, saying, "She's lost. Look, no tags," as if that were all the explanation needed. The potpourri she'd introduced to the bathroom I could not throw away even after it had disintegrated to red dust. The miniature toys lined on the windowsill were reminders of our trip to Belgium, where, instead of cerise and framboise, we ate too many egg-shaped chocolates that opened to reveal plastic surprises. I'd had to move to another part of the city just so Lillian would not pop up suddenly while I was on line at the supermarket, show her face in the bathroom mirror as I shaved, slip her way to the side of the bed at night as I willed myself to sleep.

The routine we've fallen into: I see Alicia every week now. Since Radiation Oncology is next to my office, I drive her home. It's no way for a weak woman to travel, waiting for a public bus, inhaling exhaust, and pushing through the crowd for a seat. She thanks me profusely.

They've stepped up her treatment so that in addition to the radiation, she's on chemotherapy. She's thinning out, not so much in her torso, but in unexpected places like her neck and elbows. Her ankles and knees look like skin coming loose.

Since I won't take money for gas, Alicia insists on stopping for coffee and muffins, though she usually doesn't buy anything for herself. As the summer progresses, we drive to the harbor. She's from Chicago and says the ocean opens her lungs up. The chemo makes her skin turn a dry brown in the sun, and so we sit in the car and roll down the windows and breathe in the ocean. These are not dates. But when there is the protection of clouds, we walk along the water and eat ice cream. Later, when she becomes too weak, we sit in the car and watch joggers and bicycles zip by.

I wonder if Lillian's traveled this far, or if she's already passed out of the Atlantic, floated down to the Caribbean Sea. Things have an odd way of traveling in open water. Perhaps the bits of Lillian have swum their way to all parts of the world. I'd once read about toy ducks that fell off a freighter container and all over South America, Northern Europe, and Africa, beachgoers found armies of smiling yellow ducks bobbing in over the surf and nesting among the sea-gulls.

"What did you do in Chicago?" I ask Alicia as the early evening strollers begin to descend en masse.

"You name it. I've done it. I was a nanny. I worked as a secretary to a pervert. I walked a herd of dogs for yuppies. You know Ann Sathers?"

"The cinnabuns?"

"I worked in the factory."

"Really?"

"Quality assurance. I ate a lot of cinnabuns."

I wonder if that's why she still smells like cinnamon.

On days when Alicia is well enough, she's famished. Today, she wants hot dogs. "You can't deny food to a woman who has cancer!" She has no qualms about playing the sympathy card. She piles on mustard and ketchup and then sauerkraut on two franks. "Ketard! Get it?" she jabs me with a weak elbow and I let out a small laugh. She's chewing grape gum — something that she says helps her nausea — and from time to time, I catch flashes of purple between teeth and tongue.

"Where's your little boy?" she asks as we sit down at a bench table. "I mean, when you're not watching him. Is there somebody who takes care of him?" She spits out the gum into her hands and I can't focus on anything because I'm wondering what she's done with it. I'm tempted to duck my head under the table to see if she's playing with it between her fingers.

"Where there're colleges, there're babysitters," I say, and she seems satisfied.

"So I'm freezing my eggs. Do you think it'll work? It's still not a sure thing, but you can conserve them. You know, fertilize them later. A lot of women on chemo are doing it now."

"That's a smart thing to do."

"They basically drain the eggs out of you and keep them floating in liquid nitrogen."

"That sounds splendid. Sounds like one of Nick's science projects."

"Your son must be great. Kids are great."

"Most of the time."

"I thought I'd have plenty of time to have kids."

I'm not sure how to respond, and when she sees me just staring at the water, she says, "I had chances to, you know?" She smiles. "Shit happens, as they say."

Alicia chews hungrily, only intermittently bothering to wipe the orange mix of ketard from the corners of her mouth. There's something admirable in her embrace of joy, however temporary. Even if it will make her sick, even if in two hours she could throw it all up, she won't be denied satiation.

When I tell Alicia about Tanya, she's amazed. We're comparing our biggest bragging rights. She says she once guessed the number of jellybeans in a giant jar and won two thousand dollars, and I come back with, I once dated a woman who made a living in bra and panties. She wants pictures of her. "You're bullshitting," she says. "That's the oldest lie in the book."

For the next week, I search for Tanya in Macy's flyers. She modeled regularly for their lingerie section, and now she's apparently moved on to modeling business suits for them.

"You're kidding," Alicia says when I hand her the clipped flyer. Today, we've driven to a different pier to watch the late afternoon sun paint the bay in shifting colors of emerald green and pink.

"I'm not a pictures guy."

She flashes a smile. "A true romantic. Wow. Is that her?"

"It wasn't a big deal."

"Gosh. I've never looked like that in my life." With the dramatic weight loss, Alicia's deep-set eyes seem to burrow toward the back of her head. Her thinning hair is now brassy. She leafs through the rest of the flyer. "This is depressing. I've never been in a dress that resembles anything like these, you know?"

"What do you mean?"

"You know, I've never felt — pretty. Like one of those girls with perfect hair and skin. The kind that know how to flirt with guys." She catches me open and close my mouth, fishing for something to say. "The only good thing about getting sick is I'm finally skinny."

"I remember," she continues when I don't respond, "I went to the prom with a family friend my mother basically strong-armed into taking me. Mortifying, right? Well, I thought, hey, I'll make the best of it. I'll at least get a nice black dress. I thought those were so elegant. So royal. But of course the only thing that fit me and I could afford was this puffy magenta thing. It made me look like a giant cherry! I spent half the night in the bathroom. I just wanted to disappear down the toilet."

"Don't talk like that," I say, and Alicia looks at me with some expectation. "Don't ever think that again. You're beautiful," I add after a while.

The way her face opens up, the way Alicia's eyes become liquid, suddenly make even the possibility of her disappearance unbearable. I think, maybe I've never realized the possible permutations of beauty.

For her birthday, Alicia has decided to throw herself a backyard barbecue party. She's insisted I come with Nick. *I'd love to meet your son, and there'll be other kids,* she urged. She's set up an inflatable pool and a trampoline.

When we get there, the only kids I see are infant twins. There're fewer than ten people, all neighbors. Alicia emerges from the kitchen with a tray of hot dogs. She has on a sundress and a wide-brimmed hat. She's wearing makeup, and she smiles at me with two lines of thin red lips. For the first time, I notice freckles that fan out from one ear to the other.

"Hey there," she says when Nick hands her a bouquet of flowers. "Aren't you just a charmer! Well, I heard you like brownies. Guess what we're making!" She lets Nick mix the batter. He licks his fingers while Alicia clowns around, smearing chocolate on his cheeks. They turn on the oven light and watch the brownies rise.

While we eat, Nick has his run of the yard. He does impossible jumps on the trampoline. "Wonderful," Alicia says. "It must be wonderful having him in your life. We should do this more. My nephews are back in Chicago. I miss having kids around." She lights a cigarette. "I don't know why I've put my life on hold for so long. You know, now it's like I don't want to waste another minute. I'm doing all these things I've always wanted to do, because what am I waiting for? Carpe diem."

"What kinds of things?" I ask.

"Oh, the South Pacific. I've been watching these travel videos. I've always wanted to go there."

"What else?" I ask. I don't imagine even she can see herself getting on a long plane ride anytime soon.

"Well, getting involved with somebody, I guess." She crushes her cigarette under her sandals. "So how come you never moved on? You know, really moved on? I mean, do you ever think Nick would want someone in his life again?"

As if summoned by his mention, Nick runs up to us, asking Alicia to jump with him on the trampoline. "Oh, Nick, I don't know if I can do that," she says. "But do you want to watch videos? Have you been to an island where there're pirates?" Nick stops talking and his eyes widen. "You know what they have in the South Pacific? Cocoa trees. That's where chocolates come from." From the confusion on his face, I see Nick can't imagine chocolate that isn't wrapped in foil. "I'm planning to go there. Maybe we can all go together if your dad lets you. Would you like that?" she asks with a wink.

On the drive back, Nick recounts the ways in which he loves Alicia. *I like her pool. I like her jumping thing,* he says. *She's the best brownie maker.* "Can we come play next Saturday?" he pleads.

"Maybe, Nick."

"She said I can come over anytime."

"We'll see about that."

"Why do we have to see?" he asks in a voice like a goat's bleat. I see in the rearview mirror his eyes begin to tear.

What three-month checkups reveal: In the fall, Alicia comes in for her exam, cheerful as though she were only stopping by for a social visit.

"I'm having another get-together this weekend," she says, sliding up to me while I help a patient with his forms. I tell her that things are too busy and she says, "Okay, sure," but she lingers. "Another time then?" she asks when the assistant comes to lead her away.

She doesn't seem a bit embarrassed while the intern helps her at the machine. She doesn't cringe as the stranger's hands shift her breasts now here and then there. It's the response of a woman whose body has become a thing of science, who's stripped repeatedly for doctors and nurses and technicians. Her body has been poked at, argued about by oncologists, examined with cold instruments, described only in clinical terms. I catch a glimpse of her bra as she redoes her gown. It's a white cotton thing. No frills. No contraptions to lift and push together. Plain as day.

I stand over the technician as he processes her pictures. I want to shut my eyes when a new mass comes to life, because there it is, in her thigh, a stubborn growth that has planted despite the dual attacks by radiation and chemicals.

I file an updated report: Distant osteolytic metastasis to femur in left leg.

What I want to tell her: You should be spared. If I had the power to rip this thing out of you, if only I could sieve the little cells of poison swimming around in your lymph and blood.

What's ahead: Bone pain. And the slow perforation of the skeleton.

I call to tell her the news myself. She says, "Give it to me straight, doc."

"Don't call me that."

"Okay, Sean. Lay it on me. Tell me how bad it's gonna be."

"It's spread." There's no way to soften the blow. "It's gone into your bones."

"I see."

"You'll probably have to increase the treatment. I called your doctor already. This isn't uncommon. They have medicines for every complication." I let myself believe what my patients often say: that fighting cancer is 99 percent mental.

"You're a sweetie. Give my love to Nick. I'd love to see him again."

What I withhold from her: Only 10–20 percent make it at this stage. After the leg, the cancer will wind its way to the pelvis. Then: to the lungs and then shortness of breath. Next: the liver. Her skin will yellow and become puffy. There'll be an unprecedented loss of weight until finally, Alicia will not be able to eat. Then: the brain.

With her new treatment, I can't drive Alicia home because she's in and out by the early afternoon. But when I catch glimpses of her in the hospital, I see there's a definite yellowness to her face. The roundness of her cheeks is gone. Her skin, darkened by the chemicals pumped into her body, is dry. It reminds me of cracked African earth after years of drought.

Today, she has a fantastic green scarf on her head. She looks like some odd goddess heralding the spring, except there's no trace of vitality about her anymore. We comment on the rain and she jokes about her hair falling out.

"Positive attitude's the cure, right?" she asks.

"That's the key."

"Hey, how about a ball game sometime? Nick would like that, wouldn't he?"

"We should do that," I say, my tone betraying the conviction of my words.

Alicia lets out a small laugh. "Sean," she says. "Did I do something? I mean, I thought we were all getting along great."

"It's not that."

"What is it then?"

I let a minute pass while we walk down the hall. After a few paces, she says, "C'mon, I can handle it."

"It's just that," I say, then can't finish.

"What is it just?" She stares, unflinching. "What?" she asks more sharply.

"It's Nick. He latches on."

She scrutinizes my face, waiting for more explanation, and I have to look away. "I don't want to hurt him again." The resolution of my voice surprises me.

"Oh. I see." She twirls the ends of her scarf. "Ah, now I got you."

"Alicia." I reach to touch her arm but she shies away.

"No, that's all right. It's all right." We've reached the hospital exit, and she peers out the glass doors, checking the rain outside. "See you around," she says. When she walks away, all she leaves is a muddy boot print.

*

Months later, I'm woken up by a call.

"This is Ed. I'm Alicia Straninsky's ex," a deep voice announces.

"Ex?"

"Husband. Geez. Did I wake you? I didn't think you'd be sleeping."

"No, no." I start to explain how I've been working late hours. "Is she okay?" I manage to mumble. I can't find my glasses.

"Not quite. She's had a fall, doc. She broke her hip. You were listed on her emergency contact form."

I put on my glasses and the room comes into sudden focus. "Husband?" I ask in a more clear tone.

"Well, from years ago."

I wouldn't know it's sleeting except the minute I'm out of the car, my wet clothes freeze onto my skin. I don't even remember turning on the wipers.

In the emergency room, the nurse points me to Ed, a man considerably older than Alicia. A woman in her twenties is holding his hand. Ed has a scruffy look like most people here, but with him, it seems possible that even without an emergency, he might look exactly this way. His hair is a nest of dark brown and he's wearing a Black Sabbath T-shirt with PARANOID written across his chest. The shirt is tattered in unexpected places: near the bellybutton, on his upper arm, by the clavicle. He shakes my hand vigorously and thanks me.

"How's she doing?"

"We haven't been told anything, except to wait." The young woman nods her head. She can't be more than a college kid.

"I wish she'd told me. I had no idea." Ed scratches his head for a long time. "Thank God she still had me on the forms. We made each other health proxies, but that's when we were married. That's Alicia for you. Good with planning. Not so good with the follow-through."

We make small talk. Ed teaches sociology. He and Alicia were married for less than a year. He wanted children. She didn't. We chat about the weather.

"It's not my business, I suppose, but I thought you were her doctor. I wouldn't have woken you. It said Dr. Sean so I thought we'd better call you."

"Well, I'm her radiologist."

"I see," Ed says, looking puzzled. "Like you take her x-rays?"

When we're finally taken to see Alicia, she's lying with a pillow between her legs. They'll take her into surgery, reconnect her hips with screws. "Oh, hi," she says, not directed at either of us. She looks to Ed and says, "Good to see you," and waves to me. "I can't believe you both are here," she says shyly, as if we've thrown her some surprise party.

Ed fills her in on the new college where he teaches. I show them pictures of Nick in his Halloween costume. *So it takes a little boy to make you a pictures guy,* Alicia says. I stay to help Ed with the forms, but leave before they wheel Alicia back, still fractured, in pain, held up with metal. I've never known how to say a proper goodbye.

In March, Alicia is back to check for more distant metastasis. She comes in in a wheelchair. Even seated, she seems barely capable of holding up her weight. Her lips are pale and cracked. Her breathing is labored for the brief time we chat. She asks if Nick is well and I say we should go to the harbor sometime, grab hot dogs. *Sure,* she says, emptily. Later, Alicia waves a wan hand and mouths a soft *Bye.* I pretend I'm busy with paperwork and nod a quick acknowledgment. *Heartless,* we call oncologists who abandon the patients they cannot save. *Cowards,* we say of husbands who flee rather than see their wives suffer. I place the x-ray vest too hard on a fifty-five-year-old man who's come in for a pelvic exam. I shuffle through his charts with some force.

What would otherwise be a perfect day: When the second call comes from Ed, it's a beautiful, dry June day. Nick has agreed to try a baseball day camp and I'm plotting the rest of our summer — Little League, season tickets behind the dugout at Camden Yards, and a trip to Hershey Park where Nick can discover chocolate heaven. It's been weeks since he's asked about Alicia. There is no hint of humidity, no heavy rains, and I sit in my car and wait patiently for the traffic to thin out from the afternoon game. In all of Baltimore, it's a perfectly ordinary day.

I see Ed in the hospital ward, next to a young woman rubbing his shoulders. I can't be sure it's the same girlfriend from the winter. He gets up to shake my hand. He's a broken man.

"Thanks for coming. I know she would've wanted you here. She considered you a friend. She didn't really have a network here."

His eyes fill with tears. The girlfriend strokes his arm and Ed holds up a hand to signal that he's okay. "Anyway, you were on the short list. Told you she was organized. There was a sort of phone chain. Well, she didn't know that many people. I have no fucking idea how these things work," he says, waving an arm over the empty corridor. There's the distinctive odor of antiseptic, evidence of eradication, of something made absent.

For days, I take the long way from the basement elevator to my office, knowing she's somewhere in the morgue's drawers smelling of all kinds of noxious chemicals.

The memorial the night before the burial is a New Age thing arranged by Ed. It's not an open casket event, but I'm still surprised to see there isn't even a coffin, no photos of Alicia as a kid or smiling with Ed in healthier days.

Ed has asked everyone to bring things that remind them of Alicia. I couldn't settle on anything, and on the way over, bought a cheese Danish when I couldn't find a cinnamon bun. A woman walks up to the lectern holding an almanac. "Alicia was all brains," she says rather gravely, and people clap. A man produces a bamboo stick and says, "Alicia was all strength." Another woman waves a copy of *To Kill a Mockingbird.* "For our stubborn tomboy," she says to a room that breaks out in laughter. I hold on to my Dunkin' Donuts bag while people shoot me curious looks.

When the ceremony is over, Ed is surrounded by people extending condolences. He spots me and says, "Ah, the good doc. Great that you made it."

"Wouldn't have missed it. Nice event. I mean, you know, for what it is." We let a soundless minute pass while Ed nods to several people. "No pictures?"

"Alicia wanted it this way. She was never showy. Never thought she was much to look at."

"Is there anything I can do?" I ask.

"No, no. You've done so much already. Thank you."

Outside, I cool my temple against the window of the Camry as car after car turns on its lights and winds its way out of the parking lot. Ed catches me as I'm about to turn the keys in the ignition. He angles his head in. "Actually, Sean, could you do me this one big favor? I've been going nuts here. Her mom is flying in and then her cousins are coming, and of course I have to pick them all up. Since you live in the neighborhood, would you mind dropping this off at the funeral home in the morning? It's her clothes."

"Anything to help."

Then, as if remembering something, he blurts, "Can you believe her mother didn't come to the memorial? She thinks we're hippies, I suppose. That's Mrs. Straninsky for you. She hated me, that despicable old woman," he says with a distant look.

"Don't worry. I got it, Ed."

"Yes, tomorrow, if you can go to the Funeral King, it'd be great." He hands me a shopping bag.

The end of the college semester has sneaked up on me, and I can't find a babysitter for the weekend. I drive to the Morell Park Funeral Home with Nick asleep in the back seat. It's a stately Gothic Revival manor, a castlelike structure that sits on acres of manicured gardens and reflecting pools. The funeral director is a colorful man widely known as the Funeral King, in part because he holds a monopoly on the burial business, and because he appears in TV ads promising, "We treat your loved ones like royalty."

It takes a long while before the Funeral King himself answers the bell.

"I'm sorry for your loss," he says in a deep voice.

"Thank you." I hand over the bag. "This is for Ms. Straninsky."

"Ah. Lady Straninsky. Come in, come in, please." I walk a few steps into the parlor and point to Nick in the car. We watch Nick press his mouth against the window and puff his cheeks out like a blowfish. "I'm sorry, you're . . ."

"Her radiologist. I was also a friend. Is she . . ." I begin to mutter but can't stomach the thought that she's steps away in the basement on some cold, metal table, her body drained of its fluids and her face powdered and rouged to an obscene color.

"She's almost ready," the Funeral King says, placing a hand on my arm. "She's comfortable now."

I think of how comfortable she might have been in her last days. I wonder whether Ed would've known to increase the pain medication only as needed to maximize its numbing effect. I wonder whether he would've soaked her feet in warm water, changed her sheets twice a day, massaged her sores, made her final moments somehow bearable. In her last week, she would've been incapable of communicating her most basic wishes — a shave of ice for her dry mouth, another drop of morphine, the need to be shifted in bed every few hours to relieve the pressure of one limb pressing on another. It should've been me there to listen for the mysterious rhythm of her final breaths.

"She's almost ready," the Funeral King says in a soothing baritone, his voice seeming to travel to me from somewhere far away. "I'll just make sure that everything's here." He ruffles through the bag. "Well, actually, you seem to have forgotten her . . . undergarments. Don't worry," he says when I stare, puzzled. "You're not the first. It's usually the thing people will forget." He opens the bag for me to examine. There's a white hat and gloves, along with a blue dress — a real '50s outfit. I wonder if Ed is out of his mind. There are even nylon stockings, but no underwear. "We usually keep some extras around, but I'm sorry, we've been so busy and this is really cutting it close. If you wouldn't mind just bringing some of her garments, we can take care of everything." He anticipates my objection. "I would suggest, there is a mall a mile or so away. Don't worry," he says again. I must've looked terrified then. "This happens all the time."

In the Victoria's Secret, Nick tries to don a giant pair of angel wings. "Oh, honey," a flustered saleswoman yells, "those wings aren't for playing." Then she turns in my direction. The smell of her perfume hits me before she reaches me.

I apologize and she says with a broad smile, "All the kids love that. Are you looking for anything in particular?"

"Yes, I'm looking for underwear. And bras."

"Sure."

"It should be something special."

"Of course." She eyes Nick, who is now tugging the arm of a teddy bear that's part of a display. I make a face at him to stop.

"No. Something very special. For a beautiful woman."

"Well, we have many special things. We have these of course," she says, holding up a thong. "These are very popular."

"We need something classy."

"Is there a specific color you had in mind?"

"Let's see. Her dress is blue."

"Well, how about this in royal blue?" She holds up a modest set of satin underwear. "Classy but beautiful. It's what she's wearing." The saleswoman points to a large poster of a thin, voluptuous model she explains is Brazilian. "Quite stunning," she says to herself. I buy the set and have her throw in the straps the model sports that seem to do nothing but connect her stockings to her underwear. "Practical and elegant," the saleswoman admires. "Would you like some body lotion? It's called Amazon Goddess. It smells like the rainforest." I want to ask if she's ever smelled the rainforest, but I purchase a small bottle anyway.

I think, For one day, Alicia, you will be the princess of Morrell Park, of ketard on hot dogs, of small breasts.

ARYN KYLE

Allegiance

FROM PLOUGHSHARES

ON HER FIRST DAY at the American school, Glynnis's class dissects earthworms. At her old school, the fourth-graders dissected cow eyes that came delivered in a plastic jug. But here, the worms aren't delivered. After lunch, the class has to find their own worms in the mud outside, then rinse them off in the bathroom sinks. Glynnis's new teacher partners her with Leora Faust, a girl with crooked teeth and patchy brown bruises on her knees. Everyone else already has a partner.

That morning, Glynnis's father drove her to the new school on his way to work. Her mother had refused to come along. "American children bring guns to school," she said, and kissed Glynnis on the top of the head. "So try not to piss anyone off." Her father grew up in this town, and along the drive he pointed out things he remembered: a tire store that used to be an ice cream shop, a small park that used to be a big park, a bank that has always been a bank but used to have a different name.

Glynnis got to sit at her desk while the rest of the class stood to say the Pledge of Allegiance. She told her teacher that it would be treason for her to say it, that if they found out in England, they could have her head chopped off. Miss Glen cocked her head to one side and said, "Well, we wouldn't want that, would we?" Until Glynnis was paired with Leora Faust, no one else had spoken to her.

Glynnis stands to the side, watching as Leora reads the directions from her science book. At the desk behind hers, a boy uses his knife to lift a sliver of guts from his worm. "Hey, Mary Poppins!" he says, and thrusts his knife toward Glynnis.

Two girls with matching Princess Leia buns in their hair laugh as

Glynnis darts sideways. "Jer-e-*mi*-ah!" they squeal, and Glynnis tries to smile, tries to take the joke. At her old school, the disturbed children had their own classroom in the basement, and even in there, Glynnis is pretty sure they weren't allowed to hold knives.

It's a mess, this new school, a dirty scab of a place with orange carpet in the hallways and soggy hamburgers at lunch. Because the rain made the playground muddy, the class has to take their shoes off when they come inside and pile them up next to the door. Glynnis has spent the whole day feeling cold and grubby in her socks. In England, they always got to wear their shoes inside.

"Check it out," Jeremiah says to the Princess Leia girls and aims his knife at Leora Faust. As she bends forward over her science book, Jeremiah flicks his knife, springing worm guts onto the back of her head. Leora continues reading, keeping her place with her finger while the guts stick in her hair, dangling like a tiny slick sausage.

Miss Glen is circling through the classroom, answering questions and leaning over to inspect work. When she comes up behind them, Glynnis holds her breath. Someone will have to tell. It isn't like Jeremiah made a nasty face or called Leora a name. There are *dead* parts hanging in her hair. Glynnis is sure the Princess Leia girls will say something. At her old school, it was always girls against boys.

Miss Glen stops just behind Glynnis and touches her crimson fingernails to one of the girls' perfect braided buns. "Megan R. and Megan C.," she says. "You two always have the prettiest hair." Glynnis waits. This is the time to tell. Miss Glen is on their side.

"My mom does it," one of the Megans says. "Megan C. comes over before school, and my mom does us both."

The Megans turn back to their work. Miss Glen is walking past. Glynnis stares down at her desk so that she won't have to see the worm guts, the slick greasy string of them, shivering in Leora's hair. So this is America, then. Nobody is going to do anything.

While Glynnis and her father eat supper that night, her mother sits at the table, smoking cigarettes and drinking red wine from a paper cup. "Aren't you eating?" her father asks.

"I hate the food here," her mother says, and waves her cigarette in front of her. "Everything tastes like cheese or chocolate."

"It's just *soup,*" says her father.

"It's easy for you," her mother says. "You've been eating so much of this garbage, you stink of it. Both of you." Glynnis puts her spoon down and sniffs at her shoulder. The new house smells like fresh paint and carpet cleaner. The yard smells like wet dirt. But her shoulder smells regular enough.

Glynnis's father smiles and blinks his eyes quickly. "How about we try to be a little positive? Glynnis?" He raises his eyebrows at her. "Tell us one thing about your new school."

Glynnis opens her mouth to tell about Jeremiah throwing worm guts into Leora's hair, but before any sound can come out, her father holds up his hand. "No," he says. "Something *good.*"

Glynnis stops. Her father is watching, tapping his plastic spoon on the edge of his paper bowl. "I don't know," she says finally.

"Your teacher's pretty," he says, and her mother makes a choking noise in the back of her throat. "Don't you think?"

Glynnis hasn't really thought about it, but she supposes Miss Glen is all right. She isn't old or fat or covered with big hairy moles. "Sure," Glynnis says. "She's pretty enough."

She can see the cords in her mother's neck tightening, the skin around her lips pulling thin. "Well," she says to Glynnis's father. "Thank *God-bless-America* for that."

"Taxation without representation. What does that even *mean?*" her mother asks while Glynnis is in the bathtub. Glynnis is trying to explain about the Social Studies lesson. They love their wars, Americans, love to talk about them and watch filmstrips about them and look at pictures of them in books. Only her first day and already Glynnis knows all about George Washington and the Redcoats and Paul Revere screaming his head off across the countryside. *The British are coming! The British are coming!*

"You'd think they would have gotten over it by now," her mother says. "A slight overcharge for tea, and we're still on their list."

"Miss Glen says it was a long time ago," Glynnis tells her mother. "She says that America saved us in a couple of big wars, and so we're all great friends again."

"She sounds like a nincompoop," her mother says, and bends over Glynnis, clipping the wet ends of her hair to the top of her head with a barrette. This is their time together, *girl time,* her mother calls it. Her father never bothers them, never knocks or calls or tries to come in. But still, her mother locks the door.

"Did you make any friends?" her mother asks, and sits down on the lid of the toilet.

Glynnis scrubs herself hard with the soap, just in case the food smell is still on her. "There was one girl," she says. "We cut up a worm together."

Her mother's face freezes.

"It was for Science," Glynnis says. "Miss Glen made us partners."

Her mother closes her eyes and smiles. "Oh," she says. "That doesn't count, then. You didn't make a friend." She stands up and peels out of her blue jeans and sweater, dropping them onto the floor. "Scoot up," she says. "I'm getting in."

Glynnis moves forward, pulling her knees to her chest as her mother lowers herself into the water behind her. She rubs Glynnis's back with the heel of her hand. "Was school terrible?" she asks, and Glynnis slides back between her mother's legs, leaning onto her chest.

"They never raise their hands," she says. "Nobody talks to me, and the classroom smells like dirty feet."

"It's the same way here," her mother says. She touches her mouth to the top of Glynnis's head. "I miss home."

"So do I," says Glynnis.

"I was *born* there," her mother whispers.

"So was I," says Glynnis.

Her mother touches one wet finger to the curve of Glynnis's ear, tracing the lobe with her fingernail. "What does your teacher look like?"

Glynnis tries to think. "She has black hair and brown eyes," she says. "She paints her fingernails red. And she smiles a lot."

Glynnis can feel the rise and fall of her mother's chest against her shoulder blades. "Can I sleep in your bed tonight?" her mother asks, and Glynnis nods. Her mother circles her wet arms around Glynnis's shoulders. "Nobody loves you as much as I do," she says.

"I know," says Glynnis.

Her mother tightens her arms and dips her head forward so that Glynnis can feel her breath on the back of her ear. "Now you say it to me," her mother whispers.

"No one loves you as much as I do."

The cafeteria doesn't have enough chocolate milk for everyone in line. Because of this, it is a race to be first. Miss Glen tries to make it fair. "Today," she says to the class, "people with the letter *M* in their name may be the first in line." Megan R. and Megan C. clap their hands and run to the door, cramming their feet into matching pink sneakers. Glynnis puts her chin in her hand and waits. Next come people with *B*'s, then *H*'s. Most of the class is in line, and Glynnis feels the sadness inside her like a bag of wet sand. She doesn't even like chocolate milk.

When Miss Glen calls *L*, Glynnis slides out of her desk and follows Leora Faust to the back of the line. Miss Glen starts to lead the class into the hallway, and Glynnis hurries to get her laces tied.

"My shoe's gone!" Leora yells, and Miss Glen stops. "Somebody stole my shoe!"

Miss Glen walks to the back of the line, her bright mouth puckered like a prune. "Leora," she says, and she sounds tired. "No one *stole* your shoe. Let's hurry now so that we don't make everyone late for lunch."

Leora looks like she is about to cry. Everyone is watching. Crying is the absolute wrong thing to do. "I can't find my shoe," Leora says, and her voice is small and squeaky.

Miss Glen closes her eyes and rubs her forehead with her fingers. "Let's all look for Leora's shoe," she says, and sighs at the ceiling.

When Jeremiah pulls the shoe out of the trash can, he swings it at Leora by its laces. "Somebody must have thought it was garbage," he says.

On the way to the lunchroom, the hallway echoes with shouts of "Leora-shoe-germs! No touch-backs!" One by one, the shoe germs pass down the line. Glynnis walks behind Leora, who hasn't taken the time to put her shoes all the way on and clip-clops down the hallway with her heels bunched out over the backs. When the germs pass to Leora, they stop. She does not turn around to pass her own germs to Glynnis.

In the cafeteria, Glynnis eats lunch by herself. At the table beside hers, Megan R. is passing out pink envelopes with stickers on them. "It's a slumber party," she tells the girls at her table. "My mom is buying mud masks and cucumbers so we can do facials."

"Your birthday parties are always the best, Megan," says one of the girls.

"I know," says Megan R. "But it's going to be expensive, and my mom won't let me have as many people this year. We have to keep it a secret." The rest of the girls smile, and Megan R. lowers her voice. "I don't want people to have their *feelings* hurt."

It is simple who is to blame for this. At some point in the early party-planning, parents said how many people got to come, how many friends your life had room for. Sometime, weeks before Glynnis even existed at this school, Megan R.'s mother had said a number. A list was made. Glynnis sits alone at her table, sipping her plain white milk and waiting for the bell to ring so that she can throw her food away and go back to the classroom.

After school, Glynnis sits cross-legged on her bed while her mother stands naked in front of the closet. At the new house, all the closet doors are made of mirrors, and this is what her mother does now while her father is at work — look at herself naked.

"There's one girl at school that everybody's mean to," Glynnis tells her mother. "Even the teacher."

Her mother is standing sideways in the mirror, pulling the skin on her stomach smooth, then letting it pooch again. "It's like that sometimes," she says. "For some people, it's like that." This is something that Glynnis appreciates about her mother, the way she doesn't pretend like she can fix things.

"Why?" Glynnis asks, and her mother shrugs.

"Some people just make it too easy," she says. "They make it too easy for people to be mean."

Glynnis thinks about this. At her old school there was a girl who said loud, screechy prayers before every meal and every exam, always *Jesus* this and *Jesus* that. But nobody ever threw her shoes in the garbage can. Nobody ever passed her germs around. "But why doesn't she have any friends?" Glynnis asks, and her mother turns to look at her.

"*I* don't have any friends," she says.

"At home you do," Glynnis says. "You have lots."

"No." Her mother crosses her arms over her breasts, pressing them flat against her body. "I don't."

Glynnis uses her fingernail to scrape a piece of dried mud off the bottom of her shoe. "What about Judy?" she asks, and flicks the clump of mud off the bedspread. "What about Rachel and Linda and Katie Bell from across the street? They're all your friends."

"Not anymore," her mother says. "I don't have any friends anymore."

The girls, that's what her mother called them. They had grown up together, had gone to the same schools, listened to the same music, told the same stories about the same people. When Glynnis came home in the afternoons she would find them on the back porch, smoking cigarettes and sipping cocktails out of fancy glasses. *"Girls,"* they whispered to each other when they had something important to say. Glynnis would sit on her mother's lap and take tiny sips from her frosted glass while they talked about old boyfriends and first kisses, women they'd known who had gotten fat or poor or divorced. They finished one another's sentences, her mother's friends, clipping their stories together, filling in one another's missing details, telling jokes in unison, screaming with laughter at the mention of a name, a place, a word that meant nothing to Glynnis.

Her mother's friends called her father *the American,* and when he came home from work they would take turns dancing with him around the kitchen table. "You're lucky," they told him while the radio played in the background. "American women are loud and fat. They chew with their mouths open." He wagged his finger at them while Glynnis and her mother laughed into their hands. "Don't you ever let him steal you away," they said to Glynnis's mother, and she promised that she wouldn't.

"How come they're not your friends anymore?" Glynnis asks. "Is it because we moved?"

Her mother is staring at her reflection, tracing the tips of her fingers along her lips, pressing them into the hollows beneath her eyes. "Ask your father," she says, and Glynnis sits up straight.

"Why did we come here?" she asks.

Her mother looks down at the carpeting, pushing the knobs of her knees together as she lifts up onto her toes. "He lied," she says. "He lied to me."

Glynnis thinks about this. One little lie doesn't seem like such an important thing. If that's the only reason, then maybe they don't have to stay here. They're not even unpacked yet. "Maybe he's sorry," Glynnis says, and climbs to her knees. "*Really* sorry, I mean. Like that time I spilled grape soda on the carpet and blamed it on the lady who used to clean our house? Maybe it's like that!"

"It isn't," her mother says. "It isn't at all like that." She narrows her eyes at Glynnis in the mirror. "And you can just stop bouncing up and down because we aren't going back."

Glynnis sinks back onto her heels, and her mother lifts her breasts, pinching the nipples between her fingers. "Do you think I'm ugly?" she asks.

"No," Glynnis says, and her mother sighs.

"You have to say that," she says. "You look just like me."

For supper, her mother gives them cheese macaroni on paper plates, then sits at the table smoking a cigarette and drinking from her paper cup. Her father takes a big bite of macaroni and then gives them the thumbs-up sign. "Super!" he says, and her mother makes a hissing noise in the back of her throat. "Not eating?" he asks, and when her mother doesn't answer, he claps his hands and rubs them together. "Well," he says, smiling. "Let's hear something good about school, Glynnis."

Glynnis looks at her mother to see if she has to answer, but her mother's head is tilted backward, blowing smoke rings at the ceiling. "The coolest girls are Megan R. and Megan C.," she says. "They wear matching hair and pink shoes, and everybody wants to be friends with them."

"That's nice," her father says.

"It's Megan R.'s birthday on Friday, and she's having a slumber party. Only the best girls get to go."

Her mother's head snaps up. "A slumber party!" she says, and shimmies her shoulders over the table. "I *loved* slumber parties. We used to laugh until we threw up!"

"Charming," her father says, but her mother ignores him.

"We used to put a girl's fingers in warm water while she was sleeping so that she would wet herself." Her mother dips her head forward, laughing into her chest. "Then when she woke up, we'd lock her outside so that she'd have to ring the doorbell and walk through the house in front of everyone!"

"You did that to your friends?" Glynnis asks, and her mother cocks her head.

"Of course not," she says. "Well, not to the *good* ones, anyway."

"Why would you do that to anyone?" Glynnis asks, and her mother rolls her eyes.

"For *fun*," she says.

"It doesn't *sound* like fun," Glynnis says, and her father coughs into his shoulder.

"Maybe not to *you,*" her mother says. "You're such a stick."

"I'm not invited to go, anyway," Glynnis says, and her father looks up.

"Why not?" he asks.

Glynnis blinks at her plate of macaroni. "I'm new."

Her father reaches across the table and puts his hand on top of hers. "You won't be new for long," he says, and squeezes her fingers. Glynnis feels a knot pressing into the back of her throat. She wants to close her eyes and lean her head forward onto the back of her father's wrist.

"You were supposed to be a Megan," her mother says, and Glynnis looks up at her. "Up until the very last second. But your father changed his mind."

"What?" Glynnis asks.

"Oh," he says. "Yeah. It reminded me of breakfast. Eggs and bagels or something. I don't know. I liked Glynnis." He smiles at her across the table. "Aren't you lucky to be one of a kind?"

Her mother watches as Glynnis slides her hand away from her father and drops it into her lap.

After her bath that night, Glynnis sits on her bed while her mother plays with the radio, turning through static until she finds a station with bright, bouncy music. "Want me to paint your fingernails?" she asks, and Glynnis shakes her head. Her insides are still jumping at the near miss of her own stupid name.

"I'm really tired," Glynnis says, but her mother shakes the little bottle in front of her.

"Oh, come on," she says. "It'll make you pretty."

At lunch the next day, Miss Glen announces that people with pink fingernails can be first in line, then winks one almond-shaped eye at Glynnis. There is groaning. Both of the Megans have normal, naked fingernails.

While Glynnis is waiting to get her tray, she hears a rustling behind her and turns to see the Megans leaning out of line. "New Girl," Megan R. whispers, and waves to get her attention. "Get us a chocolate milk." She thrusts her hand forward, and Glynnis looks down at the money.

Nothing good can come of this. If Glynnis takes the money, the Megans will think she is weak, willing to give something for nothing. If she doesn't, they will hate her forever. The Megans narrow their eyes, and the rest of the class watches. This is the choice: enemy or servant. Glynnis doesn't know which is worse.

When Leora Faust steps out of line, her eyes are wide and serious. "It's against the rules," she says to Glynnis. "It's cheating, and it's against the rules."

"M-Y-O-B," says Megan C., and Leora touches Glynnis on the arm.

"You're not supposed to, Glynnis. Miss Glen might call your mom, and then you'll get in trouble." Leora's fingers feel smooth and cold in the crook of Glynnis's elbow, and for a second, she wants to put her hand on Leora's bony little shoulder. She wants to tell her not to worry, that everything is going to be fine.

But the Megans turn to each other, speaking with the silent language of their eyes. It is something Glynnis has seen her mother do with her friends, a lengthening of the neck, a raised eyebrow, a slow curl at one side of the mouth. In a moment it will be too late. She has to do something.

"Don't touch me," Glynnis says, and yanks her arm away. "*I* don't want your stinky germs."

Leora's breath comes out in one hot gasp. "I'll tell," she says, but her voice is small, buried somewhere deep inside her chest. "I'll tell Miss Glen on all of you."

Megan R. steps forward, resting her hand on one cocked hip. "Then we'll all say you're lying," she says. Leora looks down at her scruffy brown shoes, and Glynnis snatches the money from Megan R. A second, maybe less, and they are all back in line.

"I was almost a Megan," Glynnis says when they sit down at her table. She passes them each a chocolate milk, and Megan C. looks at her doubtfully.

"*Almost?*" she asks.

"It's my mother's favorite name in the world," Glynnis tells them. "But my father changed it at the last second."

"Why didn't your mom stop him?" Megan R. asks. "If that's what she wanted to name you?"

Glynnis thinks about this. "He lied," she says after a moment. "He changed it without telling her, and she didn't find out till after."

"That sucks," says Megan R., but she is looking over the top of Glynnis's head, waving to get the attention of the girls who usually sit at her table.

"She's still ripped up about it," Glynnis says. "My mother only calls me *Megan*."

"We have one too many people," Megan R. says, counting chairs around the table. "We'll have to squeeze."

The table fills in around them, and Glynnis sits with her elbows pinched to her sides while the other girls talk about the slumber party. "My dad's going to make oysters Rockefeller," Megan R. says. "They're my favorite."

"Oysters?" Glynnis asks, and Megan straightens.

"Have you ever *had* them?" she asks, and Glynnis blushes.

"My dad doesn't cook," she says, and Megan smiles at the rest of the table.

"Well," she says. "You don't know what you're missing."

Glynnis pokes at her lunch. The gravy on her chicken-fried steak is brown and clumpy, and she scrapes it to the edge of her tray while the other girls plan prank phone calls and talk about what movies Megan R. should ask her mother to rent for the party.

"At my old school, we used to put a girl's hand in warm water and make her wet herself at slumber parties," Glynnis says, and the rest of the girls look at her.

"Wet herself?" Megan C. asks. "Like, pee her pants?"

Glynnis nods. "We waited for someone to fall asleep, and then after we made her wet, er, pee her pants, we'd lock her outside." For one glorious moment, the Megans look at Glynnis, and she can feel the doors of her future swing wide open. She will buy pink tennis shoes. She will wear her hair in fancy braids. She will be the Megan with interesting stories — the *Continental* Megan.

But even as Glynnis is imagining the three-way phone calls and notes passed in class, the Megans turn toward each other. They touch fingers. Glynnis can feel her lungs empty like two shriveled balloons. It doesn't matter how many stories she has, how many cafeteria rules she breaks. She could eat lunch at this table every day for the rest of her life, go to every party, share in every conversation. Still, she won't ever know them as well as they know each other.

"We have to do that," Megan R. whispers. "Who could we do that to?"

"The water has to be really warm," Glynnis says. "Or else it won't work."

"Leora," Megan C. says. "We should do that to Leora."

Glynnis moves her food around on her tray while the rest of the girls discuss the best way to convince Megan's mom to let her invite an extra person. They will say Leora helped with a Social Studies project. It might work. Megan R. stands up and crosses the cafeteria to the table where Leora is sitting alone.

Glynnis cannot watch. Leora Faust is small and strange-looking, with greasy hair and dirty fingernails. But she has never done anything to Glynnis. Leora can't know the way the world has been planning against her. Glynnis's mother, Megan R.'s mother, they all had a part. Strangers bumped into each other's lives, moved things around without credit or knowledge or blame. One day, Glynnis and her mother had seen her father sitting in the window of a restaurant, sharing a soda with Katie Bell from across the street. And then they'd moved. Snip, snip, snip. The old world fell away, and Glynnis was left in this new one. Megan R. was wrong when she said that Glynnis didn't know what she was missing. The whole wide world was just a big pile of strangers, thinking all the time about everything they were missing.

Glynnis's father says that she cannot eat Pop-Tarts for dinner. He peels back the bread from his cheese sandwich and shakes the salt and pepper shakers over the square of yellow cheese. "I've been working all day," he says to her mother. "You could at least unpack some boxes. You could at least *heat something up.*"

Her mother doesn't answer. She holds her paper cup against her chest and sways her hips around the kitchen counter, like she is listening to music. Glynnis sits down at the table and uses her teeth to tear open the foil wrapper of her Pop-Tart. Her father looks up at her. "I said no," he says. "Not for dinner, Glynnis."

Glynnis looks at her mother, waiting to be told what to do. Her mother glances at the Pop-Tart and then at Glynnis's father. She yawns and clutches her paper cup in both hands as she twirls around the counter and sways quietly out of the room. When Glynnis looks back at her father, he is watching her hard, his mouth small and tight in the corners. Glynnis keeps her eyes on his as she folds back the foil wrapper. He shakes his head, a warning, and Glynnis stares straight at him. Very slowly, she fills her mouth with Pop-Tart and makes her face big with chewing.

When her father stands up, Glynnis is afraid he is going to hit her. He raises his hand, and the Pop-Tart turns to concrete inside her mouth, grit and dirt and gravel. But her father doesn't hit her. Instead, he hits the table. He slams the flat of his hand down hard so that the table shakes over Glynnis's legs and the salt and pepper shakers tip sideways, spilling across the wood. "God*damn* it!" he yells.

The words stay in the room even when the sound has stopped. The walls hold them there like a cold, creeping fog. Glynnis stares down at all the salt and pepper loose across the table. She sits in her chair long after her father has left the kitchen, using the ridge of her fingernail to separate the salt and pepper into little piles, salts with salts, peppers with peppers, so they will be with their friends. So they won't be afraid.

"Friday Flip-Up Day!" Jeremiah screams on the playground before school starts. Leora Faust is wearing a skirt with big cartoon frogs on it, and the boys chase her around the tire swing, catching the hem of her skirt in their fingers and lifting it over her white underpants.

"Stop it!" she screams, spinning in circles and swatting their hands away like bees. "Leave me alone!"

Jeremiah laughs. "You *know* what Friday is," he tells her. "You shouldn't have worn a skirt."

Leora breaks away, sprinting across the muddy grass to the classroom. Glynnis leans back against the brick wall with the Megans, tugging at her corduroy pants and thanking God that all her skirts are still packed in boxes somewhere.

"Leora's mom said she could come to my party," Megan R. says when the bell rings. "You're so cool for thinking of that warm water thing. I really wish I could invite you, too."

Glynnis follows them into the classroom. "I'm sure your party will be really fun," she says politely. But her head is loose and swimmy on the cord of her neck, her limbs slow and heavy. Glynnis sits through the morning with her head propped on both hands. Her stomach feels like a cold wet rag, and she pushes her fist into it, trying to make it believe she isn't hungry. Glynnis's mother had been asleep by the time she finished with the salts and peppers. She climbed into bed without a bath and pressed her body against her mother's. She had stayed awake all night, listening to the sounds of her stomach sloshing and to the slow, wheezy snorts of her father's breathing coming from the big bedroom where he slept alone.

At recess, Glynnis begins to follow the Megans, but Miss Glen calls her back. "You're looking a little scruffy today," she says. Glynnis looks down to make sure that her blouse is clean, that she's put her shoes on the right feet. "Would you like me to fix your hair for you?" Miss Glen asks, and Glynnis runs her fingers over the back of her head. Her mother was still asleep when Glynnis left for school, and she had tried to put her own hair in a French braid. She worked until her fingers ached, but it had come out wrong, crooked and lumpy.

Glynnis stands perfectly still while Miss Glen uses her fingers to comb out her hair. "So," she says as she divides Glynnis's hair into sections. "It must be hard to be so far from home."

"I guess so," Glynnis says. She doesn't want to think about England or her old school or the house she used to live in. What's the point? She can't go back.

"Of course, *this* is your home, too," Miss Glen says.

Glynnis is quiet. It would be rude to argue with her teacher.

"Your father's American?" Miss Glen asks. Glynnis can feel Miss Glen's hands tugging on her hair as she nods. "So you are, too. You have *dual citizenship*. Do you know what that means?" When Glynnis doesn't answer, Miss Glen sighs. "It means you're very special," she says. "You have *two* countries. Everyone else at this school only has one. I think we can all learn *a lot* from each other."

Glynnis is facing the bulletin board, where Miss Glen has taped up a construction-paper version of Betsy Ross's flag. "What if there's a war?" she asks, and the words feel loose and clunky inside her mouth. "Like before?"

Miss Glen snaps the rubber band around the end of Glynnis's braid. "You don't have to worry," she says. "That won't ever happen." She squeezes Glynnis's shoulders. "All done."

Glynnis's hair feels smooth and tight around her face, like it is pulling her mouth back and holding her eyes wide open. "Thank you," she says. But as she leaves the classroom, Glynnis can feel the doubt creeping up the back of her throat. *Ever* is an awfully long time.

Outside, Glynnis looks around for the Megans. They are on the monkey bars, but before she can cross to them, she sees Leora Faust, slouched and shaking on the grass. "Are you sick?" Glynnis asks. "Should I get Miss Glen?"

Leora is on her hands and knees, raking the wet grass with her fingers. When she lifts her head to look at Glynnis, her whole face is red and patchy with crying. "I lost a button," she says between hiccups. "A button off my shirt. I lost it."

"Don't be such a bawl-baby," Glynnis says, and glances over her shoulder to make sure the Megans aren't watching. "Get off the ground."

"I'll get in so much trouble," she wails. "You have to help me find it." Leora reaches up and grabs Glynnis's arm with her wet, muddy hand. "Please, Glynnis. Help me."

This is all she needs. If the Megans look over and see Glynnis with Leora, they'll think she *wants* to be here. They'll think she's made a choice. "It's just a button," Glynnis says, but Leora is crying too hard to hear.

Leora slaps the ground, the wet grass sticking to the backs of her hands. "No-no-no-no-*no*," she says. "Oh please, *please* no." Her face is slick with tears and snot, and she uses the backs of her wrists to wipe her eyes as she crawls through the grass, smearing wet, grimy streaks across her forehead. Glynnis cannot walk away. She cannot leave her here like this.

"My mom will *kill* me!" Leora shrieks, and Glynnis winces in the direction of the Megans. She leans forward and pretends to look in the grass.

"Maybe it fell off in the classroom," she says. "It's probably on the floor by your desk."

Leora shakes her head, spinning on her knees to feel the grass behind her. "The boys were pulling at my shirt," she says. "When I was over here. It *must* be over *here!*" She is yelling now, choking on her own screechy voice. "Please, Glynnis. Please help me find it."

"Shut up, then," Glynnis hisses. "People are looking."

Out of the corner of her eye, Glynnis can see the boys on the basketball court glancing in their direction. Her ears prickle with heat, and she feels her way down the front of her blouse until she reaches the last button. It doesn't put up much of a fight. One good yank, and it pops right off in her fingers. Glynnis is about to hold it out, about to say, "Here, you big crybaby, just take this and stop wailing," when Leora leans forward onto her elbows, her bony spine heaving.

"I won't be able to go to the party now," Leora says, and Glynnis goes still. "I've never been invited to a slumber party."

Glynnis strokes the button with her thumb and forefinger. "You haven't?" she asks. "Not ever?"

Leora turns her face sideways on the ground. "I already got a present and everything," she sniffs. Glynnis squeezes the button in her palm, and Leora turns on her back, letting one arm fall loosely across her chest. "I got her a book of different braids she can do with her hair," she says. "It came with ribbons and sparkly barrettes and things. I thought her mom could use it when she does her and Megan C.'s hair before school."

Leora raises one knee, and her skirt falls up around her white thighs. Glynnis looks away, embarrassed. Can't Leora see the way things are? Did she ever stop to wonder why Megan R., who, as far as Glynnis can tell, has never said a single nice thing to Leora, would suddenly up and invite her to a birthday party? No. She just went running out and bought a present.

Glynnis feels the button, smooth and silky between her fingers. It is nothing, really — a piece of plastic. She looks down at Leora, at the wet skirt tangled around her muddy legs, the hint of underpants peeking out beneath the bunched-up hem, and suddenly Glynnis hates her. She hates Leora for being so weak, for making it so easy. Glynnis squeezes the button in her fist. "I don't think we're going to find it," she says.

When the recess bell rings, Leora stands up, her bare legs streaked with dirt and grass. As they file into the classroom, Miss Glen sighs through her teeth and points at Leora. "You're a mess," she says. "Go to the girls' room and clean yourself up."

Glynnis keeps her head down as she pushes her shoes off in the doorway. On her way to her desk, she opens her hand and lets the button fall into the trash can.

Glynnis is waiting for the school bus when her father's car pulls up in the parking lot. "Why aren't you at work?" Glynnis asks.

"Come on," he says to her. "It's starting to rain."

Glynnis climbs into the car, and mud flakes off her shoes onto the floor. "I thought we could go get something to eat," her father says. "Just you and me. We can go to a restaurant and order whatever we want. It'll be like a date." Glynnis can feel the grumbling in her stomach, and she thinks of a warm, cozy booth where they will share French fries and get cheesecake for dessert. But then she thinks of her mother, alone and naked in the new house, waiting for her.

"I have homework," she says.

"It's Friday," her father tells her. "You have the whole weekend."

"I have a lot," she says. "We start the Civil War next week."

Her father sighs. "Fine," he says.

When they come through the front door, Glynnis's mother walks into the living room, tying her bathrobe around her waist. Her lips are purple with wine. "What are you doing here?" she asks.

Her father stands in the front hallway, looking through the mail. "I took the afternoon off," he says. "I picked Glynnis up from school."

Her mother nibbles at the rim of her paper cup. "What happened to your hair?" she asks, and Glynnis reaches back to feel her braid.

"Miss Glen did it for me," she says.

"Looks nice," her father says without lifting his head.

"I lost a button," Glynnis tells her mother, and holds out the bottom of her blouse. "At school. It fell off or something."

Her mother glances down at the shirt. "Throw it away," she says, and Glynnis's father looks up. Her mother smiles at him. "Daddy'll buy you a new one."

When the phone rings, Glynnis leaves her parents staring at each other in the front hallway to answer. It's Megan R.

"Glynnis?" she says. "Leora's mom just called. Leora can't come to my party."

Glynnis can feel her heartbeat in the back of her throat. "I didn't think her mother would really say no just because of a button," she says, and there is silence on the other end of the phone.

"What?" asks Megan. "She's sick, that's what her mom said."

"Sick?" Glynnis asks. "She seemed fine at school."

"I guess so," says Megan. "But who cares? I told my mom all about you, about how you're new, but you're super cool, and she said you can come instead of Leora. Isn't that the best news ever?"

Glynnis says that it is. Maybe Leora really is sick. She *did* spend all that time rolling around on the wet grass. And if she *is* sick, it would only make things worse to lock her outside after she had wet herself.

"I know it's last minute," Megan tells her. "But my mom says we can come pick you up, if that makes it easier."

When Glynnis walks back to her parents, they are still in the front hallway. Her mother is stroking the collar of her robe with one hand and balancing her paper cup in the other. "That was Megan R.," Glynnis says. "Inviting me to her slumber party tonight." She pulls at her mother's arm. "We have to hurry," she tells her. "We need to find a present."

Her mother looks at her blankly. "You'd spend the night?" she asks. "The *whole* night?"

"It's a slumber party," Glynnis says again, and her mother bites her lip.

"I don't know," she says, and holds one hand to her forehead. "I don't think I want you to do that." Glynnis opens her mouth, but before any words come out, her father interrupts.

"Why?" he asks, and Glynnis and her mother look at him. "Why can't she go?"

Her mother shakes her head and turns to walk into the den. Glynnis and her father follow. "I don't know these people," she says. "And I won't have her going off with strangers."

"You can meet them," Glynnis tells her. "And then they won't be strangers."

Her mother chews her purple lips with her teeth. "I want you here," she says in a small voice. "With me."

"Don't do this," her father says, and his voice is low and serious. "Do it to yourself if you have to, but don't do it to Glynnis."

"What are you talking about?" her mother asks, and turns to face her father.

"This is home now," he says. "We live *here*."

"Whose fault is *that*?" her mother asks, and her face tightens into something mean and ugly. Glynnis watches her father straighten and broaden across the shoulders, making himself look larger than he is. Her knees begin to wobble. Her hands and feet go cold.

"It's just for one night," she whispers, but no one is listening.

"You," her father says. "You're the one who said we had to move. I would have stayed. But you said no."

Glynnis looks at her mother. This can't be true. It can't be.

Her mother's head snaps up, and her eyes narrow. "You and Katie Bell," she says. "How could I have stayed after that?"

"We've talked about this," her father says in a low voice. "It was *over*. I *made* my choice."

Her mother drops her chin to her chest and squeezes her paper cup until it caves in on one side. "You took *everything,*" she whispers. "You let them laugh at me."

Her father goes still. "No one was laughing at you," he says, and his voice is softer. "They were your friends. They were never laughing."

Glynnis's mother begins to cry, and her father reaches for her. But as his hand closes around her arm, she yanks away, and her paper cup tilts sideways, spilling red wine in an arch across the white carpet. Her mother looks down at the spill, then drops the cup to the floor and runs out of the room.

Glynnis and her father stand, staring down at the stain. "Go," he says to Glynnis. "Go see if she's all right."

Glynnis looks for her mother in the bedroom, but she isn't there. She calls down the hallway and peeks around corners. She is about to go back to her father, about to tell him that her mother must have sneaked out the back door, but then she passes the bathroom. The door is open a crack, and it is dark inside. As Glynnis edges the door open, a bar of light falls across the tile floor, and on the other side of the bathroom, she can make out the shape of her mother in the darkness, sitting in the bathtub.

As Glynnis creeps across the floor, the toe of her shoe catches on the silk of her mother's bathrobe, which is lying like a dark puddle on the floor. Her mother sits with her knees pulled to her chest, naked in the empty bathtub.

"Mom?" Glynnis whispers, but her mother is shaking, her head lowered over her bare knees. She doesn't look up. "Mom, are you okay?"

Her mother doesn't answer, doesn't move, doesn't make a sound. Her skin looks blue in the darkness, and her hair spills in messy tangles down the ridge of her spine. Glynnis stands, watching. Those are her mother's hands, her mother's ankles, her mother's narrow shoulder blades. Glynnis has seen her mother's body so many times that it is as familiar as her own. She knows every curve and angle, every knobby joint. But standing in the bathroom, Glynnis stares at her mother and feels nothing. She is a stranger. Glynnis has never seen her before in her life. She backs out of the room and closes the door, leaving her mother there, alone in the darkness.

When Glynnis walks back into the den, her father is on his hands and knees, scrubbing at the stain with a paper towel. The red wine is turning black on the carpet, and the paper towel is shredding into scraps as her father rubs harder and harder. *That won't work,* thinks Glynnis, but she doesn't say anything.

"Well?" her father asks without looking up.

"She's fine," Glynnis says. "She just wants some time to herself."

Her father nods at the stain, and Glynnis kneels beside him. She watches his hand move across the spill, pressing the pieces of paper towel into the carpet, trying to mop up what has already been absorbed, trying to fix what will be there forever.

Outside there is the low rumble of a car pulling into the driveway, the slam of a car door. Glynnis leans her shoulder against her father's and puts her hand over his. "The party, Daddy. Can I go?"

BRUCE McALLISTER

The Boy in Zaquitos

FROM FANTASY AND SCIENCE FICTION

The Retired Operative Speaks to a Class

YOU DO WHAT YOU CAN FOR your country. I'm sixty-eight years old and even in high school — it's 2015 now, so that was fifty years ago — I wanted to be an intelligence analyst . . . an analyst for an intelligence agency, or if I couldn't do that, at least be a writer for the United States Information Agency, writing books for people of limited English vocabularies so they'd know about us, our freedoms, the way we live. But what I wanted most was to be an analyst — not a covert-action operative, just an analyst. For the CIA or NSA, one of the big civilian agencies. That's what I wanted to do for my country.

I knew they looked at your high school record, not just college — and not just grades, but also the clubs you were in and any sports. And your family background, that was important too. My father was an Annapolis graduate, a Pearl Harbor survivor, and a gentle Cold War warrior who'd worked for NATO in northern Italy, when we'd lived there. I knew that would look good to the Agency, and I knew that my dad had friends who'd put in a good word for me, too, friends in the Office of Naval Intelligence.

But I also knew I had to do something for my high school record; and I wasn't an athlete, so I joined the Anti-Communist Club. I thought it was going to be a group of kids who'd discuss Marxist economics and our free-market system, maybe the misconceptions Marx had about human nature, and maybe even mistakes we were making in developing countries, both propaganda-wise and in the kind of help we were giving them. I didn't know it was just a front for Barry Goldwater and that all we were going to do was make election signs, but at least I had it on my record.

Because a lot of Agency recruiting happens at private colleges, I went to one in Southern California — not far from where my parents lived. My high school grades were good enough for a state scholarship, and my dad covered the rest. It was the '60s, but the administration was conservative; and I was expecting the typical Cold War Agency recruitment to happen to me the way it had happened to people I'd heard about — the sons of some of my dad's friends. But it didn't. I went through five majors without doing well in any of them; and it wasn't until my senior year, when I was taking an IR course with a popular prof named Booth — a guy who'd been a POW in World War II — that I mentioned what I wanted to do. He worked, everyone said, in germ warfare policy — classified stuff — at Stanford; and I figured that if I was about to graduate I'd better tell someone, anyone, what I really wanted to do in life: not sell insurance or be a middle manager or a government bureaucrat, but work for a civilian intelligence agency — get a graduate degree on their tab maybe — and be an analyst.

I could tell he wanted to laugh, but he didn't. He was a good guy. The administration didn't like him because he never went to faculty meetings; and he didn't act like a scholar, even though he had his doctorate, and he wasn't on campus much. But when they tried to fire him, the students protested — carried signs, wrote letters, and caused enough of a scene that they kept him. This was back in the '60s when you did this kind of thing.

He was smiling at me and I could see those teeth — the ones he hadn't taken good enough care of in the POW camp, the ones that had rotted and were gone now, replaced years ago with dentures.

He looked at me for a long time, very serious, and said, "I could put in a good word for you at the USIA. You're a good writer, Matt."

"I'd rather be an analyst."

"Have you thought about the FBI?"

I had to laugh at that.

"Okay," he said, laughing too.

"I shouldn't be doing this. Your grades are terrible and I can't say much about you except that you're a good writer. In fact, I'm not sure why I'm even considering this. You're a pretty tame guy. You're even tamer than I was at your age and I was pretty tame. I stole hubcaps at least."

We both laughed.

He got serious. "You want to do something for your country, right?"

"Yes."

"But you don't want to join the military like your father did. You love and admire him, but you don't want to join the military."

"Right."

"No one's enlisting these days anyway," he said. "Can't blame them. JFK and his brightest aren't fighting this war very well. Look at the Chinese — how those cross-border ops brought them in. Jack's green-beanie darlings."

"Yes, sir."

"And the army won't take you anyway, right?"

"Yes. I've got some scoliosis, and you can see how thick my glasses are, sir."

"That's what I thought. What you need to do is send for the Agency application. Make two Xeroxes of it, send one to me, fill out one for yourself rough draft, send a copy of that to me, and I'll help you with it. You'll have to have a physical, just like the army, and a polygraph, and you'll have to have your doctor send your records. How does your dad feel about this?"

"My dad's always been for it," I answered.

"He's not very political, is he."

That was true.

"No," he said quickly, grinning, "I haven't been talking to your dad, but people say he's a good man."

What people?

"You're right," I said. "He's not political, and neither am I, I guess."

"Maybe that's why I'm doing this."

"Sir?"

"You can't analyze a situation if you're blinded by your own politics, Matt."

"You've taught us that, sir."

He laughed again.

"And you don't have to kiss ass, Matt. Remember that in the interview. Either they want you or they don't, and either way you'll never figure out exactly why."

*

Some people — maybe one in one hundred thousand — can get infected by an epidemic disease and not get sick and die. They don't even get the symptoms, but they can carry it and they can give it to others. They're called "chronic asymptomatic carriers," or CACs. You've heard of Typhoid Mary maybe, in health class or history. She was one. Not to the degree that the history books say she was, but she was. She didn't even know she was one until they told her how many people she'd probably killed; but she was one and it drove her crazy to find out. It drove her crazy and the government dropped their case against her. That was about 1910, I think, and it was here in America, during an epidemic.

That's how hard it can be on a person when they find out they're a carrier. That's what I'm saying, I guess.

I don't know whose pull did it. I know it wasn't my record. The Anti-Communist Club certainly wouldn't have been enough and my grades in college weren't very good, though Booth was right. I was a good writer. Both of my parents were good writers. My mom had a master's degree and my dad did a lot of writing for the admirals he served. Maybe it was the writing, but I also knew they could get all the 1600 SAT and 4.0-GPA graduates they wanted — who were better writers than I was — so it had to be something else. It had to be Booth or one of my father's friends or even the fact that my dad was about to retire as a rear admiral.

However it happened, I got called into an interview in Los Angeles in the middle of summer after graduation. The man wore a short-sleeve shirt with a loud red tie and didn't seem very interested. I panicked, thinking, "Shit, he's just interviewing me so the Agency can tell Booth or my dad's friends they did, but they're not really interested." That's how it felt. At one point the man did look up at me with interest, like he was waking up, when I said stupidly, "I feel like I really don't have a country."

"What do you mean by that?"

Uh oh, I thought, and tried to backpedal. "I don't mean that in patriotic terms. I don't mean —"

"I know you don't mean it in patriotic terms," he said impatiently. "You're the Cold War son of a Cold War father, Mr. Hudson. Even if you had long hair and were running around with posters saying KILL THE FASCIST PIGS! you'd still be your father's son and I wouldn't doubt your patriotism." He stopped himself and I didn't know whether to believe him. "So how *do* you mean it?" he said.

I took a deep breath. "My dad's a career Navy man, and my mother's a teacher. We moved around a lot and my father is a kind man and my mother loves people of all races, all cultures, so it's a little hard to talk about hometowns and wave the American flag the way some people wave it . . ."

He didn't say anything for a moment.

"You're a perceptive young man, Mr. Hudson. That's what we're looking for, but I don't think you've finished your answer, do you?"

"Sir?"

"How *do* you wave the American flag?"

"I guess I don't, sir. It's not my style. I don't burn the flag — that would be wrong — but I don't wave it. I don't need to. I see the United States as a good country, one that should be defended at all costs because history doesn't see enough good countries."

"You learn that in college?"

"I was thinking it before — when my dad was stationed with NATO in Italy, when I was younger — but, yes, I learned that from a college professor of mine, too."

He was nodding.

"I think I know which prof you're talking about, and he's right. It's an experiment, our society — the most successful experiment in the history of humankind — and certainly worth protecting."

"Yes, sir."

"Thank you for coming in today, Mr. Hudson. We'll let you know if we decide another interview would be helpful."

What they were looking for was not just somebody who could carry the plague without getting sick — your normal CAC — but someone whose body could get rid of the disease fast with the right antibiotics — what you'd call "designer antibiotics" these days. Experimental. Even classified. And definitely not yet FDA-approved. And it couldn't be a genetically engineered plague. That would be discovered pretty quickly and you wouldn't be able to deny it. Everyone would know it was GW — germ warfare — so they had to use good old-fashioned plague. Bubonic, the Black Death of the Middle Ages, the Great Dying. History's had a lot of names for it. It had to be "natural."

And it wasn't any good if it took the carrier days or a week or more to get clean. If it still showed in his blood, he'd never be able to get out of the quarantine areas; he'd never be able to get out of the field and sit the crisis out — back in the States or somewhere — until he was needed again.

They'd already found one carrier — a guy they could use — but he went crazy in the field halfway through his first mission and they had to pull him.

I didn't hear about him until much later. I wish I'd heard earlier.

I waited two months working in the sports section of a K-Mart. I'd given up, in fact, on ever hearing from them when a different guy called to set up another interview, this time in Riverside. There would be a physical just after the interview, he said, and I needed to be able to give urine and blood samples.

I don't remember exactly what I said in the interview or even what the guy said. He was interested at first, asking me about my relationship with my father — which I told him was great — and about any research papers I'd found most rewarding in my college courses. One on "economic sanctions and North-South relations," I said, and another on the impact of military invasion on the cultural history of Vietnam. He perked up hearing that, but after that lost interest again. I don't know whether it was the questions he had to ask — they bored him — or my answers to them — which were boring too — but all I remember is saying "Yes" and "No" a lot and not much else.

So I wasn't surprised two weeks later to get a letter turning me down. I knew I'd get something in writing so they could tell Booth and my dad's friends and anyone else that they'd considered me "very carefully" and sent me a nice letter.

I was getting ready to apply — my father had offered to help and I had some savings — to graduate school, for an MBA at a state college, when someone called from the L.A. office again. The voice sounded not just interested, but even a little urgent. They wanted me to come in for another interview and more blood tests.

I couldn't imagine what had changed their minds.

I should explain what a "vector" is? A vector is how a disease — an epidemic — is spread. In the case of *Yersenia pestis* — the classic plague — it's carried not by a rat, but by a flea on the rat. It's very interesting, actually. There are three main forms of plague: bubonic, pneumonic, and septicemic. Bubonic is the most famous. It's the form you see in etchings from the Middle Ages — what was called the Black Death. Incubation — which is how long it takes you to come down with it — is two to five days, and your lymphatic system tries to deal with it, but can't. Your lymph nodes swell up and they're so full of the bacteria, the bacteria's toxins, that they're like knobs on your skin. These are called "buboes" — and why it's called bubonic — and eventually they burst and run. You also get a red rash. This is the "ring around the rosies" that the old nursery rhyme is referring to. It's a terrible way to die. Your temperature gets up to 103–106. Your blood pressure's so low you can't stand up, and you've got to watch these things, these big bumps, growing on you. You're becoming something else — your body is changing completely — and even if you're delirious, you hate what you're becoming. You're rotting, actually rotting, and you can smell it.

I've never had the symptoms, but I know what that feels like — to hate what you're becoming.

The second form is called "pneumonic" — like the word *pneumonia.* It fills your lungs. You get it from what's called "aerial droplet transmission" — which means from the air. It goes straight to your lungs and you come down with a pneumonia that's actually plague. You can even get it from your cat or your dog. From their saliva or their sneezing. This kind takes half as long to come down with. You get a splitting headache, chills, fever, and before you know it you're coughing up blood. It looks like strawberry jelly — even the doctors describe it that way. Your lungs are dying and you get to watch. With this kind if you don't get treatment, you always die.

The worst form — septicemic — isn't very common, fortunately, but I should mention it anyway, so you'll know. In this kind the flea is so full of the germ that when it bites you — just one bite — when it tries to suck blood from you — the germs backwash into your bloodstream, and you get infected instantly. You die in twenty-four hours. Your blood is crawling with the bacteria — it just can't handle it — and that's how you die, poisoned by living things crawling through your bloodstream.

Actually there's a fourth type, a meningitis plague — a brain membrane kind. I'd forgotten that, but it's even less common. Its code in epidemiological circles is A20.7. You don't hear about it.

The kind they wanted me to spread — the only kind I could spread — was pneumonic. I'd cough, and the coughing would spread it, but once the pneumonic gets started you see the first type too, the bubonic. That's what they wanted. Something fast to get it started, but then both kinds appearing so that it couldn't be traced.

It's important to know the history of things. That's what Booth always said and that's what they said at Langley, and it's true. In the old days — when they first had a drug for the plague, in the early 1900s — they used sulfonamides. That's the fancy name for sulfur drugs. Back in the Middle Ages the guy with all the prophecies — Nostradamus — was so smart he invented an herbal treatment that was actually pretty good. It had rose petals, evergreen needles, and a special root in it, but you couldn't save the entire population of Europe with that. You couldn't even save 20 percent. Even if everyone had believed it would work, there wouldn't have been enough roses.

So the sulfur drugs in the early 1900s weren't very good, but they were better than nothing and they could have cut the Black Death mortality rate by 50 percent. Later, what's called the tetracycline drugs came in and these cured people quickly. That's why you get only a couple of plague cases every year in the United States, and they're out on Indian reservations or in the woods in a national park somewhere, someone getting bitten by a squirrel maybe.

But if you've got a Third World country, what we used to call an "LDC" — a Lesser Developing Country — you couldn't necessarily get the drugs, either quickly or at all, and maybe thousands would get infected and thousands would die. Especially if you didn't want them to get the drugs. If, say, the president of a little country was a leftist and you didn't want that kind of leadership in that country — where American businesses had factories and relied on certain kinds of privileges, and because you saw communism as a threat to our way of life — you could keep the drugs from getting to it. If the country couldn't get the drugs fast enough and enough people died, the country would become "destabilized." And if there was a group like the military or a landowner with the army's backing ready to overthrow the president, that was the time to do it. You know what I'm saying. I'm not talking politics here. I'm just saying how it was back then.

I'm sure you've heard about some of these things before. In

World War II the Japanese tried plague on China and killed a couple of hundred Chinese, but also one of their own companies of soldiers. They were also, later in the war, planning to try it on San Diego, California, but then Hiroshima and Nagasaki happened and they signed the surrender. And all the old Agency stories — the news media coverage, the "black ops," the assassinations of heads of state, the secret support of coups d'état — all those covert actions that got the intelligence community in trouble in the 1970s. You've heard about those things, I'm sure.

They didn't want me as an intelligence analyst. They wanted me to do this other work for them — in countries where they needed it done. I needed training for that — any twenty-two-year-old would have — and it was the kind any overseas operative would get. In my case it was training for South America. It lasted sixteen weeks — they taught me Spanish and E&E, escape and evasion — and gave me some medic training, some reporter-skills training (I'll talk about that in a minute), and some firearms training — which was pretty funny with my bad eyesight. Right before I left for all that training I went to visit my parents. I couldn't tell them anything, but I wanted them to be proud of me. All I could say was "I'm about to work for the intelligence community, Dad. But not as an analyst. I'm heading out in two days for sixteen weeks of training."

"I thought that might be what was happening, Matt," he told me with a smile, but I could tell he was worried. Analysts live safe lives. Field operatives don't always. "You haven't been saying much recently."

"You're right," I said. "That was why."

I couldn't tell them what I'd be doing. I couldn't tell anyone. Even if I'd been allowed to, how could I?

"I know I can't ask you anything about it, Matt, and that's okay," my dad said. "During the war in the Pacific we couldn't tell our families. No places, people, events. Just what we were feeling. Whenever you want to tell us how you're feeling, we'd like to hear. We're very happy for you."

I didn't become what I would become until maybe the second mission. I didn't develop the habits, I mean — the crazy ways of thinking, feeling, and acting that you develop when you know that if you touch someone you love, you may be giving them a disease that will kill them — until later. Those things didn't really start until after the first mission, though during that mission I'd meet people I liked and they'd be in the city where I needed to start the thing, and I had no choice — it was important that I start it there, in that city, if what we needed to have happen was to happen.

I remember a young woman in . . . a midsized city — let's call it Santa Livia. That's not its real name, but I still can't use the real names. She was an ex–Peace Corps worker and back in the States I'd have asked her out; but when I met her she was in — in Santa Livia working for a civilian aid organization. And that was the city where they wanted me to crack the hollow thing in my tooth to start it. All I needed to do after I cracked it was take the train from Santa Livia to the next two cities on the train route and cough a lot. It was in my bloodstream and that's all it would take. I'd cough, put my hand over my mouth, cough some more, touch the railings and doors of the train as I left and entered each car along the way. It was easy. You weren't sick yourself — you didn't have the symptoms — and the first time you did it you couldn't believe you were starting an epidemic. How could you be starting an epidemic just by doing that? You didn't believe it. You were just doing what they wanted you to do.

When I'd reach the third city, I'd crack the other three fillings on the other side of my mouth and the antibiotic would kill the *Yersenia* in my bloodstream; and I'd continue on the train to — let's call them Santo Tomás, and Santa Carolina . . . and Morela. If anyone tried to track the spread of it, the "vector trail," as they called it, would end in Morela; but only the World Health Organization would know how to track it and by the time they did, my train trip would be lost in the epidemic. Everyone — the cities, the government, the aid organizations — would be overwhelmed in days by the infected and no one could charge the United States with anything even if we got what we wanted. The disease would move from city to city within a day, and there'd be geometric spread — the kind you get in urban areas with rats, fleas, and aerial transmission — out from those cities. I'd be evacuated along with other nonquarantined Americans before the disease could hit the capital, where I was staying.

Spreading it that way made it look natural. That was, as I think I said, the main reason to have someone — a human carrier — do it — do it "by hand," as we liked to say — in a couple of cities and then let it spread. Looking natural was important. The word you hear all the time in CIA movies — "deniability" — is true. It's not just a Hollywood idea. That was the guiding principle. You don't have to have it deniable in economic warfare, the way we do things now; but you do in covert-action matters. Economic warfare — public sector and private sector both — works better anyway.

She had blue eyes and she liked me, I think. I didn't know if she got out. I didn't want to know. She was in the first city and maybe that gave her a chance, unless she chose to stay — to help. With pneumonic, if it's an untreated population, you can have 90 to 100 percent mortality. With bubonic it tends just to be 50 to 60 percent, so I didn't know.

After doing those three cities, I took the train back to the capital and found myself not looking at women or children. If I looked at them, I felt like they were going to die, that I was going to kill them — which could have been true, but not in the way it felt at the moment. I felt that my eyes — just my eyes — could do it. If I looked at them, they'd die. And with the women, if I thought they were beautiful, they'd also die because I thought it — because I thought they were beautiful.

Later, it would get a lot worse — the superstitions and habits — but that's how it started, on the first mission. Not looking at women and children.

Or anyone who looked at all like my parents.

It started with toothbrushes, I guess. That's when I first really noticed it. Not just averting my eyes on a train, but actual things I could touch — that I took home with me, and couldn't get away from. I wasn't supposed to do anything to draw attention to myself when I was in the field; but after the first mission, it was like I couldn't get the taste out of my mouth, so I started buying toothbrushes, one for every day; and I'd wrap up each one in a plastic bag at the end of the day. I started doing this when I was still in the field the second time. It was in the capital city, when all of the uninfected Americans and Europeans and Chinese and Japanese were being rushed out by jet. I used up ten toothbrushes in six days — that's more than one a day — right before I was evacked.

Back in the States, they had me live in Minneapolis. Why, I don't know. They didn't check me in at Langley — Agency headquarters — when I got back. Not at first. They put me in Walter Reed, the big military hospital in D.C. I was there for three days to make sure I wasn't still carrying, and then I did go to Langley for debriefing, a week of it, if I remember correctly. And then finally to Minneapolis, where they wanted me low profile until they needed me again, which wouldn't be for another six months. I kept buying the toothbrushes — a different one, sometimes two, for each day, and eventually rubber gloves to hold them with and plastic bags to put them in. I'd put them in the blue dumpsters behind my apartment. I wanted to burn them in a furnace, but the building didn't have one.

I noticed too that I didn't touch things out in public, or where other people could touch what I'd touched. I could have hired a maid — the Agency would have paid for it — but I wouldn't hire a maid. I didn't want her touching what I'd touched in the apartment. Out in public if I touched things it would be with my left hand, the hand I never let come near my mouth.

I was back in my own country again — with people I'd grown up with and cared about — and if I wasn't careful (a voice was telling me), I could start it here. I know that doesn't make any sense, but that's how it felt. I was clean, completely clean, but that's how it felt.

I had no social life, even though my case agent — let's call him Rod — kept telling me I needed one. "It's easier in D.C.," I'd tell him. "There's no social life in Minneapolis."

"That's not the reason, Matt," he'd say, "and you know it."

"What are you talking about?" I'd say, pretending I didn't know.

"You're agoraphobic and you need to work your way out of it. It happens. It's going to happen in work like this. Do you want to see an Agency shrink?"

"No." I wanted to work it out myself. I didn't want to be in a shrink's office where I could touch things and the shrink might die.

Sometimes Rod would visit me — maybe four times while I was there, during those six months — and his visits helped. Someone who knew me and thought I was okay — despite what kind of work I did — who wasn't afraid to sit near me or touch me. He was a short, squat man, and pretty gruff — a little like Joe Friday, real old school, OSS originally — but he reminded me of Professor Booth, because he also seemed to care. I'm not sure he did — that either of them really cared — but that's how it felt, and it helped.

I certainly didn't date. I didn't have to work. I had all this free time, but I didn't socialize unless I had to. I told people in the building that I was a writer and I know they thought I was some rich kid who didn't have to work, who could just write a book while everyone else worked. They didn't like that, which meant no one wanted to be around me — which was great. I had a different name, different social security number, the usual witness-protection kind of cover; and everyone assumed I was a trust-fund kid, I'm sure. I had all the time in the world, so I read a lot. When you read a lot you don't meet a lot of people. You don't meet a lot of girls.

But there was one — her name was Trisha — she lived down the hallway — but when I thought of dating her, I saw myself sitting in my car and watching it happen. They'd given me a car, a '68 Mustang fastback — the kind of car a trust-fund kid would have — and I saw myself sitting in it with her and, though she wanted me to kiss her, I couldn't. Why? Because if I did she'd jerk back like she'd been shot and I'd have to watch her get sick and die.

It would be like time-lapse photography, like a flower in a Disney nature movie blooming real fast, the buboes blooming like flowers, and then she'd be dead.

That's what I'd see if I thought of asking her out, but I finally did — maybe because I thought I should. I knew I was going crazy and maybe it would help. She wouldn't die — I knew that — and seeing that she didn't die might just help. But when I did ask her, when I got off the phone after asking her out, I threw up. I threw up on the bed where I'd made the call. I couldn't stop shaking and I didn't pick her up that Saturday. I never called her again, I avoided her in the hallway, and I didn't return her call the one time she called me two weeks later.

I also had a chance to see my parents during those six months and didn't. I couldn't.

I'd phone and tell my dad that they had me real busy, that even when I was out of the field they were keeping me busy, and he'd say, "That's fine, Matt. I know how it goes. My good friend Gavin from the Academy was ONI and he was the busiest man I ever knew. Just hearing your voice is wonderful. Call us when you can."

Or he'd tease me and say, "You're not trying to avoid us, are you?" and I'd lie and say, "You know me better than that." I'd say it to my mom, too. "You know I love you both. If I'm not going to get to see you, I want at least to call. I want you to at least hear my voice."

"You know we're proud of you," they'd both say, and they'd mean it. I didn't let myself wonder what they'd think if they knew what I was doing. Maybe they wouldn't want to know.

My dad died of a heart attack right after my third mission and I wanted to make it to the funeral, but I just couldn't do that either. I talked to my mom for a long time on the phone, trying to explain why I couldn't, inventing all sorts of things; and though I know she believed me — I know it made her proud — I know she was disappointed. But she'd been married to a Navy man, so she knew what sacrificing for your country was.

I was sitting watching television in my apartment in Phoenix — this time they had me in Arizona — when my dad's funeral started four hundred miles away. I remember looking at my watch every five minutes for an hour. I don't remember what was on television. I remember hearing in my head what I would have said about him if I'd been there. I remember imagining his body in a casket, starting to smell, the rash and bumps, and stopping myself — and then just seeing my mother's face and hugging her and telling her I loved her and what a wonderful man he'd been, which was true.

At first they lied to me and said the ex–Peace Corps woman — the woman in Santa Livia, the one I'd liked — had made it out okay; but two years later — after two more missions — they admitted she hadn't, that she'd been one of five Americans who'd died in the city because the WHO's medical shipment to the center of the epidemic took ten days, not three; and the five were sick and so they couldn't be evacuated. We'd delayed the WHO's shipment, of course. It was easy to do. I'd killed her. That was the truth of it. I hadn't delayed the shipment, but I'd killed her.

It was knowing that she'd died that made me do what I did in the city of — the city of Zaquitos. I'm sure it was. It wasn't a young woman, though. It was a boy, one who looked like a kid I'd played with — a friend — in the fourth grade in Florida, when my dad was stationed there. In the next country I was sent to I saw a lot of young women who were beautiful. Maybe their arms had little nicks and scars from a hard life. Maybe they were dirty from the dust and heat, but they were beautiful. People are beautiful wherever they are, whether it's war or peace or famine or floods they're living in. But it wasn't a woman I decided to save, it was a boy. I remember thinking: *This is someone's kid. You're going to have kids someday, Matt — if you're lucky, if you make it through this — and this is someone's kid.*

He was a *mezcla* — a mixed-blood kid at the bottom of the social ladder. His hair was kind of a bronze color, the way hair sometimes is from Brazil and the Azores. My friend in the third grade was from the Azores. This boy in Zaquitos had light brown eyes just like my friend. His skin was dark, but he had that bronze hair and, believe it or not, a couple of freckles on his nose, too. There'd been a lot of Irish and Germans in that country in the beginning and they'd mixed and maybe it was Irish blood coming through in this kid.

He lived on a famous dump in Zaquitos — the dump I'd gone to write a story about. I was there to write a story about how terrible conditions were for the people in that country's north. They'd left the drought-stricken countryside and ended up in the *favelas,* the slums, and that wasn't any better. It was worse, in fact, and that's what I was writing about. I was a reporter for a liberal English-language paper out of the capital city; that's what I was supposedly doing there. The agency had figured out how to use my writing skills and that was my — as they say — cover. I'd been interviewed by the newspaper the way any applicant would and I'd been hired the way anyone would be. At least that's how it looked. A paper trail in case one was needed. I wasn't comfortable with the job. I didn't talk leftist jargon well enough to feel comfortable when I met other leftist journalists, but my case agent said, "Don't worry. They can't fire you." The newspaper, it turned out, was funded by the Agency. Some of the editors worked for the Agency and could pipeline agents like me, and the other editors just didn't know. That's how it was in those days. It's an old story now and pretty boring; but for two missions that was my cover, and it was a good one because I got to be alone a lot of the time.

I had to make myself step up close to the boy — the one I'm talking about in the dump. Stepping up to him was hard to do because I wasn't supposed to do that with anyone I cared about. But I did it and I asked him in Spanish if I could take his picture. Some of you know Spanish, I'm sure. I said, "*¿Puedo fotografiarte?*" and he cocked his head, and for a moment I was back in the third grade and my friend Keith was looking at me. I jumped back and nearly tripped on the garbage. I wanted to run. But in that moment I was also myself twenty years in the future looking down at my own son and feeling a love I'd never felt before. No one, especially guys, ever feels a love like that — for children, I mean — when they're twenty-two. It's just not what life is like when you're twenty-two — unless you're a father already. But that's what I felt and that's what kept me from running away.

There were dirty streaks on the boy's neck from all that sweat and dirt. His ears were dirty and all he wanted to do when he saw me was beg. He kept shaking his head and putting out his hand and saying in English, "*Very poor! Very poor!*" He'd try to touch me — my camera, my sleeve — and I'd step back, shaking my head, too, because I was terrified. But I made myself do it. I gave him what I had — some coins and some bills. I was shaking like crazy because I was *touching* the money — *touching it and then giving it to him* — and as I did it I could see him dying right before me. But he didn't die, so I asked him again: "*Can I photograph you?*"

"Yes!" he said, happy now, the coins and bills in his hands. "*Foto! Foto!*" He'd gotten what he wanted and now I could snap his picture, just like any tourist would.

I took his picture and went back to my hotel downtown. Even though I didn't have the roll I'd taken at the dump processed, I didn't need to. I could see his face as I fell asleep. I dreamed about him; and I could see his face as I woke up and got ready to go back to the dump, where I was supposed to start the "distraction" — that's what we called it — that morning. The *favelas* were a logical place for it — with all the urban rats and the incredible transiency. Everyone in that country and in bordering countries and at WHO and the UN was waiting for some epidemic to start in that country. It was a time bomb. Cholera, typhoid, something. But if we — if the Agency — could get a big enough one going, there was a 90 percent chance that the government of — the government of that country — would topple. The military was ready for a coup. It had already tried once.

So I stood on the dump — in all that stink and garbage — and I just couldn't do it. I couldn't do it with the boy there somewhere — a boy who looked like my friend and a boy who was someone's kid — so I went looking for him, and it took an hour, but I found him. He was with his father and brothers, and I said, "*Debe llevarse a su familia a otra ciudad — ahora! Cosas malas llegan!*" That meant: *You've got to move your family to another city — right now! Bad things are com-*

ing! They looked at me like I was crazy, so I said it again and I got out the five hundred American dollars I'd had my department wire me. *Living expenses,* I'd explained, and that was fine with them. I said in Spanish, "I want you to be safe. You need to leave this place immediately. Do the boys have a mother?" No, she'd died, the father said. "I will give you five hundred American dollars if you will leave today — if you will leave now!"

The father looked at me and I knew damn well what he was thinking: *Crazy American.* The kind that tries to "save you." That sends money to your country because of a television show and if it gets to you it's a penny rather than a dollar.

He was willing to take the money, but you could tell he wasn't going to pack up and move — not today, maybe not ever. They had friends here, other families. You don't give that up even for five years of income, do you?

I looked at them and waited and finally I said, "If you don't go today, I'll take my money back. I'll call the police and tell them you robbed me, and I'll take my money back."

When he got the point, when he saw I was dead serious, he led me to the shack they lived in — the cardboard and corrugated metal shack that had no running water or sewage — and helped his boys get things together. I just stood there. I couldn't touch anything — anything they were going to bring. I wanted to put on rubber gloves so I could help them, but I couldn't do that either. They'd be insulted, and I didn't want to insult them. The boys gathered up six toy soldiers — two apiece — hammered from tin cans, a broken plastic gun, and two big balls of twine, and the father gathered up four dirty blankets, a can opener that looked bent, two pairs of pants for each of them, and a bag filled with socks, shoes, plastic plates, and cups. That's what they had. They'd slept on the dirt floor on those blankets. I'd never really thought of how people like this lived, and here it was. How do you live like that and not stop caring? I don't know.

I waited for them, and when they were ready we trudged back across the refuse and smells of the dump to the first paved road, where I took the bus with them to Parelo, where they said they had family in the *favela* there. They did. I paid for a taxi for us, sat in the front seat by myself, and dropped them off with the father's sister, who didn't look happy until she saw how much money it was. The *favela* wasn't much better than the dump, but it was two hundred miles away from where the epidemic would start, and it was a lot of money.

It was a dangerous thing for me to do — being that visible — but I didn't have any choice. I knew that if I didn't do it I'd see the boy's face forever, like a photograph in my head. I wasn't acting very normally then — I couldn't touch people — I started shaking even when I thought of touching anyone — but I knew I had to try to save this one kid. If anyone was following me, they'd wonder what the hell I was doing. That much money. A dump family. Getting them out of town and spending eleven hours on the bus with them. They might put two and two together later — someone might — but in a country this poor who'd be watching me? I was a leftist journalist and the regime was leftist. Who'd be watching a leftist reporter? And once the epidemic started, who'd be free to watch me?

I was much more worried about what my case agent and his boss and the DDP would say. "You did what?" they'd say. How do you tell someone?

I returned to Zaquitos — which took me a day.

The next morning I went back to the dump and started it. I bit down, heard the little crack, coughed into my hand, and began touching things when I got to the cemetery and crematorium, and the cars and little stores after that.

I tried not to look at anyone as I did it, especially anyone old or a woman or kids. Those were the ones who bothered me most. It was hard not to look, because you wanted to know, but I'd had a lot of practice not looking by then. *Just don't look,* a voice would say to me and I wouldn't.

The next day I took the train to the next two decent-sized cities; and when I was through with both of them, I stopped, cracked the other fillings, went to the capital, and flew back to the States before the quarantines could even get started.

I kept seeing the boy's face, sure, but it made me happy.

You're wondering why they let me talk about all of this — "top-secret your-eyes-only" kinds of things. The kinds of things that in the movies, if someone tells you, it gets you killed, right? They let me talk not only because they're not worried — how much damage can one guy who's not very credible, who's had mental problems, do? — but also, and this is the other half of it, because it's *old news.* It's actually there in the *Pentagon Papers* — that old book — if you look closely enough, and it's even mentioned — indirectly, of course — in Richard Nixon's autobiography, along with the planned use of a single-k nuclear device to end the war in Vietnam. It's old news and I get to talk about it now because it doesn't matter anymore. I guess that's what I'm saying. No one really cares. Vietnam doesn't care whether we were planning to detonate a nuclear device to flood Hanoi — they just want favored trade status now — and those countries in South America have each had half a dozen governments since then, and they want to forget too. Ancient history. Besides, the Agency has better things to do. They've got covert economic programs you wouldn't believe and designer diseases they haven't even used yet. This is the new war. The Army's got mines that can weigh you — tell you how much you weigh — and whether you're an adult or a child and whether you're carrying a gun. Other mines that land and become dozens of little mobile mines that go out looking for you instead of waiting for you to come to them. They've got suits that, if you're a soldier and wounded, will give you an antibiotic, or if you're poisoned, give you the antidote, or if you're out of water it will recycle your urine for you. You don't have to think. The suit thinks for you. They've got these things and they're using them. This is what warfare is now, so how important is a guy who can break a filling in his tooth and start some plague from the Middle Ages — something that crude and messy?

That's how they're thinking, believe me.

I did catch hell from my boss and his boss and the DDP when they found out what I'd done with the boy. I said, "That should tell you something. It should tell you that you don't really want me to do this for you anymore."

They actually let me quit. That surprised me. I didn't think you could quit. I'd seen too many movies, I guess, where no one could quit the Agency, like no one could quit the Mafia. They said they didn't really want me if my heart wasn't in it. But I don't think that was the real reason. I think it was that they just didn't need the program anymore. They were getting better programs.

They made me sign papers promising for twenty-five years not to write about what I'd done — what they'd had me do for my country — or talk about it publicly or to anyone who'd make it public —

and then they let me leave. I had all these interpersonal problems, as I've been saying, but I did go back to school and, I'm proud to say, got my MBA. I wanted to get a degree I could use anywhere. I started out as a manager of a drugstore, but that was because of the interpersonal problems; and when I could finally go to company meetings and not act strange, I started moving up the ladder. In three years I was in management at corporate headquarters, and that's where I met my wife. It took a few more years of therapy — of Agency shrinks at the VA hospital actually — to get over it enough to really function. The toothbrushes, the not touching people you loved, the nightmares and the flashbacks — all those things I needed to work through. My wife hung in there with me throughout it all — that I'll be forever grateful for — and we've got two kids almost grown now, both of them boys.

I don't know where that boy from Zaquitos is now, or if he's still alive. You don't live long in those countries. The Luz de Muerte paramilitary units — the ones that could make you "disappear" — started up under the military regime after I did what I was sent there to do. The new government was tied to a group called the Society for Church, Family, and Tradition, and those units were operating there for ten years at least. If the boy had any leftist leanings, he might not have made it through that. Or he could have been killed for no reason. Or, if he didn't get out of the *favelas,* he might have died of typhus or cholera or dengue fever. You lose a lot of Third World people to those diseases even now, and they're natural ones.

I think about that boy a lot. What if someone started a plague in the United States, maybe at the White House in a tour group, or maybe in a big airport like LAX — to turn the tables, to "destabilize" *us?* I think about that. I think of my own boys dying, no one around to save them the way I saved that boy and his brothers and father. One family's not very much, but it's something. That's what I tell myself anyway.

I guess that's it. I've gone way over my time, I know. Thanks for inviting me to speak today. It's good to have an audience. It's good to know that people, especially young people, are still interested in things like this. After all, I did what I could for you.

ALICE MUNRO

Dimension

FROM THE NEW YORKER

DOREE HAD TO TAKE three buses — one to Kincardine, where she waited for one to London, where she waited again, for the city bus out to the facility. She started the trip on a Sunday at nine in the morning. Because of the waiting times between buses, it took her until about two in the afternoon to travel the hundred-odd miles. All that sitting, either on buses or in the depots, was not a thing she should have minded. Her daily work was not of the sitting-down kind.

She was a chambermaid at the Comfort Inn. She scrubbed bathrooms and stripped and made beds and vacuumed rugs and wiped mirrors. She liked the work — it occupied her thoughts to a certain extent and tired her out so that she could sleep at night. She was seldom faced with a really bad mess, though some of the women she worked with could tell stories to make your hair curl. These women were older than her, and they all thought that she should try to work her way up. They told her that she should get trained for a job behind the desk, while she was still young and decent-looking. But she was content to do what she did. She didn't want to have to talk to people.

None of the people she worked with knew what had happened. Or, if they did, they didn't let on. Her picture had been in the paper — they'd used the photo he took of her with all three kids, the new baby, Dimitri, in her arms, and Barbara Ann and Sasha on either side, looking on. Her hair had been long and wavy and brown then, natural in curl and color, as he liked it, and her face bashful and soft — a reflection less of the way she was than of the way he wanted to see her.

Since then, she had cut her hair short and bleached and spiked it, and she had lost a lot of weight. And she went by her second name now: Fleur. Also, the job they had found for her was in a town a good distance away from where she used to live.

This was the third time she had made the trip. The first two times he had refused to see her. If he did that again she would just quit trying. Even if he did see her, she might not come again for a while. She was not going to go overboard. She didn't really know what she was going to do.

On the first bus she was not too troubled. Just riding along and looking at the scenery. She had grown up on the coast, where there was such a thing as spring, but here winter jumped almost directly into summer. A month ago there had been snow, and now it was hot enough to go bare-armed. Dazzling patches of water lay in the fields, and the sunlight was pouring down through naked branches.

On the second bus she began to feel jittery, and she couldn't help trying to guess which of the women around her might be going to the same place. They were women alone, usually dressed with some care, maybe to make themselves look as if they were going to church. The older ones looked as if they were going to strict old-fashioned churches where you had to wear a skirt and stockings and some sort of hat, while the younger ones might have belonged to a livelier congregation, which accepted pantsuits, bright scarves, earrings, and puffy hairdos. When you took a second look, you saw that some of the pantsuit women were quite as old as the others.

Doree didn't fit into either category. In the whole year and a half that she had been working she had not bought herself a single new piece of clothing. She wore her uniform at work and her jeans everywhere else. She had got out of the way of wearing makeup because he hadn't allowed it, and now, though she could have, she didn't. Her spikes of corn-colored hair didn't suit her bony bare face, but it didn't matter.

On the third bus she got a seat by the window, and tried to keep herself calm by reading the signs — both the advertising and the street signs. There was a certain trick she had picked up, to keep her mind occupied. She took the letters of whatever word her eyes lit on, and she tried to see how many new words she could make out of them. "Coffee," for instance, would give you "fee," and then "foe," and "off" and "of," and "shop" would provide "hop" and "sop" and "so" and — wait a minute — "posh." Words were more than plentiful on the way out of the city, as they passed billboards, monster stores, car lots, even balloons moored on roofs to advertise sales.

Doree had not told Mrs. Sands about her last two attempts, and probably wouldn't tell her about this one, either. Mrs. Sands, whom she saw on Monday afternoons, spoke of moving on, though she always said that it would take time, that things could not be hurried. She told Doree that she was doing fine, that she was gradually discovering her own strength.

"I know those words have been done to death," she said. "But they're still true."

She blushed at what she heard herself say — *death* — but did not make it worse by apologizing.

When Doree was sixteen — that was seven years ago — she'd gone to visit her mother in the hospital every day after school. Her mother was recovering from an operation on her back, which was said to have been serious but not dangerous. Lloyd was an orderly. He and Doree's mother had in common the fact that they were both old hippies — though Lloyd was actually a few years the younger — and whenever he had time he'd come in and chat with her about the concerts and protest marches they'd both attended, the outrageous people they'd known, drug trips that had knocked them out, that sort of thing.

Lloyd was popular with the patients because of his jokes and his sure, strong touch. He was stocky and broad-shouldered and authoritative enough to be sometimes taken for a doctor. (Not that he was pleased by that — he held the opinion that a lot of medicine was a fraud and a lot of doctors were jerks.) He had sensitive reddish skin and light hair and bold eyes.

He kissed Doree in the elevator and told her that she was a flower in the desert. Then he laughed at himself, and said, "How original can you get?"

"You're a poet and don't know it," she said, to be kind.

One night her mother died suddenly, of an embolism. Doree's mother had a lot of women friends who would have taken Doree in — and she stayed with one of them for a time — but the new friend

Lloyd was the one Doree preferred. By her next birthday she was pregnant, then married. Lloyd had never been married before, though he had at least two children whose whereabouts he was not certain of. They would have been grown up by then, anyway. His philosophy of life had changed as he got older — he believed now in marriage, constancy, and no birth control. And he found the Sechelt Peninsula, where he and Doree lived, too full of people these days — old friends, old ways of life, old lovers. Soon he and Doree moved across the country to a town they picked from a name on the map: Mildmay. They didn't live in town; they rented a place in the country. Lloyd got a job in an ice cream factory. They planted a garden. Lloyd knew a lot about gardening, just as he did about house carpentry, managing a wood stove, and keeping an old car running.

Sasha was born.

"Perfectly natural," Mrs. Sands said.

Doree said, "Is it?"

Doree always sat on a straight-backed chair in front of the desk, not on the sofa, which had a flowery pattern and cushions. Mrs. Sands moved her own chair to the side of the desk, so that they could talk without any kind of barrier between them.

"I've sort've been expecting you would," she said. "I think it's what I might have done, in your place."

Mrs. Sands would not have said that in the beginning. A year ago, even, she'd have been more cautious, knowing how Doree would have revolted, then, at the idea that anybody, any living soul, could be in her place. Now she knew that Doree would just take it as a way, even a humble way, of trying to understand.

Mrs. Sands was not like some of them. She was not brisk, not thin, not pretty. Not too old, either. She was about the age that Doree's mother would have been, though she did not look as if she'd ever been a hippie. Her graying hair was cut short and she had a mole riding on one cheekbone. She wore flat shoes and loose pants and flowered tops. Even when they were of a raspberry or turquoise color these tops did not make her look as if she really cared what she put on — it was more as if somebody had told her she needed to smarten herself up and she had obediently gone shopping for something she thought might do that. Her large, kind, impersonal sobriety drained all assaulting cheerfulness, all insult, out of those clothes.

"Well, the first two times I never saw him," Doree said. "He wouldn't come out."

"But this time he did? He did come out?"

"Yes, he did. But I wouldn't hardly have known him."

"He'd aged?"

"I guess so. I guess he's lost some weight. And those clothes. Uniforms. I never saw him in anything like that."

"Wasn't he once an orderly?"

"It wasn't the same."

"He looked to you like a different person?"

"No." Doree caught at her upper lip, trying to think what the difference was. He'd been so still. She had never seen him so still. He hadn't even seemed to know that he should sit down opposite her. Her first words to him had been "Aren't you going to sit down?" And he had said, "Is it all right?"

"He looked sort of vacant," she said. "I wondered if they had him on drugs?"

"Maybe something to keep him on an even keel. Mind you, I don't know. Did you have a conversation?"

Doree wondered if it could be called that. She had asked him some stupid ordinary questions. How was he feeling? (Okay.) Did he get enough to eat? (He thought so.) Was there any place where he could walk if he wanted to? (Under supervision, yes. He guessed you could call it a place. He guessed you could call it walking.)

She'd said, "You have to get fresh air."

He'd said, "That's true."

She'd nearly asked him if he had made any friends. The way you ask your kid about school. The way, if your kids went to school, you would ask them.

"Yes. Yes," Mrs. Sands said, nudging the ready box of Kleenex forward. Doree didn't need it; her eyes were dry. The trouble was in the bottom of her stomach. The heaves.

Mrs. Sands just waited, knowing enough to keep her hands off.

And, as if he'd detected what she was on the verge of saying, Lloyd had told her that there was a psychiatrist who came and talked to him every so often.

"I tell him he's wasting his time," Lloyd said. "I know as much as he does."

That was the only time that he had sounded to Doree anything like himself.

All through the visit her heart had kept thumping. She'd thought she might faint or die. It cost her such an effort to look at him, to get him into her vision as this thin and gray, diffident yet cold, mechanically moving yet uncoordinated man.

She had not said any of this to Mrs. Sands. Mrs. Sands might have asked — tactfully — whom she was afraid of. Herself or him? But she wasn't *afraid.*

When Sasha was one and a half, Barbara Ann was born, and, when Barbara Ann was two, they had Dimitri. They had named Sasha together, and then they made a pact that he would name the boys and she would name the girls.

Dimitri was the first one to be colicky. Doree thought that he was maybe not getting enough milk, or that her milk was not rich enough. Or too rich? Not right, anyway. Lloyd had a lady from the La Leche League come and talk to her. Whatever you do, the lady said, you must not put him on a supplementary bottle. That would be the thin edge of the wedge, she said, and pretty soon you would have him rejecting the breast altogether. She spoke as if that would be a major tragedy.

Little did she know that Doree had been giving him a supplement already. And it seemed to be true that he preferred that — he fussed more and more at the breast. By three months he was entirely bottle-fed, and then there was no way to keep it from Lloyd. She told him that her milk had dried up, and she'd had to start supplementing. Lloyd squeezed one breast after the other with frantic determination and succeeded in getting a couple of drops of miserable-looking milk out. He called her a liar. They fought. He said that she was a whore like her mother.

All those hippies were whores, he said.

Soon they made up. But whenever Dimitri was fretful, whenever he had a cold, or was afraid of the older children's pet rabbit, or still hung on to chairs at the age when his brother and sister had been walking unsupported, the failure to breast-feed was recalled.

The first time Doree had gone to Mrs. Sands's office, one of the other women there had given her a pamphlet. On the front of it were a gold cross and words made up of gold and purple letters:

"When Your Loss Seems Unbearable . . ." Inside, there was a softly colored picture of Jesus and some finer print that Doree did not read.

In her chair in front of the desk, still clutching the pamphlet, Doree began to shake. Mrs. Sands had to pry it out of her hand.

"Did somebody give you this?" Mrs. Sands said.

Doree said, "Her," and jerked her head at the closed door.

"You don't want it?"

"When you're down is when they'll try and get at you," Doree said, and then realized that this was something her mother had said, when some ladies with a similar message came to visit her in the hospital. "They think you'll fall on your knees and then it'll be all right."

Mrs. Sands sighed.

"Well," she said. "It's certainly not that simple."

"Not even possible," Doree said.

"Maybe not."

They never spoke of Lloyd, in those days. Doree never thought of him if she could help it, and then only as if he were some terrible accident of nature.

"Even if I believed in that stuff," she said — meaning what was in the pamphlet — "it would only be so that . . ." She meant to say that such a belief would be convenient because she could then think of Lloyd burning in Hell, or something of that sort, but she was unable to go on, because it was just too stupid to talk about. And because of a familiar impediment that was like a hammer hitting her in the belly.

Lloyd thought that their children should be educated at home. This was not for religious reasons — going against dinosaurs and cavemen and monkeys and all that — but because he wanted them to be close to their parents and to be introduced to the world carefully and gradually, rather than thrown into it all at once. "I just happen to think they are my kids," he said. "I mean they are our kids, not the Department of Education's kids."

Doree wasn't sure that she could handle this, but it turned out that the Department of Education had guidelines, and lesson plans that you could get from your local school. Sasha was a bright boy who practically taught himself to read, and the other two were still too little to learn much yet. In the evenings and on weekends Lloyd taught Sasha about geography and the solar system and the hibernation of animals and how a car runs, covering each subject as the questions came up. Pretty soon Sasha was ahead of the school plans, but Doree picked them up anyway and put him through the exercises right on time so that the law would be satisfied.

There was another mother in the district doing homeschooling. Her name was Maggie and she had a minivan. Lloyd needed his car to get to work, and Doree had not learned to drive, so she was glad when Maggie offered her a ride to the school once a week to turn in the finished exercises and pick up the new ones. Of course they took all the children along. Maggie had two boys. The older one had so many allergies that she had to keep a strict eye on everything he ate — that was why she taught him at home. And then it seemed that she might as well keep the younger one there as well. He wanted to stay with his brother and he had a problem with asthma, anyway.

How grateful Doree was then, comparing her healthy three. Lloyd said that it was because she'd had her children when she was still young, while Maggie had waited until she was on the verge of menopause. He was exaggerating how old Maggie was, but it was true that she had waited. She was an optometrist. She and her husband had been partners, and they hadn't started their family until she could leave the practice and they had a house in the country.

Maggie's hair was pepper-and-salt, cropped close to her head. She was tall, flat-chested, cheerful, and opinionated. Lloyd called her the Lezzie. Only behind her back, of course. He kidded with her on the phone but mouthed at Doree, "It's the Lezzie." That didn't really bother Doree — he called lots of women Lezzies. But she was afraid that the kidding would seem overly friendly to Maggie, an intrusion, or at least a waste of time.

"You want to speak to the ole lady. Yeah, I got her right here. She's rubbing my work pants up and down the scrub board. See, I only got the one pair of pants. Anyway, I believe in keeping her busy."

Doree and Maggie got into the habit of shopping for groceries together, after they'd picked up the papers at the school. Then sometimes they got takeout coffees at Tim Horton's and took the children to Riverside Park. They sat on a bench while Sasha and Maggie's boys raced around or hung from the climbing contraptions, and Barbara Ann pumped on the swing and Dimitri played in the sandbox. Or they sat in the mini, if it was cold. They talked mostly about the children, and things they cooked, but somehow Doree found out about how Maggie had trekked around Europe before training as an optometrist and Maggie found out how young Doree had been when she got married. Also about how easily she had become pregnant at first, and how she didn't so easily anymore, and how that made Lloyd suspicious, so that he went through her dresser drawers looking for birth-control pills — thinking she must be taking them on the sly.

"And are you?" Maggie asked.

Doree was shocked. She said she wouldn't dare.

"I mean, I'd think that was awful to do, without telling him. It's just kind of a joke when he goes looking for them."

"Oh," Maggie said.

And one time Maggie said, "Is everything all right with you? I mean in your marriage? You're happy?"

Doree said yes, without hesitation. After that she was more careful about what she said. She saw that there were things that she was used to that another person might not understand. Lloyd had a certain way of looking at things; that was just how he was. Even when she'd first met him, in the hospital, he'd been like that. The head nurse was a starchy sort of person, so he'd called her Mrs. Bitch-out-of-hell, instead of her name, which was Mrs. Mitchell. He said it so fast that you could barely catch on. He'd thought that she picked favorites, and he wasn't one of them. Now there was somebody he detested at the ice cream factory, somebody he called Suck-stick Louie. Doree didn't know the man's real name. But at least that proved that it wasn't only women who provoked him.

Doree was pretty sure that these people weren't as bad as Lloyd thought, but it was no use contradicting him. Perhaps men just had to have enemies, the way they had to have their jokes. And sometimes Lloyd did make the enemies into jokes, just as if he were laughing at himself. She was even allowed to laugh with him, as long as she wasn't the one who started the laughing.

She hoped that he wouldn't get that way about Maggie. At times she was afraid she saw something of the sort coming. If he prevented her from riding to the school and the grocery store with Maggie it would be a big inconvenience. But worse would be the shame. She would have to make up some stupid lie, to explain things. But Maggie would know — at least she would know that Doree was lying, and she would interpret that, probably, as meaning that Doree was in a worse situation than she really was. Maggie had her own sharp no-nonsense way of looking at things.

Then Doree asked herself why she should care, anyway, what Maggie might think. Maggie was an outsider, not even somebody Doree felt particularly comfortable with. It was Lloyd and Doree and their family that mattered. Lloyd said that, and he was right. The truth of things between them, the bond, was not something that anybody else could understand and it was not anybody else's business. If Doree could watch her own loyalty it would be all right.

It got worse, gradually. No direct forbidding, but more criticism. Lloyd coming up with the theory that Maggie's boys' allergies and asthma might be Maggie's fault. The reason was often the mother, he said. He used to see it at the hospital all the time. The overcontrolling, usually overeducated mother.

"Some of the time kids are just born with something," Doree said, unwisely. "You can't say it's the mother every time."

"Oh. Why can't I?"

"I didn't mean *you*. I didn't mean you can't. I meant couldn't they be born —"

"Since when are you such a medical authority?"

"I didn't say I was."

"No. And you're not."

Bad to worse. He wanted to know what they talked about, she and Maggie.

"I don't know. Nothing, really."

"That's funny. Two women riding in a car. First I heard of it. Two women talking about nothing. She is out to break us up."

"Who is? *Maggie?*"

"I've got experience of her kind of woman."

"What kind?"

"Her kind."

"Don't be silly."

"Careful. Don't call me silly."

"What would she want to do that for?"

"How am I supposed to know? She just wants to do it. You wait.

You'll see. She'll get you over there bawling and whining about what a bastard I am."

And in fact it turned out as he had said. At least it would certainly have looked that way, to Lloyd. She did find herself at around ten o'clock one night in Maggie's kitchen, sniffling back her tears and drinking herbal tea. Maggie's husband had said, "What the hell?" when she knocked — she heard him through the door. He hadn't known who she was. She'd said, "I'm really sorry to bother you —" while he stared at her with lifted eyebrows and a tight mouth. And then Maggie had come.

Doree had walked all the way there in the dark, first along the gravel road that she and Lloyd lived on, then on the highway. She headed for the ditch every time a car came, and that slowed her down considerably. She did take a look at the cars that passed, thinking that one of them might be Lloyd. She didn't want him to find her, not yet, not till he was scared out of his craziness. Other times she had been able to scare him out of it herself, by weeping and howling and even banging her head on the floor, chanting, "It's not true, it's not true, it's not true," over and over. Finally he would back down. He would say, "Okay, okay. I'll believe you. Honey, be quiet. Think of the kids. I'll believe you, honest. Just stop."

But tonight she had pulled herself together just as she was about to start that performance. She had put on her coat and walked out the door, with him calling after her, "Don't do this. I warn you!"

Maggie's husband had gone to bed, not looking any better pleased about things, while Doree kept saying, "I'm sorry. I'm so sorry, barging in on you at this time of the night."

"Oh, shut up," Maggie said, kind and businesslike. "Do you want a glass of wine?"

"I don't drink."

"Then you'd better not start now. I'll get you some tea. It's very soothing. Raspberry-camomile. It's not the kids, is it?"

"No."

Maggie took her coat and handed her a wad of Kleenex for her eyes and nose. "Don't try to tell me yet. We'll soon get you settled down."

Even when she was partway settled down Doree didn't want to

blurt out the whole truth, and let Maggie know that she herself was at the heart of the problem. More than that, she didn't want to have to explain Lloyd. No matter how worn out she got with him, he was still the closest person in the world to her, and she felt that everything would collapse if she were to bring herself to tell someone exactly how he was, if she were to be entirely disloyal.

She said that she and Lloyd had got into an old argument and she was so sick and tired of it that all she'd wanted was to get out. But she would get over it, she said. They would.

"Happens to every couple sometime," Maggie said.

The phone rang then, and Maggie answered.

"Yes. She's okay. She just needed to walk something out of her system. Fine. Okay then, I'll deliver her home in the morning. No trouble. Okay. Good night.

"That was him," she said. "I guess you heard."

"How did he sound? Did he sound normal?"

Maggie laughed. "Well, I don't know how he sounds when he's normal, do I? He didn't sound drunk."

"He doesn't drink, either. We don't even have coffee in the house."

"Want some toast?"

In the morning, early, Maggie drove her home. Maggie's husband hadn't left for work yet, and he stayed with the boys.

Maggie was in a hurry to get back, so she just said, "Bye-bye. Phone me if you need to talk," as she turned the minivan around in the yard.

It was a cold morning in early spring, snow still on the ground, but there was Lloyd sitting on the steps without a jacket on.

"Good morning," he said, in a loud, sarcastically polite voice. And she said good morning, in a voice that pretended not to notice his.

He did not move aside to let her up the steps.

"You can't go in there," he said.

She decided to take this lightly.

"Not even if I say please? Please."

He looked at her but did not answer. He smiled with his lips held together.

"Lloyd?" she said. "Lloyd?"

"You better not go in."

"I didn't tell her anything, Lloyd. I'm sorry I walked out. I just needed a breathing space, I guess."

"Better not go in."

"What's the matter with you? Where are the kids?"

He shook his head, as he did when she said something he didn't like to hear. Something mildly rude, like "holy shit."

"*Lloyd.* Where are the kids?"

He shifted just a little, so that she could pass if she liked.

Dimitri still in his crib, lying sideways. Barbara Ann on the floor beside her bed, as if she'd got out or been pulled out. Sasha by the kitchen door — he had tried to get away. He was the only one with bruises on his throat. The pillow had done for the others.

"When I phoned last night?" Lloyd said. "When I phoned, it had already happened.

"You brought it all on yourself," he said.

The verdict was that he was insane, he couldn't be tried. He was criminally insane — he had to be put in a secure institution.

Doree had run out of the house and was stumbling around the yard, holding her arms tight across her stomach as if she had been sliced open and was trying to keep herself together. This was the scene that Maggie saw, when she came back. She had had a premonition, and had turned the minivan around in the road. Her first thought was that Doree had been hit or kicked in the stomach by her husband. She could make nothing out of the noises Doree was making. But Lloyd, who was still sitting on the steps, moved aside courteously for her, without a word, and she went into the house and found what she was now expecting to find. She phoned the police.

For some time Doree kept stuffing whatever she could grab into her mouth. After the dirt and grass it was sheets or towels or her own clothing. As if she were trying to stifle not just the howls that rose up but the scene in her head. She was given a shot of something, regularly, to quiet her down, and this worked. In fact she became very quiet, though not catatonic. She was said to be stabilized. When she got out of the hospital and the social worker brought her to this new place, Mrs. Sands took over, found her somewhere to live, found her a job, established the routine of talking with her once a week. Maggie would have come to see her, but she was the one person Doree could not stand to see. Mrs. Sands said that that feeling was natural — it was the association. She said that Maggie would understand.

Mrs. Sands said that whether or not Doree continued to visit Lloyd was up to her. "I'm not here to approve or disapprove, you know. Did it make you feel good to see him? Or bad?"

"I don't know."

Doree could not explain that it had not really seemed to be him she was seeing. It was almost like seeing a ghost. So pale. Pale loose clothes on him, shoes that didn't make any noise — probably slippers — on his feet. She had the impression that some of his hair had fallen out. His thick and wavy, honey-colored hair. There seemed to be no breadth to his shoulders, no hollow in his collarbone where she used to rest her head.

What he had said, afterward, to the police — and it was quoted in the newspapers — was "I did it to save them the misery."

What misery?

"The misery of knowing that their mother had walked out on them," he said.

That was burned into Doree's brain and maybe when she decided to try to see him it had been with the idea of making him take it back. Making him see, and admit, how things had really gone.

"You told me to stop contradicting you or get out of the house. So I got out of the house."

"I only went to Maggie's for one night. I fully intended to come back. I wasn't walking out on anybody."

She remembered perfectly how the argument had started. She had bought a tin of spaghetti that had a very slight dent in it. Because of that it had been on sale and she had been pleased with her thriftiness. She had thought that she was doing something smart. But she didn't tell him that, once he had begun questioning her about it. For some reason she'd thought it better to pretend that she hadn't noticed.

Anybody would notice, he said. We could have all been poisoned. What was the matter with her? Or was that what she had in mind? Was she planning to try it out on the kids or on him?

She had told him not to be crazy.

He had said that it wasn't him who was crazy. Who but a crazy woman would buy poison for her family?

The children had been watching from the doorway of the front room. That was the last time she'd seen them alive.

So was that what she had been thinking — that she could make him see, finally, who it was that was crazy?

When she realized what was in her head, she should have got off the bus. She could have got off even at the gates, with the few other women who plodded up the drive. She could have crossed the road and waited for the bus back to the city. Probably some people did that. They were going to make a visit and then decided not to. People probably did that all the time.

But maybe it was better that she had gone on, and seen him so strange and wasted. Not a person worth blaming for anything. Not a person. He was like a character in a dream.

She had dreams. In one dream she had run out of the house after finding them, and Lloyd had started to laugh in his old easy way, and then she had heard Sasha laughing behind her and it had dawned on her, wonderfully, that they were all playing a joke.

"You asked me if it made me feel good or bad when I saw him? Last time, you asked me?"

"Yes, I did," Mrs. Sands said.

"I had to think about it."

"Yes."

"I decided it made me feel bad. So I haven't gone again."

It was hard to tell with Mrs. Sands, but the nod she gave seemed to show some satisfaction or approval.

So when Doree decided that she would go again, after all, she thought that it was better not to mention it. And since it was hard not to mention whatever happened to her — there being so little, most of the time — she phoned and canceled her appointment. She said that she was going on a holiday. They were getting into summer, when holidays were the usual thing. With a friend, she said.

"You aren't wearing the jacket you had on last week."

"That wasn't last week."

"Wasn't it?"

"It was three weeks ago. The weather's hot now. This is lighter but I don't really need it. You don't need a jacket at all."

He asked about her trip, what buses she'd had to take from Mildmay.

She told him that she wasn't living there anymore. She told him where she lived, and about the three buses.

"That's quite a trek for you. Do you like living in a bigger place?"

"It's easier to get work there."

"So you work?"

She had told him last time about where she lived, the buses, where she worked.

"I clean rooms in a motel," she said. "I told you."

"Yes. Yes. I forgot. I'm sorry. Do you ever think about going back to school? Night school?"

She said that she did think about it but never seriously enough to do anything. She said that she didn't mind the work she was doing.

Then it seemed as if they could not think of anything more to say.

He sighed. He said, "Sorry. Sorry. I guess I'm not so used to conversation."

"So what do you do all the time?"

"I guess I read quite a bit. Kind of meditate. Informally."

"Oh."

"I appreciate you coming here. It means a lot to me. But don't think you have to keep it up. I mean, just when you want to. Just come when you want to. If something comes up, or if you don't feel like it — What I'm trying to say is, just the fact that you could come at all, that you even came once, that's a bonus for me. Do you get what I mean?"

She said yes, she thought so.

He said that he didn't want to interfere with her life.

"You're not," she said.

"Was that what you were going to say? I thought you were going to say something else."

In fact, she had almost said, What life?

No, she said, not really, nothing else.

"Good."

Three more weeks and she got a phone call. It was Mrs. Sands herself on the line, not one of the women in the office.

"Oh, Doree. I thought you might not be back yet. From your holiday. So you are back?"

"Yes," Doree said, trying to think where she could say she had been.

"But you hadn't got around to arranging another appointment?"

"No. Not yet."

"That's okay. I was just checking. You are all right?"

"I'm all right."

"Fine. Fine. You know where I am if you ever need me. Ever just want to have a talk."

"Yes."

"So take care."

She hadn't mentioned Lloyd, hadn't asked if the visits had continued. Well, of course, Doree had said that they weren't going to. But Mrs. Sands was pretty good, usually, about sensing what was going on. Pretty good at holding off, too, when she understood that a question might not get her anywhere. Doree didn't know what she would have said, if asked — whether she would have backtracked and told a lie or come out with the truth. She had gone back, in fact, the very next Sunday after he more or less told her that it didn't matter whether she came or not.

He had a cold. He didn't know how he'd got it.

Maybe he had been coming down with it, he said, the last time he saw her, and that was why he'd been morose.

Morose. She seldom had anything to do, nowadays, with anyone who used a word like that, and it sounded strange to her. But he had always had a habit of using such words, and of course at one time they hadn't struck her as they did now.

"Do I seem like a different person to you?" he asked.

"Well, you look different," she said cautiously. "Don't I?"

"You look beautiful," he said sadly.

Something softened in her. But she fought against it.

"Do you feel different?" he asked. "Do you feel like a different person?"

She said she didn't know. "Do you?"

He said, "Altogether."

Later in the week a large envelope was given to her at work. It had been addressed to her care of the motel. It contained several sheets of paper, with writing on both sides. She didn't think at first of its being from him — she somehow had the idea that people in prison were not allowed to write letters. But, of course, he was a different sort of prisoner. He was not a criminal. He was only criminally insane.

There was no date on the document and not even a "Dear Doree." It just started talking to her in such a way that she thought it had to be some sort of religious invitation:

> People are looking all over for the solution. Their minds are sore (from looking). So many things jostling around and hurting them. You can see in their faces all their bruises and pains. They are troubled. They rush around. They have to shop and go to the laundromat and get their hair cut and earn a living or pick up their welfare checks. The poor ones have to do that and the rich ones have to look hard for the best ways to spend their money. That is work too. They have to build the best houses with gold faucets for their hot and cold water. And their Audis and magical toothbrushes and all possible contraptions and then burglar alarms to protect against slaughter and all ~~neigh~~ neither rich nor poor have any peace in their souls. I was going to write "neighbor" instead of "neither," why was that? I have not got any neighbor here. Where I am at least people have got beyond a lot of confusion. They know what their possessions are and always will be and they don't even have to buy or cook their own food. Or choose it. Choices are eliminated.
>
> All we that are here can get is what we can get out of our own minds.
>
> At the beginning all in my head was purturbation (Sp?). There was everlasting storm, and I would knock my head against cement in the hope of getting rid of it. Stopping my agony and my life. So punishments were meted. I got hosed down and tied up and drugs introduced in my bloodstream. I am not complaining either, because I had to learn there is no profit in that. Nor is it any different from the so-called real world, in which people drink and carry on and commit crimes to eliminate their thoughts which are painful. And often they get hauled off and incarcerated but it is not long enough for them to come out on the other side. And what is that? It is either total insanity or peace.
>
> Peace. I arrived at peace and am still sane. I imagine reading this now you are thinking I am going to say something about God Jesus or at any rate Buddha as if I had arrived at a religious conversion. No. I do not close my eyes and get lifted up by any specific Higher Power. I do not really know what is meant by any of that. What I do is Know Myself. Know Thyself is some kind of Commandment from somewhere, probably the Bible so at least in that I may have followed Christianity. Also, To Thy Own Self Be True — I have attempted that if it is in the Bible also. It does not say which parts — the bad or the good — to be true to so it is

not intended as a guide to morality. Also Know Thyself does not relate either to morality as we know it in Behavior. But Behavior is not really my concern because I have been judged quite correctly as a person who cannot be trusted to judge how he should behave and that is the reason I am here.

Back to the Know part in Know Thyself. I can say perfectly soberly that I know myself and I know the worst I am capable of and I know that I have done it. I am judged by the World as a Monster and I have no quarrel with that, even though I might say in passing that people who rain down bombs or burn cities or starve and murder hundreds of thousands of people are not generally considered Monsters but are showered with medals and honors, only acts against small numbers being considered shocking and evil. This being not meant as an excuse but just observation.

What I Know in Myself is my own Evil. That is the secret of my comfort. I mean I know my Worst. It may be worse than other people's worst but in fact I do not have to think or worry about that. No excuses. I am at peace. Am I a Monster? The World says so and if it is said so then I agree. But then I say, the World does not have any real meaning for me. I am My Self and have no chance to be any other Self. I could say that I was crazy then but what does that mean? Crazy. Sane. I am I. I could not change my I then and I cannot change it now.

Doree, if you have read this far, there is one special thing I want to tell you about but cannot write it down. If you ever think of coming back here then maybe I can tell you. Do not think I am heartless. It isn't that I wouldn't change things if I could but I can't.

I am sending this to your place of work which I remember and the name of the town so my brain is working fine in some respects.

She thought that they would have to discuss this piece of writing at their next meeting and she read it over several times, but she could not think of anything to say. What she really wanted to talk about was whatever he had said was impossible to put in writing. But when she saw him again he behaved as if he had never written to her at all. She searched for a topic and told him about a once famous folksinger who had stayed at the motel that week. To her surprise he knew more than she did about the singer's career. It turned out that he had a television, or at least access to one, and watched some shows and, of course, the news, regularly. That gave them a bit more to talk about, until she could not help herself.

"What was the thing you couldn't tell me except in person?"

He said that he wished she hadn't asked him. He didn't know if they were ready to discuss it.

Then she was afraid that it would be something she really could not handle, something unbearable, such as that he still loved her. "Love" was a word she could not stand to hear.

"Okay," she said. "Maybe we're not."

Then she said, "Still, you better tell me. If I walked out of here and was struck down by a car then I would never know, and you would never have the chance to tell me again."

"True," he said.

"So what is it?"

"Next time. Next time. Sometimes I can't talk anymore. I want to but I just dry up, talking."

I have been thinking of you Doree ever since you left and regret I disappointed you. When you are sitting opposite me I tend to get more emotional than perhaps I show. It is not my right to go emotional in front of you, since you certainly have the right more than me and you are always very controlled. So I am going to reverse what I said before because I have come to the conclusion I can write to you after all better than I can talk.

Now where do I start?

Heaven exists.

That is one way but not right because I never believed in Heaven and Hell, etc. As far as I was concerned that was always a pile of crap. So it must sound pretty weird of me to bring up the subject now.

I will just say then: I have seen the children.

I have seen them and talked to them.

There. What are you thinking at the moment? You are thinking well, now he is really round the bend. Or, it's a dream and he can't distinguish a dream, he doesn't know the difference between a dream and awake. But I want to tell you I do know the difference and what I know is, they exist. I say they exist, not they are alive, because alive means in our particular Dimension, and I am not saying that is where they are. In fact I think they are not. But they do exist and it must be that there is another Dimension or maybe innumerable Dimensions, but what I know is that I have got access to whatever one they are in. Possibly I got hold of this from being so much on my own and having to think and think and with such as I have to think about. So after such suffering and solitude there is a Grace that has seen the way to giving me this reward. Me the very one that deserves it the least to the world's way of thinking.

Well if you have kept reading this far and not torn this to pieces you must want to know something. Such as how they are. They are fine. Really happy and smart. They don't seem to have any memory of anything bad. They are maybe a little older than they were but that is hard to say. They seem to understand at different levels. Yes. You can notice with Dimitri that he has learned to talk which he was not able to do. They are in a room I can partly recognize. It's like our house but more spacious and nicer. I asked them how they were being looked after and they just laughed at me and said something like they were able to look after themselves. I think Sasha was the one who said that. Sometimes they don't talk separately or at least I can't separate their voices but their identities are quite clear and I must say, joyful.

Please don't conclude that I am crazy. That is the fear that made me not want to tell you about this. I was crazy at one time but believe me I have shed all my old craziness like the bear sheds his coat. Or maybe I should say the snake sheds his skin. I know that if I had not done that I would never have been given this ability to reconnect with Sasha and Barbara Ann and Dimitri. Now I wish that you could be granted this chance as well because if it is a matter of deserving then you are way ahead of me. It may be harder for you to do because you live in the world so much more than I do but at least I can give you this information — the Truth — and in telling you I have seen them hope that it will make your heart lighter.

Doree wondered what Mrs. Sands would say or think, if she read this letter. Mrs. Sands would be careful, of course. She would be careful not to pass any outright verdict of craziness but she would carefully, kindly, steer Doree around in that direction. Or you might say she wouldn't steer — she would just pull the confusion away so that Doree would have to face what would then seem to have been her own conclusion all along. She would have to put the whole dangerous nonsense — this was Mrs. Sands speaking — out of her mind.

That was why Doree was not going anywhere near her.

Doree did think that he was crazy. And in what he had written there seemed to be some trace of the old bragging. She didn't write back. Days went by. Weeks. She didn't alter her opinion but she still held on to what he'd written, like a secret. And from time to time, when she was in the middle of spraying a bathroom mirror or tightening a sheet, a feeling came over her. For almost two years she had not taken any notice of the things that generally made people happy, such as nice weather or flowers in bloom or the smell of a bakery. She still did not have that spontaneous sense of happiness, exactly, but she had a reminder of what it was like. It had nothing to do with the weather or flowers. It was the idea of the children in what he had called their Dimension that came sneaking up on her in this way, and for the first time brought a light feeling to her, not pain.

In all the time since what had happened had happened, any thought of the children had been something she had to get rid of, pull out immediately like a knife in her throat. She could not think their names, and if she heard a name that sounded like one of theirs she had to pull that out, too. Even children's voices, their shrieks and slapping feet as they ran to and from the motel swimming pool, had to be banished by a sort of gate that she could slam down behind her ears. What was different now was that she had a refuge she could go to as soon as such dangers rose anywhere around her.

And who had given it to her? Not Mrs. Sands — that was for sure. Not in all those hours sitting by the desk with the Kleenex discreetly handy.

Lloyd had given it to her. Lloyd, that terrible person, that isolated and insane person.

Insane if you wanted to call it that. But wasn't it possible that what he said was true — that he had come out on the other side? And who was to say that the visions of a person who had done such a thing and made such a journey might not mean something?

This notion wormed its way into her head and stayed there.

Along with the thought that Lloyd, of all people, might be the person she should be with now. What other use could she be in the world — she seemed to be saying this to somebody, probably to Mrs. Sands — what was she here for if not at least to listen to him?

I didn't say "forgive," she said to Mrs. Sands in her head. I would never say that. I would never do it.

But think. Aren't I just as cut off by what happened as he is? Nobody who knew about it would want me around. All I can do is remind people of what nobody can stand to be reminded of.

Disguise wasn't possible, not really. That crown of yellow spikes was pathetic.

So she found herself traveling on the bus again, heading down the highway. She remembered those nights right after her mother had died, when she would sneak out to meet Lloyd, lying to her mother's friend, the woman she was staying with, about where she was going. She remembered the friend's name, her mother's friend's name. Laurie.

Who but Lloyd would remember the children's names now, or the color of their eyes? Mrs. Sands, when she had to mention them, did not even call them children, but "your family," putting them in one clump together.

Going to meet Lloyd in those days, lying to Laurie, she had felt no guilt, only a sense of destiny, submission. She had felt that she was put on earth for no reason other than to be with him and try to understand him.

Well, it wasn't like that now. It was not the same.

She was sitting on the front seat across from the driver. She had a clear view through the windshield. And that was why she was the only passenger on the bus, the only person other than the driver, to see a pickup truck pull out from a side road without even slowing down, to see it rock across the empty Sunday-morning highway in front of them and plunge into the ditch. And to see something even stranger: the driver of the truck flying through the air in a manner that seemed both swift and slow, absurd and graceful. He landed in the gravel at the edge of the pavement, on the opposite side of the highway.

The other passengers didn't know why the driver had put on the brakes and brought them to a sudden uncomfortable stop. And at first all that Doree thought was, How did he get out? That young man or boy, who must have fallen asleep at the wheel. How did he fly out of the truck and launch himself so elegantly into the air?

"Fellow right in front of us," the driver said to his passengers. He was trying to speak loudly and calmly, but there was a tremor of amazement, something like awe, in his voice. "Just plowed across the road and into the ditch. We'll be on our way again as soon as we can and in the meantime please don't get out of the bus."

As if she had not heard that, or had some special right to be useful, Doree got out behind him. He did not reprimand her.

"Goddamn asshole," he said as they crossed the road and there was nothing in his voice now but anger and exasperation. "Goddamn asshole kid, can you believe it?"

The boy was lying on his back, arms and legs flung out, like somebody making an angel in the snow. Only there was gravel around him, not snow. His eyes were not quite closed. He was so young, a boy who had shot up tall before he even needed to shave. Possibly without a driver's license.

The driver was talking on his phone.

"Mile or so south of Bayfield, on 21, east side of the road."

A trickle of pink foam came out from under the boy's head, near the ear. It did not look like blood at all, but like the stuff you skim off the strawberries when you're making jam.

Doree crouched down beside him. She laid a hand on his chest. It was still. She bent her ear close. Somebody had ironed his shirt recently — it had that smell.

No breathing.

But her fingers on his smooth neck found a pulse.

She remembered something she'd been told. It was Lloyd who had told her, in case one of the children had an accident and he wasn't there. The tongue. The tongue can block the breathing, if it has fallen into the back of the throat. She laid the fingers of one hand on the boy's forehead and two fingers of the other hand under his chin. Press down on the forehead, press up on the chin, to clear the airway. A slight firm tilt.

If he still didn't breathe she would have to breathe into him.

She pinches the nostrils, takes a deep breath, seals his mouth with her lips, and breathes. Two breaths and check. Two breaths and check.

Another male voice, not the driver's. A motorist must have stopped. "You want this blanket under his head?" She shook her head tightly. She had remembered something else, about not moving the victim, so that you would not injure the spinal cord. She enveloped his mouth. She pressed his warm fresh skin. She breathed and waited. She breathed and waited again. And a faint moisture seemed to rise against her face.

The driver said something but she could not look up. Then she felt it for sure. A breath out of the boy's mouth. She spread her hand on the skin of his chest and at first she could not tell if it was rising and falling, because of her own trembling.

Yes. Yes.

It was a true breath. The airway was open. He was breathing on his own. He was breathing.

"Just lay it over him," she said to the man with the blanket. "To keep him warm."

"Is he alive?" the driver said, bending over her.

She nodded. Her fingers found the pulse again. The horrible pink stuff had not continued to flow. Maybe it was nothing important. Not from his brain.

"I can't hold the bus for you," the driver said. "We're behind schedule as it is."

The motorist said, "That's okay. I can take over."

Be quiet, be quiet, she wanted to tell them. It seemed to her that silence was necessary, that everything in the world outside the boy's body had to concentrate, help it not to lose track of its duty to breathe.

Shy but steady whiffs now, a sweet obedience in the chest. Keep on, keep on.

"You hear that? This guy says he'll stay and watch out for him," the driver said. "Ambulance is coming as fast as they can."

"Go on," Doree said. "I'll hitch a ride to town with them and catch you on your way back tonight."

He had to bend to hear her. She spoke dismissively, without raising her head, as if she were the one whose breath was precious.

"You sure?" he said.

Sure.

"You don't have to get to London?"

No.

EILEEN POLLACK

The Bris

FROM SUBTROPICS

WHEN MARCUS PACKED FOR FLORIDA, he harbored no illusions about what would happen when he got there. His father's liver soon would fail, and, without a transplant, he couldn't survive the week. "Why waste a miracle on an elderly man like me?" his father scoffed. He pooh-poohed the new liver as if it were a slightly used sports car Marcus insisted he buy. "At least let me put your name on the waiting list," Marcus said, but his father blew raspberries through the phone. "Give that same liver to someone young, and he or she could get another fifty years out of the goddamn thing."

And so, with a heavy carry-on and an even heavier heart, Marcus flew to West Palm Beach. He rented a car and drove to the hospital in Boca Raton where his father had been taken after his last collapse. As he checked in at Registration and followed the arrows to the room, he prepared for the likelihood that in another few days he would be arranging his father's funeral. What he couldn't have predicted was that first he would be called on to arrange his father's bris.

"Your bris, Pop?" Marcus laughed, although his father rarely joked; for a former hotelkeeper in the Catskills, he was a singularly humorless man. His request that Marcus find a *mohel* who would circumcise him before he died could only be an effect of the drugs he was taking or the poison seeping from his liver. "Don't worry, Pop. All of that was taken care of a long time ago."

His father waved a bloated yellow arm. Hooked up to an IV, he reminded Marcus of an inflated creature in the Thanksgiving Day parade. "A lie," his father gasped. "Everything has been a lie."

"What, Pop? What lie?" If there was one thing Marcus knew, it was that his father didn't lie, any more than he ate shellfish or pork. When Marcus had been a boy, his father made such a megillah about never telling lies or playing tricks that Marcus imagined he must once have been the victim of some terrible prank or hoax. That his guileless, defenseless father had been wounded by someone's lie made Marcus resolve never to lie himself. When he started his first accounting job in Manhattan in the eighties, he couldn't bring himself to fudge even the tiniest account his employer expected him to fudge. A quarter of a century later, he still had trouble living in the world of shaded truths most New Yorkers lived in. "Don't talk to me about lying," he told his dad. "You're the most truthful man I know."

His father squinched his lips and shrugged, a gesture meant to convey that he wasn't the saint everyone took him to be. "They won't let me be buried —" He sucked oxygen from the tube inside his nose. "In the plot. Beside your mother."

Marcus was seized by the premonition that his father was about to reveal a sordid and completely out-of-character affair with the woman who used to work as the social director at the family's hotel. While Marcus's mother had been alive, his father had treated Liddy Newman's voluptuous advances as a burden to be endured rather than a pleasure to be pursued. But Marcus's mother had dropped dead of a heart attack while working in the kitchen one particularly stressful night when Marcus was fifteen, and he had never understood how or why his father found the self-control not to fool around with Liddy after that.

When his father finally sold Lieberman's — gave it away was more like it, to a group of Brooklyn Hasids who promised they would use it as a camp for retarded teenagers, then used it as a getaway for themselves — he moved to a retirement community in Boca, where the widows hounded him so ferociously he took a few to lunch. Maybe he took a few to bed. But how could that deny him the right to be buried with Marcus's mother?

"The cemetery," his father rasped. In his younger days he had been a tall, fair broomstick of a man, with mild blue eyes and a generous expression; he reminded Marcus of a scarecrow begging the crows to take his corn. But this last bout of hepatitis had puffed his face and limbs and turned his irises and skin such a bilious yellow-orange that he looked as if vandals had stuffed him with extra straw and jammed a rotting pumpkin on his neck.

"The cemetery," Marcus repeated dully, the reality sinking in that within a few days both his father and his mother would be lying in the ground.

Although apparently not together.

"The cemetery is only for Orthodox Jews." Marcus's father's hand drifted to his groin, which he clutched as if it pained him. "And that is something I am not. Not only am I not an Orthodox Jew, I am not a Jew of any kind."

Marcus hadn't been aware that he had been holding his breath until he let it out. "Pop, if you haven't been a good enough Jew, no one ever has." He recited his father's acts of charity — his quiet beneficence to the poor, his selfless attentions to Marcus's mother and her parents, the litany of favors he had extended to the guests, employees, and hangers-on at Lieberman's Mountain Rest.

His father chopped off the recitation. "None of that is relevant. You might as well say that actions such as these make a man a good Christian."

Marcus rubbed his eyes. He had been up late the night before deciding whether to propose to his girlfriend, Vicki, despite her desire to have a child, something Marcus was loath to promise. His flight from LaGuardia had left at six. On the plane he couldn't sleep, mostly because the harried young man beside him couldn't control his son. The boy kept vaulting Marcus's knees and bounding down the aisle, colliding with the flight attendants; Marcus took this as a sign that he was too old to have a child. Not that Vicki had made having a child a prerequisite to getting married. But how could he live with the knowledge that he had deprived the woman he loved of what she wanted most?

"I wasn't born a Jew," his father cried. "And I never converted. It was such a little thing. But I couldn't face the prospect of anyone coming near me with a knife — down there. The very thought made me woozy."

The force of his father's revelation set in. Short and solid as he was, Marcus swayed like a beachfront high-rise in a hurricane. He sat heavily on the bed and tucked his head between his legs. "This isn't making sense. All these years and, what, you've been *pretending* to be a Jew?"

His father nodded and turned away. What little Marcus knew of his father's early life came back to him. Orphaned young, he had deserted his rural Texas town to escape "a lack of opportunities" that Marcus had always assumed to be the result of anti-Semitism. His father had lied about his age, enlisted in the army, spent two years overseas, and suffered a minor wound. A veteran at nineteen, he had landed in New York and found a job in the garment district winding ribbon on cardboard spools; he went to school at night and earned his diploma, then used his GI loan to finance a few semesters at NYU, after which he took a summer job waiting tables in the Catskills, where he fell hopelessly in love with the owners' daughter, married her, and never left. Now, as Marcus listened to a revised and expanded version of those events, he understood that the astonishing gaps in his father's history — Marcus had never seen a photo from the years before New York, never met a Texas relative — had disturbed him so much that he'd never dared to ask for an explanation.

In truth, his father had been the only child of narrow Baptist parents who were indifferent to his survival, let alone his desire to find a less restricted, warmer, more cosmopolitan way of life. "It was one of those Christian homes where the only book is the Bible. They were scornful of anything that brought comfort to a boy. Music. Art. A kind word. A pat on the shoulder. One time, my father found a drawing of a pretty girl, a classmate, I had sketched in a notebook. It wasn't meant to be crude. I had never seen a naked female and I was trying to visualize . . . My father beat me and broke my hand." He teared up even now. "To draw a beautiful girl is a sin, but breaking a young boy's fingers isn't?" He took another gasp of oxygen. "That was the first instance I ran away. I hid in the back of a bus to Lubbock, which was the nearest big town, and I sneaked in a theater to see my first movie show. I was so sick with guilt that before the picture started I needed to go to the men's room and vomit. But it was entirely worth the fear. The movie was a Marx Brothers feature. Can you imagine what it was like for me to see those four brothers act in such a way? In the movie, the brothers live in a made-up country, but in my mind, they might have lived on Mars."

That his father, as a boy, had had his hand broken for sketching a female classmate and run away to see *Duck Soup* filled Marcus with a pity so profound it nearly burst his chest. Certainly, this explained why his father used to drop whatever he was doing, even on the busiest weekend of the year, to turn on the little black-and-white TV set in Marcus's bedroom and spend two hours watching whatever Marx Brothers movie happened to be on. Until now, Marcus had attributed his father's fondness for the Marx Brothers to the fact that only these four comedians could make him laugh. And yet, thinking back on those afternoons when he and his father had sat at the foot of Marcus's single bed watching *Horsefeathers* or *A Night at the Opera,* he felt sadly left out, as if his father and the Marx Brothers, instead of playing their tricks on some overly zealous cop or a wealthy snobbish matron, had been playing a trick on him.

His father wiped his eyes. "You can imagine the beating I got when I returned home. My father could only think that I had gone to town to visit a house of prostitution. Prostitutes! It had taken all my courage just to sketch that naked girl! I can't imagine how I made it through another year in that house. But where was I to go? This is a terrible thing to admit, but I was glad there was a war. How else could I have gotten away so young?"

Here, the new version of his father's autobiography merged with the version Marcus already knew. "I was so tall, I had no trouble passing for two years older. But what a shock, meeting those older men. The way they cursed! What they said about women! Imagine what I felt, finding people who believed that Christ was no more than a carpenter who had lived in Galilee a long, long time ago." Not that his conversion had been immediate. He simply felt so much more at home among the Jews he met in the army and in Manhattan that he absorbed their culture and religion, their love for music, art, and books.

"I had been told that Jews were stingy. But to my way of thinking, they gave too much of everything. They talked too loudly, too much. They studied too hard, made too much fuss about their health, about everyone's health, about this or that injustice. They made a lot of money, but they gave so much away. And food! The mountains of food they ate! It came to me that Christians lied about Jews to hide their own guilt at being so stingy, not only with their money but with their love."

He hadn't taken the job at Lieberman's with the intention of passing as a Jew. It was just that once he got there, everyone assumed he was one.

"I told your mother. *She* knew the truth. And I would have converted. For your mother, I would have done anything. I wanted to be a Jew. In my heart, I already was one." He rose from his pillow. "But every time I thought of being circumcised . . ." He turned a paler shade of yellow. Beads of oily sweat popped out on his brow. "Your mother, *oleha ha sholem,* took pity on my dilemma. She wanted to be married to a Jew, but she loved me too much to insist that I suffer anything I couldn't suffer willingly."

It came to Marcus that he had never seen his father's genitals. For all the years they had shared a house, for all the times they had changed together in a locker room, he had never caught his father naked. If he had thought anything, he had assumed that his father was excessively shy or afflicted with some embarrassing deformity — his balls were strangely shaped, his penis too small or oddly bent. The realization that his father's obsessive modesty had been a deliberate sham made Marcus feel as foolish as a shtetl wife who has learned that she's been the dupe of a Yentl-like deceiver, so ignorant of the facts of life she couldn't figure out that her "husband" was a woman dressed up as a man.

His father's eyes were closed. The tracings on the monitor flowed as quietly as the ripples on a pond. He jostled his father's hip. "Pop, it's all right. Whatever it is, I forgive you."

Without opening his eyes, his father patted Marcus's hand. "For your forgiveness I thank you. But what I need from you now is not your forgiveness but your help."

Not ask his forgiveness? He remembered all those Saturdays when his father had carried him to shul, slipped a yarmulke on his head, wrapped him in a tallis, then sat beside him on the bench and helped him follow the Hebrew prayers. (Did his father even know Hebrew? When would he have learned? More likely, he had glanced at their neighbors' books, spied the right page, and followed as best he could.) When Marcus lost his faith and considered canceling his bar mitzvah, his father listened to his objections and quietly and persuasively reinstated his belief, if not in God then at least in being Jewish. None of these things had done Marcus any harm. Yet there seemed something unsavory in their having been performed by a gentile. It was as if a man pretending to be a doctor had removed Marcus's appendix, and even though the operation had proved a success, Marcus couldn't help but be shaken to learn that the surgeon had been a quack.

"In other ways I'm not a coward," his father said. "In the war, I ran across a field while bullets were being shot and I dragged a man to safety. I saw terrible bloody sights a man ought never see."

A long time went by. The elderly man in the next bed passed gas so forcefully that Marcus jumped. "*Oy, gevalt,*" the man moaned. "Tell me, dear God, what I did to deserve such misery!" As if every human fart were under God's control.

Marcus plucked a Kleenex and wiped his father's brow. His father opened his eyes and pressed Marcus's palm to his lips. "You are a good boy, and I am sorry if I failed you. What little I know about being a parent I had to teach myself. My own father cared only that I never drink or dance. He died a few months after I ran away. My mother couldn't be bothered to make inquiries. She died when you were four. Who was there to say I wasn't actually a Jew?"

The onslaught of revelations, including a gentile grandmother who had still been alive in Texas when Marcus was a child, rendered him mute. He wanted to get away and think. Or rather, he wanted to call Vicki and ask her what he ought to be thinking. "Pop," he said, "this isn't doing either of us any good. Why not take a nap? I'll drive to the condo and eat a bite, then come back and see you later."

His father grabbed his wrist; it felt as if he were being touched by a rubber glove full of lukewarm water. "We don't have much time."

"Time? Time for what? Don't tell me that you intend to get circumcised now."

"That is exactly what I do intend."

"Oh, Pop, can't we just get the folks who run the cemetery to make an exception? Would they actually refuse to allow you to be buried with Mom?"

"Of course they would refuse! Ahavath Yisroel is only for Orthodox Jews. And to be an Orthodox Jew, a man must be circumcised. The night before the funeral, the members of the burial society must sit up and wash the body, and the individuals on that committee would immediately notice what was what. If they made an exception for me, why not make an exception for everyone?" He shook his head miserably, the plastic tube from the oxygen mask waving like a tusk.

Marcus had never seen his father's face so troubled. His lips were dry and rough, and he kept licking them as he spoke. "Pop, I don't get it. Why did you bury Mom in Bubbe and Zayde's plot if you knew you wouldn't be allowed to be buried there with her?"

The tracings on the monitor erupted, as if a meteor had hit the pond. "You know how much your mother loved her parents! How could I deny her the right to spend eternity beside them?" And — what he didn't mention — how much he had loved them, too, the Jewish parents he'd never had. "They gave us those spaces as a wedding gift. If we had refused to be buried in their plot, we would have needed to explain the reason. I was still a young man. I thought I had all the time in the world. I assumed there would be advances."

"Advances? You were expecting the doctors were going to come up with a pill you could swallow and your foreskin fell off? Believe me, Pop, that sort of research is not high on the list of medical priorities." The mere mention of someone's foreskin falling off caused his head to swim. The two times he had been invited to a bris, Marcus had needed to sit on the stoop outside until the cutting part was over. "There's no use discussing it. Your body couldn't stand the shock."

His father wrapped his hands around the rail and pulled himself to sit. "I'm going to die anyway. I might as well die a Jew."

"Pop, I can't."

"Have I ever asked you anything? Have I ever, in all your years, asked you a single thing?"

No, Marcus thought, he hadn't. His father had taught him how to swim — albeit, so Marcus could supervise the hotel pool — and his happiest memories were of him and his dad washing off the stink of serving the evening meal by taking a midnight swim. His father had bought a book and used it to teach the two of them to hit a tennis ball on the single cracked court at Lieberman's. True, this was partly so Marcus could provide a partner for the guests, but he and his dad had enjoyed many a cutthroat set in the mystical predawn hour before the guests got up and started clamoring for their lox and eggs. His father had given Marcus everything a father could give — and what a mother could give as well. He had cooked for him and cleaned. He had nursed Marcus through the mumps, mononucleosis, diarrhea, and upset stomachs. Marcus felt like a gambler who could never repay his bookie. Better to change your name and run away, start a new life, put your debts behind you.

Which, except for the name change, was exactly what Marcus had done. He had moved to Manhattan, gotten his degree in accounting, and set up the kind of life in which he was free from obligations, even to himself. Rather than cook, he ate out. He sent his dirty clothes to a laundry and hired a maid to clean. He lived within his means and paid off his college loans. For Christ's sake, he didn't even own a cell phone. He owed nothing to anyone. Except, it seemed, his father.

"Pop, if the people in the burial society see a recent scar, won't they be suspicious?"

His father held up a finger, as if Marcus finally had asked a question worthy of an answer. "If the foreskin has been removed and the survivors of the deceased can provide a certificate of conversion, the officials must accept that the individual is a Jew. As it happens, I have a friend who is a rabbi. Twice a week I attend the services that Rabbi Dobrinski conducts at the condo shul. Three times a week, we play tennis as partners. At first, he wasn't so enthusiastic. But I kept speaking from the heart, and he began to see my point. Also, I agreed to leave my money to his synagogue. If you add your plea to mine, he won't refuse."

Marcus was incensed to learn that his father had pledged his few hard-earned dollars to bribe some unscrupulous rabbi into performing a religious rite that he ought to perform for free. He wondered if his father meant that Marcus ought to add his own money to his father's "donation" in the hope that this larger bribe would persuade the rabbi to do their bidding.

"Once the rabbi is on board," his father went on, "all that will remain is finding a *mohel* who will perform the circumcision."

"Sure," Marcus said, "that's all. And who do you suppose is going to circumcise a dying man?"

His father motioned toward the cart beside the bed. Marcus opened the little drawer and found a newspaper clipping about a pediatrician named David S. Schiffler, who, in his spare time, performed ritual circumcisions for the newborn Jewish males of Boca Raton. "That's quite an interesting sideline," Marcus said. "And lucrative as well."

"Don't make fun. You think a man like this, a professional man, needs what he earns performing a bris? He donates his fee to the Boca March of Dimes. Also, he is performing a service for the community. He comes in the home, but he does the procedure in a sanitary, modern way; the baby isn't traumatized."

Marcus was about to remind his father that he wasn't a baby when a nurse bustled in.

"Now we will be having a soothing, refreshing bath," the woman said with a Jamaican lilt. "We can't let a man get all smelly, now can we?"

"The rabbi," his father said. "You can find him on the tennis court. He plays a doubles match at four."

The nurse drew the curtain around the bed. "First we will wash down as far as possible." She dipped a sponge in a pan of soapy water and squeezed out the excess. "Then we will wash up as far as possible." Giggling, she reached for his father's gown. "And then we must wash possible!"

As thoroughly as it irked him that a stranger would get to view what had been hidden from him so long, Marcus was horrified at the prospect. In his mind, his father's penis grew and grew and grew, a pointy-headed rocket zooming for outer space. Before the nurse could expose his father's "possible," he dashed out into the hall. Weaving to avoid the patients and their relatives who hobbled along the corridors three- and five-abreast, he headed for the lobby. Outside, he found his car and reached for the key, only to find the clipping about Dr. Schiffler still crumpled inside his fist.

During his father's previous bouts with hepatitis, Marcus had become acquainted with the route from the hospital to the condo. Still, he lost his way. He pulled off on the shoulder near an intersection where a cheerless man in overalls was selling the *Homeless Times* and a girl in a green bikini hawked hot dogs from a cart. The father he had known for forty-eight years was dying, as was the father who had grown up in a poverty-stricken Baptist town and had his hand broken for drawing a picture of a girl, then glimpsed redemption in a universe ruled by Groucho Marx. In the months and years to come, whenever a question about this gentile Texas father sprang to Marcus's mind, there wouldn't be a soul to answer it.

How could such an honest man have lived such a whopping lie? And how could he have made such a tsimmes about the shame a lie could bring? Then again, who else was qualified to issue such a warning? For thirty-three years, the poor man had lived without sex to avoid the need to explain to a Jewish woman why he wasn't circumcised. Marcus almost wished that his father had been the kind of person who would sleep with someone he had no intention of ever marrying. *Oh, Pop, wasn't the urge to make love stronger than your fear of having your foreskin cut off?*

He knew he ought to go. With the way the retirees down here drove, if he sat here long enough someone would plow into him. Bits of red plastic from an earlier victim's taillight still littered the intersection. But Marcus couldn't move. His poor mother! It must have made her sad to know that she wasn't really married to a Jew. Or to a man who loved her enough to face his worst fear for her sake. How isolated she must have felt, how cut off from her parents.

Unless her parents knew. How could they not have known? Now that Marcus thought about it, his father didn't look the least bit Jewish. His name was James Sloan. There had been so few available Jewish men during the war that Marcus's mother was twenty-seven when they met, six years older than her suitor. How could her parents have objected to a handsome, generous man who was willing to marry their spinster daughter and live a Jewish life and run the hotel they loved? The only detail they hadn't guessed was that, unlike most American men, their son-in-law wasn't circumcised. Marcus did the math. Was it possible that his father had been only forty-three when Marcus's mother died? Then again, Marcus had been so absorbed in pretending that his mother's death hadn't nearly killed him that he barely had noticed his father's grief, let alone his age.

Once a week, after the guests checked out on Sunday, they had driven to the little Jewish cemetery on the outskirts of town, where Marcus shuffled down the path with the feigned indifference of an adolescent hiding his bitter urge to fall on his mother's grave and weep. Even now, he sometimes rented a car and drove up to visit the plot where his mother and grandparents lay beneath a monument engraved with the family name. Most of the surrounding monuments also bore the names of Catskills resorts, which reinforced Marcus's notion that owning a hotel and serving people killed you. Certainly it had killed his mother. She might have been overweight, but trying to feed 250 guests without a salad man or a dishwasher could have killed a thinner woman with a much healthier heart.

Yet who was he to say? His mother had loved running Lieberman's. If such interments had been permitted, she would have asked to be buried on the front lawn. He missed the hotel, too. Whenever he visited his mother's grave, he sat with his back to his grandfather's stone and imagined they were all waiting for his father, the way they used to wait for him to finish some repair or settle some dispute and join them in the dining room before the Sabbath meal.

And his father had screwed it up. He'd had thirty-three years to muster the courage to check into the hospital and allow the doctors to trim his foreskin — under anesthesia, after all — and he'd put it off and put it off. Maybe it wasn't only the fear of the operation. Maybe he hadn't been able to face the idea of giving up that last little bit of the man he used to be.

But did his father actually believe that this Dr. Schiffler would agree to perform a circumcision on a dying man? For a moment, Marcus wondered if a *mohel* would circumcise his father *after* he was dead, but the notion made him ill.

The homeless man tapped on his window, and Marcus shook his head to indicate that he didn't want to buy a newspaper. It bothered him that the man wasn't allowed to beg but had to pretend to sell a newspaper no one wanted to read. These days, no one was allowed to give anything away for free, not even charity. Marcus saw the girl in the green bikini pointing to her cart and miming the act of eating a hot dog, so he pulled onto the road again. He was hungry enough that he could have wolfed down several hot dogs, but he didn't want anyone to think that he was one of those men who would buy a woman's wares so he could look down her cleavage when she leaned in the window and set his hot dogs in his lap.

The condo development where his father lived was populated almost exclusively by Orthodox Jews. No rules excluded gentiles, but what Christian would want to settle in a place where the country club served heavy kosher meals, the tennis courts and pool were locked from sundown Friday to sundown Saturday, and nearly all the residents attended services at the dumpy concrete synagogue within the development's walls? While the guard checked Marcus's name against a list, he felt the impulse to reveal his father's lie. He couldn't have said why. He felt no less Jewish than before. He had inherited his *zayde* Lieberman's dark Hebraic looks. That his mother had been a Jew guaranteed that Marcus would be certified as a Jew by even the strictest rabbi. He had attended Hebrew School, well, religiously, and — thanks to his father — been circumcised and bar mitzvahed. His father had lived a completely Jewish life for nearly seven decades. How could this one act of sacrifice — which most Jewish male babies underwent when they were drunk on Manischewitz the *mohel* had given them to suck from a bit of cloth — count for so much?

The guard waved Marcus through. Of course he wouldn't reveal his father's origins. He didn't wish him any harm. As for his father's right to live in this development, God would be issuing His own eviction notice soon enough.

He parked in his father's space and let himself into the condo, which was stuffy and stank of mold. His father had never been a hoarder and, in recent years, had given away most of what he owned. Every time Marcus flew down for a visit, he flew back to New York with a moth-eaten cardigan or a set of wooden coat-hangers or a box of jellied fruit slices some kindly female neighbor had given his father for Passover the year before. Little remained on the condo's shelves except the novels of Leon Uris, some kitschy figurines of Jewish peddlers, and his grandparents' brass menorah. Marcus turned on the air conditioner, but the unit was so palsied that his khakis and shirt were plastered to his skin before the place cooled down. The apartment, which until then had held only pleasant associations, now harbored a sinister possibility in every nook, as if the harmless geckos flitting here and there might suddenly hiss and bite.

He looked up Dr. Schiffler's number, picked up his father's rotary phone, and dialed. When he finally got through, he told the receptionist that he needed to discuss a circumcision. "There are . . . let's call them complications," Marcus said, and she agreed to let him speak to the pediatrician at 6:15, when his regular appointments were done.

Marcus lingered by the phone. If only he could talk to Vicki. But he needed to get to the tennis courts in time to catch Rabbi Dobrinski before his doubles match at four.

The air was so humid he could hardly catch his breath. He crossed the parking lot and reached the pool, which shimmered seductively in the sun, then walked along the path that skirted the development's man-made lagoon. The water was a sludgy brown that concealed who-knew-what creatures. Alligators? Snakes? From earlier explorations, Marcus knew the shore was lined with the sandy mounds of fire ants. Yet he entertained the fantasy of running down the bank and diving in.

Finally he reached the tennis club, whose palm-shaded courts and coolers of icy water beckoned like an oasis. Marcus had played his father here three times, and all three times he'd lost. As kind as his father was, he turned fiendish on a tennis court. No matter where Marcus hit the ball, his father, with his willowy arms and legs, could reach it and hit it back. Even now that Marcus's father had grown too old to run, he could still slice a ball so deftly that it traced corkscrews in the air before landing just shy of Marcus's racket.

He stepped into the clubhouse, where the air conditioning froze his sodden clothes. Beyond the racks of colorful nylon shorts, he found a woman in her fifties standing behind the desk. She had brassy red hair and enormous blue-framed glasses. Racket-shaped earrings dangled from her ears.

"Excuse me," Marcus said. "I'm looking for Rabbi Dobrinski. My father said he always plays a doubles match at four."

The woman startled Marcus by reaching across the counter and taking his hand in both of hers. "You must be James's son. How is he? What a dear, dear man. Please, next time you see him, tell him Rita Crookstein sends her love."

She wasn't his father's type, but it pained Marcus that Rita Crookstein probably felt real affection for his dad and had little or no idea why he'd never asked her out. The clubhouse door swung open and three leathery, fit old men came in. All three wore white shorts, white polo shirts, white cotton knee-highs, and various bandages and supports around their limbs. Two of the men had fluorescent green yarmulkes bobby-pinned to their hair.

"Excuse me," Marcus said, "I'm looking for Rabbi Dobrinski."

The shortest of the three men lifted the tinted lenses clipped to his regular frames. He looked Marcus up and down.

"My father is in the hospital," Marcus said. "He's very ill. He sent me to ask a favor."

The rabbi took out a handkerchief and blew his nose. "I'm sorry he's in the hospital. But your father already asked his favor, and already I told him no."

Marcus rose to full height. Even at five foot six he was taller than the rabbi. What kind of spiritual leader would act in such a peremptory way to the son of a dying man? Extortionists like Dobrinski were exactly the reason Marcus didn't belong to a congregation. You joined, and right away someone demanded to see your tax returns and dunned you 5 percent, then hit you up for pledges to the building fund and the mortgage fund, donations to the UJA, and service on committees. In return, all you got was a seat for Rosh Hashanah and a place to say kaddish when one of your parents died. Like Diogenes with his lamp, Marcus longed to find a spiritual leader who didn't see his position as an opportunity to take advantage of a person in need. "My father told me you'd consented —" He glanced at the other men, who pretended to be examining a rack of shirts. "To do what he asked."

The rabbi unzipped his racket. "Your father believes what he wants to believe." He said this in such a loud voice that the other men and Rita Crookstein couldn't pretend they hadn't heard. "What I told him was, I will come when he is dying and offer what prayers I can. If he takes this to mean I will issue some sort of paper that says he is a Jew, he is badly misinformed."

"But if a dying man wishes to convert to Judaism? If he wishes to be buried beside his wife? After all, my father lived most of his life as a Jew."

Dobrinski bounced his racket against his fist. "I have known your father nine years. We play tennis. We play golf. We discuss politics and theology. More than that, we are friends. So, you don't think it's a shock, all of a sudden he tells me he's not a Jew? Against non-Jews I have nothing. But against non-Jewish friends who pretend to be Jewish . . . Pardon me if I do not believe that the reward for so many years of deceit should be an easy deathbed conversion." The rabbi flipped down his lenses and started toward the courts.

"Rabbi Dobrinski." Marcus raised his voice. "My father is dying. You say he is your friend. Yet you can't find it in your heart to stretch the rules?" Something came back to him from his years in Hebrew School. "I thought that any rule could — and should — be broken to save a dying man."

Rabbi Dobrinski stopped. "To *save* a dying man. Not to hasten his death. If this truly were a matter of bringing about *shalom biet,* peace in the family . . . But it is only about allowing your father the convenience of being buried as a Jew."

"But think of the peace it will bring my mother. Think of the peace it will bring to me!"

"I am not entirely without sympathy for your case. *Your* case, not your father's. But a conversion must come about as a complete change of heart. The act of circumcision, followed by immersion in the ritual bath, the mikvah, must be experienced by the convert as a blessing. Your father wants his conversion should entail a sleight of hand. He wants the *mohel* and I should say abracadabra while he's lying there unconscious and suddenly he's a Jew. And not just any kind of Jew, but an Orthodox Jew, an observant Jew —"

The telephone rang, and Rita Crookstein answered it. "Yes," she said, "the three of them are here. I'm so sorry. I'll let them know." She hung up and primped her hair. "Rabbi Dobrinski? That was Mr. Markowitz. His wife suffered another stroke. He's calling from the hospital. He can't make your doubles match today."

All three men looked as disappointed as if the messiah weren't coming. Then they turned to Marcus.

"If you are your father's son," Dobrinski said, "you know your way around a tennis court."

Marcus almost said no, but his vanity wouldn't allow it. "I play. But tennis wasn't on my mind when I packed to come down here." Nothing his father owned would fit. The sneakers would be too tight, and the ancient racket his father played with was made of some heavy metal Marcus could barely lift.

Dobrinski motioned to the desk. "Rackets she has plenty." He looked at Marcus's feet. "Size nine, a common size. There is a dress code at this club, but I am sure you will find a suitable shirt and shorts in Ms. Crookstein's lost and found."

"You expect me to play tennis at a time like this?"

"Let me put it this way. If you fill out our fourth, I will see what I can do about your father's request."

It took Marcus a while to get the rabbi's point. Already this Dobrinski had extracted a donation to his shul from Marcus's father. Now he was trying to extract a doubles game from Marcus. "Fine," Marcus said, "but only for an hour."

"An hour is all we play. In case you hadn't noticed, we are not such young men." He introduced Marcus's partner, Victor Eisen, and the rabbi's partner, Isaac Karsh. Rita Crookstein loaned Marcus a shirt and shorts. The racket's frame was dented, as if someone had smashed it against the court, and the strings were strung too loose, but as keyed up as he was, Marcus felt confident that he could beat the rabbi and Isaac Karsh with a fly swatter.

Yet once they were on the court, Marcus muffed shot after shot. The ball failed to clear the net or went sailing out of bounds. He dribbled in serves so weak they could have been returned by a crippled Girl Scout. Sweat cascaded down his brow and made the racket slip inside his grip. He had never before played on a clay court and this threw off his rhythm. His opponents' yarmulkes were the same fluorescent green as the balls and constantly misled his gaze. (No doubt this was intentional. Who had ever seen yarmulkes in such an obnoxious hue?) Worse, his mind was on his father. Marcus would have given anything — gallons of blood, a kidney, the very marrow from his bones — to save his father's life. Instead, he had been asked to play a game of tennis in the Florida heat so that his father could have a bris, and this he couldn't do.

In no time, Marcus and his partner were behind five games to love. Marcus found it difficult to hit his most powerful shots against two such frail old men. What if Rabbi Dobrinski ran for a shot and fell? What if Isaac Karsh suffered a heart attack and died?

Nor was Marcus's partner in healthy shape. When Dobrinski tossed up a lob, Eisen shaded his eyes, scuttled backward like a crab, then shrugged and let the ball drop without trying to smash it. "Stenosis of the spine," he explained to Marcus. "I lean too far back, I could snap something in my neck and be paralyzed for life." When Eisen played at net and a shot came whizzing toward him, he stepped aside and let it pass. Worse, he was nearly deaf and couldn't hear the strategies for a comeback that Marcus whispered in his ear when they switched sides between games.

Karsh was no Rod Laver, but Dobrinski must have known that he was giving Marcus the weaker partner. Marcus suspected the rabbi would try to cheat, but if anything, he was a stickler for the rules. Repeatedly, he called foot faults on Marcus, which no one had ever done, and questioned his every call, demanding to see the skid marks for any shot that landed anywhere near a line. Marcus got so rattled that he and his partner lost the first set six games to love, then started going under in the second set.

"Either you're not much of a player," the rabbi gloated, "or you're not trying. I won't even consider doing what your father asks unless you win two games."

Marcus was enraged. The rabbi had mentioned nothing about how many games he needed to win to fulfill their bargain. As Dobrinski prepared to serve, Marcus bent low, weaving and bobbing, forgetting everything except his desire to smash the return of serve crosscourt as deep and hard as possible. The rabbi tossed the ball, and the serve came looping high and wide with a devious slice. But Marcus had played enough games against his father, who used a similarly deceptive spin, to know just what to do. He let the ball drop, drew his racket back and down, then whipped it across his chest. The rabbi, who had come to net for what he assumed to be a winner, took Marcus's return in his face. His glasses went flying — the tinted lenses came off, as if a bird had lost its wings in flight — and he dropped to his knees and screamed.

Eisen helped him to a chair. Karsh doused a towel with water and laid it across the rabbi's eyes.

Marcus crouched beside the rabbi. "Are you all right? Can you see?" He was appalled at what he'd done but couldn't keep from glancing at his watch; he had less than an hour before he was due to meet Schiffler. "You have to admit, I satisfied what you asked. If I get a *mohel* to perform the bris, will you sign a certificate of conversion?"

The rabbi raised his fist. "Not in a million years! This is the Almighty's way of reminding me what happens to those who turn a blind eye to deception."

"Oh come on," Marcus scoffed. "You can't seriously believe —"

The rabbi peeled off the towel, and Marcus could see red skid marks above and below the eye. "No," he said, "I don't. But you knocked some sense back into me. I can't be party to more betrayals. I love your father. He is a very good man. But I will not sign some phony document of conversion." Squinting, he peered from the teary eye, moaned, and shook his head. "And now will someone please drive me to the emergency room before I lose what little sight God has seen fit to spare?"

Blinding a rabbi was no small matter. Had Marcus helped his father's cause or ruined it? He had no time to carry out his usual calculation as to who owed what to whom. If Schiffler performed the circumcision, the burial society might assume that the wound had been the result of a medical procedure in his father's final days and see no reason to ask for a certificate of conversion.

He removed his borrowed clothes in the locker room, stepped into the shower, and lathered up. He soaped his belly then his balls. How could the sight of his own circumcised prick not remind him of his father? What a little thing it seemed to have one's foreskin snipped off. What if Vicki had asked that he chop off his little finger? Would he do it?

No. Not even for Vicki. Did that mean he didn't love her? What would Vicki do for *him?* He had toyed with the idea of asking her to lose a few pounds. Paula, his ex-wife, had been Manhattan thin, which at the time had turned him on. He'd never imagined that he could make love to an overweight woman. But Vicki's extra weight served as an aphrodisiac. Marcus would catch himself thinking of all those rolls of flesh, the pillowed breasts and rounded thighs, the soft warm welcome of her vagina, and he would find that he was hard. Even now his prick reared its foamy head. He worked it in his hand, then braced himself and came; a sad spurt of semen spattered the stall as Marcus wept and cursed.

By that time, he had less than ten minutes to put on his clothes and drive across town in rush-hour traffic to speak to Dr. Schiffler. He arrived twenty minutes late, parked, and ran inside. The waiting room was full; the doctor had been delayed by an emergency and was running late. Marcus was glad that he hadn't missed his appointment, but it seemed some kind of punishment that in a city reserved for the very old he should be compelled to spend an hour in a room full of kids.

He took the one remaining seat. Scattered around the carpet were miniature trucks and buses with bobble-headed passengers that fit on pegs inside. On a table the height of Marcus's shin sat an elaborate wire structure along which a pixie-ish Hispanic child of indeterminate gender slid colorful beads. When Marcus was young, doctors had provided nothing to keep a child amused except tattered copies of *Highlights,* whose goody-goody articles and harsh black-and-white illustrations had irritated him to tears; it wasn't bad enough that you had to get a shot, you had to be subjected to pious sermons by a poorly drawn bear.

He tried to read a magazine, but the articles on newborn colic and toddlers' tantrums made him sweat. His mind wandered to his daughter, who lived on Staten Island with her mother. He loved Michelle. But she was tied up in his mind with the grudge his ex-wife held against him for not providing enough help around the house or enough money to support them. He had married in his thirties, waiting until he found a woman as self-sufficient as he was, independent to the point of fierceness, a lawyer whose job was to ferret out fraud in the banking system of New York State.

But his plan had gone too far. The day they'd moved in together, Paula had tacked up a chart on which they could record how much time each of them spent doing chores. Likewise, she insisted they spend exactly the same amount on necessities for the apartment. Marcus could understand that a woman of Paula's generation might fear that her talents would be wasted in the service of her husband's career. But he wasn't an ambitious man. He had grown up with a father who wasn't ashamed to lift a mop. The very fact that she felt the need to keep track of what he did or didn't give made him surly and defensive.

After the divorce, Paula's scorekeeping had grown even more precise. The amount for Michelle's upkeep was deducted from Marcus's bank account, but Paula — who earned as much as Marcus — demanded his share of extras such as ballet and summer camp, and she kept track of every minute he spent with their daughter, offering monthly statements of both accounts, until Marcus felt as if the girl were a commodity in which he had purchased so many shares.

It struck him that his marriage, like most of his friends' marriages, had failed because each member of the couple had been so wary of being asked to give more than his or her fair share. What he loved about Vicki was her generosity. Like Paula, she worked hard. She was the founder of a bakery that sold muffins and croissants to yuppie groceries around the city. (As her accountant, Marcus had advised her to use less expensive ingredients, to which Vicki replied that she would rather not bake at all than sell pastries made with axle grease masquerading as a dairy product.) But her philosophy seemed to be that if two people loved each other, they did everything possible to make each other happy. She assumed Marcus to be as generous as she was, and her love and good opinion kindled in his heart a desire to give.

"Mr. Sloan?" Marcus looked up. The waiting room was empty. The receptionist led Marcus to an office in which a weedy, popeyed man sat behind a desk. The diplomas on the wall were surrounded by photos of Dr. Schiffler handing oversized checks to the chairpersons of Boca charities, snapshots of children's circumcision ceremonies and birthday parties, and thank-you letters from grateful parents.

The doctor shook Marcus's hand. "I understand this has something to do with a circumcision. With complications, you said? An interfaith marriage, I take it? Perhaps your wife and in-laws are upset or confused about the ritual?" The pediatrician smoothed his tie, which was printed with those colorful costumed children found on products sold by UNICEF. "Tell me about your problem and I will do everything I can to make this event a *simcha* even for the non-Jewish individuals involved."

Buoyed by Schiffler's open-mindedness, Marcus related his quandary, although even as he spoke he wondered what kind of madman would be telling such a tale. Usually, when he entered a doctor's office, it was in his capacity as an accountant and the doctor was the one who had something unsavory to explain. Now Marcus was the schnorrer. It was not a position he favored. In high school they'd read a play in which Marcus found a line that encapsulated his own philosophy: *Neither a borrower nor a lender be.* Yet here he was, begging favors from everyone. Only the fact that he was begging these favors on his father's behalf lent the begging some air of nobility.

The pediatrician picked up a pencil and, to Marcus's amazement, used it to clean his ears. He wiggled the pencil briskly, as if to dislodge the screwy request, then said that he couldn't possibly circumcise a dying man. "I would need to put your father under general anesthesia, and between that and the procedure itself, I would be hastening his death. I might even kill him outright. The hospital would never allow such a thing. And my conscience would not permit it."

Marcus was reluctant to push the matter further, but he had invested so much time in his scheme already that he tried another tack. Perhaps Dr. Schiffler might be willing to perform the circumcision on his father at home? "Not under general anesthetic, but the way you do with babies. I mean, maybe we could get him drunk?"

The doctor glanced around as if he expected Alan Funt to step out of a closet and ask him to smile. "You aren't serious. Are you? What do you think I am? I could lose my license for a stunt like that!"

Marcus raised his palms. "The joke of a desperate man. I appreciate your taking the time to listen." He reached in his pocket and removed his checkbook. "I don't suppose a . . . donation would change your mind?"

Schiffler looked around again. By now he seemed frantic, as if he were being set up for a sting.

"What I mean is, in return for taking up your valuable time, I am happy to write a check to your favorite charity. But maybe you would prefer that I send it directly to the Boca March of Dimes rather than making it out to you?"

The doctor smiled wanly. "Yes. Certainly. Thank you. I must have misunderstood." He rose and held the door. "I'm afraid that my receptionist has gone home for the day. Just follow the signs to the waiting room, then let yourself out."

Retracing his steps, Marcus passed a nurse's station on the top of which sat a cardboard box of lollipops, a pad of the doctor's letterhead, and a stack of bandages and gauze. He didn't yet have a plan. But the moment he placed the lollipop, the letterhead, and the packet of gauze in his trouser pocket, the plan began to sprout.

He found his father sleeping. His skin glowed eerily against the sheets.

"Mr. Sloan?" Marcus turned. His father's gerontologist beckoned from the hall. "I'm glad you were able to get here in time." Marcus was suspicious of any doctor who worked in Florida — they seemed a pack of jackals that had migrated south to take advantage of the dying Jews — but his father's gerontologist, Dr. Persky, was a compassionate, warm-hearted man. Boyishly thin and sweet faced, with stooped shoulders and curly silver hair, he gave the impression of eternal youth combined with extreme old age, as if he had taken on himself the burdens of his patients. "I'm sorry to have to tell you, but it doesn't look good. We don't usually suggest this, but if he continues to refuse the transplant, which, to be honest, I completely understand, there isn't anything we can do for him here. I was wondering how you would feel about taking your father home."

Home to die, the doctor meant. Marcus's stomach shrank. He had never seen anyone die. The night his mother's heart had given out, Marcus had been at a rock concert in Monticello, his parents having granted him the evening off from his job as headwaiter in the children's dining room. At the time, he had been relieved that he hadn't seen his mother's corpse, but later he'd regretted that he hadn't had the chance to ask her forgiveness for all his snotty backtalk. And the chance to say goodbye. He wasn't about to make the same mistake with his father. *Goodbye, Pop, forgive me. Goodbye, goodbye, goodbye.*

The doctor lifted his hands. "Of course, there's always the hospice. But in your father's condition, it won't be more than a few days. And having him die at home might have its advantages."

Advantages, Marcus thought. "Yes. I would prefer it if my father were able to die at home."

"Take a while to think it over. Make sure you're up to the strain. But if you do choose to have your father die at home, a visiting nurse will stop by to keep him comfortable." He gripped Marcus's hand, and Marcus was touched to see that the corners of his eyes were wet.

Marcus went back in and sat by his father's bed, stroking his yellow arm. Just as he was about to leave, his father's eyelids fluttered open.

"Hey, Pop. It's Marcus."

"Your mother . . ." He used his tongue to wet his lips. "I dreamed Claire was here. Beside me. In this bed."

Marcus shrugged to say *who knew?* "How would you like to go home?" He could see this information flatten his father's face. "Of course, if you'd rather stay here . . . Or we could move you to a hospice."

His father shook his head. "Home," he said. "No hospice." Again he licked his lips. "And the other? Dobrinski? Schiffler?"

Marcus fought his qualms and lied. "Everyone's on board. When the time is right, they've agreed to do what needs to be done."

His father sank back and closed his eyes. Marcus was surprised he didn't ask for details. He probably didn't want to know.

The wife of the man in the next bed reminded her daughter-in-law to bring a box of cookies for the nurses. "They work hard," the woman said. "They deserve some recognition."

"What Mom is saying," the son chimed in, "is if you give them the cookies, they'll come running faster if Dad needs them."

"And what's wrong with that? A box of cookies never hurts. And make sure you don't get the cheap ones from Publix. Go to that nice bakery in the mall. Get some elephant ears, a dozen rugelach. Don't skimp, we shouldn't look cheap."

Just as Marcus thought he could stand the conversation no longer, his father opened his eyes and asked, "What about the woman?"

"Woman, Pop?"

"The baker."

Marcus assumed his father was referring to the conversation

about the cookies. But his father made a wavy shape in the air with one hand. "Zaftig," he said, and Marcus knew he meant Vicki. It wasn't hard to see why his father liked her. Marcus cooked so rarely that he owned only two pots, one without a handle, but in honor of his father's visit to Manhattan Vicki had prepared a magnificent meal, beginning with a mushroom barley soup whose flavors brought tears to his father's eyes and ending with a peach strudel so rich that Marcus's father had felt impelled to kiss Vicki's hand. In Boca, Vicki had taken one peek in his father's cupboard and immediately gone out shopping; she returned with six big bags of staples and a selection of gourmet items that Marcus was sure his father would never eat, although the next time he came to visit, all these items were gone. "I like a woman who's got some meat and potatoes," his father said, a preference borne out by the fact that Marcus's mother had been anything but svelte. Which, no doubt, was why Marcus used to be attracted only to skinny women. Who wanted to think he was making love to his mother? But Vicki's extra weight seemed a sign of a more general sloppiness — her inability to keep a neat house, her tendency to throw out receipts and bills before Marcus had the chance to see them and chide her yet again about staying clear of debt.

"Marry her!" his father whispered hoarsely. And Marcus didn't argue.

The drive to the condo took forever, as did placing the call to Vicki. *Come on,* he thought, *come on,* urging the signal north.

"Sweetheart!" she cried, her voice clotted with whatever pastry she'd been tasting. "I've been thinking about you and your father all day. How did it go? How is he?"

And out it all came, in a wholehearted, uncensored way that Paula would never have allowed. Not that she wouldn't have cared. But she would have been waiting for her turn so she could tell him what had gone wrong at her office that day.

"Oh, Marcus," Vicki said, "I can't think of anything more upsetting. Do you want me to come down there? I could hop on the next plane."

Oh no, he said, she shouldn't even think of coming. Whatever his father asked, Marcus had to be the one to do it. Still, Vicki's willingness to listen calmed him. When they had exhausted every possibility for solving his father's problem and had hashed out at least a few of the implications of his father's revelation about not being Jewish, Marcus felt stable enough to ask what was new with her.

"Nothing you need to worry about. That pastry guy I hired left a stack of towels too near the stove. You can imagine all the smoke. We lost most of a day before we could get back in the kitchen."

It touched Marcus that, to avoid upstaging his trials in Florida, she had minimized what must have been a frightening event and a serious financial strain. "I love you," he said.

"I love you too," she said, which was followed by a pause in which she must have been wondering what he had decided about getting married. "I miss you. Call me anytime."

He almost blurted out that if having fifteen children was the price he had to pay for keeping her in his life, then fifteen children they would have. But she took another bite, and the sound of her mastication prevented him from saying any more than "I'm sorry about the fire" before he hung up.

The next morning, the ambulance drove up and the EMTs unloaded Marcus's father and carried him to his bedroom. As his father lay in the musty condo drifting in and out of sleep, Marcus sat beside him, unable to think of anything except how much he owed this man and how little he could do to pay him back. Maybe that was the source of the resentment in so many families. The parents stewed about how much they had sacrificed for their kids while the children chafed at the burden of being saddled with all that guilt. What changed the equation for Marcus was his new understanding that his father hadn't sacrificed quite as much as Marcus had always thought.

For an entire day and night, his father barely surfaced from the depths. Marcus couldn't focus enough to read *Exodus* or *Reader's Digest.* He ripped the skin from a blister he must have gotten playing tennis. He bit the cuticles around his nails, peeled the calluses from his feet. To keep from giving himself a whole-body circumcision, he rummaged through the drawers. To find what, a cache of gay porn? A syringe and a vial of heroin? In the bathroom, Marcus found nothing more questionable than a pack of bubblegum flavored floss; in the den, nothing but an envelope whose contents verified that his father had indeed left half of the few pennies in his account to Rabbi Dobrinski's shul. Marcus didn't mind about the money. What made him feel cheated was the wealth of information his father would take to his grave. How had Marcus's grandparents ended up in Texas? What country had they come from? Had any of Marcus's ancestors fought in the Civil War, and, if they had, on the Northern or Southern side? What had his father's baptism been like? Had he grown up eating pork, and, if so, had he liked it?

In the kitchen drawers he found plastic forks and coupons and a stack of Christmas cards from a man who appeared to be his father's buddy from the war. The man's greetings seemed effusive. Had the sender of these cards been the soldier his father saved? Marcus would need to let him know that his father had passed away. But the cards were bare of envelopes. Hoping to find an address book, he emptied the drawer. At the bottom lay a directory of Jewish services in Boca Raton. Marcus thumbed the pages, and there, under RITUAL CIRCUMCISIONS, he saw a list of three *mohels*.

The first number was disconnected, and whoever answered the second number didn't have a clue what a *mohel* was; the directory, Marcus saw, was five years out of date. But the third *mohel* not only answered, but he said that he would be happy to meet Marcus that afternoon.

"To tell the truth," the *mohel* said in a heavy old-world accent, "business hasn't been so good lately." He laughed a wheezy laugh. "I have nothing on my agenda. I am not the type to play tennis or golf."

"I'll be there in an hour," Marcus said. When the visiting nurse stopped by, he was halfway out the door before she set down her bag.

The address the *mohel* gave him was in the only shabby section of Boca that Marcus had ever seen. The crooked mossy lanes were lined with stunted palms and flimsy pastel cottages that hadn't been painted since the fifties. Marcus's knock echoed, and when the old man let him in, the un-air-conditioned air, laden with the stench of pipe smoke and salted fish, nearly knocked him out. By the time the *mohel* led him to his "study" — a tiny room with a folding metal chair, a child-sized desk, and shelves and shelves of books in Hebrew — Marcus was already soaked. The man offered him a glass of hot tea, but the idea of drinking anything hot appalled him. "Nothing, I'm fine, but thank you."

The *mohel* sat heavily. "Mazel tov on the son." He slapped his thighs, his rheumy eyes shining. But as Marcus explained why he had come, the *mohel* bowed his head; his beard brushed his chest, which was bare to the sternum, the shirt unbuttoned to either side. After Marcus finished, the *mohel* lifted his chin and stroked his beard. "So, this is quite a situation you've gotten yourself into. I suppose you would pay a considerable sum to convince me to perform this bris."

Why, the wily old bastard! Of course, given the man's poverty, such a shakedown made sense. The *mohel*'s shirt was so old that the fabric had turned as yellow as Marcus's father's skin. His trousers were threadbare, and he wasn't wearing shoes; his cheap white cotton socks had a hole in each big toe.

The old man grinned — gray teeth, gums an unhealthy brown. "I suppose a successful man like you has a fair amount of money in his wallet."

As a matter of fact, he did. On his way to the airport, Marcus had stopped at an ATM and withdrawn five hundred dollars, of which he'd spent forty. He removed the wad of cash and held it toward the *mohel*. In a way, it would be a mitzvah to give a bribe to such a poor man. Pediatricians like Schiffler probably were putting their more traditional competitors out of business.

Slowly, the *mohel* stood. He held out a thick-nailed hand and made a gimme-gimme motion. When Marcus didn't move, the hand darted out and snatched the cash. Marcus jumped back, and the *mohel* startled him even more by dashing the money to the floor and stomping on it as if it were a roach. With one white-socked foot planted across the bills, the *mohel* began to shout. "To be a Jew there are no shortcuts! God demanded that Father Abraham be circumcised at ninety-nine, and because Abraham agreed, God told him that his seed would be as numerous as the sands on the beach. Abraham didn't try to sneak out of the operation. He didn't wait until he was dying and no longer conscious of the pain. Think of all the pain *one* child can cause. How should Abraham have become father to *millions* of Jews with no pain at all?" Shakily, the *mohel* bent, scooped the money in his fist, and shook it at Marcus. "Get out, and take your filthy money with you!"

A moment later, Marcus stood by his car, holding the bills and trembling. It was a relief to be outside, but he was dizzy and out of breath. How was it fair to punish a person for handing over a bribe he'd been finagled into offering? And that speech about Father

Abraham . . . He dropped to his knees. *Oh, God, don't let me pass out here.* He glanced at the *mohel*'s house and saw the curtain flicker. The heat blared. A lizard skittered past his hand. He touched his forehead to the sidewalk, fighting the urge to crawl back to the *mohel*'s house, scratch at the door, and beg to be let back in.

That's when he heard the voice. Or rather, a wordless chant, a honeyed vibrating hum. He looked up at the sun, whose rays poured down and blinded him, wave after wave of light and heat and hum. He understood what he understood. Things were what they were. His father was what he was. *Oh, God,* he thought, *thank you.* He staggered to his feet, brushed the broken seashells from his palms, found a sprinkler on a ratty lawn a few houses down the block, wet his face, then drove back to his father's condo to wait and let whatever might happen happen.

He resumed his bedside vigil. And the longer he sat, the more he came to see that unless he took matters into his own hands — literally — neither he nor his father would have any chance of peace. He wanted desperately to talk to Vicki, but if he spoke to her now he would feel compelled to reveal his plan, and she would tell him that he was nuts.

"Claire!" His father's arm flailed across the mattress, groping for his wife. Then: "Reuven!" and "Hattie!" — Marcus's grandparents' names. "Reuven! Hattie! Claire!" Soon he would slip below the surface a final time. The visiting nurse arrived and left. The evening stretched ahead.

Marcus got a tumbler from the kitchen, then found his father's stash of Manischewitz and carried the bottle and cup to his father's room. He shook his father's arm. "Dad? It's time. Wake up."

Remarkably, his father opened his eyes. "Time? Schiffler's coming?"

Marcus held out the cup. "He told me to get you good and drunk."

Though his father looked frightened, he tried his best to smile. "Sure, I'm a regular *shikker,*" he said, and Marcus had to laugh. Neither of his father's two religions, the real or the adopted, encouraged the use of alcohol. But Jews at least allowed themselves a sip of candyish wine to commemorate important rites. His father gulped down the Manischewitz, then motioned for Marcus to pour another cup and slugged that one down, too. He closed his eyes and lay back, a purple mustache above his lip, and soon he was sound asleep.

Marcus counted to a hundred, then clapped his hands by his father's ear. When his father didn't stir, he went to the den and rummaged through the trousers he had worn to visit Schiffler. He found the items he had pilfered from Schiffler's office and laid them next to his father's bed, then took a very long breath, peeled back his father's sheet, and lifted his hospital gown.

There it was, neither overly large nor small, not so badly wrinkled, an orange-yellow mouse curled in its nest of silky white hair. The foreskin dangled like the tip of an uninflated condom. Intellectually, Marcus knew this was the natural state of the male organ, but the hood on his father's penis seemed devious, as if it were hiding something. And the penis was nothing like his own.

How can you be my father? How can I be your son?

So it was with anger as well as love that he gripped his father's cock and twisted it, this way, then that, and, for good measure, twisted it again, as if, by sheer force, he could twist off his father's foreskin. Tears rose in his eyes. *I'm sorry, Pop,* he thought, then opened a pack of gauze. Clumsily, he stuck a pad to either side of his father's cock, which was red now as well as yellow, and wrapped the whole thing in tape so it stood away from his father's groin like an obscenely prominent erection. Marcus printed a few hasty lines on the pediatrician's letterhead, then set it beside the lollipop.

His father jerked awake. He looked up at Marcus with pleading, befuddled eyes. "So? Is it done?" Gingerly, he caressed his swaddled cock.

Marcus nodded.

"The pediatrician? Schiffler?"

Again Marcus nodded, as if, as long as he didn't speak, he couldn't be accused of lying. Although really, what was so awful about a lie? The immorality lay in the cowardice the lie was meant to hide.

"It hurts," his father said, "but not nearly as bad as I thought it would." His father smiled — a genuine smile this time — and Marcus's heart fluttered.

He handed his father the lollipop. "Here. He said you were such a good patient you deserved a treat."

His father took the candy by the stick and waved it. "A fine man, didn't I tell you? A real mensch." A look of concern crossed his face. "What did he charge? I wouldn't want the fee should come out of your pocket."

Marcus picked up the sheet of letterhead and passed it to his father, who passed it back and motioned that Marcus should read it aloud.

"'One adult circumcision, local anesthetic. Fee: contribution in the amount of $500 to the March of Dimes of Boca Raton, Florida.'"

His father beamed. "See? This is how a real Jew behaves." He closed his eyes to savor the bliss not only of waking to find himself circumcised but also of receiving proof that the world held righteous men. Then he opened his eyes and moaned. "Did he by any chance leave something for the pain?"

Marcus hadn't planned another lie, but this one came out as if he'd scripted it. "Not with the shape your liver is in. Schiffler said that even one Tylenol might finish you off."

His father shrugged. "My comeuppance for waiting so long. Soon the pain won't matter." He closed his eyes and, still smiling, drifted back to sleep.

Marcus used the chance to call Dobrinski. "You can come or not come, but there isn't much time."

The rabbi's answer was noncommittal. "I'm not forgetting you nearly blinded me."

"Rabbi Dobrinski, my father is dying. I'm only calling to inform you of his condition. If you can see your way toward coming, my father would be obliged. If you can't, we'll get along without you." He hung up and went back in.

His father was awake. "I was thinking. A convert is supposed to bathe in the mikvah. Of course, if it's too much trouble . . . But even a dip in a tub or pool . . ."

Marcus went to the window and peered between the jalousies. The sun was almost down, but the streetlights gave off the same incandescent yellow glow as his father's skin. "Sure, Pop. It won't be official, but we'll do the best we can." Tenderly, he wrapped his father in the sheet and lifted him in his arms. His father was so full of fluids he nearly sloshed, but Marcus had little trouble carrying him across the lot. Unfortunately, the pool was locked. Marcus could have scaled the fence, but not while he was carrying his father.

He continued along the path. His father looked up with a quizzical expression, then shrugged and turned his face against Marcus's chest. Marcus saw the rabbi walking toward him. Dobrinski wore a white shirt, dark pants, a white yarmulke, and street shoes, as if death, like tennis, had a dress code. If not for the eye patch, he might have looked like a rabbi. But the closer Dobrinski came, the more Marcus felt pursued by a shifty old pirate determined to steal the treasure from his arms.

Marcus veered off the path, his feet sliding on the stiff slick grass. Peering at the shadowy ground to avoid stepping in a nest of fire ants, he approached the lagoon. Something in the distance splashed — a frog, he hoped, or a turtle. To be a true mikvah, a body of water had to be free flowing, which Marcus doubted this lagoon to be. Then again, all water came from somewhere. And flowed to somewhere else.

His shoes filled with lukewarm sludge. Another step and he sunk in to his calves. His father opened his eyes and looked up. Marcus looked up, too. The sky was wild with stars, the kind of spectacular array Marcus never saw in the city.

He dipped his father in the lake and bathed him the way a parent bathes a child. The way, if all went well, he would soon bathe the child to whom his wife would give birth. The sheet absorbed the sludge and the burden grew so heavy he could barely lift his arms. What a bother it would be to disinter his mother and her parents from the plot at Ahavath Yisroel and move their remains to a more ecumenical cemetery where his father could join them, as could Marcus and Vicki and whatever children they might have, and, for all Marcus knew, his daughter and former wife. Let everyone in the world who wanted to be buried in the Sloan-Lieberman family plot be buried at his expense. The more guests checked in, the merrier it would be.

Above him, on the bank, Dobrinski slipped and cursed, although the curse, being in Yiddish, sounded more like a blessing. Dobrinski limped to the shore beside him, adjusted his eye patch, and started chanting a Hebrew prayer whose melody and words Marcus had never heard. Nothing the rabbi said or did now would exert the slightest effect on his father's religious status. But the simple fact of the rabbi's presence might bring his father peace, and for that Marcus was glad.

Oh Pop, Marcus thought, *you were such a generous man. Why did you stop a few millimeters short of doing all you could?* Because even if a person was asked to cut off his foreskin, or, for that matter, cut off his entire cock, he had to give and give and give, no matter how frightened the giving made him, no matter how much it hurt.

Marcus raised his face to the star-drenched sky, and even as the rabbi sang whatever prayer he saw fit to sing in a circumstance such as this, he composed his own prayer of thanks for having been allowed to repay his father even a part of all he owed. Although really, it didn't make much sense to keep track of such matters, any more than it made sense to measure what the sun and stars gave a person as opposed to what that person gave the sun and stars.

KAREN RUSSELL

St. Lucy's Home for Girls Raised by Wolves

FROM GRANTA

> Stage 1: The initial period is one in which everything is new, exciting, and interesting for your students. It is fun for your students to explore their new environment.
>
> — from *The Jesuit Handbook on Lycanthropic Culture Shock*

AT FIRST, our pack was all hair and snarl and floor-thumping joy. We forgot the barked cautions of our mothers and fathers, all the promises we'd made to be civilized and ladylike, couth and kempt. We tore through the austere rooms, overturning dresser drawers, pawing through the neat piles of the Stage 3 girls' starched underwear, smashing light bulbs with our bare fists. Things felt less foreign in the dark. The dim bedroom was windowless and odorless. We remedied this by spraying exuberant yellow streams all over the bunks. We jumped from bunk to bunk, spraying. We nosed each other midair, our bodies buckling in kinetic laughter. The nuns watched us from the corner of the bedroom, their tiny faces pinched with displeasure.

"*Ay caramba,*" Sister Maria de la Guardia sighed. *"Que barbaridad!"* She made the Sign of the Cross. Sister Maria came to St. Lucy's from a Halfway House in Copacabana. In Copacabana, the girls are fat and languid and eat pink slivers of guava right out of your hand. Even at Stage 1, their pelts are silky, sun-bleached to near invisibility. Our pack was hirsute and sinewy and mostly brunette. We had terrible posture. We went knuckling along the wooden floor on the callused pads of our fists, baring row after row of tiny, wood-rotted teeth. Sister Josephine sucked in her breath. She removed a yellow wheel of floss from under her robes, looping it like a miniature lasso.

"The girls at our facility are *backwoods,*" Sister Josephine whispered to Sister Maria de la Guardia with a beatific smile. "You must be patient with them." I clamped down on her ankle, straining to close my jaws around the woolly XXL sock. Sister Josephine tasted like sweat and freckles. She smelled easy to kill.

We'd arrived at St. Lucy's that morning, part of a pack fifteen-strong. We were accompanied by a mousy, nervous-smelling social worker; the baby-faced deacon; Bartholomew the blue wolfhound; and four burly woodsmen. The deacon handed out some stale cupcakes and said a quick prayer. Then he led us through the woods. We ran past the wild apiary, past the felled oaks, until we could see the white steeple of St. Lucy's rising out of the forest. We stopped short at the edge of a muddy lake. Then the deacon took our brothers. Bartholomew helped him to herd the boys up the ramp of a small ferry. We girls ran along the shore, tearing at our new jumpers in a plaid agitation. Our brothers stood on the deck, looking small and confused.

Our mothers and fathers were werewolves. They lived an outsider's existence in caves at the edge of the forest, threatened by frost and pitchforks. They had been ostracized by the local farmers for eating their silled fruit pies and terrorizing the heifers. They had ostracized the local wolves by having sometimes-thumbs, and regrets, and human children. (Their condition skips a generation.) Our pack grew up in a green purgatory. We couldn't keep up with the purebred wolves, but we never stopped crawling. We spoke a slab-tongued pidgin in the cave, inflected with frequent howls. Our parents wanted something better for us; they wanted us to get braces, use towels, be fully bilingual. When the nuns showed up, our parents couldn't refuse their offer. The nuns, they said, would make us naturalized citizens of human society. We would go to St. Lucy's to study a better culture. We didn't know at the time that our parents were sending us away for good. Neither did they.

That first afternoon, the nuns gave us free rein of the grounds. Everything was new, exciting, and interesting. A low granite wall surrounded St. Lucy's, the blue woods humming for miles behind it. There was a stone fountain full of delectable birds. There was a statue of St. Lucy. Her marble skin was colder than our mother's nose, her pupilless eyes rolled heavenward. Doomed squirrels gamboled around her stony toes. Our diminished pack threw back our heads in a celebratory howl — an exultant and terrible noise, even without a chorus of wolf-brothers in the background. There were holes everywhere!

We supplemented these holes by digging some of their own. We interred sticks, and our itchy new jumpers, and the bones of the friendly, unfortunate squirrels. Our noses ached beneath an invisible assault. Everything was smudged with a human odor: baking bread, petrol, the nun's faint woman-smell sweating out beneath a dark perfume of tallow and incense. We smelled one another, too, with the same astounded fascination. Our own scent had become foreign in this strange place.

We had just sprawled out in the sun for an afternoon nap, yawning into the warm dirt, when the nuns reappeared. They conferred in the shadow of the juniper tree, whispering and pointing. Then they started toward us. The oldest sister had spent the past hour twitching in her sleep, dreaming of fatty and infirm elk. (The pack used to dream the same dreams back then, as naturally as we drank the same water and slept on the same red scree.) When our oldest sister saw the nuns approaching, she instinctively bristled. It was an improvised bristle, given her new, human limitations. She took clumps of her scraggly, nut-brown hair and held it straight out from her head.

Sister Maria gave her a brave smile.

"And what is your name?" she asked.

The oldest sister howled something awful and inarticulate, a distillate of hurt and panic, half-forgotten hunts and eclipsed moons. Sister Maria nodded and scribbled on a yellow legal pad. She slapped on a nametag: HELLO, MY NAME IS_______! "Jeanette it is."

The rest of the pack ran in a loose, uncertain circle, torn between our instinct to help her and our new fear. We sensed some subtler danger afoot, written in a language we didn't understand.

Our littlest sister had the quickest reflexes. She used her hands to flatten her ears to the side of her head. She backed toward the far corner of the garden, snarling in the most menacing register that an eight-year-old wolf-girl can muster. Then she ran. It took them two hours to pin her down and tag her: HELLO, MY NAME IS MIRABELLA!

*

"Stage 1," Sister Maria sighed, taking careful aim with her tranquilizer dart. "It can be a little overstimulating."

> Stage 2: After a time, your students realize that they must work to adjust to the new culture. This work may be stressful and students may experience a strong sense of dislocation. They may miss certain foods. They may spend a lot of time daydreaming during this period. Many students feel isolated, irritated, bewildered, depressed, or generally uncomfortable.

Those were the days when we dreamed of rivers and meat. The full-moon nights were the worst! Worse than cold toilet seats and boiled tomatoes, worse than trying to will our tongues to curl around our false new names. We would snarl at one another for no reason. I remember how disorienting it was to look down and see two square-toed shoes instead of my own four feet. Keep your mouth shut, I repeated during our walking drills, staring straight ahead. Keep your shoes on your feet. Mouth shut, shoes on feet. Do not chew on your new penny loafers. Do not. I stumbled around in a daze, my mouth black with shoe polish. The whole pack was irritated, bewildered, depressed. We were all uncomfortable, and between languages. We had never wanted to run away so badly in our lives; but who did we have to run back to? Only the curled black grimace of the mother. Only the father, holding his tawny head between his paws. Could we betray our parents by going back to them? After they'd given us the choicest part of the woodchuck, loved us at our hairless worst, nosed us across the ice floes, and abandoned us at the Halfway House for our own betterment?

Physically, we were all easily capable of clearing the low stone walls. Sister Josephine left the wooden gates wide open. They unslatted the windows at night, so that long fingers of moonlight beckoned us from the woods. But we knew we couldn't return to the woods; not till we were civilized, not if we didn't want to break the mother's heart. It all felt like a sly, human taunt.

It was impossible to make the blank, chilly bedroom feel like home. In the beginning, we drank gallons of bathwater as part of a collaborative effort to mark our territory. We puddled up the yellow carpet of old newspapers. But later, when we returned to the bedroom, we were dismayed to find all trace of the pack musk had vanished. Someone was coming in and erasing us. We sprayed and sprayed every morning; and every night, we returned to the same ammonium eradication. We couldn't make our scent stick here; it made us feel invisible. Eventually we gave up. Still, the pack seemed to be adjusting on the same timetable. The advanced girls could already alternate between two speeds, "slouch" and "amble." Almost everybody was fully bipedal.

Almost.

The pack was worried about Mirabella.

Mirabella would rip foamy chunks out of the church pews and replace them with ham bones and girl dander. She loved to roam the grounds wagging her invisible tail. (We all had a hard time giving that up. When we got excited, we would fall to the ground and start pumping our backsides. Back in those days we could pump at rabbity velocities. *Que horror!* Sister Maria frowned, looking more than a little jealous.) We'd give her scolding pinches. "Mirabella," we hissed, imitating the nuns. "No." Mirabella cocked her ears at us, hurt and confused.

Still, some things remained the same. The main commandment of wolf life is Know Your Place, and that translated perfectly. Being around other humans had awakened a slavish-dog affection in us. An abasing, belly-to-the-ground desire to please. As soon as we realized that others higher up in the food chain were watching us, we wanted only to be pleasing in their sight. Mouth shut, I repeated, shoes on feet. But if Mirabella had this latent instinct, the nuns couldn't figure out how to activate it. She'd go bounding around, gleefully spraying on their gilded statue of St. Lucy, mad-scratching at the virulent fleas that survived all of their powders and baths. At Sister Maria's tearful insistence, she'd stand upright for roll call, her knobby, oddly muscled legs quivering from the effort. Then she'd collapse right back to the ground with an ecstatic *oomph!* She was still loping around on all fours (which the nuns had taught us to see looked unnatural and ridiculous — we could barely believe it now, the shame of it, that we used to locomote like that!), her fists blue-white from the strain. As if she were holding a secret tight to the ground. Sister Maria de la Guardia would sigh every time she saw her. *"Caramba!"* She'd sit down with Mirabella and prise her fingers apart. "You see?" she'd say softly, again and again. "What are you holding on to? Nothing, little one. Nothing."

Then she would sing out the standard chorus, "Why can't you be more like your sister Jeanette?"

The pack hated Jeanette. She was the most successful of us,

the one furthest removed from her origins. Her real name was GWARR! but she wouldn't respond to this anymore. Jeanette spiffed her penny loafers until her very shoes seemed to gloat. (Linguists have since traced the colloquial origins of "goody two-shoes" back to our facilities.) She could even growl out a demonic-sounding precursor to "Pleased to meet you." She'd delicately extend her former paws to visitors, wearing white kid gloves.

"Our little wolf, disguised in sheep's clothing!" Sister Ignatius liked to joke with the visiting deacons, and Jeanette would surprise everyone by laughing along with them, a harsh, inhuman, barking sound. Her hearing was still twig-snap sharp. Jeanette was the first among us to apologize; to drink apple juice out of a sippy cup; to quit eyeballing the cleric's jugular in a disconcerting fashion. She curled her lips back into a cousin of a smile as the traveling barber cut her pelt into bangs. Then she swept her coarse black curls under the rug. When we entered a room, our nostrils flared beneath the new odors: onion and bleach, candle wax, the turnipy smell of unwashed bodies. Not Jeanette. Jeanette smiled and pretended she couldn't smell a thing.

I was one of the good girls. Not great and not terrible, solidly middle-of-the-pack. But I had an ear for languages, and I could read before I could adequately wash myself. I probably could have vied with Jeanette for the number one spot; but I'd seen what happened if you gave in to your natural aptitudes. This wasn't like the woods, where you had to be your fastest and your strongest and your bravest self. Different sorts of calculations were required to survive at the Home.

The pack hated Jeanette, but we hated Mirabella more. We began to avoid her, but sometimes she'd surprise us, curled up beneath the beds or gnawing on a scapula in the garden. It was scary to be ambushed by your sister. I'd bristle and growl, the way that I'd begun to snarl at my own reflection as if it were a stranger.

"Whatever will become of Mirabella?" we asked, gulping back our own fear. We'd heard rumors about former wolf-girls who never adapted to their new culture. It was assumed that they were returned to our native country, the vanishing woods. We liked to speculate about this before bedtime, scaring ourselves with stories of catastrophic bliss. It was the disgrace, the failure that we all guiltily hoped for in our hard beds. Twitching with the shadow question: *Whatever will become of me?*

We spent a lot of time daydreaming during this period. Even Jeanette. Sometimes I'd see her looking out at the woods in a vacant way. If you interrupted her in the midst of one of these reveries, she would lunge at you with an elder-sister ferocity, momentarily forgetting her human catechism. We liked her better then, startled back into being foamy old Jeanette.

In school, they showed us the St. Francis of Assisi slide show, again and again. Then the nuns would give us bags of bread. They never announced these things as a test; it was only much later that I realized that we were under constant examination. "Go feed the ducks," they urged us. "Go practice compassion for all God's creatures." *Don't pair me with Mirabella,* I prayed, *anybody but Mirabella.* "Claudette," Sister Josephine beamed, "why don't you and Mirabella take some pumpernickel down to the ducks?"

"Ohhkaaythankyou," I said. (It took me a long time to say anything; first I had to translate it in my head from the Wolf.) It wasn't fair. They knew Mirabella couldn't make bread balls yet. She couldn't even undo the twist tie of the bag. She was sure to eat the birds; Mirabella didn't even try to curb her desire to kill things — and then who would get blamed for the dark spots of duck blood on our Peter Pan collars? Who would get penalized with negative Skill Points? Exactly.

As soon as we were beyond the wooden gates, I snatched the bread away from Mirabella and ran off to the duck pond on my own. Mirabella gave chase, nipping at my heels. She thought it was a game. "Stop it," I growled. I ran faster, but it was Stage 2 and I was still unsteady on my two feet. I fell sideways into a leaf pile, and then all I could see was my sister's blurry form, bounding toward me. In a moment, she was on top of me, barking the old word for tug-of-war. When she tried to steal the bread out of my hands, I whirled around and snarled at her, pushing my ears back from my head. I bit her shoulder, once, twice, the only language she would respond to. I used my new motor skills. I threw dirt, I threw stones. "Get away!" I screamed, long after she had made a cringing retreat into the shadows of the purple saplings. "Get away, get away!"

Much later, they found Mirabella wading in the shallows of a distant river, trying to strangle a mallard with her rosary beads. I was at the lake; I'd been sitting there for hours. Hunched in the long cattails, my yellow eyes flashing, shoving ragged hunks of bread into my mouth.

I don't know what they did to Mirabella. Me they separated from my sisters. They made me watch another slide show. This one showed images of former wolf-girls, the ones who had failed to be rehabilitated. Longhaired, sad-eyed women, limping after their former wolf packs in white tennis shoes and pleated culottes. A wolf-girl bank teller, her makeup smeared in oily rainbows, eating a raw steak on the deposit slips while her colleagues looked on in disgust. Our parents. The final slide was a bolded sentence in St. Lucy's prim script:

DO YOU WANT TO END UP SHUNNED BY BOTH SPECIES?

After that, I spent less time with Mirabella. One night she came to me, holding her hand out. She was covered with splinters, keening a high, whining noise through her nostrils. Of course I understood what she wanted; I wasn't that far removed from our language (even though I was reading at a fifth-grade level, halfway into Jack London's *The Son of the Wolf*).

"Lick your own wounds," I said, not unkindly. It was what the nuns had instructed us to say; wound licking was not something you did in polite company. Etiquette was so confounding in this country. Still, looking at Mirabella — her fists balled together like small white porcupines, her brows knitted in animal confusion — I felt a throb of compassion. How can people live like they do? I wondered. Then I congratulated myself. This was a Stage 3 thought.

> Stage 3: It is common that students who start living in a new and different culture come to a point where they reject the host culture and withdraw into themselves. During this period, they make generalizations about the host culture and wonder how the people can live like they do. Your students may feel that their own culture's lifestyle and customs are far superior to those of the host country.

The nuns were worried about Mirabella too. To correct a failing, you must first be aware of it as a failing. And there was Mirabella, shucking her plaid jumper in full view of the visiting cardinal. Mirabella, battling a raccoon under the dinner table while the rest of us took dainty bites of peas and borscht. Mirabella, doing belly flops into compost.

"You have to pull your weight around here," we overheard Sister Josephine saying one night. We paused below the vestry window and peered inside.

"Does Mirabella try to earn Skill Points by shelling walnuts and polishing Saint-in-the-Box? No. Does Mirabella even know how to say the word *walnut?* Has she learned how to say anything besides a sinful 'HraaaHA!' as she commits frottage against the organ pipes? No."

There was a long silence.

"Something must be done," Sister Ignatius said firmly. The other nuns nodded, a sea of thin, colorless lips and kettle-black brows. "Something must be done," they intoned. That ominously passive construction; a something so awful that nobody wanted to assume responsibility for it.

I could have warned her. If we were back home, and Mirabella had come under attack by territorial beavers or snow-blind bears, I would have warned her. But the truth is that by Stage 3 I wanted her gone. Mirabella's inability to adapt was taking a visible toll. Her teeth were ground down to nubbins; her hair was falling out. She hated the spongy, long-dead foods we were served, and it showed — her ribs were poking through her uniform. Her bright eyes had dulled to a sour whiskey color. But you couldn't show Mirabella the slightest kindness anymore — she'd never leave you alone! You'd have to sit across from her at meals, shoving her away as she begged for your scraps. I slept fitfully during that period, unable to forget that Mirabella was living under my bed, gnawing on my loafers.

It was during Stage 3 that we met our first purebred girls. These were girls raised in captivity, volunteers from St. Lucy's School for Girls. The apple-cheeked fourth-grade class came to tutor us in playing. They had long golden braids or short, severe bobs. They had frilly-duvet names like Felicity and Beulah; and pert, bunny noses; and terrified smiles. We grinned back at them with genuine ferocity. It made us nervous to meet new humans. There were so many things that we could do wrong! And the rules here were different depending on which humans we were with: dancing or no dancing, checkers playing or no checkers playing, pumping or no pumping.

The purebred girls played checkers with us.

"These girl-girls sure is dumb," my sister Lavash panted to me between games. "I win it again! Five to none."

She was right. The purebred girls were making mistakes on purpose, in order to give us an advantage. "King me," I growled, out of turn. "I SAY KING ME!" and Felicity meekly complied. Beulah pretended not to mind when we got frustrated with the oblique, fussy movement from square to square and shredded the board to ribbons. I felt sorry for them. I wondered what it would be like to be bred in captivity and always homesick for a dimly sensed forest, the trees you've never seen.

Jeanette was learning how to dance. On Holy Thursday, she mastered a rudimentary form of the Charleston. "Brava!" the nuns clapped. "Brava!"

Every Friday, the girls who had learned how to ride a bicycle celebrated by going on chaperoned trips into town. The purebred girls sold seven hundred rolls of gift-wrap paper and used the proceeds to buy us a yellow fleet of bicycles built for two. We'd ride the bicycles uphill, a sanctioned pumping, a grim-faced nun pedaling behind each one of us. "Congratulations!" the nuns would huff. "Being human is like riding this bicycle. Once you've learned how, you'll never forget." Mirabella would run after the bicycles, growling out our old names. "Hwraa! Gwarr! Trrrrrrr!" We pedaled faster.

At this point, we'd had six weeks of lessons, and still nobody could do the Sausalito but Jeanette. The nuns decided we needed an inducement to dance. They announced that we would celebrate our successful rehabilitations with a Debutante Ball. There would be brothers, ferried over from the Home for Man-Boys Raised by Wolves. There would be a photographer from the *Gazette Sophisticate.* There would be a three-piece jazz band from West Toowoomba, and root beer in tiny plastic cups. The brothers! We'd almost forgotten about them. Our invisible tails went limp. I should have been excited; instead I felt a low mad anger at the nuns. They knew we weren't ready to dance with the brothers; we weren't even ready to talk to them. Things had been so much simpler in the woods. That night I waited until my sisters were asleep. Then I slunk into the closet and practiced the Sausalito two-step in secret, a private mass of twitch and foam. Mouth shut — shoes on feet! Mouth shut — shoes on feet! Mouthshutmouthshut . . .

One night I came back early from the closet and stumbled on Jeanette. She was sitting in a patch of moonlight on the windowsill, reading from one of her library books. (She was the first of us to sign for her library card too.) Her cheeks looked dewy.

"Why you cry?" I asked her, instinctively reaching over to lick Jeanette's cheek and catching myself in the nick of time.

Jeanette blew her nose into a nearby curtain. (Even her mistakes annoyed us — they were always so well intentioned.) She sniffled and pointed to a line in her book: "The lake water was reinventing the forest and the white moon above it, and wolves lapped up the cold reflection of the sky." But none of the pack besides me could read yet; and I wasn't ready to claim a common language with Jeanette.

The following day, Jeanette golfed. The nuns set up a miniature put-put course in the garden. Sister Maria dug four sand traps and got Clyde the groundskeeper to make a windmill out of a lawnmower engine. The eighteenth hole was what they called a "doozy," a minuscule crack in St. Lucy's marble dress. Jeanette got a hole in one.

On Sundays, the pretending felt almost as natural as nature. The chapel was our favorite place. Long before we could understand what the priest was saying, the music instructed us in how to feel. The choir director — aggressively perfumed Mrs. Valuchi, gold necklaces like pineapple rings around her neck — taught us more than the nuns ever did. She showed us how to pattern the old hunger into arias. Clouds moved behind the frosted oculus of the nave, glass shadows that reminded me of my mother. The mother, I'd think, struggling to conjure up a picture. A black shadow, running behind the watery screen of pines.

We sang at the chapel annexed to the Halfway House every morning. We understood that this was the human's moon, the place for howling beyond purpose. Not for mating, not for hunting, not for fighting, not for anything but the sound itself. And we'd howl along with the choir, hurling every pitted thing within us at the stained glass. "Sotto voce." The nuns would frown. But you could tell that they were pleased.

Stage 4: As a more thorough understanding of the host culture is acquired, your students will begin to feel more comfortable in their new environment. Your students feel more at home and their self-confidence grows. Everything begins to make sense.

"Hey, Claudette," Jeanette growled to me on the day before the ball. "Have you noticed that everything's beginning to make sense?"

Before I could answer, Mirabella sprang out of the hall closet and snapped through Jeanette's homework binder. Pages and pages of words swirled around the stone corridor, like dead leaves off trees.

"What about you, Mirabella?" Jeanette asked politely, stooping to pick up her erasers. She was the only one of us who would still talk to Mirabella; she was high enough in the rankings that she could afford to talk to the scruggliest wolf-girl. "Has everything begun to make more sense, Mirabella?"

Mirabella let out a whimper. She scratched at us and scratched at us, raking her nails along our shins, so hard that she drew blood. Then she rolled belly-up on the cold stone floor, squirming on a bed of spelling-bee worksheets. Above us, small pearls of light dotted the high tinted window.

Jeanette frowned. "You are a late bloomer, Mirabella! Usually, everything's begun to make more sense by Month Twelve at the latest." I noticed that she stumbled on the word *bloomer.* HraaaHA! Jeanette could never fully shake our accent. She'd talk like that her whole life, I thought with a gloomy satisfaction, each word winced out like an apology for itself.

"Claudette, help me," she yelped. Mirabella had closed her jaws around Jeanette's bald ankle and was dragging her toward the closet. "Please. Help me to mop up Mirabella's mess."

I ignored her and continued down the hall. I only had four more hours to perfect the Sausalito. I was worried only about myself. By that stage, I was no longer certain of how the pack felt about anything.

At seven o'clock on the dot, Sister Ignatius blew her whistle and frog-marched us into the ball. The nuns had transformed the rectory into a very scary place. Purple and silver balloons started popping all around us. Black streamers swooped down from the eaves and got stuck in our hair like bats. A full yellow moon smirked outside the window. We were greeted by blasts of a saxophone, and fizzy pink drinks, and the brothers.

The brothers didn't smell like our brothers anymore. They smelled like pomade and cold, sterile sweat. They looked like little boys. Someone had washed behind their ears and made them wear suspendered dungarees. Kyle used to be the blustery alpha male BTWWWR!, chewing through rattlesnakes, spooking badgers, snatching a live trout out of a grizzly's mouth. He stood by the punch bowl, looking pained and out of place.

"My stars!" I growled. "What lovely weather we've been having!"

"Yeees," Kyle growled back. "It is beginning to look a lot like Christmas." All around the room, boys and girls raised by wolves were having the same conversation. Actually, it had been an unseasonably warm and brown winter, and just that morning a freak hailstorm had sent Sister Josephine to an early grave. But we had only gotten up to Unit 7: Party Dialogue; we hadn't yet learned the vocabulary for Unit 12: How to Tactfully Acknowledge Disaster. Instead, we wore pink party hats and sucked olives on little sticks, inured to our own strangeness.

The sisters swept our hair back into high, bouffant hairstyles. This made us look more girlish and less inclined to eat people, the way that squirrels are saved from looking like rodents by their poofy tails. I was wearing a white organdy dress with orange polka dots. Jeanette was wearing a mauve organdy dress with blue polka dots. Linette was wearing a red organdy dress with white polka dots. Mirabella was in a dark corner, wearing a muzzle. Her party culottes were duct-taped to her knees. The nuns had tied little bows on the muzzle to make it more festive. Even so, the jazz band from West Toowoomba kept glancing nervously her way.

"You smell astoooounding!" Kyle was saying, accidentally stretching the diphthong into a howl and then blushing. "I mean . . ."

"Yes, I know what it is that you mean," I snapped. (That's probably a little narrative embellishment on my part; it must have been months before I could really "snap" out words.) I didn't smell astounding. I had rubbed a pumpkin muffin all over my body earlier that morning to mask my natural, feral scent. Now I smelled like a purebred girl, easy to kill. I narrowed my eyes at Kyle and flattened my ears, something I hadn't done for months. Kyle looked panicked, trying to remember the words that would make me act like a girl again. I felt hot, oily tears squeezing out of the red corners of my eyes. Shoesonfeet! I barked at myself. I tried again. "My! What lovely weather . . ."

The jazz band struck up a tune.

"The time has come to do the Sausalito," Sister Maria announced, beaming into the microphone. "Every sister grab a brother!" She switched on Clyde's industrial flashlight, struggling beneath its weight, and aimed the beam in the center of the room.

Uh-oh. I tried to skulk off into Mirabella's corner, but Kyle pushed me into the spotlight. "No," I moaned through my teeth, "noooooo." All of a sudden the only thing my body could remember how to do was pump and pump. In a flash of white-hot light, my months at St. Lucy's had vanished, and I was just a terrified animal again. As if of their own accord, my feet started to wiggle out of my shoes. *Mouth shut,* I gasped, staring down at my naked toes, *mouthshutmouthshut.*

"Ahem. The time has come," Sister Maria coughed, "to do the Sausalito." She paused. "The Sausalito," she added helpfully, "does not in any way resemble the thing that you are doing."

Beads of sweat stood out on my forehead. I could feel my jaws gaping open, my tongue lolling out of the left side of my mouth. What were the steps? I looked frantically for Jeanette; she would help me, she would tell me what to do.

Jeanette was sitting in the corner, sipping punch through a long straw and watching me with uninterest. I locked eyes with her, pleading with the mute intensity that I had used to beg her for weasel bones in the forest. "What are the steps?" I mouthed. "The steps!"

"The steps?" Then Jeanette gave me a wide, true wolf smile. For an instant, she looked just like our mother. "Not for you," she mouthed back.

I threw my head back, a howl clawing its way up my throat. I was about to lose all my Skill Points, I was about to fail my Adaptive Dancing test. But before the air could burst from my lungs, the wind got knocked out of me. *Oomph!* I fell to the ground, my skirt falling softly over my head. Mirabella had intercepted my eye-cry for help. She'd chewed through her restraints and tackled me from behind, barking at unseen cougars, trying to shield me with her tiny body. "*Caramba!*" Sister Maria squealed, dropping the flashlight. The music ground to a halt. And I have never loved someone so much, before or since, as I loved my littlest sister at that moment. I wanted to roll over and lick her ears; I wanted to kill a dozen spotted fawns and let her eat first.

But everybody was watching; everybody was waiting to see what I would do. "I wasn't talking to you," I grunted from underneath her. "I didn't want your help. Now you have ruined the Sausalito! You have ruined the ball!" I said more loudly, hoping the nuns would hear how much my enunciation had improved.

"You have ruined it!" my sisters panted, circling around us, eager to close ranks. "Mirabella has ruined it!" Every girl was wild-eyed and itching under her polka dots, punch froth dribbling down her chin. The pack had been waiting for this moment for some time. "Mirabella cannot adapt! Back to the woods, back to the woods!"

The band from West Toowoomba had quietly packed their instruments into black suitcases and were sneaking out the back. The boys had fled back toward the lake, bow ties spinning, suspenders snapping in their haste. Mirabella was still snarling in the center of it all, trying to figure out where the danger was so that she could defend me against it. The nuns exchanged glances.

In the morning, Mirabella was gone. We checked under all the beds. I pretended to be surprised. I'd known she would have to be expelled the minute I felt her weight on my back. Clyde had come and told me this in secret after the ball, "So you can say yer goodbyes." I didn't want to face Mirabella. Instead, I packed a tin lunch pail for her: two jelly sandwiches on saltine crackers, a chloroformed squirrel, a gilt-edged placard of St. Bolio. I left it for her with Sister Ignatius, with a little note: *Best wishes!* I told myself I'd done everything I could.

"Hooray!" the pack crowed. "Something has been done!"

We raced outside into the bright sunlight, knowing full well that our sister had been turned loose, that we'd never find her. A low roar rippled through us and surged up and up, disappearing into the trees. I listened for an answering howl from Mirabella, heart thumping — what if she heard us and came back? But there was nothing.

We graduated from St. Lucy's shortly thereafter. As far as I can recollect, that was our last communal howl.

Stage 5: At this point your students are able to interact effectively in the new cultural environment. They find it easy to move between the two cultures.

One Sunday, near the end of my time at St. Lucy's, the sisters gave me a special pass to go visit the parents. The woodsman had to accompany me; I couldn't remember how to find the way back on my own. I wore my best dress and brought along some prosciutto and dill pickles in a picnic basket. We crunched through the fall leaves in silence, and every step made me sadder. "I'll wait out here," the woodsman said, leaning on a blue elm and lighting a cigarette.

The cave looked so much smaller than I remembered it. I had to duck my head to enter. Everybody was eating when I walked in.

They all looked up from the bull moose at the same time, my aunts and uncles, my sloe-eyed, lolling cousins, the parents. My uncle dropped a thighbone from his mouth. My littlest brother, a cross-eyed wolf-boy who has since been successfully rehabilitated and is now a dour, balding children's book author, started whining in terror. My mother recoiled from me, as if I were a stranger. TRRR? She sniffed me for a long moment. Then she sank her teeth into my ankle, looking proud and sad. After all the tail wagging and perfunctory barking had died down, the parents sat back on their hind legs. They stared up at me expectantly, panting in the cool gray envelope of the cave, waiting for a display of what I had learned.

"So," I said, telling my first human lie. "I'm home."

RICHARD RUSSO

Horseman

FROM THE ATLANTIC MONTHLY

> Whenever the moon and the stars are set,
> Whenever the wind is high,
> All night long in the dark and wet,
> A man goes riding by.

ALTHOUGH IT WAS only four in the afternoon, it was almost dark outside, and the wind was blowing hard enough to set the branches of the quad's trees in motion. The nearest branch scratched insistently, like a memory, on Janet Moore's office window. Was it the turbulence outside that had invited the horseman to gallop into her consciousness, or the silence of the sullen boy across from her? The lines she was remembering were from a children's poem, the one her husband, Robbie, read to Marcus, their son, every night before he went to sleep, and they haunted her with the force of a childhood memory, even though she'd first heard the poem only a decade ago, when she was a grad student at the university. Now it kept her awake nights, long after Robbie had fallen asleep beside her — *all night long in the dark and wet* — and sometimes she'd wake up in the middle of the night with the verses still echoing. Had they been part of her actual sleep, repeating on some sort of endless loop? Lately, the horseman had appeared in her waking thoughts as well. When she jogged in the woods behind the New England college where she taught, she'd realize she was running to that unwelcome, unforgiving iambic cadence — *whenever the moon and the stars are set* — as if she were a horse. And then the familiar heartsickness, as if she were suddenly clomping not through the woods but through an endless cemetery.

*

A moment before she had been feeling both anger and self-righteousness. These were easy, unambiguous emotions to which, in the present circumstance, she felt entitled. She was angry, and rightly so, that students cheated more often in her classes than in those of her male colleagues, just as they were more often tardy, more openly questioning of her authority, and more often gave her a mediocre evaluation at the end of each term. Even worse, the fact that they held her to a higher standard was unwitting. Had anyone asked them if they were prejudiced against their female professors, not one would have answered yes. Hooked up to a lie detector, every one of them would pass.

Maybe even this one, this James Cox, seated before her now, with one sockless, boat-shoed foot balanced on a J. Crew–chinoed knee, still smug, though the fact that she had him dead to rights seemed to be dawning on him. He was studying, or pretending to study, the two typed pages she'd given him — the one with his own name in the upper right-hand corner, and the other that had been handed in to her four years earlier — with feigned astonishment, as if the similarities between them were just the damnedest thing, amazing, really, like frogs, thousands of them, falling from a cloudless June sky.

Next door she heard Tony Hope, her best friend in the department, leave his office, the door banging shut behind him. She'd told him earlier that she had a plagiarism case to deal with, and he'd offered to loiter outside, just in case. These days, all teachers were vulnerable. Cornered female students would sometimes charge male professors with having made sexual advances, while similarly cornered males would sometimes become belligerent with their female teachers. But James Cox had been late, and Tony was meeting a couple of his seniors at the Hub Pub. When Tony appeared in her half-open doorway, eyebrow arched, she gave him the sign that everything was fine, that it was okay for him to leave. Probably it was.

When she heard the double doors at the end of the corridor clang shut, Janet turned her attention back to her student, whose demeanor had dramatically changed. The feigned astonishment had evaporated. He slumped in his chair now, like a beaten fighter in the late rounds, just enough cognition left to recognize futility when he saw it up close. He met her eye for a split second. Had he held it for a beat longer, Janet would have been the one to turn away, but the branch scratching at the window attracted his attention, and he stared outside at the small cyclones of dead leaves in the windy quad.

Had he cheated before? she wondered. Was cheating the habit of his short lifetime? It didn't really matter. Even if he'd never cheated before, he'd cheated now, in her class, and she'd caught him. She'd had to ransack four years' worth of files to find the essay. Hours, it had taken, hours she didn't have, not now, two days before Thanksgiving. Knowing how long the search would take, she'd almost let it go. After all, she hadn't been certain. The essay *felt* familiar, but she might have just been recalling one with a similar topic and thesis. And even if she was right and the essay was plagiarized, what would her reward be for finding it? The knowledge that she had a good memory for ideas? (She already knew that.) Justification for disliking this particular student? (She already had sufficient reason.) Hadn't he alternated, all semester, between sullen inattention and stubborn obstruction in class, and then, outside in the hall, plied her with half-apologies and assurances that he didn't mean to be a pain in the ass? "But you *are* a pain in the ass." This had been on the tip of her tongue since September.

But maybe she'd been wrong, because now that he saw he was lost, he dropped his bravado. In fact, he looked like someone who'd been waiting so long in the doctor's office that when the feared diagnosis was finally delivered, it was a relief.

"So," he said, handing the identical pages back to her.

She waited until it became clear that he did not intend to go on. "So?"

"So, you got me, right?" Then he made a pistol of his thumb and forefinger, put the barrel to his temple, and pulled the trigger, his head jerking, as if struck by an invisible bullet. Sure, the gesture was symbolic, but she was still startled by the boy's willingness to metaphorically off himself.

Finally she said, "Do you want to tell me why?"

"It was easy. My fraternity keeps files."

"So do professors."

Again he made her wait. Then he asked, "What do you want?"

The question, so direct and simple, caught her off guard. "What do I *want*?"

He shrugged. "Well, this is where I get what's coming to me, no?"

"And what do you think you've got coming to you?"

"Not up to me, is it," he said, getting to his feet, terminating the interview. How brash males are, she thought. How controlled, even in defeat. "Whatever you decide."

At the door he paused, his back to her, his head canted at an odd angle, as if listening for something. What he said then surprised her. "My advice? Don't hold back."

And then he walked out.

Almost a decade earlier, on the morning of her first conference with the great Marcus Bellamy, Janet had parked in the dusty, unpaved X Lot on the farthest reaches of the university campus, the only place graduate students could afford to park in, and trekked across campus in the sweltering Southwest heat to Modern and Romance Languages. The Faculty Lot was right across the street. She saw Bellamy arrive in his vintage Mustang and then, in a breathtakingly confident move, stride off, leaving the convertible's top down. She checked to see if anyone was around who knew her and might be watching, and then she altered her course so she could pass by the Mustang for a closer look. Amazing! The front passenger seat was littered with cassette tapes, jazz mostly, and she could see the corner of a box that likely contained a dozen or so others. Did the man have some reason to believe his music would not be stolen? Everyone knew Marcus Bellamy, of course — he was the department's one true academic superstar — so maybe he felt protected by his reputation. Or perhaps the F Lots were monitored by cameras. She'd never noticed any, but it was possible. Even so, afternoon thunderstorms were predicted. Did Bellamy believe his status warded off not just music thieves but the elements themselves?

She had a full day before her — a comp class to teach, her Henry James seminar to attend, a stack of essays to start grading if the entire weekend wasn't to be ruined — but she could think of little but her conference with Bellamy. At lunch Robbie had remarked on how preoccupied she was, and as the afternoon wore on she'd felt increasingly lightheaded, at times almost ill. Robbie also had a conference with Bellamy that afternoon, and Janet was glad his and her own weren't back to back. No doubt Bellamy had noticed she and Robbie were a couple, but she preferred he not think of her as part *of anything. For this first conference she saw no need for context beyond the essay they would be discussing. She'd spent a long time on it, and they had a good deal to talk about. She'd signed up for the last conference slot of the afternoon, so they could run long if they needed to.*

Bellamy's office was the largest on the corridor, its most ostentatious fea-

ture a large, working fireplace. Janet's first thought upon entering was that if things went well this semester, maybe by the holidays she'd be invited in for — what? — brandy and eggnog before a roaring fire? Probably it would never get cold enough in the desert to justify that, but the fantasy was pleasant enough. The rest of the office was crammed with books and periodicals on floor-to-ceiling built-in shelves. In the unlikely event she ever managed to snag an office like this one, she thought, she'd stay put. What possessed a man with such a cushy life to pack up all those books and move every couple of years, as Bellamy did? He'd no sooner arrived on this campus than the speculation had begun about how long he'd stay, where he'd go next, what would be needed in the way of salary and perks to lure him away. Brilliant black English professors were in demand, as Bellamy well knew, and some students whispered he was already receiving and weighing offers for the year after next. That was why Janet had wanted so desperately to study with him now, this term. His class in proletarian fiction was wildly oversubscribed. Even the linguistics and creative-writing majors wanted in. And so far, the course had been electrifying.

Bellamy greeted her at the door with a warm smile, but they were no sooner seated than he said, rather ominously, "Ms. Moore, in conference I always like to be forthright."

To which she murmured something silly, pretty close to the exact opposite of the truth. She said that she assumed he would be forthright, or hoped he would be, or — worse — that she was always grateful for any honest, rigorous appraisal of her work.

"Excellent," he said, handing back her essay. "Because though it has much to recommend it, I have serious misgivings about your work."

So it was true. Yesterday she'd overheard one of her classmates claiming that Bellamy was reading not only the papers they'd just turned in, but previous efforts from other courses as well, everything he could get his hands on. She hadn't believed it — who but a madman would take on so much extra work? — but there it was, on the desk between them, a big blue Graduate Office folder with her name on it, containing, by the look of it, a dozen or so of her essays from past semesters. When he said he had misgivings about her work, could he possibly mean all *of it? Work that had already established her as perhaps the most promising scholar in the program?*

She examined the essay he'd just handed her. She saw no letter grade on the cover page, and Janet had marked enough freshman compositions to know what this could portend. She herself always put a poor grade, along with her reasons for awarding it, on the back of the last page, safe from prying eyes. Though it was probably the wrong thing to do, she quickly turned the essay over to see if Bellamy handled weak efforts in the same fashion, only to discover that the back page was blank as well. As were all the others. If he had found "much to recommend" in the essay, weren't those things worth mentioning? "Misgivings?" she said finally, her voice sounding strange, distant, whiny, frightened.

Bellamy had risen and was now scanning his bookshelves, and he didn't answer immediately. Turning his back on her had the effect of compounding her fears. "I'll try to explain, but it's going to be easier to show you . . ."

"Actually, I thought my essay was good," she ventured. "I spent a long time on it." She couldn't believe she was saying this. How many times had she told her own students that the amount of time you spent on something was immaterial?

"I'm sure you did, Janet. It's meticulous. Flawless." He stepped back for a better angle at the books and periodicals on the top shelves. "It's just not really yours."

"I don't know what you mean," she replied, swallowing hard. "Are you saying it's plagiarized?"

"Good heavens, no. Relax."

As if.

"Actually," he went on, still not turning around, "theft would have been more revealing. Then at least I'd have known what you admired, whereas I can't locate you in what you *did* write, anywhere. The same is true with your previous essays. It's as if you don't exist . . . Ah, here we are!" The volume he'd been looking for was on the top shelf. Bellamy was a tall man — a skilled basketball player, according to Robbie, who'd reported this fact half apologetically, as if he felt personally responsible for perpetuating a stereotype — but he still had to use a footstool to reach it. Stepping down again, he placed the journal, a twenty-year-old issue of *American Literature*, on the desk between them, then sat back down.

"But . . . I *do* exist," she offered, suddenly unsure that she was entitled to this opinion. Would he attempt to reason her out of it? Would he succeed?

"Indeed," he said. "Here you are. In the flesh."

The word *flesh*, spoken in such an intimate setting, in a room that contained a leather sofa in front of a fireplace, made her apprehensive. Earlier that morning, stepping from the shower, she'd imagined this meeting with pleasure. Nothing sexual, of course, or even terribly intimate. She'd imagined neither the fireplace nor the sofa — just that their conversation, the first of many, would go well, and that Bellamy would admire her, as she admired him. He'd certainly seemed responsive to her in class — though, it was true, he was no more responsive to her than to her classmates. He obvi-

ously knew better than to display overt signs of favoritism. In conference was where you let your guard down a bit, showed your enthusiasm for good work. She'd felt confident that this was what would happen today. Maybe after they were done he'd suggest a beer at the Salty Dog, where grad students hung out and Robbie's band played on Saturday nights.

"I thought," *she said carefully, rubbing her moist palms against the cushion of her chair, "that was the whole idea of literary criticism. Isn't the 'I' supposed to disappear? Isn't the argument itself what matters?"*

"That's what we teach," he conceded. He'd taken his glasses off and was cleaning them with a handkerchief — unnecessarily, it occurred to her, an affectation. "It's what I was taught, and I used to believe it. Now I'm not so sure. The first-person pronoun can be dispensed with, it's true. But not the writer behind the pronoun."

"I guess I don't know what you mean, then," she said, aware that this was the second time she'd resorted to those exact words. Oh God — she "guessed" she didn't understand? If one of her freshmen had written that, she'd have scratched "Can't you be certain?" in the margin.

"It's true the writer shouldn't intrude upon the argument," Bellamy admitted, "but that's not the same as saying he should disappear, is it?"

She caught herself this time. A third "guess" would have been disastrous. "Isn't it?"

"Okay, let's back up. Why did you write about Dos Passos?"

"I was interested —"

"But why? Why were you interested?"

Now she was squirming, angry. Because he'd interrupted her? Not given her a chance to explain? Or was it the challenge implied in his question?

"Did you choose a topic you had a real connection to? Or just one you knew I *was interested in?"*

Well, sure, Bellamy's enthusiasm for Dos Passos had been the main reason, but to her way of thinking that merely predicted a good starting point for their ongoing dialogue. Wasn't the study of literature supposed to be a dialogue? a series of dialogues between writer and reader, reader and teacher? Why was he challenging a conversation so recently begun? Had he already concluded that it would go nowhere? What evidence might have led him to such a conclusion? She tried to concentrate on what he was saying, to not personalize, to not be overwhelmed by disappointment. But with each new question — What are you risking in this essay? From what passion in your life does it derive? Where did you grow up? What did your parents do? Did you attend private school or public? — she felt herself flushing. What had her life to do with anything? She'd come prepared to argue her essay's nu-

ances, to accept her professor's suggestions for bolstering its thesis, even to hear him question its validity, but here he was, wanting to talk about her, *as if what she'd produced didn't matter. It was as if he'd asked her to take off her clothes.*

"Look, Janet," he said, perhaps sensing her distress. "The truth is, I can teach you very little. You have a lively intellect and genuine curiosity, and you work hard. You read carefully, you synthesize well, and you know how to marshal evidence. If a scholar's life is what you want, you're well on your way. That's the good news. But one last piece of the puzzle is missing. The bad news is that it's a big one, and for some people it can be elusive."

Still a big piece of the puzzle missing? She didn't want to believe that. Her other professors all agreed that she was close, probably ready to start submitting her work to academic journals. (Bellamy knew the editors of these journals personally, and a word from him . . .) And if the piece she was missing was "big," how could it be elusive? The charge didn't make sense.

Then again, what if what he was saying was true? Hadn't she sometimes worried, in the aftermath of extravagant praise, that something was *missing? Hadn't she sometimes had the distinct feeling that what she'd really succeeded in doing was fooling them again? Was that what Bellamy was getting at? Had he seen something in her work, or the absence of something? He was arguing — she understood this much — for some kind of passionate, personal connection, but what if that connection wasn't there? What if what she possessed — what her other professors admired — was merely a facility? What if she was just doing what she was good at, and nothing deeper? "This elusive thing?" she heard herself say, in a frightened, childlike voice. "I won't succeed until I find it?"*

"Oh, you'll succeed just fine," he told her, waving that concern aside. "You'll just never be any good."

But the two cases were hardly analogous, she told herself as she emerged into the quad. James Cox, the little prick, was a plagiarist, a cheat. When Bellamy had said that her essay wasn't really hers, she'd thought that was what he was getting at. But no. His "misgivings" about her work had been vague, abstract, spectral, whereas her objection to James Cox's essay was concrete, clear-cut, and accusatory. The two things were similar, not parallel. So forget it. Go home.

She was halfway to her car, near the entrance to the student union, when a Frisbee whistled overhead, too close for comfort, causing her to duck. Normally, it would have run out of air and skimmed along the surface of the brown grass and come to rest there, but this particular Frisbee was riding a gust of wind that had tunneled down the quad (*whenever the wind is high* — the words were suddenly there), so on it flew, gaining altitude.

Her first thought was that someone must have thrown it at her intentionally (James Cox?), but turning around she saw that it could only have been tossed by one of two students who stood on the lighted library steps a good two hundred yards up the hill. Apparently someone had left the Frisbee on the steps, and the boy who'd thrown it wanted to see how far it would travel on such an impressive tailwind. "Whoa!" she heard him shout as it continued on down the terraced lawn, all the way to the macadam road, where it struck a passing pickup truck in the windshield with a loud *whump*. The truck immediately skidded to a halt, and the driver, either a townie or someone from Grounds and Maintenance, got out, glared at Janet, and yelled, "Hey!"

"Yeah, right," she called down the hill, though in fact she couldn't really blame the fellow for jumping to the wrong conclusion. Except for the two figures on the library steps, an impossible distance away, she was the only person in the deserted quad.

"The hell's wrong with you, anyway?" the man wanted to know, his voice all but lost in the wind.

"Search me," she called back, and then, when he looked like he might want to make something of it, she made a sharp right and headed down the student union steps into the Hub Pub, a place she normally avoided, having no desire to run into students — those old enough to drink legally — or, worse, her grousing department colleagues. So she was relieved to discover that, late on the Tuesday afternoon before Thanksgiving, the place was almost as deserted as the quad. One large circular table was occupied by a group of students playing a drinking game that involved bouncing quarters off the tabletop. In the far corner, Tony Hope and his seniors occupied a booth. The students were cramming papers into overstuffed backpacks, their meeting concluded.

"Remember," Tony was telling them. "In effaced, you can't have it both ways. If you're dunna dit in, dit in. If you're dunna dit out, dit out."

The students, apparently understanding this advice, nodded agreement, slid out of the booth, and wished him a happy Thanksgiving.

Sliding onto the bench, she said, "That was truly bizarre advice. 'Effaced'?"

Tony chuckled, clearly pleased by her mystification. He pushed what she hoped was an unused glass in her direction and poured the last of the pitcher into it. "Effaced point of view," he explained. "Sort of like a camera eye. The writer disappears. Just reports what the characters do and say without revealing their thoughts and motivations. No judgments. Totally objective."

"'If you're dunna dit in, dit in'?"

"My father had a speech impediment. When we went to the drive-in for burgers, all us kids would get out of the car and run around. We were always slamming the car doors. When he couldn't stand it anymore, he'd yell, 'If you're dunna dit in, dit in. If you're dunna dit out, dit out. No more doddamn dittin' in, dittin' out.'"

"And your students understand such references?"

"They know the story, yeah."

"Teaching creative writing really is a scam, isn't it. How do I join the club?"

"Did your father have a speech impediment?"

"No."

"Well, there you go. Sorry. Don't you tell your students anything about yourself?"

"No, I teach literature, remember? We have actual texts to occupy our attention. Things would have to go terribly, terribly wrong before I'd resort to personal anecdote." Such reticence, she knew all too well, ran counter to the entire culture, but she hadn't the slightest interest in the confessional mode, nor did she intend to Oprah her classes, to reduce the study of literature to issues, to ratchet up interest by means of irrelevant autobiography. Besides, what would she tell them? Did you know I have a damaged son? (I do!) Guess how long it's been since my husband and I had sex? (Here's a hint: a long time!)

"Don't you people believe everything is a text these days?" Tony objected. "Tolstoy? *Us Weekly?* A tattooed buttock?"

"Oh, stop."

"And speaking of living texts, here's one of your favorites."

In the entryway, Tom Newhouse, professor emeritus, was hanging his tweed hat on a peg. Forced into retirement at age seventy, Newhouse continued to teach the Joyce seminar for which he was famous among students (for his bonhomie) and infamous among his colleagues (for his critical misreadings). Turning, feet planted wide apart, he surveyed the disappointing scene before him. His white hair was utterly wild.

"Looks like he's got his usual load on," Tony observed.

"Don't," Janet pleaded, when Tony started to wave. "Maybe he won't notice us."

"He's just lonely, Janet," Tony said.

"It's not *your* ass he's going to grab when he comes over here," she reminded him.

"That wasn't true, in case you're interested," Tony replied. Earlier in the semester a young woman had accused Newhouse of inappropriate touching. ("*Inappropriate,*" Tony had remarked at the time. "There's a word I wouldn't mind never hearing again.") The charge had been dropped after a suggestion that the victim must have been acting on an overheard suggestion, from a women's studies professor, that someone ought to put a stop to the old fool's groping. "Besides," Tony went on, "you're sitting. Don't stand up, and you're safe."

"*That's* your solution?"

"No, it's yours. I don't require a solution."

The bartender was drawing Newhouse a pitcher of beer. Not a good sign, though perhaps Newhouse intended to send the beer over to the student table. His wife having died a decade earlier, his house and car paid off, Newhouse was famous for his largesse, especially with his seniors.

Janet leaned forward and planted her elbows on the wet tabletop, hoping that if Newhouse saw her and Tony with their heads together in close conversation he would not intrude.

"Are you going anywhere over break?" she asked. Tony usually fled for New York or Boston after his last class. When they first met, Janet had assumed he was gay, but apparently he was not. In fact, he'd dated most of the college's eligible female faculty, as well as a few of the administrative staff, and recently she'd heard a rumor about a custodian. Which made her wonder why he'd never shown any interest in *her.* True, she was married, but he'd never even flirted with her, at least not seriously.

"No, I'm staying put," Tony said, surprising her. "My brother and his wife are visiting from Utah, if you can believe it."

Janet risked a barward glance and saw that the bartender was now drawing Newhouse a second pitcher. "I didn't know you had a brother."

"We don't see that much of each other," Tony said. "He and the little woman are both strict Mormons, which means that I'm not even going to be able to anesthetize myself. They're determined to experience a genuine New England Thanksgiving, and they don't seem to understand that such a thing simply can't be done sober. What are you and yours up to?"

She'd been dreading the holiday all week, and now realized that this dread probably accounted for her willingness to spend all those hours searching her files for the Cox essay. The task had let her avoid confronting the awful, endless day ahead. Robbie would cook a huge meal for just the three of them. Two, really — Marcus would eat only what he ate every day: a grilled-cheese sandwich, and then only if Robbie cut off any cheese that had turned brown on the bottom of the pan. He might not eat anything at all if he was out of sorts, which he was likely to be. When his regular TV programs weren't on, he often became agitated and inconsolable. Last year the balloons of the Macy's parade had upset him, and it had taken forever to calm him down. Her own presence was another issue. Marcus did best when his routine was not violated. Janet's being home on a weekday often made him restless, as if he were waiting for her to go away, for things to return to normal. Robbie claimed this wasn't true, and swore that Marcus loved her. But it seemed true to Janet. The doctors had warned them that children like Marcus sometimes chose one parent over another. They usually chose the mother, though Marcus had not. She'd been told that it was nothing personal — but what could be more personal than someone's preference for one person over another? Wasn't that what the word *personal* meant?

"Moooooore!" Tom Newhouse bellowed as he came toward them, beer slopping over the lip of the pitcher in his hand. He'd dropped the other pitcher off at the undergraduate table. He slid into their booth — on Janet's side, naturally — and she moved as far away from him as she could, until her right shoulder was against the brick wall.

"You *know* what I like about you, Moore?" Newhouse called everyone, students and colleagues alike, by their last names. His other irritating habit was dramatically emphasizing, at deafening volume, one word in nearly every sentence.

Yes, Janet thought, you like my boobs. He was always ogling them, and he appeared to be ogling them now.

"Do you know what I *like* about Moore?" he asked Tony, when Janet declined to speculate aloud.

"Sure," Tony said. "The same thing we all like."

Newhouse blinked at Tony drunkenly, then fixed Janet with a rheumy gaze. "*He* has a dirty mind."

"You arrived at that conclusion how?" Janet asked, causing the man to scroll back, then break into a big grin.

"I see what you mean," he said. "It's *my* mind that's dirty, isn't it." He turned back to Tony. "What I was *going* to say was, what I like about this lady is that she's a good dancer."

"That's what we *all* like about her," Tony said.

"You've never seen me dance, Professor Newhouse." She was sure she hadn't danced in public since joining the college faculty, seven years before.

"I've heard *stories,*" he said, turning to Tony to pursue his argument. "Besides, you can tell by the way a woman walks if she's got the music in her. And *this* lady's got the music."

"Nice rack, too," Tony added.

Newhouse absorbed this comment thoughtfully, then turned back to Janet. "Now *that* time it was him, not me. You can't blame me for *that* one."

"I guess you're right," she said. "Just this once, I'll let you skate."

He topped off their glasses. "*Thank* you," he said, fixing his eye on Tony again. "That's the problem these days: nobody lets anybody skate on anything." He still hadn't forgiven Tony for serving on the committee that had recommended he take a sensitivity seminar as a condition of dropping the "inappropriate touching" charge.

"That's one of the problems," Tony agreed cheerfully.

"We have a *student* in common, you and I," Newhouse said to Janet, leaning toward her, as if what he was about to impart were a secret to be kept from Tony Hope at all costs. His elbow came to rest against her left breast. Tony noticed and grinned. "*That* one." Newhouse offered his index finger for her to sight along. She recognized one of the students at the round table, though his back was to them.

"*Cox,*" Newhouse thundered. "James Cox. Wrote the best paper on *Dubliners* I ever read."

"Who do you think wrote it?" she asked.

"He could *publish* the damn thing," Newhouse went on, an alcoholic beat behind. Then: "What do you mean, who wrote it? James Cox *wrote* it."

"Okay."

Now Newhouse leaned away from her. "Why would you suspect *Cox?*"

"If you aren't suspicious, fine," she said, lowering her voice in the vain hope that he would lower his as well.

"I'm *not* suspicious. Why would *you* be suspicious?"

"Do you get a lot of publishable work from undergraduates?" Tony, bless him, asked innocently.

"*You,*" Newhouse said. "You stay out of this. I want this lady to tell me why I should suspect *Cox.*"

"Maybe I'm wrong," Janet told him.

"You *are* wrong," he said, sliding out of the booth and grabbing the pitcher. His face had gone beet red. "You *are* wrong. You're *worse* than wrong." He turned to Tony, then. "And *you.*"

"Yes, Tom?"

"*You* aren't even a good dancer."

And with that Newhouse pivoted and returned to the bar to drink alone. "What's 'worse than wrong,' do you suppose?" Janet asked Tony when Newhouse was out of earshot.

By the time Janet emerged from Modern and Romance Languages, the sky had grown menacingly dark and a hot desert wind, full of electricity, had sprung up, auguring rain. Good, she thought. In the air conditioning of Bellamy's office she'd not sensed the gathering storm, which probably meant that he hadn't either. Otherwise, he'd be headed for his top-down Mustang at a dead run. By the time the rain hit his office window, it would be too late.

She held in her hand the old issue of American Literature. *He'd turned down the corners of the two articles he wanted her to read. One, he'd explained, was his first published essay, written when he was a grad student, a careless effort that contained, by his count, no fewer than six errors, every one of which had been pointed out to him over the years by fastidious fact-gatherers who seemed to believe that mistakes, no matter how innocent or inconsequential, were unforgivable. He hoped she'd see why the essay, despite its flaws, had been worth publishing. Though he hadn't said it in so many words, her assignment, apparently, was to look for the signs of the Bellamy passion that had led, inevitably, to greatness, to the best office on the corridor and the vintage Mustang in the F Lot.*

The other essay he suggested Janet look at was by one Patricia Anastacio; in this one (here again he had more implied this than stated it) she would find admirable but distinctly minor (feminine, no doubt) virtues — industriousness, organizational skills, attention to detail — that were predictive of a workmanlike but uninspired scholarly career. ("You read carefully, you synthesize well, and you know how to marshal evidence.") Really, the man's arrogance was breathtaking. He'd cast himself as Tennyson's Ulysses, fearlessly sailing uncharted waters, while she (like the other girls?) would remain behind like Telemachus, blamelessly tending the household gods. Okay, Telemachus wasn't a girl — but the gender prejudices at the core of Bellamy's assumptions would have been infuriating even coming from a white man. How much worse to have them served up by a black one, who should have known better.

At the bottom of the steps was a metal trash can, and Janet had to restrain herself from tossing in the periodical. What prevented her was an even better idea: she'd drop it onto the front seat of the Mustang. When the skies opened, it would swell up like the man's bloated ego. If he said anything later, she could claim innocence, tell him she'd xeroxed the essays and was simply returning the magazine to its owner. That story didn't really track, but nothing about it was grossly unbelievable, nothing he could call her on.

She was still so worked up when she arrived at the F Lot that she was totally unprepared for the strange sight she encountered there. Standing next to Bellamy's Mustang was a young man dressed in brightly mismatched clothes. He had a large shaved head, and his arms were flailing about wildly, as if he were doing battle with invisible demons. As she drew near, he let out a startling howl. Had his eyes not been clamped shut, he'd have been looking right at her, which was no doubt why she briefly entertained the irrational notion that it was her own approach that he was so determined to fend off. He looked like some sort of demented, idiot genie summoned by her proximity for the express purpose of protecting Bellamy's car.

These were, of course, the impressions of an instant. Later, guiltily, she would try to reconstruct exactly what had happened and why. The young man was *a frightening apparition, his arms thrashing about his head, as if he'd just received an electrical charge. (Did he mean to share that jolt with her if she came close enough to touch?) But by the time she'd taken her first, instinctive step around him, she'd known the truth — that he was blind, and that the hot wind, gusting fiercely and carrying all manner of grit, had frightened and disoriented him. His white cane lay under the Mustang's bumper. Why, then, once she'd apprehended the truth, was it so hard to banish the original, clearly false impression of the young man as someone to be feared, someone determined to transfer his demons to her?*

And then, as if a switch had been thrown, his howling and gyrations stopped, and he cocked his head. Did he sense her nearness? Did he mean to cast a spell? To grant her a wish she'd later come to regret? Slowly, he turned toward her. Had his eyes not been clamped shut, he'd again have been looking right at her, and the two of them stood there frozen, a couple of feet apart, until the young man finally threw back his head and howled, "Pleeeeeease!"

As if in answer, the rains came, the first fat drop hitting Janet on an eyebrow, releasing her, and she ran.

Robbie looked up and smiled when she came in through the garage and hung her shoulder bag on the wall hook. Marcus was sitting next to him on the sofa. They were watching cartoons, which Robbie, at least, seemed to be enjoying. Marcus's face was blank, as usual, but he was caressing his father's earlobe between his thumb and his forefinger, as was his habit when he was calm. The significance of that gesture was one of the many things Robbie and Janet couldn't agree on. Robbie thought it was sweet that their son found his earlobe comforting. Until recently, Marcus had forbidden touching of any sort, so Janet supposed that, yes, it might be an encouraging sign, but she was troubled that Marcus still didn't like to *be* touched, and also that Robbie's earlobe was the only one he seemed comforted by. When she'd pointed this out to her husband, he'd reminded her of their doctors' repeated admonitions. "And besides," he'd said. "Have you noticed it's only my right earlobe? I've tried putting him on the other side of the sofa and letting him play with the left one, but no dice. It's the right one or nothing."

"He doesn't want either of mine."

"I'm the one who's around. If you were here all day, it'd be you." When she replied that she didn't think so, he said, "I guess we'll never know." He said this without sarcasm, a simple fact, one of the many simple facts that made up Robbie's life, none of which he seemed to resent.

In graduate school, he'd been a year behind her. Though universally well liked, he was generally considered the least-gifted student in the doctoral program. The others had all done their master's work elsewhere, but Robbie was a holdover, admitted at the last minute when a more highly regarded Ivy Leaguer had backed out. At least once a term, he'd had to be persuaded not to drop out of the program. Since Janet had accepted her tenure-track position at the college, Robbie had been writing grants for local nonprofits, a job he could do at home while taking care of Marcus. The year before, when she'd been up for tenure and working long hours on the book that would justify the college's awarding it, they'd seemed to be drifting toward divorce, but now that her job was secure, things seemed a little better. They'd found a morning-care program for Marcus, which meant Robbie could finally finish his dissertation — though so far he'd shown no such inclination. His rationale was that the college already had someone with his specialty, so what difference did it make? Even if a better position at a research university came along for Janet, he'd still be considered baggage. To Janet the idea of not finishing something you'd worked on for so long was beyond baffling. But that was Robbie.

"The grant came through," he told her, nudging Marcus gently. "Move over, sport. Let's make room for Mom. She looks like she's had a rough day." And she's late, was what he didn't say. Late coming home on a day when she might have been expected to return early.

"That's okay," she told him. "I'm going to change. Which grant? How much?"

"The Contemporary Art Institute. Seventy-five K. They're over the moon."

"They should be. Congratulations." And how much did *you* get? she thought. Why do you let these people take advantage of you, working for peanuts, making them look good?

In their bedroom she shed her work clothes and pulled on a pair of jeans. Outside it had begun to rain. The bedroom blinds were drawn shut, but she could hear the first raindrops hitting the window in wind-driven splashes. *Why does he gallop and gallop about?*

Why had she returned to the F Lot? She remembered telling herself that she just wanted to make sure that the young man was all right. If he was still in distress, she'd call the campus police, who, after all, were paid to handle such situations. But even at the time she'd known she was more curious than concerned. Had he tried to cross the street and been run over? (Would that be her fault?) Or, in his literally blind rage, had he assaulted the next passerby (proving how wise she'd been to steer clear of him)?

At least ten minutes had elapsed, so she wasn't surprised to see that someone had the young man in hand now. But she hadn't expected it to be Bellamy. He had the boy (he looked younger now, for some reason) by the elbow and was preparing to help him cross the now-flooded street. She considered just driving by, but what if Bellamy recognized her? Did he know her car?

"Janet," he said, when she pulled up next to them, "you're a lifesaver." He led the boy around to the passenger side of her car, helping him into the front seat, an accusation — See how harmless he is?

"God bless you," the boy muttered as Bellamy, still out in the rain, got him situated, fastening his seat belt.

"God bless you." Was she included in this blessing? The boy faced forward, as if unaware of her. Did he imagine the car drove itself? Or had he caught a whiff of her in the lot before she darted off, and recognized her scent now? Another possibility also occurred to her. What if the boy was only partially blind? Maybe that was why he refused to look in her direction.

"Here," Bellamy said, taking the boy by the wrist and putting his cane in his hand.

"God bless you."

"William here needs a lift to the Newman Center," Bellamy said (he already knew the boy's name?), and then he slid into the back seat, dripping, diamonds in his hair.

"Where's that?"

"Turn right on Glenn. Two blocks, on the left," Bellamy told her. Was he Catholic? Why else would he know where the Newman Center was? She tried to picture The Great Bellamy on his knees, praying.

The rain was falling even harder now, but straight down; the wind had abated some. "Do you want to put your top up?" she asked, indicating the Mustang.

Bellamy regarded her curiously, perhaps surprised that she knew which car was his, then burst into laughter. "That's hilarious," he said.

"Everything okay?" Robbie wanted to know. He was standing in the doorway, regarding her wistfully as she sat on the edge of the bed in her bra, and she felt a wave of something like nausea pass over her as past and present merged. "You looked like you were about to cry."

She rose, went over to the dresser, took out a sweatshirt, and pulled it over her head. "I'm fine. Just had to deal with a plagiarism."

"Those are always fun," Robbie said. "Did he come clean?"

She nodded. "Then, to make matters worse, I ran into Tom Newhouse." She wouldn't mention that this had happened in the Hub Pub. One of Robbie's complaints, back when it looked like they might divorce, was that except for the rare dinner party, they never went out anymore. He loved live music, even the kind of junky garage bands that played loud blues in the mill-town dives that ringed the campus, the kind he'd played in himself back in their university days.

"Turns out my plagiarist is taking a class with him too, and Tom starts raving about this Joyce paper the kid wrote. Then he gets mad at me when I suggest he might want to look into it."

Robbie frowned. "Why did you do that?"

"Do what?"

He just shrugged.

"No, what are you saying?"

"Don't get angry. I was just remembering high school. I always hated it when the nuns compared notes. If I got into trouble in one class on Monday afternoon, by Tuesday morning they were all pissed at me. It didn't seem fair."

"The solution to that problem was not to fuck up with the first nun."

He shrugged again, unwilling, as usual, to take the bait. "You want me to cook something, or go out for pizza?"

"Whichever."

"Pizza, then. Marcus can come with me. He loves Pizzoli's."

Really? How can you tell? Not saying this, of course. Because it probably wasn't the real reason he was taking Marcus with him. It was just better not to leave him alone with her.

"It's the greatest of mysteries, I think," Bellamy said later. She'd waited in the car while he walked the boy into the Newman Center, then she gave him a lift back to his waterlogged Mustang. Though she'd run all the way to the X Lot, she'd been soaked to the skin by the time she got there, and she was aware that her shirt was now semitransparent. If Bellamy noticed, he gave no sign. "What it's like to be another person, to be William. What it feels like, I mean. Literature. Life. They give us little glimpses, leaving us hungry for more."

When she said nothing he finally glanced over at her, then away again. "I'm sorry I pushed you so hard today," he said. "I like to know who people are, but I sometimes forget it's none of my business."

Go away, she remembered thinking. Please stop talking and go away. His kindness toward the blind boy had stolen her righteous anger, leaving her hollow, in need of another emotion, though she couldn't think of one she was entitled to, unless it was despair.

She was sobbing now, her body shaking violently, and for a long time she could not stop. Only when she quit trying did she feel herself begin to come out the other end. How long did the jag last? She wasn't sure, but probably no more than half an hour, or Robbie and Marcus would have returned with the pizza. The face that stared back at her from the bedroom mirror — pale, swollen, naked — was barely recognizable as her own. It wasn't a face she wanted Robbie or Marcus to see. Their son seemed to have no emotions of his own other than anger and fear, but those of others often upset him. She did not want to be in the house, looking like this, when they returned.

Backing out of their driveway, she had no idea where she was going — didn't know, in fact, until she got to the end of their street and turned left onto College Avenue. Was she losing her mind? What could she possibly hope to accomplish by returning to campus? James Cox and his friends were probably long gone, the pub locked up. But she knew now what she wanted to say to him, what she should have said earlier. And suddenly the idea of waiting until after the Thanksgiving break was insupportable. The resumption of classes was too far in the future. She couldn't risk forgetting, couldn't risk the return of her sanity, her emotional equilibrium. Given time and opportunity, she'd reason herself out of saying the words. For her own sake more than his, she needed to say what she believed, this very moment, to be true: that his dishonesty wasn't a condition; it was nothing but a habit, and habits could be broken. Just cheating once didn't make you a cheater, not if you stopped. He could begin his new life by writing a new essay. Something by James Cox, not some long-forgotten fraternity brother. Maybe in the writing he'd locate a James Cox who wasn't lazy or incompetent, sullen or belligerent. Maybe he could find a better self. "Don't hold back," he'd advised her, and she didn't plan to. She would make him understand.

But by the time she arrived back at the Hub Pub, James Cox and his friends were gone, and the disappointment she felt was crushing, out of all proportion. To make matters worse, Tom Newhouse was seated right where she'd left him at the bar. He hadn't seen her come in. She could slip out, and he'd never know. You could do that in life — just slip away before you were noticed. What was the term Tony had used? *Effaced.* You could become effaced.

"Moore," Newhouse said when she slid onto the barstool next to him. "You're *back.*" His smile suggested that either he'd forgotten she'd recently angered him or he'd already forgiven her.

"Would you like to join us for Thanksgiving dinner, Tom?" she heard herself say.

He blinked at her, and didn't answer immediately. "What are you serving?"

She laughed out loud. "What do you mean, what are we serving?"

"Sommelier!" he called over to the bartender. "A glass for the lady. A *clean* one. This is Professor Moore. You *know* Professor Moore? Our rising star?"

The boy behind the bar put a glass in front of her, which Newhouse proceeded to fill to the brim and then over.

"What I *mean* is, I'm weighing several options. I assume you're serving a roast *fowl* of some sort?"

"Turkey, yes."

"Will it be a *stuffed* turkey?"

She said yes, she thought it probably would.

"Will there be *cran*berries? *Yams?*"

"Why not?"

He regarded her seriously with bleary-eyed benevolence. "Well, then. It all comes down to *pie,* doesn't it?"

"What kind of pie do you like, Tom? What would seal the deal?"

*"Mince*meat."

"You're kidding me."

"Pumpkin would be okay. What *time?"*

"Midafternoon?"

"And I can bring *what?"*

"A mincemeat pie, if you really want mincemeat pie."

When she slid off the barstool again, he said, "You're leaving? You just *got* here."

"Robbie and Marcus went out for a pizza. I forgot to leave them a note, so . . ."

"I'll see you Thursday."

"I should warn you," she told him, feeling her throat constrict, "my son has good days and bad. If he's having a bad one, you may wish you hadn't come."

He lumbered down from his barstool then and gave her a hug. She didn't resist. "You're okay, Moore."

It did not escape her that her professional life at this moment was bracketed by two scholars, one a legendary critic, several of whose books were still considered classics, the other the local Mr. Chips, a man who was struggling to not let alcohol and loneliness undermine his legacy. Two men with nothing in common but an innate generosity. Each disposed, for reasons both mysterious and profound, to think better of people than perhaps they deserved — whereas her own inclination had always been to think less of them. Bellamy had tried to warn her. He'd seen how skilled she was, how coldly persuasive she could be; he'd known that she would use the study of literature to distance herself. Maybe he even foresaw how things would go for her and Robbie, how she'd win every argument in their marriage until finally the marriage was gone.

"I'm sorry," she said, when Tom Newhouse finally released her. "I must look awful."

"You've looked better," he conceded. "*I've* looked better. We've *all* looked better." Then, after a beat: "So James *Cox* didn't write that essay."

"Oh, I don't know. It's possible he did," she admitted. "But no, I don't think so." The accusation was the same one she'd made before, but it felt different this time, and Newhouse seemed willing to accept it now.

"Well, *shit,*" was all he said.

"You were right about one thing, though," she told him. "I *am* a good dancer. Or I was. When I passed my prelims, Robbie invited everyone in the department to help us celebrate. His band played, and they were so great that night. I used to sing one song with them — Jefferson Airplane's 'Somebody to Love.'" Newhouse had clearly never heard of either the song or the group. The very thought of Grace Slick had Janet on the verge of tears again. "We ended up at a biker joint at three in the morning. I danced on the bar."

"That must have been something," he said. "I wish I'd *been* there."

"Yeah, well, you missed it," she said.

"Hey," he said, planting a kiss on her forehead. "Just because I wasn't there doesn't mean I can't remember it."

Back home, Robbie's car was in the driveway, and when she got out she could see her husband and her son through the dining room window. Robbie was opening the pizza box and Marcus was closing his eyes, breathing in — re-creating, perhaps, every single detail of the pizza parlor that, according to Robbie, he loved. So this, she thought, was heartbreak. She'd read about it, and she wasn't sure she wanted to get any closer. She'd always suspected that epiphany was overrated. Even now her inclination was to remain right where she was, the dining room window between herself and her husband and child, safe from them and they from her.

The night she'd passed her prelims and danced on the bar, Bellamy had been there, and when the biker bar closed they'd all adjourned to a truckstop, where they'd ordered huge breakfasts. Waiting for the food to arrive, they'd argued, the way only happy, drunken graduate students can, about which was the greatest lyric poem ever written. You could nominate a poem only if you were able to recite it, start to finish, from memory. Then you had to make the case for its greatness. Robbie had surprised her by reciting *Kubla Khan* in its entirety, to wild applause. When it was Bellamy's turn, he'd recited "Windy Nights," a children's poem everyone but Janet remembered. He emphasized its childish iambic downbeat by slapping the table so hard the water glasses jumped, and by the time he finished the entire group was weak with laughter. "Okay, okay, okay. Now the explanation," someone insisted. "Tell us why that's the greatest poem ever in the English language."

"Because," Bellamy said, suddenly serious, his eyes full, "when I speak those words aloud, my father is alive again."

He left the following year, as predicted, and went back to the Ivy League, but not before he'd recommended her for a prestigious postdoctoral fellowship, a much-needed port in the academic storm for her and Robbie. Why had he done it? Maybe for Robbie. She'd come to believe that Bellamy knew, that he'd arrived on the scene that afternoon in time to see her flee from the blind man. If so, he'd apparently not held her cowardice against her. Could he possibly have wanted, like Tom Newhouse, to express through the fellowship his optimistic view that in the end she'd be all right? If that was what he had truly believed, could she be certain he was wrong? Tomorrow she'd find the journal Bellamy had loaned her all those years ago, containing the essays she'd stubbornly refused to read. She already knew what she'd find in them. In Bellamy's, she'd find Bellamy, the man they'd all known, his human presence tangible in every word. Authorial. What he'd learned, from literature and life, made him hungry for more, and this hunger was what drew people to him. Robbie had wept when he read her Bellamy's obituary from the *Times* the same year she accepted her tenure-track position at the college, and Robbie had wanted to name their son in Bellamy's memory. She'd argued for other names, names that originated in her family or his, but she couldn't make him understand. "What's wrong with *Marcus?*" he kept asking, until she finally gave in.

In the other essay, she'd find what Bellamy had found in hers: an absence. An implied writer. A shadow. A ghost. "But I *am* real," she'd insisted that day, imagining that he meant to talk her out of it, when in reality he was merely urging her to find that last elusive thing, a self worth being, worth becoming, and, finally, worth revealing. Yes, even though she knew what she'd find in those two essays, she would read them. She owed Bellamy that much. He'd given her an assignment, and she'd finish it. After which, she suspected, he'd haunt her no more.

Robbie was peering out the dining room window. He'd no doubt heard her car pull in and was wondering what she was doing out there *in the dark and wet.* He had set the table for three. Tonight they'd eat pizza. Tomorrow she'd find out what the hell mincemeat was. Then they would celebrate Thanksgiving. After that, who knew?

JIM SHEPARD

Sans Farine

FROM HARPER'S MAGAZINE

MY FATHER, Jean-Baptiste Sanson, had christened in the church of Saint-Laurent two children: a daughter, who married Pierre Hérisson, executioner of Melun, and a son, myself. After my mother's death, he remarried, his second wife from a family of executioners in the province of Touraine. Together they produced twelve children, eight of whom survived, six of whom were boys. All six eventually registered in the public rolls as executioners, my half brothers beginning their careers by assisting their father and then myself in the city of Paris.

My name is Charles-Henri Sanson, known to many throughout this city as the Keystone of the Revolution, and known to the rabble as Sans Farine — without flour — a pun based on my use of emptied bran sacks to hold the severed heads. I was named for Charles Sanson, former adventurer and soldier of the king and, until 1668, executioner of Cherbourg and Caudebec-en-Caux. My father claimed he was descended from Sanson de Longval and that our family coat of arms derived from either the First or Second Crusade. Its escutcheon represents another pun: a cracked bell and the motto *San son:* without sound.

You want to know — all France wants to know — what takes place in the executioner's mind: the figure who before the Revolution wielded the double-bladed axe and double-handed sword, and who branded, burned, and broke on the wheel all who came before him. The figure who now slides heads through what they call the Republican Window on the guillotine. Does he eat? Does he sleep? Do his smiles freeze the blood? Is he kind to those he kills? Does he touch his wife on days he works? Does he reach for you with blood-rimmed fingernails? Did he spring full-blown from a black pit to send batch after batch through the guillotine?

Becoming shrill, my wife calls it, whenever I get too agitated in my own defense.

"What struck people's minds above all else," Livy, the great Roman, wrote in his *History* on Brutus' sacrifice of his own sons for the good of the Republic, "is that his function as consul imposed on the father the task of punishing his sons, and that his unbendingness compelled him personally to order the execution, the very sight of which was not spared him." In Guerin's rendering of the scene, the hero turns away but does not blanch. Standing before it in the old Royal Academy with Anne-Marie, I told her that perhaps that way we attain the sublime: by our fierce devotion to the required. She was not able to agree.

I am a good Catholic. The people's judges hand out their sentences, and mine is the task of insuring that their words become incarnate. I am the instrument, and it is justice that strikes. I feel the same remorse as anyone required to be present at an execution.

Before the Revolution, justice was apportioned and discharged in the name of the king, who ruled by divine right as one of God's implements. And the punishment of malefactors was God's will and earned, therefore, for his sovereign minister, God's grace and esteem. But for most, that grace and esteem did not extend as far as the sovereign's hand servant. Before the Revolution, daughters of executioners were forbidden to marry outside the profession. When their girls came of age, such families had to display on their doors a yellow affidavit clarifying the family's trade and acknowledging the taint in their bloodline. Letters of commission and payments were not passed into their hands but dropped before them. They were required to live at the southern ends of towns, and their houses had to be painted red.

Before the Revolution, a woman with whom I dined at an inn demanded I be made to appear in court to apologize for having shared with her a dinner table. She petitioned that executioners be made to wear a particular badge or color upon their coats or singlets, so that all would know their profession. Before the Revolution, our children were allowed no playmates but one another.

For lunch today there was egg soup with lemon juice and broth, cockscomb, a marrow bone, chicken fried in breadcrumbs, jelly, apricots, bread, and fennel comfits. Clearing the table, Anne-Marie reminisced about a holiday we took when the children were small. When she speaks to me, she holds the family before us like a pleasing little stove. Before, she was able to treat this terrible time as a brigand unable to trespass upon the better world she bore within.

With children, everything and nothing registers. My earliest memory is of the house outside Paris, and the height of the manure pile, and the muck dropped by the household geese. I remember flies whenever one went outside. I remember my mother's calm voice, and associate it with needlework. She was fond of saying that I had no ideas of grandeur and that she would wish that to continue. My grandmother always chided me for losing even a crumb of my bread, since, as she put it, I couldn't make for myself even that. My father was a quiet man who resolved that his little boy should become a person capable of self-sufficiency, when it came to understanding the world, and so he allowed me to negotiate my own passage through that household. I was perceived to be headstrong but inhibited. I was sent away at an early age and then pitched from school to school, since the moment my classmates uncovered my family's profession, life became unbearable again. I wrote my mother a series of supplications outlining my misery and pleading for a response. In a cheerless chapel in a school in Rouen — my fourth in as many years — I received my father's letter informing me of her death.

He remarried; the house was repopulated with half brothers and half sisters; I stayed away at my schools. I matured into a beanstalk whose expressions excited pity on the street. My teachers knew me as dutiful, alert, frugal, and friendless: a nonentity with ambitions. I was often cold and known for my petitions to sit nearer the room's hearth. I volunteered for small errands so that in solitude I might gather the strength to face the rest of the day. I wrote to myself in my notebooks that I felt my bleak present within me, and ached to my bones with wondering if loneliness would always be the measure of my days.

Anne-Marie was a market gardener's daughter in Montmartre, her father's establishment a luncheon stop on my infrequent visits home from school. She was his eldest. She was born the same day as myself, and when we first conversed, I imagined that we had loved each other from that date, unawares.

Her first act in my presence was to scratch at a rash on her foot until chided by her father, entering the room with the roast. She visited the water closet and, back at the table, returned my gaze as if examining a distant coastline. She was still chewing a bit of carrot. From that first meeting I have perched perpetually, in a kind of dreamy distress, on the very edge of relieving my longings. Her lovely large mouth and deep-set eyes, with their veiled expression, and her child's posture have been my harbor and receding horizon. Her seat, that first luncheon, was in the sun, and her skin was so fine I could see the circulation of her blood. When she blushed, I could feel the warmth.

I contrived to visit more often. She confided her various sadnesses, her mother having led a life regulated by an intricate and dispiriting routine, much of which was centered on the needs of her younger sister. Her father's health and general cheerlessness prevented him from finding solace in anything. But even in that company, she found the resources to engage, with animation, in any society offered her, as if the seas that swamped other shipping beat upon her little boat in vain.

With her I tended toward passionate recollection of my own imagined virtues. Without her my private life had been a record of uninterrupted emptiness and misery. Her first letter to me upon my return to school concluded, "I seem to have written you a newspaper instead of a note, as was my intention. My conduct is most mysterious. Well. Until later —"

She saw in me a perceptive enough boy, self-educated in a variety of disciplines, from astronomy to law, from medicine to agronomy. I was tall. I was charitable, and kind to the poor. I played the cello, and seemed someone with whom a good home could be constructed. Her family was poor enough that an executioner's son was still a possibility, but respected enough that she was as good a match as my family would find. For her, marriage to someone like me meant renouncing vanities she had never possessed, and for which she had no desire.

Soon after our marriage I related to her the story of my first execution, a story designed to elicit her pity. I had been sixteen. When home from school, I had been my father's assistant from the age of eleven. He had retired and I had been left alone on the scaffold with a few of his assistants, now mine. A man named Mongeot was to be bludgeoned and then broken on the wheel for having murdered his mistress's husband. His mistress was to be held under guard and made to witness what transpired. A snowstorm had enveloped the scaffold, then a kind of sleet, and I stood in the wind clutching my collar against the wet while my mulatto did the bludgeoning. The man's mistress shrieked and clawed at her guards' faces, and tore at her hair. It took Mongeot two hours to die. I'd worn the wrong boots, and my feet were soaked through and freezing. I could not see for my weeping and misheld the lever when we were in the act of breaking his legs. My grandmother, bundled in robes and representing the family, lost patience and shouted at me. The crowd hissed and showered me with contempt.

Anne-Marie pitied me for such stories but, after an expression of sympathy, maintained a wary silence. Our newlyweds' happiness was then colored by a kind of quiet. There were other stories I didn't share with her. After Mongeot, a man named Damiens, who had tried to stab the king, was sentenced to be drawn and quartered. No one had been quartered in France since Ravaillac, more than a century before. I went to my father, but he said he had no advice to give. I offered to resign my commission, but my grandmother summoned my uncle, executioner of Reims, to steady me. Our assistants were to handle the preliminaries and on the appointed day drank until they could barely stand. They tottered between the instruments while the crowd jeered at their fumblings and shouted abuse. The hand that had held the knife was severed, and boiling oil and lead were poured into the wound. The man's screams were such that we could not hear one another's instructions. Then the horses only dislocated his limbs without separating them from the trunk. The executioner's sword lodged in one of his shoulder joints. I had to run and find an ax.

Some three months after the fall of the Bastille, the National Assembly took up the issue of renovating the penal code, and in the middle of those proceedings, Dr. Joseph-Ignace Guillotin, deputy from Paris and professor of anatomy on the Faculty of Medicine, set forth his argument in favor of a fixed punishment for the same crimes, regardless of the convicted's rank and estate.

He reminded the Assembly of the infamies of the unenlightened past and proposed a less barbaric method of capital punishment: automatic decapitation by a mechanism yet to be developed. A Jesuit, he'd left the order, choosing a ministry of the body over that of the soul. He wanted the machinery of execution to be fearful but the death to be easy. There was enthusiasm for his proposal among the revolutionaries: a capital punishment that was mercifully quick and democratic was seen as another step in the regeneration of society. It was pointed out that while the executioner's sword might require two or three strokes, with a machine the condemned man would not be kept waiting. Lally-Tollendal's name was resurrected. Some years before, I'd proven unable to dispatch him, and my father had had to take over the blade.

After some delay the measure was adopted in the new penal code, and the next challenge became how to cut off all those heads. I was invited to submit a memorandum sharing my views in which I pointed out that with any multiple execution, the sword is not fit to perform after the first, and needed to be reground and sharpened, which meant an impractical number of swords, depending on the number condemned. I also pointed out that for an execution by sword to arrive at the result prescribed by the law, the executioner must be consistently skillful and the condemned at least momentarily steadfast, and that in the event of multiple executions, there would be the issue of blood in such quantities that it would affect even the most intrepid of those to be executed, so that it would be indispensable to find some means by which the condemned could be secured for the blow and the public order protected.

Dr. Guillotin had begun to lose interest in his idea, but Dr. Antoine Louis, secretary of the Academy of Surgeons, engaged a German piano maker to build the prototype. There was some difficulty finding men to do the job. They had to be exempted from signing the usual working papers, so that their identities could remain a secret.

The result is what my assistants call the Great Machine. At the heart of its design are two uprights, five meters high and fifty centimeters apart, which flank a blade weighing seven kilos. Bolted to the top of the blade is a thirty-kilogram iron bar to accelerate its descent. The assembly falls from top to bottom in three quarters of a second. The cutting edge is slanted so that the blow, as it penetrates into the parts it divides, acts as a saw of lightning efficiency. The blow lands at the head of a narrow tablelike arrangement for the condemned. From a distance the whole thing has the austerity of a diagram. The grooves are rubbed down with soap before each use. Disassembled, it's stored in a shed known as the Widow's House.

My sons and I supervised its first test at the Bicêtre Hospital on the outskirts of Paris. Before us and the assembled dignitaries, Dr. Louis beheaded a bundle of straw, a live sheep, and several corpses. The last corpse was not beheaded after three tries, so it was decided to extend the height of the uprights and add weight to the blade. At that very first demonstration, I was heard to wonder aloud whether the machine's very efficiency would prove to be a source of regret.

So on the twenty-second of March in the year 1792, the Abbé Chappe bestowed his invention, the telegraph, upon the Assembly. A month later, Dr. Guillotin and Dr. Louis's machine was inaugurated. The culprit was strapped facedown on the plank, which was then tilted to the horizontal and run on grooves forward until his neck slid onto the lunette, a semicircular block. The block was not struck by the falling blade but grazed at high speed, so that the head was planed off. In an eye blink it leapt seventeen or eighteen inches from the trunk. For some, the head was gone before the eye could trace the blow. It became clear that the minimum size for the basket must be that of an infant's bathtub. The executioner's role in the proceedings consisted of giving a little tug on a lever. The crowd saw the blade but not the hand that moved it. Much time was consumed afterward with the mess. Four buckets of water alone were used on the grooves and block.

I used to have a constitution able to endure labor that might have hamstrung a team of oxen. Now my complaints include dizziness, inflammation of the eyes, colic and digestive troubles, and rheumatic pains.

What talk I have with Anne-Marie occurs in the early mornings before the workday begins. I'll pass her on her way out of our little courtyard, hanging laundry to dry, if it's warm enough, or plucking salad herbs. Across from us a shop sells brushes of every manner and use. Its proprietor is a drunk and in all weather slumps beside its door in an old wreck of an iron chair. We can hear the knife grinder's bell as he makes his rounds.

For the past three months, I've approached her heartbroken with the misfortune I helped author, because in August, at the execution of three men accused of forging promissory notes, our youngest boy, Gabriel, fell when exhibiting one of the heads, fracturing his skull and dying before my eyes. He was twenty-one. There'd always been in our family puzzled concern about him, since he'd kept hidden his aspirations and inner life. What we knew was that he was great for peeling oranges when they were in season. In response to interrogatives he stroked his upper lip with his forefinger and seemed to wait for the intelligent part of the question to emerge. He'd wanted to try his hand at another profession, and Anne-Marie had wanted the same for him. But I'd reminded her of his cousin's experience of having apprenticed himself to a locksmith only to find that no one would patronize their shop. The subject had been dropped. Then Gabriel had offered to join the National Guard. His older brother had asked if he thought himself too refined for the family business. His uncles hadn't been even that kind. I had done my best to comfort him but had also requested that he remain a realist about his future.

That morning the clouds had poured forth rain, the sky churning as if with empyrean seas. Up on the scaffold, our hair was whipped by the wind. It had rained, and the wood was slick and the cobblestones below greasy with mud. There'd been the usual silence while the executioner and his assistants had walked about the platform. Each had a special task, one assistant handling the strapping to the plank, one seeing to the remaining condemned, one adjusting the heads in the lunette while wearing an ankle-length waxed apron. Each assistant is given a chance at one point or another to display one of the heads.

Gabriel I usually allowed to see to the remaining condemned. He moved about his responsibilities like a child resignedly attending a new school. The third head pitched from its lost shoulders. It was his turn to reach his arm down into the basket. I could not see from where I stood whether his expression as he held it up by the hair was one of fascinated horror or queasy forbearance or distracted indifference. The rain and the three men's blood made the front of the scaffold as slick as soap. There was no rail.

Perseus hoisted Medusa's head. Judith, Holofernes'. David, Goliath's. The head warns of the consequences of violating the sovereign peace. Held by the hair and presented at the scaffold, it represents the government's discharge of its promise to maintain order. An executioner's reputation depends to a large extent upon his efficiency and élan with that display. Doing his best to manifest the head to as much of the crowd as he could, and failing to look where he put his feet, our Gabriel slipped and split his head open on the cobblestones. The head he'd been holding scattered the crowd. We carried him back to our house in the cart that had brought the condemned.

It's said that, losing his wife and crazed with grief, Robespierre's father abandoned his four children, the eldest being only seven, and traveled in turn through England and the German states, eventually dying in Munich. And that young Robespierre, at seven, had become the implacable and unhappy figure he remains today. All through the early morning hours of that terrible night, Anne-Marie lay like one of the Furies on her bed and would not be consoled. I was not allowed into the room.

A week passed before she addressed me. Her misery was a well from which her spirit refused to surface. I saw only stiffness and mistrust when I got too near. All of her gestures seemed devitalized, as if viewed in weak candlelight. If not for her capacity for work, she would have seemed imprisoned in a perpetual exhaustion.

It was a busy time for the executioner. She tracked without comment my unimpaired predilection for order, my consistency of demeanor, and my undiminished capacities of concentration.

We both remembered a time, after the imprisonment of the king, when I'd been of a sudden possessed by an ungovernable rage with all of those in power who had brought our nation to her present catastrophe, and had resolved to leave Paris. Gabriel in particular had loved the idea. But my passion had subsided, and I'd understood just a bit of what such a decision would involve. Was everyone to abandon his post every time the country took a turn for the worse? Was it left to each servant of the State to decide which laws he would carry out and which he would not? Did anyone but the highest ministers have sufficient information on which to base their opinions?

Yesterday there was a hard frost, and we woke to discover the waste plug burst and the corridor floor covered in filth. Some of it had already frozen, and we scraped and chipped at it in the early morning darkness. The smell from what hadn't frozen drove us back. It was unclear to me, working beside my wife, which in me was stronger: hatred of my profession or hatred of myself. I asked her opinion and she didn't answer. Later, when making her toilet, she remarked that she found my self-contempt understandable, given the minuteness of my self-examinations.

Even with my family, she told me later, serving my supper before leaving the room, I craved the advantage of invisibility. My supper turned out to be beef and cabbage and runner beans.

I eat alone. I sit alone. Without her I have no intimate friend, no affectionate relations. For three months she's remained close-buttoned and oblique, her expressions lawyers' expressions. Some nights I sleep, when Heaven has pity on me.

The night before the waste plug burst, she woke to my weeping. She remained on her back and addressed the ceiling. She told it she'd overheard a boy on the rue de Rennes tell his wet nurse that he'd gone to see a guillotining, and oh, how the poor executioner had suffered. Her tone prevented any response.

She knows that the exclusion of our profession from society is not founded on prejudice alone. The law requires executions, but compels no one to become an executioner.

So now I carry an emptiness with me like the grief of a homesick child. I understood my wife's misery and, under the compulsion of duty, added to it. Each night I take a little brandy, hot lemonade, and toast. My belly is in constant ferment. I'm a pioneer in a Great New Age in which I don't believe. My profession has grown over us like a malevolent wood.

Another frost this morning. In our window box, frozen daisies.

The executioner has the uncontested title to all clothing and jewelry found on the men and women put to death. He pays no taxes. The condemned are subcontracted to him by the nation. The trade in cadavers with the medical profession brings in some additional revenue. But in terms of expenses, there's all household costs and salaries and repairs to the carriages and feed for the horses and any number of other constant vexations. And, of course, the expectation that the machine will be maintained and housed. My father, on execution days, wore a brocaded red singlet with the gallows embroidered across his chest in black and gold thread. In bright sun onlookers could make out a heavily worked panel of darker red satin along his spine. His culottes were of the finest silk. What do I own? A coat of black cloth, a satin waistcoat from an old-clothes shop, a pair of black breeches, a pair of serge breeches, two clothes brushes, four shirts, four cravats, four handkerchiefs, two pairs of stockings, two pairs of shoes, and a hat.

This morning in the courtyard, Anne-Marie was doing no work at all. The sun was out but it was very cold. Clouds issued from the mouth of our sleeping neighbor in his iron chair. She sat with her back to the plaster, wrapping and rewrapping a shawl. I tucked it behind her and she thanked me. We sat for half an hour. Sometimes when addressed she seemed as if she were alone. I told her that I had stopped for wine on the way home the previous evening and had overindulged. She responded that it was probably a part of my unconquerable rejection of anything that might cause me to think. And what was it I should be thinking about? I wanted to know. The world and your place in it, she said. And what was my place in it? I asked, and touched her cheek. And she stood, composing her carriage. Around me now she carries herself like the Holy Sacrament. She returned to the house. We've had two weeks of her working alone, the Austere Isolate, while the rest of us come and go, playing off one another like members of a mournful choral trio.

Perhaps, I told her at dinner, my curse from God was that I lacked that stone tabernacle within the soul in which I could treasure absolute truths. We were having soup, skate, and artichokes. She answered, after some thought, that I was killing her, but that I was also teaching her how to die.

We kept to ourselves the rest of the evening. At one point we had to consult over the household's ledger books.

Ask any soldier what his profession entails. He'll answer that he kills men. No one flees his company for that reason. No one refuses to eat with him. And whom does he kill? Innocent people, people who are only serving their country.

Together, Anne-Marie and I have negotiated, like wood chips in a waterfall, the Revolution itself, with its shocks and transformations: the trial and condemnation of the king; his execution; and all the deprivations of the war with the Allied powers. We covered our heads and hurried past each disaster, sometimes speaking of it afterward, sometimes not. The poor king's troubles began when he was dragged into the unhappy affair with America. Advantage was taken of his youth. In financing his support of America's revolution, he fell victim to that belief of monarchs that expenditure should not be governed by revenue but revenue instead should be governed by expenditure. And then nature provided its additional burden: the summer of 1788 and its unprecedented drought. We saw starvation in our own neighborhood. And everyone was busy holding forth on the subject of just which radical changes needed to be made, each to his own attentive audience.

So events took their course, thanks to that crowd of minor clerks and lawyers and unknown writers who went about rabble-rousing in clubs and cafés. From such crumbling mortar was the Edifice of Freedom built. De Launay was decapitated after the Bastille's fall by a pocketknife used to saw through his neck. Foulon, accused of plotting the famine, had the mouth of his severed head stuffed with grass. It was proclaimed that the great skittle row of privilege and Royalism had been struck to maximum effect, revealing a new and cleared space for civic responsibility. The Treasury was refilling, the corn mills turning, the traitors in full flight, the priests trampled, the aristocracy extinct, the patriots triumphant. The king did nothing, apparently believing the more extreme sentiments to be a fever that had to run its course.

Anne-Marie took up needlework, and then abandoned it as unsatisfying.

The National Assembly had announced only the abolition of royalty. Everyone saw clearly what needed to be razed or pillaged, but no one agreed what needed to be erected in its place. There was not a man near the wheels of power who was equal to the task at hand, with ever-greater tasks impending. The more radical, sensing conspiracies, wanted more surveillance, more wide-ranging arrests, more extremity. They proclaimed the maintenance of civic virtue impossible without bloodshed. They learned the hard way that *government* was impossible if the bloodshed was not monopolized and managed.

First the king's Swiss Guards were slaughtered defending him at the Hôtel de Ville. Some were thrown alive into a bonfire, others from windows onto a forest of pikes. My assistant Legros, passing the Tuileries, saw furniture together with corpses being pitched from the upper stories into the courtyard. He met us on our way home, and Anne-Marie and I had to wait at each city gate so he could shout "Vive la Nation!" like a good sans-culotte and thereby disarm the murderousness of those roaming the streets. Four times we were stopped and made to swear an oath to the new regime. At the entrance to our courtyard we found half a corpse, which I dragged out of the archway by the feet.

Then in September it was deemed necessary to weed out Royalist sympathizers after the Prussians had had some success against our armies, and People's Tribunals, set up in each of the prisons, began handing prisoners over to crowds gathered outside with butchers' implements and bludgeons. In four days 1,300 — half of all the prisoners in Paris — were massacred, including Madame de Lamballe, whose body was dragged behind a wagon by two cords tied to her feet and whose head was carried on a pike to where the royal family was imprisoned, so that it might be made to bow to the queen. One of the killers was said to have used a carpenter's saw. Each neighborhood seemed to have its own mob of National Guards and sans-culottes, a few mounted, bearing on their horses fishwives and bacchantes, filthy and bloody and drunken. At the Quai d'Orsay hung a whole row of men mangled and lanterned, their feet continually brushed and set in motion by passersby. Garden terraces in the morning sunlight were ashine with smashed bottles. It was said that Madame de Lamballe's head was found wedged upside-down on a bar in a cabaret and surrounded by glasses, as if it were serving as a carafe. She'd been famous for her fragile nerves and her penchant for fainting at the slightest unpleasantness.

As was the king. We followed his trial through the newspapers and broadsheets. Talking with Henri-François, our eldest, was like conversing with a rock garden, so Anne-Marie was left with me. During meals we were circumspect because Legros shared our table, but at night in bed some of our old intimacy returned. She argued the king's side: perhaps the mildest monarch to ever fill the throne had been precipitated from it because of his refusal to adopt the harshness of his predecessors. Throughout the proceedings, from the galleries, the Jacobins, men and women, ate ices and bawled for the death penalty. Legendre proposed to divide the accused monarch into as many pieces as there were Departments, so as to mail a bit of him to each. My wife was at a loss, reading such news: from where did such ferocity originate? I had no answer for her, just as the king had no ally in the Assembly willing to risk his own life on his sovereign's behalf. Having refused to become the patron of any one side, our helpless monarch had become the object of hatred for all.

Robespierre finally doomed him with the argument that if the king were to be absolved, what would become of the Revolution? If he was innocent, then the defenders of Liberty were malefactors and the Royalists were the true inheritors of France. To those who said that the State had no right to execute the king, he countered that the Revolution had been "illegal" from the outset. Did the deputies want a Revolution without a revolution?

We were awake the entire night before the execution. The day before, I'd been authorized to oversee the digging of a trench ten feet deep, along with the procurement of three fifty-pound sacks of quicklime. The machine was moved to the Place de la Révolution, near the pedestal from which the bronze equestrian statue of the king's father had been hacked down.

I had asked the prosecutor to be relieved of my responsibilities in the king's case. That request had been denied. I had then asked for more detailed instructions: Would the king require a special carriage? Would I accompany him alone or with my assistants? I was informed that there would be a special, closed carriage, and that I was to await the king on the scaffold. The latter instruction I understood to suggest that I myself was suspected of Royalist tendencies.

I asked Legros to wake me at five, the same hour that the king's valet, Cléry, would be waking him. I was awake before he could knock. "Please don't do this," Anne-Marie whispered from her side of the bed. Her fist pounded lightly on my rib. But she knew the danger in which we already found ourselves, and only held the pillow over her face while I began to dress.

Cléry reported to me later that the king's children had been rocking in agony as he'd prepared to depart under guard. For the previous hour they had consoled themselves with the time they had left, the little dauphin with his head between his father's knees.

Would the population rise in revolt against such an act? Had the Allies planted agents in order to effect a rescue? These questions and more terrified the deputies, who ordered each of the city's gates barricaded and manned, and provided an escort of 1,200 guards for the king's coach. The streets along the route to the scaffold were lined with army regulars. The windows were shuttered upon pain of death.

The crowd during the carriage's parade was mostly quiet. The king, when he arrived, seemed to derive much consolation from the company of his confessor. A heavy snowfall muffled the accoutrements of the carriage.

He mounted the steps. He asked that his hands be kept free. I looked to Santerre, commander of the guard, who denied the request. The king's collar was unfastened, his shirt opened, and his hair cut away from his neck. In the icy air he looked at me and then out at the citizenry, where the vast majority, because of weakness, became implicated in a crime that they would forever attribute to others.

I was assisted by my eldest son and Legros. That morning I had received absolution from a nonjuring priest — the new term for one who has not yet forsworn his allegiance to the Church. I had checked and rechecked the sliding supports on the uprights, and resharpened the blade. The king tried to address the people over the drum roll but was stopped by Santerre, who told him they'd brought him here to die, not to harangue the populace. Henri-François strapped him to the plank. Legros slid him forward. He died in the Catholic faith in which he had been raised. In accordance with the custom, the executor of justice then found the head in the basket and displayed it to the people. He lifted it by the hair, raising it above shoulder height. He circled the scaffold twice. The head sprinkled the wood below as it was swung around. There was an extended silence and then a few scattered cries of "Long Live the Republic."

The executor did not accompany the wicker basket to the cemetery. He was told that it fell from the cart near the trench, and that the crowd had then torn it to pieces. He ordered more expiatory Masses said on his own behalf. He made certain that the king's blade was never used again.

And he also made certain that his wife never discovered his trade in packets of the king's hair: his eldest son's idea. Though for months afterward she saw the broadsheets of his hand holding the king's severed head over the caption *May impure blood water our fields.*

Thereafter there seemed to be no space anywhere in our country for moderation. All dangers and all proposals conceived to counter them partook of the dire, the drastic, and the headlong. The nation was in peril, and what constitutional safeguards remained had to make way for emergency measures. Danton claimed that if a sufficiently severe Revolutionary Tribunal had been constituted that September, there would have been no massacres. The government's discipline had to be terrible or the people themselves would again spread terror. A tribunal impaneled to punish with death all assaults on the indivisibility of the Republic could operate, as he put it, with an irreducible minimum of evil.

Anne-Marie by then was a wraith, disappearing from rooms, a cough the only evidence of her presence in the house. One night she didn't come to table at all. Legros had to fetch our dinner from the kitchen. Henri-François informed me that she'd had an altercation with another woman at the bakery about her place in the bread line. He was no help with details. I waited while together we watched the shoveling motion of his spoon. Finally I asked if she'd been hurt, and he shrugged and said, "Well, she got the bread."

I found her in our root cellar, sorting through potatoes. Many had already sprouted. The skin under her eyes was blue.

"Are you well?" I asked.

"I'm unable to eat," she told me. "I'm sure it will pass."

"Are you injured?" I asked.

"I'm sound in body and mind," she answered. As if to prove her point, she showed me a potato. We could hear someone above us who'd returned to the kitchen for a second helping from the pot.

We said nothing for some few minutes, sharing the close darkness. The damp smell of the dirt was pleasant. I sorted potatoes with her.

"It's not assumed that the wife of the Executor of State Judgments will be found brawling in the street," I joked, gently.

"You thought you married a lady," she said.

"I only meant that this was not a time for public demonstrations," I told her.

"They know you by now," she said. "You're as suited to take a hand in political faction as you are to arrive on the moon."

But she underestimated me. I attended Commune sessions when I saw fit, ready to speak if the occasion warranted it. The Law of the Suspect was promulgated that September to speed the work of terrorizing foes of the Revolution. Suspects of any sort could now be denounced and detained by local Committees constituted on the spot and unfettered by the sorts of legal concerns that had no doubt already allowed too many culprits in league with our enemies to escape. And that category of suspects now extended to all foreigners residing in France; to those who speculated in any way with foreign currencies; to those who spoke too coldly of their enthusiasm for the Revolution; and finally to those who, while having done nothing in particular against the Cause, hadn't seemed to do much for it either. A prisoner might be accused at nine, find himself in court at ten, receive sentence at two, and lose his life at four. Anyone's neighbor might be an Allied agent already at work to engineer famine or defeat. The Law of the Suspect was a reminder to the populace that a nation at war might have to exterminate liberty in order to save it. Prisons like the Conciergerie tripled their detainees. In some rooms, the sewage fumes were so strong that torches, brought into them, went out.

And by such measures idlers and thugs had now become the People. Histrionic patriotism was the only requisite for public speaking, so especially those compromised by shameful pasts rushed to demonstrate their worthiness by addressing their Popular Societies, agitating in all corners, disrupting the courts and trials, searching homes themselves, denouncing and condemning and turning France into one boundless parade ground of calumny. The solution for all national troubles was understood to be an unflagging austerity of purpose in the form of an ever more passionate embrace of ruthlessness. There were mass cannonadings in Lyon. Carrier, the revolutionary representative at Nantes, sealed hundreds into the holds of barges and sank them in the Loire in what he called "vertical deportations." Saint-Just announced that the Republic consisted of the extermination of everything that opposed it. The Marquis de Bry offered to organize a force he called the Tyrannicides: freedom fighters dispatched to foreign capitals to assassinate heads of state, or anyone else the Committee might stipulate.

"The People make their demands," Henri-François remarked one night at dinner, apropos of our ever-increasing workload. His hair fell across his forehead like a scrubbing mat. He always seemed against his mother to be nursing a grim new resentment.

"Their inner lives have been made bestial," Anne-Marie said to him, after having been silent the entire meal.

"That's not entirely what she means," I told Legros, who observed her as though she were a mouse in the grain supply.

"That's exactly what she means," he answered, with some affability, and then went on with his meal.

I drove my assistants day and night, but we could not master our burden. Lethal misadventures and irregularities compounded daily as batch after batch moved out of the tumbrels and into the baskets. One Tuesday we dispatched twenty-two condemned in twenty-nine minutes. Pastry merchants divided their attention between the scaffold and their customers. Friends asked friends in the crowd if they were staying and were told, not today, that they had things to do. So much blood ran down the front of the platform supports that boots there sank into the supersaturated earth as if into a mire. One woman, eighth in line among the condemned, told me that the lunette's wet wood on the front of her neck was unpleasant. When the blade dropped, her body jerked in the straps, as if abruptly trying to find a more comfortable position.

In our home, with Legros and Henri-François sent away, we received the Sacrament from our nonjuring priest.

"They're putting the queen on trial," Anne-Marie told me one morning, once the priest had left. She said that he had confirmed the rumor. In one stroke she seemed to have resuscitated all of her old intensities. She crossed and recrossed the room. She wrung her hands in a series of nervous contractions. She was beside herself, certain that the queen would be condemned.

"Not necessarily," I told her, trying to get my bearings.

"You have to resign. You have to withdraw. You have to refuse to have any part in this," she said.

"There's nothing to refuse yet," I told her.

"You have to refuse," she cried.

I told her I would attend as much of the trial as I could. And on those days I attended, she demanded a full recounting. I spared her very little. The queen was, in those chambers, the Austrian she-wolf, the arch-tigress, the cannibal who wanted to roast alive all the poor Parisians. It was claimed she'd bitten open the cartridges for the Swiss Guards in their defense of the royal family to help speed their slaughter of the onward-charging patriots. She sat alone in the dock, a childlike figure further diminished by her incarceration. Her eyesight had begun to weaken and her hair to turn white.

She looked twenty years beyond her age. She'd been made to reply to accusations as to the incestuous nature of her relations with the dauphin. The poor boy had been made to parrot unspeakable things, and his testimony was read back to her.

Everything about the dauphin injured Anne-Marie. She knew a wife of the assistant jailer and learned the boy had just passed his eighth birthday alone. Apparently he was chronically ill and had been ministered to by his mother with unceasing tenderness until he'd been made a ward of the Republic and dragged to a cell immediately beneath hers, from which she could hear him shrieking in his terror and loneliness. He was left to himself for weeks at a time. The shoemaker appointed to be his personal jailer looked in only every so often. Even he found the boy's cries hard to take. But he also made him wear the red bonnet and sing the "Carmagnole" and the "Marseillaise" and to blaspheme God from his windows.

My wife lay awake nights, mute and suffering and considering various aspects of his plight, until she burst out with wailing, jolting me from my half-drowse. When I embraced her she demanded a promise that I wouldn't be a part of this. She needed to be sure that I wouldn't be a part of this. I wouldn't be a part of this, I assured her, and reapplied my embrace.

Only weeks after the inauguration of the machine, the medical community found itself grappling with the controversy concerning the survival of feeling and consciousness in the separated head. Did the head hear the voices of the crowd? Did it feel itself dying in the basket? Could it see the light of day above it?

The question became a more urgent one following Charlotte Corday's execution for the assassination of Marat, when Legros, apparently communing with his inner brute, saw fit to slap the severed head while he was displaying it. And the face, hanging by the hair, showed the most unequivocal signs of anger and indignation in response. There was an uproar from those in front of the scaffold, who could see it, and afterward many medical eminences were interviewed on the phenomenon for the newspapers.

Eventually I was asked to assist a Dr. Séguret, professor of anatomy, who'd been commissioned to study the problem. He set up an atelier on the same square as the machine, and my assistants delivered to it a total of forty heads. We exposed two, a man's and a woman's, to the sun's rays in his back courtyard. Their eyelids immediately closed of their own accord, in a way that was startling, and their faces convulsed in agony. One head's tongue, pricked with a lancet, withdrew, the face contorting. Another's eyes turned in the direction of our voices. One head, that of a juring priest named Gardien, dumped into the same sack with the head of one of his enemies, had bitten it with such ferocity that it took both of us to separate them.

Other faces were inert. Séguret pinched them on the cheeks, inserted brushes soaked in ammonia into their nostrils, and held lighted candles to their staring eyes without generating movement or contractions of any sort.

His report was suppressed, and he refused to have any more to do with such experiments, or with me.

"What have you decided?" Anne-Marie took to asking each day, as the queen's trial dragged on. Besides all of the other charges, there were the letters abroad, many of which had been intercepted. All military defeats were being blamed on her treachery. Her son's illness was blamed on her sexual demands. As proof of the latter, his hernia was displayed.

In bed with my weeping Anne-Marie, I tell her I see no way out: the letters demonstrate conspiracy, and in all other cases, the accusers invent the proofs they lack. We need be resigned to God's will; to prepare ourselves for it and to summon the strength to endure the terrible stroke.

"*Your* terrible stroke," she responds. "You *must not* do this. You *understand* that."

But she knows, I tell her, that God alone can alter the course of events at this point. It's His mercy for which we must ask, even as we submit to His decrees.

"I'm not appealing to you to save her," she answers. "You know what I'm requesting."

A few nights later, lying beside me in the darkness, she palms my cheeks and moves her face so close that her lips graze mine. "Listen to me," she says. "Don't dismiss me like this." She moves our bodies to their newlyweds' position. But then she says nothing else.

Henri-François brings us the news as we're sitting down to some pigeon, red currants, apricots, and wine: the tribunal, according to the declaration of the jury, and complying with the indictment of the public prosecutor, has condemned Marie Antoinette, called

Lorraine d'Autriche, widow of Louis Capet, to the pain of death, the judgment to be carried out in the Place de la Révolution, and printed and exhibited throughout the Republic.

On the appointed day, my wife is missing when I awake. Our drunken neighbor across the courtyard claims not to have seen her. She's nowhere to be found when I return. The queen flinches upon seeing the open cart in which she'll ride. She explains she'd been hoping for the enclosed carriage that carried her husband. She apologizes for treading on my foot as she climbs the steps.

My wife does not return that evening, or the next. Henri-François notes a missing trunk but mentions nothing else, contemptuous of my agony. Legros takes over the cooking. In the wee hours, I occupy my fireside chair, swigging wine. In the fire the future unfolds like a game board dotted with opponents' pieces. I envision new laws abolishing the accused's right to any defense; the frightened seeking to outpace one another with the zeal and homicidal efficiency of their patriotism; prisoners condemned in groups, identities muddled in the confusion, with sons dying in the names of fathers, and families decimated by misspellings and clerical errors. At the scaffold, a nightmarish constancy, with only the actors changing. Chemists. Street singers. Fifteen-year-old servants. An abbé who'd founded and run the orphanage for the city's chimney sweeps, most as young as five or six. Carmelite nuns. Peasant women from the Vivarais, unintelligible in their patois and bewildered at their arrest. One boy in a forgeman's cap. One in a hat of otter skin. One already bloodied and bare-headed. One with little guillotines on his suspenders. One who'd drawn in ink on his neck *Cut on the dotted line.* The executions proceeding at such a pace that the heads tip from the filled baskets and roll from the scaffold's lip. Never enough for carts, straps, bran, hay, nails, soap for the grooves, or tips for the gravediggers. Baskets changed every two weeks, the bottoms rotted through, the sides chewed by teeth. The machine frequently moved as a menace to sanitation. An old man, taking in the great pile of clothing discarded by his predecessors, and extending me his compliments, and noting that I must have the most extensive wardrobe of anyone in France.

A man climbs the stairs. He's strapped to the plank. The plank slides forward. The half-moon is brought over his neck. There's a frightful second. His open eyes see the basketful below.

And when the blade comes down, a fiery mist explodes about his eyes. It's radiant with reflected light. The light converts to pain. The pain saturates all that follows. The head suffers for three days and nights, its spark finally extinguished beside its body in the lime pit.

Sulla said he stood before all of Rome and dared to declare: "I am ready to answer for all of the blood I have poured out on behalf of the republic. I will render an exact account to anyone who comes to plead for a father, son, or brother." And he said that all Rome was silent at his offer.

What a creature is Sanson! Impassive, standing with his slightly timorous look beside his sinister friend, the black heart of the Revolution. He chops off whatever is brought to him. Does he fear being alone? He eats. He gazes at others. Their heads elude him, as his eludes theirs. Will he in his dotage have visitors, each wanting to touch the blade, peer inside the baskets, lie upon the plank? Will he become the town eccentric who plays the cello badly but remains a good neighbor, puttering with his tulips and relating anecdotes to the curious?

Through years of vigils and crises and alarms that kept men from sleeping, he was never seen unshaven. Insignificance, silence, and dissimulation were his most powerful tools. His machine was a celebration of geometry formally applied, and geometry is the language of reason.

Who presented Pompey's head to Caesar in Egypt? Who presented Cicero's to Antony? History records only whose head was presented to whom. Who did the chopping? Those impossible beings. That species unto themselves.

From his chair Sanson tends the fire and coddles the past. The past for him is his wife. On their first walks, their conversation was like the exhilaration of learning itself. When he spoke with her, she lowered her eyes. When he stopped, she lingered until he continued. He blurted during one of their partings that without her he'd be his broken cello, all tunes lost. She smiled when he was in particular need of indulgence. And when her mouth touched him, she smelled like a linen sheet in the sunshine.

In a day or so he knows he'll receive a letter, its hand uneven as though composed on a knee or post: a letter in which she advises him not to be anxious on her behalf, and to follow her steadfastness, which he should have no trouble imagining. A letter in which she tells him she has no counsel to give, and that he should follow those he needs to follow. In which she informs him that she wants nothing in the way of a settlement. In which she confides to him that the time will come when he'll be able to judge the effort she has made to write this. In which she closes by noting that she has no more paper, and that the misfortune that she's awaited has arrived, and that she claps him to her heart.

And even then he'll understand the implication that he could still renounce this life and find her where she suffers. But instead he'll sit in his house, with the face of an absconding debtor. His father told him that if he offered to carry the basket, he shouldn't complain of the weight. His grandmother told him that the tears of strangers were only water. He himself was given a miracle and threw it away. Let his society perish, then, through the ferocity of its factions. Let his city return to its original state of forest. Let his neighbors relapse into the primitive, from which they could one day start again. Let it all go on without him. He was already that head without its body, jolted with the consciousness of its own death. He was already a tiny, bat-winged machine, fluttering over a wave of corpses. He was already that empty narrow space between the raised blade and its destination: that opportunity, gone in a tenth of a second, which would never return again.

KATE WALBERT

Do Something

FROM PLOUGHSHARES

THE SOLDIERS KEEP Margaret in view. She carries her tripod, unsteadily, and an extra poncho for a bib. That they have let her come this far might be due to the weather, or possibly the kinds of amusements of which she remains unaware. Still, assume that they watch, tracking her as she stomps along the fence and positions herself by the sign that clearly states NO TRESPASSING. GOVERNMENT PROPERTY. PHOTOGRAPHY FORBIDDEN.

It has turned a wet, wet September, everywhere raining so the leaves, black and slick, stick to the soles of her boots, or Caroline's: Wellingtons borrowed from the back of the hallway closet where earlier Harry watched as Margaret rummaged, wondering where she could possibly be going in such weather.

She turned, boot in hand.

"It's raining," he repeated.

Deaf at most decibels, Harry now cast his voice into the silence, as if hoping for an echo or a nod.

"Nowhere," she had said, because this is nowhere, or anywhere, or somewhere not particularly known: an hour's drive from Wilmington if you took the busy roads, and then country, mostly, the drizzle graying the already gray landscape. Ye olde et cetera — cornfields, silos, a ravaged billboard for Daniel's peas, fresh from California, though this is technically Delaware and the land of soybeans. Ducks, too, the fall season in full swing; the drizzle split by the *crack crack crack* of the hunters' guns.

She parked near the drainage ditch that edges the fence, chain-link, as if for dogs, though there are no dogs here, only a guard tower, a landing field, and the soldiers who wait for the planes. But that isn't right, exactly. The place is vast, a city of a place, with barracks — are those called barracks? — and trucks and cul-de-sacs and no doubt children sleeping, army brats — or is this marines? — in the two-story housing labyrinth not so far from where she gets out, near the drainage ditch, near the landing field, near the place where the plane will descend. This she knows. The rest — the presence of children, the numbers involved, the ranking, the hierarchy — she truthfully has no idea.

Margaret skewers the tripod into the mud and adjusts the poncho to cover her. Today, she plans to bite skin. She can almost taste it: the salt of it, the flesh; see herself in her resistance: Margaret Morrisey, mother to Caroline and the dead one, James; wife to Harry. She mounts the camera on the track and angles the lens toward where the plane will descend — they come from the east, she has learned, out of Mecca, the bodies mostly wrapped in flags but sometimes carried in a tiny box.

"Christ, Mother," Caroline said after the first arrest, the fine. "Get a life."

"Your great-great-grandfather ate horse feed; that was his dinner. He'd soften the oats with spit. He came to this country for food. Literally."

"Apropos of . . . ?" Caroline said.

"It meant something," Margaret said. "America."

"It's illegal."

"This is a free country."

"Please," Caroline said.

The two sat at Caroline's kitchen table, Caroline in one of her suits meant for business, her cigarette burning in the misshapen ashtray a ten-year-old James had spun out of clay. Caroline's children were elsewhere, having reached the age of the disappeared — their voices shouting orders from behind the locked doors of their bedrooms or even standing present, their bodies imperfect, studded casts of their former selves; if they were somewhere within them they were very, very deep.

"I should never have told you I voted for him," Caroline said.

"I would have guessed."

"The rules have to do with respect," Caroline said. "Or something. Anyway, they're the rules. It's law. Besides, it's none of our business. None of your business."

"Says whom?" Margaret said, to which Caroline had some sort of reply.

Margaret listened for a while, and then she did not; she thought of other things, how she would like to have believed that not so long ago Caroline would have stood beside her at the fence, that her daughter would have carried a sign or at least shouted an obscenity. But this was before Caroline took that job in the Financial District. The Fucked District, she calls it, but the money's good, she says. It's serious money.

"Mother?"

"I was listening," Margaret said.

"Forget it," Caroline said. She tapped her nails, those nails, on the table, then the buzzer rang — delivery — and the conversation ended.

"Dinnertime," she yelled in the direction of the doors.

Crack. Crack. Crack.

The men have had enough. They climb down from their tower to slog through duck country, technically Delaware, the first state, though most have trouble with the history; one can hear their boots, or is that frogs? The sucking. Soon enough they'll reach her. Margaret records their magnified approach; records them unlocking the gate and stepping to the other side, records their blank expressions. The trouble is she can only pretend to hate them.

"Good morning, Mrs. Morrisey." This from the one Margaret calls Tweedle-Dee.

She straightens up, adjusts the poncho.

"We'll remind you that you're trespassing. That taking photographs is forbidden."

"Today," she says, hand on tripod, "I plan to resist."

Their arms remain folded. Four pair, as usual; a pack; a team; a unit, perhaps, or would they be a regiment? No, a regiment is bigger, a regiment is many. She tries to remember from soldier days, from mornings James explained the exact order of things — sergeant to lieutenant to captain to king — his miniature warriors arranged throughout the house in oddly purposeful groupings. She would find them everywhere, assaulting a sock, scaling the Ping-Pong table, plastic, molded men with clearly defined weaponry and indistinct faces. When she banished them to his room, fearing someone would break a neck, James had cried and cried.

"That would be more than your usual fine, Mrs. Morrisey."

He is a horse's ass, but then again, a boy once James's age who should be pitied.

"I plan to resist," she repeats. One of the Mute Ones has his hand out as if to help her across the muddy plain. They are waiting, she knows, for Margaret to do something. Collapse, she thinks, then does, more a buckle than a collapse, knowing full well the ridiculousness of it, how small she'll become. The big one bends down to help her. *Now,* she thinks, though it is not until it is done that she understands she has found the courage to do it, biting the soft part of that hand, the hammock of skin between thumb and forefinger.

Caroline sits next to Harry in the detention waiting room (she must have taken the train!), no question who's the boss. Our girl could split atoms, Harry once said. We ought to lease her to GE.

Sorry, darling, Margaret mouths to him. He looks at her with his doggy yellow eyes; then Caroline leads them both out.

In the sunshine they blink: "Look at the weather!" Margaret says, reflexively. "What a treat!"

Caroline has opened the car door.

"Get in," she says.

They sit in silence to home, the radio punched to static and static and static then punched off, again, then the familiar drive, the front door, the hallway, the kitchen. Caroline makes tea and calls a Family Meeting. There's a hole in the place where James would have been so Margaret steps in and wanders around while Caroline speaks of Responsibility and Reputation and Appropriate Behavior, and, yes, the Germs in your Mouth, and Patriotism, but mostly, mostly, mostly, Mother, Embarrassment.

"Please," Caroline says. "I'm at wit's end."

Margaret would like to cradle Caroline in her arms, Caroline sleepy and hatted and a bit jaundice yellow, but she cannot. Caroline has grown; she's taller than Margaret and twice divorced and a millionaire, she has confessed. A mill-ion-aire, she said.

"Where are your friends, Mother?" Caroline asks.

Margaret shrugs. She hasn't thought of friends recently, nor her standing Wednesday at Sheer Perfection; her hair's gone shaggy and gray and her cuticles have grown over their moons.

"I'm sorry, darling," she says. "I'll stop."

*

How has it come to this? There was Youth, Margaret thinks. Then, Love: A certain indefatigable, copper-colored Spirit. Wasn't she the one who had convinced Harry to do a U-turn on the GW Bridge? And what of Leonard Nan's retirement? She'd worn a blond wig and pharmaceutical pearls, hula-hooped her toast gyrating the thing to her knees. She used to leave it all to chance, or Certain Men, actually. Wasn't she the one with the Robert Kennedy dartboard? Didn't she support Nixon to the finish?

Now she is blindsided by fury; the tide of her anger rising at certain unpredictable moments (yes, the *tide*), as if drawn by an internal moon, waxing and waning, though mostly waning.

A disclaimer, first: she lost no one in The Tragedy, no Hero her James, just an ordinary mortal, his (by inference) an unheroic death: cancer of the blood — blah blah blah — one cell fried — blah — and then another — blah blah — until nothing remained but bone and sinew, James's lungs mechanically pumping, a ring of them singing before they turned off the machine. Godspeed. And the machine stopped. Godspeed. Which is not to say she didn't know someone who knew someone; which is not to say she forgets we are living under the Cloud of It, that there are Reliable Threats, that Evil Lurks, that there are those who seek to undermine our Way of Life.

Yet if asked she will say James's death was her 9/11.

"We all have our very own," she'll say. "Don't you agree?"

Crack. Crack. Crack.

The next time Tweedle-Dee steps away from the others, approaching alone, the Big One with the bandaged hand hanging back as if on lookout.

"Did it hurt?" she calls to him. "Am I toxic? Infectious?"

"I'll ask you to read the sign, Mrs. Morrisey," says Tweedle-Dee.

"It's a free country," Margaret says.

"Not exactly," he says. Clearly there's a manual on How to Speak to the Protesters and/or the Criminally Insane.

"I'm not interested in the bodies," she says. "It's the wildlife I'm after."

"Camera's forbidden," he says.

He stands, square and sharp against the autumnal reds, his camouflage humorless, stuck in the sole season of winter. If she could see his eyes she predicts she would see embarrassment there, but they remain mirrored lenses, and anyway she is wrong: he is doing his job.

"Glorious day," she says, but he doesn't bite.

"So you can shoot them but you can't photograph them? I find that ridiculous. Ridiculous," she calls out to the Big One. "Does it still hurt?"

She grips the camera with her dirty fingers, though it is looped around her neck and going nowhere.

"You're trespassing, Mrs. Morrisey. This is Government Property."

She plunks down in Tweedle-Dee's shadow, her arms crossed.

"In Sweden there's no such thing," she says, squinting up. "You can camp anywhere. It's allowed. You could take a walk across the entire country if you wanted and no one could say, private property. I'd call that democracy, wouldn't you?"

He looms over her like a man mountain — trees and shrubs the pattern — his mirrored glasses the stone at the top, the place of the vista that from a distance could be snow, or water; bright, regardless, in the glaring sun. She waits as he gestures to the Mute Ones, to the Big One with the bandaged hand. They are all tired of her, it's clear, and bored. They step forward, unlocking their handcuffs, clicking and unclicking as if they'd rather be elsewhere. Even Tweedle-Dee wipes his forehead in an exhausted, parched gesture. She thinks of how he sees himself now, how he *pictures* himself — soldier or statesman — protecting the all of us from God knows what: Nothing; everything: An old woman with a camera. He protects is all, he's like a postage stamp or a flag; a symbol bought and sold, something with an adhesive strip to stick on an automobile bumper or football helmet — thirty-seven cents or a dollar ten in the big bin at Rite Aid.

The handcuffs are tighter than she would have imagined, and she finds herself humming the only song she can think to hum: "Amazing Grace," knowing, even while humming, how ridiculous she sounds, how outdated it's become, even quaint: Peace. She thinks to mention this to Caroline, to somehow explain: What she is trying to do is to aim for something real, she'll tell her, something that is not just an approximation of real.

Here the two of us, she'll say, the all of us: the soldiers, the protester, were all from a scene already enacted; so that even my own inclination to *be* —

Caroline interrupts. "To what?"

The fine has already been paid, though this time they fingerprinted — "Ma'am," Tweedle-Dee had said to Caroline. "Tell your mother to keep her mouth shut."

Be, Margaret says now. "To *be.*"

"Or not," says the Millionaire.

"When did everything stop being real?" Margaret says.

"Don't bring James into it."

"He would have —"

Caroline plugs her ears; she might be eight again: a girl in braids and knee socks, six missing teeth so that she could no more blow a bubble than recite Pope, though James, a teacher at heart, had tried for weeks.

"I don't care, Mother. I mean, I do, but at some point you have to put yourself first."

"Like hell."

"What?" Caroline unplugs her ears.

"I said, I know."

"You know what?"

"I know you don't care."

The bubble burst, the lopsided attempt. James picked it himself out of Caroline's braids, though Margaret had still given him a scolding and threatened the back side of the hairbrush. James put it all in his Feelings Jar, a jar that, in its earlier life, contained dill pickles. *I was just trying to DO SOMETHING. I was just trying to teach her how to blow bubbles and you got so mad you could spit.*

"I am just trying to Do Something," Margaret says, though Caroline is busy looking for dinner inspiration, for anything other than pasta. "You don't care to understand. It's like everything. Conversation, for example, is now just approximations of opinions adopted from other opinions that were approximations of opinions, et cetera, et cetera. I'm just trying to be real when everything is an approximation."

But this is not true, exactly. Death is not an approximation. It is completely real; it is unchangeable, forever — an approximation of nothing. Hadn't she seen it that first time she'd found the base, the barracks, the military galaxy? Where had she been going? She can't remember anymore. She was lost, she knew, had taken to driving, punching the radio to listen to men and women discussing God knows what, anything to drown out her own inside voice. Use your inside voice, she used to tell the children, meaning quiet. Softly. Hers shouted now; tore its hair.

She had followed the convoy of jeeps, had stopped across the highway with the other cars, curious at the rows and rows of them idling like so many school buses by the chainlink fence that surrounded the complex of guard towers and apartments and houses and a post office there in the middle of nowhere, or everywhere: soybean fields, corn crops, a V of geese heading south and somewhere else, just beyond, an abandoned barn where starlings roost in rotted eaves and a boy necks or smokes or pings his pocketful of stones one by one against the glass, wanting breakage: all boys do. At the center sat the plane, exceedingly complicated, wings folded and a scissored tail — more like a jackknife than anything that could fly — and from it soldiers transporting bodies, their families there to receive them, to take them back as real, as dead.

"This is no approximation," Margaret says. "This is what that idiot has the audacity to hide: the one thing true in the mess of it," she says, attempting to name it all for Caroline, who some time ago surrendered, running the sauce jar under hot water, her back to Margaret though presumably listening.

Now she turns, her hand dripping.

"I hear you, Mother," she says, popping the lid; she forks a noodle from the boiling pot and holds it out to Margaret. "Finito?" she asks.

Margaret dreams of James. In this one he steps out of the Cape Cod surf (those were the years!) wet and gleaming; he is as he was, a young man, a boy who loved books, who copied passages in letters to his mother, certain things he believed she might like, understanding her taste, he once wrote, in these matters.

> Dear Mother, his name is Professor Burns, which is ironic, because he smokes like a chimney and even when not keeps the cigarette, somehow lit, behind his ear. There's a rumor his hair once caught on fire and he lost his place in his notes and for the rest of the semester kept one step ahead of the syllabus oblivious. He is a little odd, but I like him and this is my favorite class. I don't know if I love romantic poetry or just love the way he talks about romantic poetry. I don't know if I just love that anyone can talk about romantic poetry at all how many years later and still weep. Yes, he weeps. Or did the other day after his lecture on Wordsworth. A few of the girls went up to console him; maybe it was just a ploy (ha ha).

Here he is! Margaret thinks in her dream. Look, here he is! He's been swimming — that scamp — all along!

She hears the waves roll out behind him, the crash of it so clearly. She is fearful he might decide to return to that riptide; how often has she warned him it could carry you for miles! But no. He walks toward her, the sun behind him dazzling. He is a dazzling boy, a young man of promise without a single broken bone, nothing to be mended, stitched; strong-hearted. He takes no medications, she could tell you, and on that repeatedly filled-out form that has so many boxes in which to check yes he checks no, no, no, no! every time. He is no more an approximation than a red tulip in May, and here is the great joke of it: He is Real!

A delicious pain, almost sexual, wakes her. It is the great cruel trick of the night: to wake alone, regardless. She can scream or cry if she wants — Caroline's gone home, and Harry is deaf asleep, long in the habit of covering his eyes with a towel to block the light. She elbow-props herself to watch him breathe, he the father of her children, the great love of her life. He floats into outer space in his bubble. It will burst, eventually, and he, like the rest of them, will be gone.

To where?

An approximation of this, perhaps, or the curl of a shell, the color of leaves, a gesture; here but somewhere deep within.

James had once asked her what she believed; this toward the end of him, she remembers, or close enough. And she might have lied; she might have given her boy something more.

"Nothing," she had said, already furious. "Absolutely nothing."

He sat in the chair by the window. She had brought a blue shawl and oatmeal cookies she would set by the door for visitors.

"You're an original, Mom. I've meant to tell you," he said.

"Thank you, darling," she said, wanting to hear more and wanting him to stop. She stood by the edge of his bed; she liked to stand there. She even liked this room, or well enough, on the quiet floor, with its view over the low rooftops to the sliver of river when the light went right, which happened more often now, in this season. It had been autumn; the sun low, at a slant. That she found it too difficult to look at him she couldn't explain.

"And I forgive you your trespasses," he said.

"Hallelujah," she said.

If she had looked she would have noticed the blueness of the shawl, how odd to see him wrapped in blue.

"I hope you're wrong," he said.

"It wouldn't be the first time."

"If you are, I'll come back and rattle the windows," he said. "Think of it as my 'so there.'"

The windows more than rattle; so there. The wind more than blows. And somewhere else the terrified children must listen for what else — the cavalry, the infantry, the artillery — what had James taught her? Nothing. Everything. The names run together to a pooled point, the way blood will when the heart stops beating, when the machine stops. The machine stopped.

That she gets out of bed and dresses is almost beside the point. She no longer needs to write a note. She throws on loose clothing and goes, forgetting her empty camera — It was just like in the movies! she told Caroline. The soldiers rolled out the film and flung it in the garbage! They called her bite his wound! — forgetting her purse, backing the station wagon out the long drive to swerve down the once-dirt road toward the highway. At this hour there's little traffic, and she can speed as much as she likes, the cornfields and rows of soybeans saluting as she passes; in the end her only ally, the landscape, the actual black dirt of the country. Government property, my ass, she thinks.

Her headlights flood the woods she turns into: wild, brush grown, skunk cabbage in the hollows and arrowheads to be found; the all of it disturbed by this strange, Halloween wind. There might be children behind the trees, trick-or-treaters, Frankensteins and ghosts and ghouls shaking the skinny limbs of the aspen saying, I'm here! No, here! But they'd be flushed out, of course, by her, by the klieg lights on the landing field: in case of emergencies, no doubt: the jackknife slicing the air into ribbons, the families the only witness to the dead.

And what had she planned, anyway? To whom would she have shown her pictures? Harry? Caroline? Absent friends?

She parks near the guard tower and slams the door. The steel latticework seems to glow in the moonlight, rising to the little booth of their tree-house watch. She might see breath on the glass, it is that cold and not so far up, or frost; she knows he is in there and she could find him if she climbed.

When did it become the boy she is after?

*

Does a radio play? Does he write a letter home?

She wants to know where he's from, what he studied in school. She's interested in his early artwork, she could tell him. Elementary. Preschool, even. Did he begin with circles? Those circles! And then slowly, no; she had seen it in her children and her children's friends and her grandchildren, even. The loss of circles, eventually. Don't despair, she could tell him. It happens to everyone.

She would like to know where he sat in the cafeteria — with the popular children or off a little by himself, like her James, his sandwich crushed from his book bag, a tuna fish on white bread or maybe peanut butter. Did his mother include notes? An *I love you,* or *Hi, Handsome!* Perhaps he was not a son who required encouragement; perhaps he did fine on his own. His were not elaborate tastes — she can guess this — nor particularly demanding. He seemed fine with what he got until he wasn't; and when he wasn't he didn't complain. He made plans — how to leave, how to get out, how to make do, survive.

Was he interested in trains? Did he play a musical instrument?

Margaret stands at the fence looking in. The worst thing, she would tell him, is that she can no longer distinguish stars; when I think I have found one it moves out of view, just metal in orbit or a transportation vehicle. There are no longer fixed points by which to determine my direction, she would tell him. How can I ever again make a wish?

You are not responsible, she would say. It is shameful what we've done to you. We should all of us be ashamed.

"You are just like the rest of us," she says. "You are only trying to Do Something."

Does Margaret shout this or whisper? It no longer matters. She is suddenly tired and aware that she should go. She'll return home the way she came, driving back through ye olde et cetera to her rightful place beside Harry: Margaret Morrisey, mother to Caroline and the dead one, James.

Hormones, she'll tell Caroline, by way of explanation.

I miss him, too, Caroline will say, by way of apology.

"Goodbye," Margaret calls to them, though none can hear for the *crack crack crack;* the hunters particularly ravenous at dawn.

Contributors' Notes

LOUIS AUCHINCLOSS, the author of over sixty books, published his first novel, *The Indifferent Children,* in 1947. He has received the NAIBA Legacy Award for lifetime literary achievement and was the president of the American Academy of Arts and Letters. In 2000, the New York Landmarks Conservancy honored him as a "Living Landmark," and in 2005, Mr. Auchincloss received the National Medal of Arts, our country's highest recognition for artistic achievement.

▪ I had long wished to try my hand at an analysis of the lethal effect of a brilliant and egocentric parent on a jealous and less gifted child.

JOHN BARTH's fiction has won the National Book Award, the PEN/Malamud Award for Short Fiction, and the Lannan Foundation Lifetime Achievement Award. For many years he taught in the Writing Seminars at Johns Hopkins University. He and his wife live in Chestertown, Maryland, and Bonita Springs, Florida. "Toga Party" is part of a story series in progress about life in a fictional gated community on Maryland's Eastern Shore.

▪ My wife and I are not frequent partygoers, but "Toga Party" was suggested by our attendance some while ago at an amusing occasion hosted by a couple of fun-loving Florida neighbors. Any further resemblance to actual persons or events is coincidental!

ANN BEATTIE has published seven novels and eight story collections (most recently, *Follies: New Stories*) and teaches literature and creative writing at the University of Virginia.

▪ I didn't write "Solid Wood" in Key West, but when I'm not there Key West is often on my mind. It's overadvertised by the tourist board, and some days it seems the whole place is glaringly, noisily on display for everyone to gawk at: the huge cruise ships; the performers at sunset; the cats who sometimes wear more clothes than their owners. I know where a few friends' keys are hidden, where some cleverly disguised doorknockers are. I'm familiar with the feeling of relief you experience when the biographer of somebody else doesn't have a clue that you ever figured in that person's life. What more do you need to start a story?

T. C. BOYLE is the author of nineteen works of fiction, including *Talk Talk* (2006), *Tooth and Claw* (2005), and *The Inner Circle* (2004). He is a graduate of the Iowa Writers' Workshop and a member of the English Department at USC. His Web site, where all sorts of engaging, lively, and polymorphously perverse ideas are expressed, is tcboyle.com. All are welcome there.

▪ I've always been fascinated by Faulkner's intransigent characters, one of the most chilling examples of which is the father in "Barn Burning." That story puts forth the proposition that blood ties are dissolvable and that there is an ethos that stands above habit, use, and even self-preservation. The father in "Balto" may bear little resemblance to Faulkner's unyielding malcontent — he is weak and his addiction has sapped him — but the adolescents in both stories do, I think, have something in common, as do the situations in which the adults place them. Indeed, are there two kinds of truth? Or is there only one?

RANDY DEVITA received his MFA in 2006 from Bowling Green State University, where he won the Devine Award for fiction. His work has appeared in *The Fiddlehead, West Branch, Third Coast,* and *Orchid,* and it received a Special Mention in the 2007 Pushcart Prize anthology.

▪ As a boy, each summer I went out on the road with my father for a week in his truck, a black Kenworth. Many of the details in the story are salvaged from what I remember of those trips, as that uninterrupted time with my father remains bright in my memory and close to me.

I wrote the first draft of "Riding the Doghouse" in 1999, so I suppose it has a lot of mileage. At the time, I'd been writing, with alarming consistency, pretty forgettable horror stories — stories far too consciously intended to scare others. So I challenged myself to write about something I feared, in this case the loss of my father. In returning to the pile of drafts, I found the element of the fantastic existed from the start. Yet that detail sank into the background as I revised, and only when I included the argument scene between the boy and the father did the story feel fully imagined. Their argument seemed to me the real story, as it revealed something of each one's character and the relationship between them. Maybe that's enough for a story — two people speaking to each other in a closed space, unwilling or unable to say what they really mean.

JOSEPH EPSTEIN is the author of two collections of short stories, *The Goldin Boys* and *Fabulous Small Jews.* He is currently working on a book about Fred Astaire and another on gossip.

▪ "My Brother Eli" is the result of a question that has played in my mind for decades: are artists entitled to special rights and privileges? Everyone knows stories about certifiably great artists — Michelangelo, Beethoven, Tolstoy, Picasso — behaving wretchedly. When we learn about this behavior, we tend to shake our heads, think it regrettable but, somehow, given the quality of their art, excusable. If the cost of Beethoven's late quartets was his general unpleasantness, surely it was a price worth paying, and we move along, grateful for the magnificent visual art, music, literature.

But should we allow the same slack to lesser artists? Allow it or not, many of them take it, assuming that irresponsibility, betrayal, meanness are part of the psychological job description of the artist. "My Brother Eli" is about a novelist who believed and acted on this assumption, and about the consequences of his doing so. In writing this story I was reminded that the English writer Hugh Kingsmill once said that no writer "can put more virtue into his works than he practices in his life." This is a very unfashionable view, but one in which I happen to believe. My subject is a writer who preached virtue but felt he needn't practice it; my theme is the myth of the artist as someone above the code of ordinary decency. I hope that I have captured both, subject and theme, in a way that brings them alive.

WILLIAM GAY is the author of three novels and a collection of short stories, *I Hate to See That Evening Sun Go Down.* His novel *Twilight* was published in winter 2006. His fiction and essays have appeared in various magazines. He lives in rural Tennessee where he is at work on a novel.

▪ Conversation with a friend who had suffered a loss got me thinking about the complexities of grief and its depth. Around this time news stories about the ravages of crystal meth in the rural South fused with my notions about grief and gave me this story.

MARY GORDON's most recent novel, *Pearl,* was published in January 2005 by Pantheon Books. Her previous novels — *Final Payments, The Company of Women, Men and Angels, The Other Side,* and *Spending* — have been bestsellers. She has also written a critically acclaimed memoir, *The Shadow Man.* In addition, she has published a book of novellas, *The Rest of Life;* a collection of stories, *Temporary Shelter;* two books of essays, *Good Boys and Dead Girls* and *Seeing Through Places;* and a biography of Joan of Arc. Ms.

Gordon has received the Lila Acheson Wallace Reader's Digest Award and a Guggenheim Fellowship. For three years (1983, 1997, and 2000), she was the recipient of the O. Henry Award for best short story. Mary is Millicent C. McIntosh Professor of English at Barnard College.

▪ A few factors came together to create "Eleanor's Music." The first was seeing a rather elegant woman of a certain age singing in a choir. The second was meeting a young composer, who had written an opera with explicitly sexual content. The third was a green silk scarf I coveted but could not afford. The fourth was a pair of Ferragamo shoes I admired, but not for myself. The fifth was Katherine Mansfield's use of the word *Entendu* in her story "Bliss." Add water, mix, and voilà!

LAUREN GROFF is a native of Cooperstown, New York, and has an MFA in fiction from the University of Wisconsin–Madison. Her stories have appeared or are forthcoming in journals including *The Atlantic Monthly, Five Points,* and *Ploughshares,* as well as in *Best New American Voices.* She was an Axton Fellow in Fiction at the University of Louisville, and her novel, *The Monsters of Templeton,* will be published in spring 2008.

▪ I wrote this story for my second MFA workshop during a long Madison winter; it is a collision of three very different obsessions of mine.

Swimming was the first element. I had just moved that autumn from California, where the major benefit of my university job was that I could swim laps in the outdoor Olympic-sized pool during my lunch breaks. I missed that pool hugely, teased as I was by the frozen lakes surrounding Madison. I began to research old-time swimmers and eventually happened upon the figure of Ethelda Bleibtrey, whose amazing life formed the outline for Aliette Huber's. They're not the same person, but Aliette's polio and swimming successes were borrowed from Ethelda's experience.

The 1918 Spanish flu epidemic was the second element, and it came from a book of poetry that I was reading, Ellen Bryant Voigt's *Kyrie.* The book knocked my socks off, and because the news that winter was filled with dire predictions of avian flu, the subject seemed timely, so I began to research it further.

The third element was the one around which everything else crystallized, and it was also the longest-held fascination of mine: the story of Abelard and Heloise, medieval lovers whom I'd studied during my freshman year of college and whose story I'd carried with me since. I'd even tried and failed to write a novel about them.

I began the story at least three dozen times before I hit on the current first line, and it all unfolded fluidly from there. My workshop was split between ardent supporters and equally ardent detractors — as most workshops are — but by then I'd learned to listen only to what sounded true to me. Later C. Michael Curtis was kind enough to pull the story from the slush pile at *The Atlantic Monthly,* to my everlasting surprise and gratitude, and it was one of my first published stories.

BEVERLY JENSEN grew up in Westbrook, Maine, earned an MFA in acting at Southern Methodist University, and performed in regional theater before turning to writing. Between 1986 and 2003, she wrote a series of interrelated stories and plays, based on the lives of her mother, Idella, and her aunt Avis. Ms. Jensen lived in New York with her husband, Jay Silverman, and her children, Noah and Hannah. In 2003, she died of cancer at the age of forty-nine.

▪ Beverly Jensen wrote of her work that "the stories chart the lifelong journey of two sisters, Avis and Idella, from childhood to old age. The loyalty and love of these sisters, not always on the surface, rarely expressed openly, were strong in their bones. Their seemingly small lives and unremarkable appearances, when examined, reveal a dignity, an ever-present humor, and a determination to live full lives that belie their hardscrabble beginnings on a remote farm in Canada."

Ms. Jensen wrote the stories a paragraph or page at a time while raising two children and holding an afternoon office job. Some of her stories she created out of whole cloth; for others she began with an incident Idella had described and then reimagined it into a full story. "Wake" is based on real events that took place during the catastrophic ice storm of 1956. Her pleasure was in the writing — hearing Idella and Avis's conversations in her head, sometimes laughing with surprise at the things they said. Her time being scarce, she used it to write and revise rather than send out stories for publication. But when she was diagnosed with pancreatic cancer, her college roommate — unbeknownst to Ms. Jensen — sent five stories to the literary editor Katrina Kenison, who responded with praise and encouragement. And after Ms. Jensen's death, her teacher, Jenifer Levin, author of *Water Dancer,* volunteered to help Jay Silverman prepare the stories for publication. "Wake" is the first story they sent out.

ROY KESEY is the author of *All Over,* a collection of stories that will be published by Dzanc Books in October 2007, and of *Nothing in the World,* winner of the 2005 Bullfight Media Little Book Prize. His work has appeared in *McSweeney's, The New England Review, Ninth Letter, Other Voices,* and *American Short Fiction,* among other magazines, as well as in *New Sudden Fiction 2006* and the Robert Olen Butler Fiction Prize anthology. He currently lives with his wife and children in Beijing, where he spends most of his time walking around and looking at things and nodding and shaking his head.

▪ The fog at the airport mocked me gently for a very long time, and in this sense "Wait" is documentary. However, the airport in question was in

South America, not Africa, and there was no chemical spill, no kickboxing, no pageant, no meteor, and no rhombi that I remember. Also, no hashed last-minute piaffe. In fact, there was only the fog and waiting. I guess that was enough.

I remember a relatively fast first draft, and liking the spiral of the thing. I remember thinking about Julio Cortázar's most excellent "La autopista del sur" and being afraid of holding it too close, and then of holding it too far away. I remember doing research on accounting and curling and ballooning, by which I mean reading random snippets in search of cool-ass words like *backwardation* and *pyrometer.* I remember a weaker ending and good suggestions from smart friends. But mostly I remember the fog, and how it moved and then didn't for hours at a time, and how much I hated it because I didn't see it for the gift it was.

STELLAR KIM was born in Seoul, Korea, and grew up in New York City. She graduated from Boston College and completed the MFA program at CUNY Brooklyn College. Stellar has taught English at Brooklyn College and Albertus Magnus College; currently, she lives in Boston and works as a writer in the nonprofit sector. She has recently received writing awards from *The Iowa Review* and *The Atlantic Monthly.* "Findings & Impressions" is her first published story.

▪ I wrote "Findings & Impressions" as I was grappling with my father's diagnosis of advanced-stage cancer and as I watched the progression of his disease. My father didn't speak much English, so every week, for two years, I accompanied him to the hospital for his chemotherapy sessions, which left me not only to interpret what the doctors told us but also to make sense of a plethora of medical information and to filter that in a palatable way.

With this story, I wanted to capture some of that feeling of having to walk the line between keeping hope alive and letting people face the end of their days with the facts of just how their body was about to fail them. I was constantly struck by how medical reports denude all emotion from an unjust disease and a tumultuous life event, so in basing this story on the form of a quasi radiology report, I wanted to reflect the tension between the narrator's clinical world and language and what was actually happening to the people of the story, flesh and soul. The story's ending was inspired by a scene from the TV show *The Gilmore Girls,* in which a character plans someone's funeral and has to buy an outfit for the deceased, including underwear. It was a brief moment that was purely comical, but it got me thinking about what it might actually be like to have to do this in a meaningful way. For the main character here, who unexpectedly grows to care intimately about a dying patient but is unable to demonstrate his feelings through concrete action while she is alive, the ending is a final chance to say goodbye with a gesture that is surreal and dramatic, but still private and tender. To me, "Findings & Impressions" is a love story, specifically about the kind of deep love and loss you can feel before someone is actually gone.

ARYN KYLE's first novel, *The God of Animals,* was published by Scribner in March 2007. Her stories have appeared in *The Atlantic Monthly, The Georgia Review, StoryQuarterly,* and elsewhere. She received her MFA from the University of Montana and is the recipient of a Rona Jaffe Award and a National Magazine Award in fiction.

▪ I began working on "Allegiance" shortly after I completed graduate school. The story took two years to finish — much longer than it's ever taken me to write a story, longer than it took me to write my novel. Then it took nearly as long to sell.

Initially, I was interested in the cutthroat world of elementary school, the kill-or-be-killed mentality that it often takes to survive. The scenes that take place in the classroom came fairly quickly — the worm dissection, the germ passing. But time went by and I could find neither a middle nor an ending for the story. I would put it away for a month or two, then pull it out and rewrite the beginning. It was sort of pointless: each draft of the beginning looked pretty much like the draft that came before. At some point, I realized that I wasn't writing a story about the cruelty of children, but about the subtle (or not-so-subtle) ways that women manipulate each other into choosing sides. Once I realized that, I knew that the real story was not going to take place in Glynnis's classroom, but in her home. That was all it took: three days later, the story was finished.

BRUCE MCALLISTER's short fiction has appeared in national magazines, literary quarterlies, "year's best" anthologies, and college readers since the 1960s. His second novel, *Dream Baby* — based on a short story that was a finalist for the Nebula and Hugo Awards — received a National Endowment for the Arts writing fellowship and was called "one of the most memorable chronicles of the Vietnam War" by *Publishers Weekly.* "The Boy in Zaquitos" will be included in a collection of his short fiction, *The Girl Who Loved Animals and Other Stories,* due from Golden Gryphon Press in 2007. A graduate of the MFA program at the University of California–Irvine, he taught at the University of Redlands in southern California for twenty years. He now works as a writing coach and a book and screenplay consultant.

▪ In the early 1970s — just before starting a fifteen-year journey of research, interviews, friendships, risky adventures, and writing experiments that would end in a novel called *Dream Baby* — I came across an article describing how the army had, on behalf of midwestern farmers, managed to kill in a single, deft spraying two million grackles and starlings — those pesky birds that eat grain. Somehow that article sparked the vision of a naive but well-meaning young man who, as an asymptomatic carrier of plague, worked for his country's intelligence community. A lover of good thrillers at the time, and inexperienced as I was, I thought I should try a "Thomas Harris meets Robert Ludlum" version, probably at 150,000 words. I managed only the first hundred pages, and I was no Ludlum or Harris. Novelist Oakley Hall, director of the MFA program where I'd just completed my degree, kindly read those pages and, saint that he is, just as kindly told me (and without using the word *terrible*) exactly what was wrong with them. The idea haunted me through the years until it finally found a more authentic shape and voice on the page in 2005, when Gordon Van Gelder, the first editor to welcome me back to writing after a decade's hiatus, accepted it for *Fantasy and Science Fiction.*

ALICE MUNRO was born in Wingham, Ontario, to a family of fox and poultry farmers. She began writing as a teenager and published her first story, "The Dimensions of a Shadow," while a student at the University of Western Ontario. She has published twelve collections of stories — *Dance of the Happy Shades; Something I've Been Meaning to Tell You; The Beggar Maid; The Moons of Jupiter; The Progress of Love; Friend of My Youth; Open Secrets; Selected Stories; The Love of a Good Woman; Hateship, Friendship, Courtship, Loveship, Marriage; Runaway;* and *The View from Castle Rock* — as well as a novel, *Lives of Girls and Women.* During her distinguished career, Ms. Munro has received many awards and prizes, including three of Canada's Governor General's Literary Awards and its Giller Prize; the Rea Award for Short Fiction; the Lannan Literary Award; England's WH Smith Award; and the U.S. National Book Critics Circle Award. She and her husband divide their time between Clinton, Ontario, and Comox, British Columbia.

▪ I wrote this story to explore the idea that this sort of killing, this sort of crime does, in fact, happen. You read about it, think about it, and you always wonder, "What if . . . ?" I also wanted to make the leap to the killer's mind. This is a story about how such persons cope with what they do afterward, in prison, alone with only their thoughts, and how the victim is necessarily drawn to the perpetrator, because who else can share their loss? This would drive the victim into the killer's madness and keep both people in extremis.

A 1978 graduate of Yale with a BS in physics, EILEEN POLLACK earned an MFA from the University of Iowa, where she was awarded a Teaching-Writing Fellowship. She is the author of a collection of short fiction, *The Rabbi in the Attic and Other Stories;* a novel, *Paradise, New York;* and a work of creative nonfiction called *Woman Walking Ahead: In Search of Catherine*

Weldon and Sitting Bull, which was a 2003 WILLA Award finalist. A new collection of stories and novellas called *In the Mouth* is forthcoming from Four Way Books. She has received fellowships from the National Endowment for the Arts, the Michener Foundation, the Rona Jaffe Foundation, and the Massachusetts Arts Council. Her stories have appeared in journals such as *Ploughshares, Prairie Schooner, Michigan Quarterly Review, Agni,* and *New England Review;* they have won two Pushcart Prizes, the Cohen Award for best fiction of the year from *Ploughshares,* and similar awards from *Literary Review* and *MQR.* Ms. Pollack is the Zell Director of the MFA Program in Creative Writing at the University of Michigan.

▪ Some origin stories are more embarrassing than others. Marian and I had been dating for three or four years, and for reasons that ought to be obvious (hint: he's a Catholic and I'm a Jew), we were discussing the circumstances under which a middle-aged man might agree to undergo a circumcision. Marian said that no matter how much he loved a woman, he would never allow his penis to be mutilated. (His word, not mine, but also a joke between us, given his observation that at least one male character in every story I'd ever written suffered a severe trauma to a major body part.)

So you would never get circumcised? I asked. Not even with anesthesia?

To which Marian replied: Would it be kosher if I let myself get clipped after the fact?

To which I replied: How about just before the fact? Say, a few minutes before you die?

In the time it took for us to laugh, the basic situation of what would come to be "The Bris" unfolded in my mind. I didn't yet know whether the main character would find a way to get his father circumcised, but I figured if I started with the father setting his son this task, I would have a story either way. (I must say I was relieved when I got to the end and realized that the circumcision would only be symbolic. Marian was relieved as well.)

I'm not sure why, but writing this novella took far less time than usual. Or maybe it was only unusually fun to write. I showed it to my dad, who, at eighty-seven, was still a healthy man. In fact, he was so healthy he could beat me at tennis. (I'm a better-than-average player, but just for the record, I've never blinded a rabbi. The inspiration for the tennis match comes from a high school practice session in which I smacked a volley into my coach's face. A few days later, when she returned to school wearing a patch over the injured eye, she challenged me to a game to show she didn't hold a grudge. I hit her an easy lob, but when she ran back to smash the overhead, she lost her balance and broke her arm.)

My father was looking forward to seeing "The Bris" in print, but by the time it had been accepted by *Subtropics,* he had been diagnosed with cancer and given only a few months to live. He survived just long enough that I was able to show him the volume in which "The Bris" appears and watch him smile and nod. Although he was a kind and generous man whose parents owned a hotel in the Catskills, he wasn't the model for Marcus's dad. (My own father was Jewish to his core — and to all his other parts.) I wrote the story to rehearse his death, to immunize myself against a loss I couldn't imagine bearing. In some ways, this strategy worked. But as Marcus learns, no one can predict the pain and grief and darkly unnerving comedy that invariably surround a parent's death.

I want to thank Marian for giving me the idea for this story, my friends and colleagues for helping me revise it, and David Leavitt for publishing a magazine that not only prints longer-than-average stories but replies to authors in record time and pays contributors generously for their work.

KAREN RUSSELL's first collection of short stories, *St. Lucy's Home for Girls Raised by Wolves,* was published by Knopf in 2006 and is forthcoming in paperback. Her stories have recently appeared in *Conjunctions, Granta, Zoetrope, Oxford American,* and *The New Yorker.* Her work has been featured in *The New Yorker* debut fiction issue, and in 2007 she was picked as one of *Granta*'s Best of Young American Novelists. Twenty-five years old, she lives in New York City, where she is working on a novel called *Swamplandia!,* about a family of alligator wrestlers.

▪ This story began as a very bad poem: *At the Half-Way House for Girls Raised by Wolves.* The title was the best part. After that, things went way south. There was a serious overuse of the word *lupine.* There were rhymes. And to my horror, each bad stanza would spawn an even worse stanza. Reading the finished poem was like watching bad blood travel down the generations.

But I couldn't stop thinking about these feral girls. I know it's a fantastical premise, but something about their plight felt very true and very serious to me, these children of werewolves caught between the deep woods and civilization, between shared and private language, between the pack and their evolving selves. And I guess that "in between" territory became the halfway house where "St. Lucy's" takes place.

I spent my junior year in Spain, and at our study abroad orientation we each received a pamphlet called "The Wheel of Acculturation." According to "The Wheel," our homesickness would be the yardstick of our success abroad. The more we learned about the customs and foods of Spain, the more foreign our own American homes would become. That was the price of becoming bilingual. Culture shock struck me as a terrific metaphor for the process of getting socialized, assimilating, growing up. Although for these wolf-girls, I imagine that becoming human is not nearly so straightforward as the Jesuits' stages make it out to be. I think it's more like a Möbius strip of progress and loss.

What else about "St. Lucy's"? Well, I used to eat burger patties with my hands, and my parents debated sending me to Etiquette Camp. It was great fun to channel my poor table manners and the specter of Etiquette Camp into this story.

Novelist and screenwriter RICHARD RUSSO won the 2002 Pulitzer Prize for *Empire Falls*. He lives and works in Maine.

▪ I probably wouldn't have written "Horseman" if, several years ago, I hadn't been asked to give the commencement address at Colby College. My daughter Kate was in the graduating class, so I wanted to do a good job and thereby avoid humiliation (hers and my own). Commencement talks are seldom memorable or exciting, but I wanted to say something that I believed to be true and maybe even important, just in case someone happened actually to be listening. Since my own graduation in 1971, my life hadn't gone the way I'd imagined, and I wanted to suggest to Kate and her friends that theirs probably wouldn't either, and this made me think of a woman I'd known a decade earlier.

Actually, I didn't know her very well. She was a faculty member in another academic department, and we'd served on a couple of liberal arts committees together. Her name is long gone, along with my reasons for not being terribly fond of her. She was smart and attractive, but also guarded in the extreme, the way academics can be.

In the language of *Star Trek*, she'd diverted all power to her shields, which was probably why I was so startled one night when I happened to catch her with her defenses down. My wife and I had gone to a party that was a mix of faculty and grad students, the obligatory keg out back, a phalanx of cheap 1.5-liter bottles of Yugoslavian wine uncorked on the kitchen sink, music pounding in the front room, where I saw the woman in question dancing with great joy and such unexpected abandon that I found myself smiling and actually liking her for the first time. I don't know how much she'd had to drink, but I'm guessing somewhere between too much and not quite enough. Later I came upon her in the kitchen where she sat with her head in her hands, her shoulders quaking uncontrollably, the party's hostess trying desperately to console her. "All I ever wanted," she sobbed, "was to play a little rock-and-roll." What I wanted to tell my daughter and her fellow graduates was that over the next two decades they had but one real job, and that was to not become this woman. Don't, I would warn them, wake up some day to the terrible realization that you've somehow managed to ignore the simple thing you wanted most in life and know it's now too late.

After commencement, I expected to forget about the woman again, but I didn't, which led me to wonder what there was about her. It came to me — slowly, the way these things do — that she was a lot like many academics I'd observed over the years. You'd think that the life of the mind, especially the liberal arts, would make us better, if not happier, people, but too often it doesn't. The study of literature had had what I believed to be a salutary effect on my own character, making me less self-conscious and vain, more empathic and imaginative, maybe even kinder. Perhaps it's an oversimplification, but as I've gotten older I've come to wonder if maybe this is what reading all those great books is really for — to engender and promote charity. Sure, literature entertains and instructs, but to what end, if not compassion? How is it, then, that so many smart people use the study of literature to erect sturdy barriers between themselves and their lives, to become strangers to their truest desires, their best selves?

I'd never quite figured out exactly how such self-deception worked, but I suspected this woman, if I let her loose in a story, might explain it to me, especially if I framed her tale against a backdrop of some other form of cheating, like, say, plagiarism.

JIM SHEPARD is the author of six novels, including most recently *Project X* (Knopf, 2004), and two story collections, including most recently *Love and Hydrogen* (Vintage, 2004). His short fiction has appeared in, among other magazines, *Harper's Magazine, McSweeney's, The Paris Review, The Atlantic Monthly, Esquire, DoubleTake, Granta, The New Yorker,* and *Playboy,* and he is a columnist on film for the magazine *The Believer.* A third story collection, *Like You'd Understand Anyway,* and a collection of his film essays, *Heroes in Disguise,* will appear in 2007. He teaches at Williams College and in the Warren Wilson MFA program.

▪ My fascination with the French Revolution and, more specifically, with the Reign of Terror must have begun either with my first viewing of MGM's version of *A Tale of Two Cities* or, more likely, with the Classics Illustrated version (#139, *In the Reign of Terror,* with a cover that featured a Clu Gulager–like aristocrat in the foreground glancing apprehensively over his shoulder at a sans-culotte menacing him with a club from behind a fence). But it never occurred to me to write about that fascination, perhaps because I couldn't imagine myself someday reading anything aloud that would force me to pronounce French. But one day while rambling through a particularly good used-book store — Monroe Street Books, in Middlebury, Vermont, if you find yourself in the area — I came across the kind of title that always appeals to the twelve-year-old in me: *Legacy of Death.* The author was Barbara Levy, and the subtitle turned out to be *The Remarkable Saga of the Sanson Family, Who Served as Executioners of France for Seven Generations.* Now there was a family I wanted to know more about. One of those generations turned out to feature the man who ended up at the center of my story, a man whose life and profession, as the book sketched them in, seemed so stunning that I found myself very much wanting to try to imagine it more fully, despite the obvious difficulties involved. Months of ghoulish research followed. (My wife, Karen, herself a writer, likes to say that I'm the only person she knows who'll take a history of the guillotine along as beach reading.) The result was the story "Sans Farine."

KATE WALBERT is the author of the novels *The Gardens of Kyoto* and *Our Kind,* which was a finalist for the 2004 National Book Award, as well as the linked story collection, *Where She Went.* Her stories have appeared in *The New Yorker, The Paris Review, The Antioch Review, DoubleTake,* the 2000 Pushcart Prize anthology, and *O. Henry Award Prize Stories 2000,* among other publications. She lives with her husband and daughters in New York City.

▪ Many images form the genesis of "Do Something": the handful of older women and the occasional man who congregate Sunday mornings on the town green in Guilford, Connecticut — and, I imagine, many small town greens — holding placards that simply say PEACE; driving past the labyrinthine barracks of Dover Air Force base on my way to Rehoboth Beach, Delaware, knowing that for years after our invasion of Iraq no photographs of the returning dead were released to the public (a professor at the University of Delaware won a lawsuit to overturn this policy, though the government's reluctant compliance has included blacking out the faces of the attending soldiers); the image of my amazing friend Pam, who died of leukemia in 2002, wrapped in a blue shawl and sitting peacefully in her hospital room, the sun setting on the city beyond. I have never before written a story to vent anger, but this one was propelled by fury. Writing it felt like shaking my fist at something impossible to name any other way.

100 Other Distinguished Stories of 2006

SELECTED BY STEPHEN KING

ADRIAN, CHRIS
A Better Angel. *The New Yorker,* April 3, 2006.
Stab. *Zoetrope,* Vol. 10, No. 2.
ALMOND, STEVE
Tamalpais. *Virginia Quarterly Review,* Vol. 82, No. 1.
ALTSCHUL, ANDREW FOSTER
Leaving Idyllwild. *StoryQuarterly,* No. 42.
ALVAR, MIA
Roundabout. *Small Spiral Notebook,* Vol. 3, No. 2.
APPEL, JACOB
The Butcher's Music. *West Branch,* No. 58.

BAKKEN, KERRY NEVILLE
The Effects of Light. *Glimmer Train,* No. 59.
BENEDICT, PICKNEY
Pig Helmet and the Wall of Life. *StoryQuarterly,* No. 42.
BISSON, TERRY
Billy and the Fairy. *Fantasy and Science Fiction,* May 2006.
BOGNANNI, PETER
The Body Eternal. *Gulf Coast,* Vol. 18.1.
BRADFORD, ARTHUR
Snakebite. *McSweeney's,* No. 21.
BRADWAY, BECKY
Fine Stationery. *Blackbird,* Vol. 5, No. 2.
BROCKMEIER, KEVIN
The View from the Seventh Layer. *Oxford American,* No. 53.
BROOKS, KIM
The Psychiatrist's Daughter. *Epoch,* Vol. 54, No. 3.
BURKE, JAMES LEE
Jesus out to Sea. *Esquire,* April 2006.
BUSCH, FREDERICK
Patrols. *Five Points,* Vol. 10, Nos. 1 & 2.

CARLSON, MEL
Walking on Water. *Tin House,* Vol. 7, No. 2.
CASEY, JOHN
Rapunzel. *Ploughshares,* Vol. 32, No. 4.

CHAPMAN, MAILE
Bit Forgive. *A Public Space*, issue 2.
CHENEY, MATTHEW
Blood. *One Story*, No. 81.
CLEMENT, ALISON
Burying Angel O'Malley. *The Sun*, December 2006.
CONNOR, JOAN
The Landmark Hotel. *Antioch Review*, Vol. 64, No. 1.
CUMMINGS, JOHN MICHAEL
The Scratchboard Project. *The Iowa Review*, Vol. 36, No. 1.

D, RAMOLA
The Next Corpse Collector. *Green Mountains Review*, Vol. 19, No. 1.
D'AMBROSIO, CHARLES
The Dead Fish Museum. *A Public Space*, Spring 2006.
DICKINSON, STEPHANIE
Pigfarmer's Stepdaughter. *Weber Studies*, Vol. 22, No. 3.
DIXON, STEPHEN
Who He? *Boulevard*, Vol. 21, Nos. 62 & 63.
DORMEN, LESLEY
The Best Place to Be. *Glimmer Train*, No. 58.
DOWNS, MICHAEL
Mrs. Lizsak. *Five Points*, Vol. 10, Nos. 1 & 2.
DOZOIS, GARDNER
Counterfactual. *Fantasy and Science Fiction*, June 2006.
D'SOUZA, TONY
Magic Muffler. *Subtropics*, No. 2.

EARLEY, TONY
The Cryptozoologist. *The New Yorker*, January 9, 2006.
EGGERS, PAUL
Monsieur Le Genius. *Agni*, No. 63.
EISENBERG, DEBORAH
The Flaw in the Design. *Virginia Quarterly Review*, Vol. 82, No. 1.
ELLISON, JAN
The Color of Wheat in Winter. *Hudson Review*, Vol. LIX, No. 2.

GAITSKILL, MARY
The Little Boy. *Harper's Magazine*, June 2006.
GAUTREAUX, TIM
The Safe. *The Atlantic Monthly*, fiction issue.
GERSHOW, MIRIAM
A Step Ahead. *Black Warrior Review*, Vol. 32, No. 2.
GURGANUS, ALLAN
Fourteen Feet of Water in My House. *Harper's Magazine*, January 2006.
GWYN, AARON
Mate. *McSweeney's*, No. 20.

HAGY, ALYSON
The Little Saint of Hoodoo Mountain. *Shenandoah*, Vol. 56, No. 1.
HARLEMAN, ANN
Thoreau's Laundry. *Alaska Quarterly Review*, Vol. 23, Nos. 1 & 2.
HOFFMAN, ALICE
All That I Am and Ever Will Be. *Harvard Review*, No. 31.
HOLLADAY, CARY
Shades. *Epoch*, Vol. 54, No. 3.
HOUSE, TOM
Careers Day. *Antioch Review*, Vol. 64, No. 1.

KARTSONIS, ARIANA-SOPHIA
Sundress. *Glimmer Train*, No. 57.
KEAR, DAVID
Greene Park Is Burning. *Glimmer Train*, No. 58.
KIMBALL, MICHAEL
Excerpts from the Suicide Letters of Jonathan Bender. *Post Road*, No. 12.
KOHLER, SHEILA
Travelogue. *Boulevard*, Vol. 21, Nos. 2 & 3.

Koven, Stephanie
Bomb Shelter. *The Sun,* November 2006.

Kramon, Justin
Shel. *Glimmer Train,* No. 59.

Lahiri, Jhumpa
Once in a Lifetime. *The New Yorker,* May 8, 2006.

Laken, Valerie
Spectators. *Ploughshares,* Vol. 32, No. 1.

Le, Nam
Love and Honor and Pity and Pride and Compassion and Sacrifice. *Zoetrope,* Vol. 10, No 2.

Lee, Don
A Preference for Native Tongue. *Kenyon Review,* Vol. XXVIII, No. 3.

Link, Kelly
Origin Story. *A Public Space,* No. 1.

McGuane, Thomas
Tango. *The New Yorker,* December 11, 2006.

McNally, John
Creature Features. *Virginia Quarterly Review,* Vol. 82, No. 1.

Meyer, Phillip
The Wolf. *Iowa Review,* Vol. 36, No. 2.

Miller, Rebecca
Mrs. Covet. *Granta,* No. 95.

Millhauser, Stephen
The Other Town. *Tin House,* No. 28.

Moore, Lorrie
Paper Losses. *The New Yorker,* November 6, 2006.

Munoz, Manuel
Bring, Brang, Brung. *Glimmer Train,* No. 59.

Nangle, Paula
Swabs. *Glimmer Train,* No. 58.

Nelson, Randy F.
Breaker. *Glimmer Train,* No. 57.

Novack, Sandra
Memphis. *Gulf Coast,* Vol. 18.1.

Oates, Joyce Carol
A Princeton Idyll. *Yale Review,* Vol. 94, No. 4.

Ockert, Jason
Jackob Loomis. *Oxford American,* No. 53.

Pearlman, Edith
Aunt Telephone. *Antioch Review,* Vol. 64, No. 3.

Perabo, Susan
Treasure. *Missouri Review,* 28:3.
This Is Not That Story. *The Sun,* March 2006.

Pitt, Matthew
Attention, Please. *The Southern Review,* Vol. 42, No. 4.

Porter, Andrew
Azul. *One Story,* No. 72.

Morris, Ellen Prewitt
Held at Gunpoint. *Image,* No. 48.

Prose, Francine
An Open Letter to Doctor X. *Virginia Quarterly Review,* Vol. 82, No. 2.

Rash, Ron
The Graveyard Shift. *Oxford American,* No. 54.

Richerson, Carrie
. . . ~~With~~ By Good Intentions. *Fantasy and Science Fiction,* October/November 2006.

Row, Jess
Nobody Ever Gets Lost. *American Short Fiction,* No. 35.

Rowe, Christopher
Another Word for *Map* Is *Faith.* *Fantasy and Science Fiction,* August 2006.

Russell, Karen
City of Shells. *Oxford American,* No. 53.
Ava Wrestles the Alligator. *Zoetrope,* Vol. 10, No. 2.

Sanders, Mark
Why Guineas Fly. *Glimmer Train,* No. 58.

SCHLOSSER, JASON
Communion. *The Sun,* April 2006.
SCHOTTENFIELD, STEPHEN
Artie Gottlieb, Consulting Philosopher. *Virginia Quarterly Review,* Vol. 64, No 2.
SHINNER, PEGGY
Jack's Things. *Alaska Quarterly Review,* Vol. 23, Nos. 1 & 2.
SHOPPER, EVAN
Honeymoon. *Glimmer Train,* No. 60.
SILVER, MARISA
Night Train to Frankfurt. *The New Yorker,* November 20, 2006.
SMITH, MANDELIENE
Mercy. *The Sun,* May 2006.
SNYDER, SCOTT
Dumpster Tuesday. *Small Spiral Notebook,* Vol. 3, No. 2.
Wrecks. *Tin House,* Vol. 7, No. 2.
STRAIGHT, SUSAN
El Ojo de Agua. *Zoetrope,* Vol. 10, No. 1.

TANAKA, SHIMON
Favor. *The Missouri Review,* Vol. 29, No. 1.
TOMLINSON, JIM
First Husband, First Wife. *Five Points,* Vol. 10, No. 3.

UDECHUKWU, ADA
Night Bus. *The Atlantic Monthly,* fiction issue.

VAPNYAR, LARA
Cinderella School. *The New Yorker,* May 22, 2006.
VIOLA, TONY
Everybody Smells Like Fish. *Pleiades,* Vol. 26, No. 1.

WALDEN, GALE RENEE
The Train. *Antioch Review,* Vol. 61, No. 1.
WATTS, STEPHANIE POWELL
Unassigned Territory. *Oxford American,* No. 52.
WICKERSHAM, JOAN
Psychological Impact. *Hudson Review,* Vol. LVIII, No. 4.

YOON, PAUL
By Boat, Drawn by Swans. *Chelsea,* No. 80.

Editorial Addresses of American and Canadian Magazines Publishing Short Stories

African American Review
St. Louis University
Humanities 317
3800 Lindell Boulevard
St. Louis, MO 63108-2007
$40, Joycelyn Moody

Agni Magazine
Boston University Writing Program
Boston University
236 Bay State Road
Boston, MA 02115
$17, Sven Birkerts

Alaska Quarterly Review
University of Alaska, Anchorage
3211 Providence Drive
Anchorage, AK 99508
$10, Ronald Spatz

Alfred Hitchcock Mystery Magazine
Dell Magazines/Themysteryplace.com
475 Park Avenue South, 11th Floor
New York, NY 10016
$34.97, Cathleen Jordan

Alligator Juniper
Prescott College
220 Grove Avenue
Prescott, AZ 86301
$7.50, Miles Waggener

American Letters and Commentary
850 Park Avenue, Suite 5B
New York, NY 10021
$8, Anna Rabinowitz

American Literary Review
University of North Texas
P.O. Box 311307
Denton, TX 76203-1307
$10, John Tait

American Short Fiction
P.O. Box 301209
Austin, TX 78703
$30, The Editors

Another Chicago Magazine
Left Field Press
3709 North Kenmore
Chicago, IL 60613
$8, Sharon Solwitz

Antioch Review
Antioch University
150 East South College Street
Yellow Springs, OH 45387
$35, Robert S. Fogerty

Apalachee Review
P.O. Box 10469
Tallahassee, FL 32302
$15, group

Arkansas Review
Department of English and Philosophy
P.O. Box 1890
Arkansas State University
State University, AR 72467
$20, Tom Williams

Ascent
English Department
Concordia College
901 Eighth Street
Moorhead, MN 56562
$12, W. Scott Olsen

Atlantic Monthly
The Watergate
600 NH Avenue NW
Washington, DC 20037
$14.95, C. Michael Curtis

Backwards City Review
P.O. Box 41317
Greensboro, NC 27404
$10, Gerry Canavan

Baltimore Review
P.O. Box 36418
Towson, MD 21286
$15, Barbara Westwood Diehl

Bamboo Ridge
P.O. Box 6176
Honolulu, HI 96839-1781
$35, Eric Chock, Darrell H.Y. Lum

Bayou
Department of English
University of New Orleans
2000 Lakeshore Drive
New Orleans, LA 70148
$10, Joanna Leake

Bellevue Literary Review
Department of Medicine
New York University School of Medicine
550 First Avenue
New York, NY 10016
$12, Danielle Ofri

Bellingham Review
MS-9053
Western Washington University
Bellingham, WA 98225
$14, Brenda Miller

Bellowing Ark
P.O. Box 55564
Shoreline, WA 98155
$18, Robert Ward

Berkshire Review
P.O. Box 120
Lenox Dale, MA 01242
$8.95, Rodelinde Albrecht

Blackbird
Department of English
Virginia Commonwealth University
P.O. Box 843082
Richmond, VA 23284-3082
Anna Journey

Black Warrior Review
P.O. Box 862936
Tuscaloosa, AL 35486-0027
$14, Laura Hendrix

Blue Mesa Review
Department of English
University of New Mexico
Albuquerque, NM 87131
Julie Shigekuni

Bomb
New Art Publications
594 Broadway, 10th Floor
New York, NY 10012
$18, Betsy Sussler

Boston Review
35 Medford Street, Suite 302
Somerville, MA 02143
$25, Joshua Cohen, Deborah Chasman

Boulevard
PMB 325
6614 Clayton Road
Richmond Heights, MO 63117
$15, Richard Burgin

Brain, Child: The Magazine for Thinking Mothers
P.O. Box 714
Lexington, VA 24450-0714
$18, Jennifer Niesslein, Stephanie Wilkinson

Briar Cliff Review
3303 Rebecca Street
P.O. Box 2100
Sioux City, IA 51104-2100
$10, Tricia Currans-Sheehan

Bridges
P.O. Box 24839
Eugene, OR 97402
$15, Clare Kinberg

Callaloo
Department of English
Texas A&M University
4227 TAMU
College Station, TX 77843-4227
$40, Charles H. Rowell

Calyx
P.O. Box B
Corvallis, OR 97339
$19.50, Margarita Donnelly and collective

Capilano Review
Capilano College
2055 Purcell Way
North Vancouver
British Columbia V7J 3H5
$25, Sharon Thesen

Carolina Quarterly
Greenlaw Hall CB 3520
University of North Carolina
Chapel Hill, NC 27599-3520
$12, Amy Weldon

Chattahoochee Review
Georgia Perimeter College
2101 Womack Road
Dunwoody, GA 30338-4497
$16, Lawrence Hetrick

Chelsea
P.O. Box 773
Cooper Station
New York, NY 10276
$13, Alfredo de Palchi

Chicago Quarterly Review
517 Sherman Avenue
Evanston, IL 60202
$10, S. Afzal Haider, Jane Lawrence, Lisa McKenzie

Chicago Review
5801 South Kenwood
University of Chicago
Chicago, IL 60637
$18, Erik Steinhoff

Cimarron Review
205 Morrill Hall
Oklahoma State University
Stillwater, OK 74078-0135
$24, E. P. Walkiewicz

Cincinnati Review
Department of English
McMicken Hall, Room 369
P.O. Box 210069
Cincinnati, OH 45221
$12, Brock Clarke

Colorado Review
Department of English
Colorado State University
Fort Collins, CO 80523
$24, Stephanie G'Schwind

Commentary
editorial@commentarymagazine.com
Neal Kozody

Confrontation
English Department
C. W. Post College of Long Island University
Greenvale, NY 11548
$10, Martin Tucker

Conjunctions
21 East 10th Street, Suite 3E
New York, NY 10003
$18, Bradford Morrow

Connecticut Review
English Department

Southern Connecticut State University
501 Crescent Street
New Haven, CT 06515
John Briggs

Crab Orchard Review
Department of English
Southern Illinois University at Carbondale
Carbondale, IL 62901
$15, Carolyn Alessio

Crazyhorse
Department of English
College of Charleston
66 George Street
Charleston, SC 29424
$15, Carol Ann Davis

CrossConnect
CrossConnect, Inc.
P.O. Box 2317
Philadelphia, PA 12103
$12, David Deifer

Crucible
Barton College
P.O. Box 5000
Wilson, NC 27893-7000
Terrence L. Grimes

Daedalus
136 Irving Street, Suite 100
Cambridge, MA 02138
$33, James Miller

Denver Quarterly
University of Denver
Denver, CO 80208
$20, Bin Ramke

Descant
P.O. Box 314
Station P
Toronto, Ontario M5S 2S8
$25, Karen Mulhallen

Descant
TCU
Box 297270
Fort Worth, TX 76129
$12, Lynn Risser, David Kuhne

Ecotone
Department of Creative Writing
University of North Carolina–Wilmington
601 South College Road
Wilmington, NC 28403
$18, David Gessner

Edgar Literary Magazine
P.O. Box 5776
San Leon, TX 77539
Sue Mayfield-Geiger

Epoch
251 Goldwin Smith Hall
Cornell University
Ithaca, NY 14853-3201
$11, Michael Koch

Esquire
250 West 55th Street
New York, NY 10019
$17.94, Adrienne Miller

Eureka Literary Magazine
Eureka College
300 East College Avenue
Eureka, IL 61530-1500
$15, Loren Logsdon

Event
Douglas College
P.O. Box 2503
New Westminster
British Columbia V3L 5B2
$22, Cathy Stonehouse

Fairy Tale Review
University of Alabama
English Department
Box 780224
Tuscaloosa, AL 35487
$12, Kate Bernheimer

Fantasy and Science Fiction
P.O. Box 3447
Hoboken, NJ 07030
$44.89, Gordon Van Gelder

Fiction International
Department of English and Comparative Literature

San Diego State University
San Diego, CA 92182
$12, Harold Jaffe

Fiddlehead
UNB P.O. Box 4400
Fredericton
New Brunswick E3B 5A3
$20, Mark Anthony Jarman

Five Points
Georgia State University
Department of English
University Plaza
Atlanta, GA 30303-3083
$20, David Bottoms

Frostproof Review
P.O. Box 3397
Lake Wales, FL 33859
$15, Kyle Minor

Fugue
Department of English
Brink Hall 200
University of Idaho
Moscow, ID 83844-1102
$14, Ben George, Jeff P. Jones

Gargoyle
P.O. Box 6216
Arlington, VA 22206-0216
$20, Richard Peabody, Lucinda Ebersole

Georgia Review
University of Georgia
Athens, GA 30602
$24, T. R. Hummer

Gettysburg Review
Gettysburg College
Gettysburg, PA 17325-1491
$24, Peter Stitt

Glimmer Train
1211 NW Glisan Street, Suite 207
Portland, OR 97209
$36, Susan Burmeister-Brown, Linda Swanson-Davies

Grain
Box 67
Saskatoon, Saskatchewan S4P 3B4
$26.95, Kent Bruyneel

Granta
1755 Broadway, 5th Floor
New York, NY 10019-3780
$39.95, Ian Jack

Green Mountains Review
Box A58
Johnson State College
Johnson, VT 05656
$15, Jack Pulaski

Greensboro Review
3302 Hall for Humanities and Research Administration
University of North Carolina
Greensboro, NC 27412
$10, Jim Clark

Gulf Coast
Department of English
University of Houston
4800 Calhoun Road
Houston, TX 77204-3012
$14, Mark Doty

Gulf Stream
English Department
Florida International University
Biscayne Bay Campus
3000 NE 151st Street
North Miami, FL 33181
$15, John Dufresne, Cindy Chinelly

Hanging Loose
231 Wyckoff Street
Brooklyn, NY 11217
$17.50, group

Harper's Magazine
666 Broadway
New York, NY 10012
$16, Ben Metcalf

Harpur Palate
Department of English
Binghamton University
P.O. Box 6000
Binghamton, NY 13902
$16, Letitia Moffitt, Doris Umbers

Harvard Review
Poetry Room
Harvard College Library
Cambridge, MA 02138
$16, Christina Thompson

Hayden's Ferry Review
Box 871502
Arizona State University
Tempe, AZ 85287-1502
$14, Christopher Becker, Eric Day

Hobart
P.O. Box 1658
Ann Arbor, MI 48103
Aaron Burch

Hudson Review
684 Park Avenue
New York, NY 10021
$24, Paula Deitz

Idaho Review
Boise State University
1910 University Drive
Boise, ID 83725
$9.95, Mitch Wieland

Image
Center for Religious Humanism
3307 Third Avenue West
Seattle, WA 98119
$36, Gregory Wolfe

Indiana Review
Ballantine Hall 465
1020 East Kirkwood Avenue
Bloomington, IN 47405-7103
$14, Esther Lee

Indy Men's Magazine
8500 Keystone Crossing, Suite 100
Indianapolis, IN 46240
Lou Harry

Iowa Review
Department of English
University of Iowa
308 EPB
Iowa City, IA 52242
$20, David Hamilton

Iris
University of Virginia Women's Center
P.O. Box 800588
Charlottesville, VA 22908
$9, Gina Welch

Iron Horse Literary Review
Department of English
Texas Tech University
Box 43091
Lubbock, TX 79409-3091
$12, Leslie Jill Patterson

Italian Americana
University of Rhode Island
Providence Campus
80 Washington Street
Providence, RI 02903
$20, Carol Bonomo Albright

Jabberwock Review
Department of English
Drawer E
Mississippi State University
Mississippi State, MS 39762
$12, Joy Murphy

Jewish Currents
45 East 33rd Street
New York, NY 10016-5335
$20, editorial board

The Journal
Department of English
Ohio State University
164 West Seventeenth Avenue
Columbus, OH 43210
$12, Kathy Fagan, Michelle Herman

Kalliope
Florida Community College
3939 Roosevelt Boulevard
Jacksonville, FL 32205
$12.50, Mary Sue Koeppel

Kenyon Review
Kenyon College
Gambier, OH 43022
$30, David H. Lynn

Lady Churchill's Rosebud Wristlet
Small Beer Press

176 Prospect Avenue
Northampton, MA 01060
$20, Kelly Link

Lake Effect
Penn State Erie
5091 Station Road
Erie, PA 16563-1501
$6, George Looney

Land-Grant College Review
P.O. Box 1164
New York, NY 10159
$18, Tara Wray

The Literary Review
Fairleigh Dickinson University
285 Madison Avenue
Madison, NJ 07940
$18, Rene Steinke

Louisiana Literature
LSU 10792
Southeastern Louisiana University
Hammond, LA 70402
$12, Jack B. Bedell

Louisville Review
Spalding University
851 South Fourth Street
Louisville, KY 40203
$14, Sena Jeter Naslund

Madison Review
University of Wisconsin
Department of English
H. C. White Hall
600 North Park Street
Madison, WI 53706
$12, Abram Foley, Laura Weingarten

Manoa
English Department
University of Hawaii
Honolulu, HI 96822
$22, Frank Stewart

Massachusetts Review
South College
Box 37140
University of Massachusetts
Amherst, MA 01003
$22, David Lenson, Ellen Dore Watson

Matrix
1455 de Maisonneuve Boulevard West
Suite LB-514-8
Montreal, Quebec H3G IM8
$21, R.E.N. Allen

McSweeney's
826 Valencia Street
San Francisco, CA 94110
$36, Dave Eggers

Memorious: A Forum for
New Verse and Poetics
Memorious.org
Rebecca Morgan Frank

Meridian
Department of English
P.O. Box 400145
University of Virginia
Charlottesville, VA 22904-4145
$10, Caitlin Johnson

Michigan Quarterly Review
3574 Rackham Building
915 East Washington Street
University of Michigan
Ann Arbor, MI 48109
$25, Laurence Goldstein

Mid-American Review
Department of English
Bowling Green State University
Bowling Green, OH 43403
$12, Michael Czyzniejewski

Midnight Mind
P.O. Box 146912
Chicago, IL 60614
$12, Brett Van Emst

Minnesota Review
Department of English
Carnegie Mellon University
Pittsburgh, PA 15213
$30, Jeffrey Williams

Mississippi Review
University of Southern Mississippi

Southern Station, Box 5144
Hattiesburg, MS 39406-5144
$15, Frederick Barthelme

Missouri Review
1507 Hillcrest Hall
University of Missouri
Columbia, MO 65211
$22, Speer Morgan

Ms.
433 South Beverly Drive
Beverly Hills, CA 90212
$45, Amy Bloom

n+1
Park West Finance Station
P.O. Box 20688
New York, NY 10025
$16, Allison Lorentzen

Natural Bridge
Department of English
University of Missouri, St. Louis
8001 Natural Bridge Road
St. Louis, MO 63121-4499
$15, Jason Rizos

New England Review
Middlebury College
Middlebury, VT 05753
$25, Stephen Donadio

New Letters
University of Missouri
5100 Rockhill Road
Kansas City, MO 64110
$22, Robert Stewart

New Orleans Review
P.O. Box 195
Loyola University
New Orleans, LA 70118
$12, Christopher Chambers

New Orphic Review
706 Mill Street
Nelson, British Columbia V1L 4S5
$25, Ernest Hekkanen

New Quarterly
English Language Proficiency
Programme
Saint Jerome's University
200 University Avenue West
Waterloo, Ontario N2L 3G3
$36, Kim Jernigan

The New Yorker
4 Times Square
New York, NY 10036
$46, Deborah Treisman

New York Stories
English Department
LaGuardia Community College
31-10 Thomson Avenue
Long Island City, NY 11101
$13.40, Daniel Caplice Lynch

Night Train
85 Orchard Street
Somerville, MA 02144
$17.95, Rod Siino, Rusty Barnes

Nimrod International Journal
Arts and Humanities Council of Tulsa
600 South College Avenue
Tulsa, OK 74104
$17.50, Francine Ringold

Ninth Letter
Department of English
University of Illinois
608 South Wright Street
Urbana, IL 61801
$19.95, Jodee Rubins

Noon
1324 Lexington Avenue
PMB 298
New York, NY 10128
$9, Diane Williams

North American Review
University of Northern Iowa
1222 West 27th Street
Cedar Falls, IA 50614
$22, Grant Tracey

North Carolina Literary Review
Department of English
2201 Bate Building
East Carolina University

Greenville, NC 27858-4353
$20, Margaret Bauer

North Dakota Quarterly
University of North Dakota
P.O. Box 8237
Grand Forks, ND 58202
$25, Robert Lewis

Northwest Review
1286 University of Oregon
Eugene, OR 97403
$22, John Witte

Notre Dame Review
840 Flanner Hall
Department of English
356 O'Shag
University of Notre Dame
Notre Dame, IN 46556-5639
$15, John Matthias, William O'Rourke

Oklahoma Today
15 North Robinson, Suite 100
P.O. Box 53384
Oklahoma City, OK 73102
$16.95, Louisa McCune

One Story
425 Third Street, No. 2
Brooklyn, NY 11215
$21, Maribeth Batcha, Hannah Tinti

Ontario Review
9 Honey Brook Drive
Princeton, NJ 08540
$16, Raymond J. Smith

Open City
225 Lafayette Street, Suite 1114
New York, NY 10012
$32, Thomas Beller, Joanna Yas

Opium
Opiummagazine.com
1272 Page Street
San Francisco, CA 94117
Todd Zuniga

Other Voices
University of Illinois at Chicago
Department of English, M/C 162
601 South Morgan Street
Chicago, IL 60607-7120
$24, Gina Frangello

Oxford American
201 Donaghey Avenue, Main 107
Conway, AR 72035
$29.95, Marc Smirnoff

Paper Street
Paper Street Press
P.O. Box 14786
Pittsburgh, PA 15234
Dory Adams

Paris Review
62 White Street
New York, NY 10013
$34, Philip Gourevitch

Parting Gifts
3413 Wilshire Drive
Greensboro, NC 27408-2923
Robert Bixby

Passages North
English Department
Northern Michigan University
1401 Presque Isle Avenue
Marquette, MI 49007-5363
$10, Katie Hanson

Pearl
3030 East Second Street
Long Beach, CA 90803
$18, group

Phantasmagoria
English Department
Century Community and Technical College
3300 Century Avenue North
White Bear Lake, MN 55110
$15, Abigail Allen

Phoebe
George Mason University
MSN 2D6
4400 University Drive
Fairfax, VA 22030-4444
$12, Lisa Ampleman

Pinch
Department of English
University of Memphis
Memphis, TN 38152
$12, Kristen Iverson

Pleiades
Department of English and Philosophy
Central Missouri State University
P.O. Box 800
Warrensburg, MO 64093
$12, Susan Steinberg

Ploughshares
Emerson College
120 Boylston Street
Boston, MA 02116
$22, Fiction Editor

Poem Memoir Story
Department of English
University of Alabama at Birmingham
217 Humanities Building
900 South 13th Street
Birmingham, AL 35294-1260
$7, Linda Frost

Porcupine
P.O. Box 259
Cedarburg, WI 53012
$15.95, editorial group

Post Road
P.O. Box 400951
Cambridge, MA 02420
$18, Mary Cotton

Potomac Review
Montgomery College
51 Mannakee Street
Rockville, MD 20850
$20, Eli Flam

Prairie Fire
423-100 Arthur Street
Winnipeg, Manitoba R3B 1H3
$25, Andris Taskans

Prairie Schooner
201 Andrews Hall
University of Nebraska
Lincoln, NE 68588-0334
$26, Hilda Raz

Prism International
Department of Creative Writing
University of British Columbia
Buchanan E-462
Vancouver, British Columbia V6T 1W5
$22, Catharine Chen

A Public Space
323 Dean Street
Brooklyn, NY 11217
Brigid Hughes

Puerto del Sol
MSCC 3E
New Mexico State University
P.O. Box 30001
Las Cruces, NM 88003
$10, Kevin McIlvoy

Quarterly West
2055 South Central Campus Drive
Department of English/LNCO 3500
University of Utah
Salt Lake City, UT 84112
$14, Mike White, Paul Ketzle

Red Rock Review
English Department, J2A
Community College of Southern Nevada
3200 East Cheyenne Avenue
North Las Vegas, NV 89030
$9.50, Richard Logsdon

Red Wheelbarrow
De Anza College
21250 Stevens Creek Boulevard
Cupertino, CA 95014-5702
$5, Randolph Splitter

Republic of Letters
120 Cushing Avenue
Boston, MA 02125-2033
$35, Keith Botsford

River Oak Review
River Oak Arts
P.O. Box 3127

Oak Park, IL 60303
$12, Mary Lee MacDonald

River Styx
3547 Olive Street, Suite 107
St. Louis, MO 63103-1014
$20, Richard Newman

Room of One's Own
P.O. Box 46160
Station D
Vancouver, British Columbia V6J 5G5
$25, Patricia Robitaille

Rosebud
P.O. Box 459
Cambridge, WI 53523
$18, Roderick Clark

Salmagundi
Skidmore College
Saratoga Springs, NY 12866
$20, Robert Boyers

Santa Monica Review
1900 Pico Boulevard
Santa Monica, CA 90405
$12, Andrew Tonkovich

Sewanee Review
University of the South
Sewanee, TN 37375-4009
$24, George Core

Shenandoah
Mattingly House
2 Lee Avenue
Washington and Lee University
Lexington, VA 24450-0303
$22, R. T. Smith, Lynn Leech

Small Spiral Notebook
172 Fifth Avenue, Suite 104
Brooklyn, NY 11217
$12, Felicia Sullivan

Sonora Review
Department of English
University of Arizona
Tucson, AZ 85721
$12, David James Poissant, Mark Polansak

South Dakota Review
University of South Dakota
P.O. Box 111 University Exchange
Vermilion, SD 57069
$15, Brian Bedard

Southeast Review
Department of English
Florida State University
Tallahassee, FL 32306
$10, Tony R. Morris

Southern Humanities Review
9088 Haley Center
Auburn University
Auburn, AL 36849
$15, Dan R. Latimer, Virginia M. Kouidis

Southern Review
43 Allen Hall
Louisiana State University
Baton Rouge, LA 70803
$25, Brett Lott

Southwest Review
Southern Methodist University
P.O. Box 4374
Dallas, TX 75275
$24, Willard Spiegelman

StoryQuarterly
431 Sheridan Road
Kenilworth, IL 60043-1220
$12, M.M.M. Hayes

StorySouth
898 Chelsea Avenue
Bexley, OH 43209
Jason Sanford

Subtropics
Department of English
University of Florida
P.O. Box 112075
Gainesville, FL 32611-2075
David Leavitt

Sun
107 North Roberson Street
Chapel Hill, NC 27516
$34, Sy Safransky

Swink
244 Fifth Avenue, No. 2722
New York, NY 10001
$16, Leelila Strogov

Sycamore Review
Department of English
500 Oval Drive
Purdue University
West Lafayette, IN 47907
$12, Sean M. Conrey

Talking River Review
Division of Literature and Languages
Lewis-Clark State College
500 Eighth Avenue
Lewiston, ID 83501
$14, editorial board

Tampa Review
University of Tampa
401 West Kennedy Boulevard
Tampa, FL 33606-1490
$15, Richard Mathews

Third Coast
Department of English
Western Michigan University
Kalamazoo, MI 49008-5092
$11, Glenn Deutsch

Threepenny Review
P.O. Box 9131
Berkeley, CA 94709
$16, Wendy Lesser

Timber Creek Review
8969 UNCG Station
Greensboro, NC 27413
$15, John Freiermuth

Tin House
P.O. Box 10500
Portland, OR 97296-0500
$39.80, Rob Spillman

Transition
69 Dunster Street
Harvard University
Cambridge, MA 02138
$28, Kwame Anthony Appiah, Henry Louis Gates Jr., Michael Vazquez

TriQuarterly
629 Noyes Street
Evanston, IL 60208
$24, Susan Firestone Hahn

Virginia Quarterly Review
One West Range
P.O. Box 400223
Charlottesville, VA 22903
$18, Ted Genoways

War, Literature, and the Arts
Department of English and Fine Arts
2354 Fairchild Drive, Suite 6D45
USAF Academy, CO 80840-6242
$10, Donald Anderson

Wascana Review
English Department
University of Regina
Regina, Saskatchewan S4S 0A2
$10, Marcel DeCoste

Washington Square
Creative Writing Program
New York University
19 University Place, 2nd Floor
New York, NY 10003-4556
$6, James Pritchard

Watchword
P.O. Box 5755
Berkeley, CA 94705
Kasia Newman, Liz Lisle

Weber Studies
Weber State University
1214 University Circle
Ogden, UT 84408-1214
$20, Brad Roghaar

West Branch
Bucknell Hall
Bucknell University
Lewisburg, PA 17837
$10, Paula Closson Buck

Western Humanities Review
University of Utah
255 South Central Campus Drive
Room 3500

Salt Lake City, UT 84112
$16, Barry Weller

Willow Springs
Eastern Washington University
705 West First Avenue
Spokane, WA 99201
$13, Samuel Ligon

Yale Review
P.O. Box 208243
New Haven, CT 06520-8243
$27, J. D. McClatchy

Zoetrope
The Sentinel Building
916 Kearney Street
San Francisco, CA 94133
$19.95, Michael Ray

Zyzzyva
P.O. Box 590069
San Francisco, CA 94109
$28, Howard Junker

THE B·E·S·T AMERICAN SERIES®

THE BEST AMERICAN SHORT STORIES® 2007. STEPHEN KING, editor, HEIDI PITLOR, series editor. This year's most beloved short fiction anthology is edited by Stephen King, author of sixty books, including *Misery, The Green Mile, Cell,* and *Lisey's Story,* as well as about four hundred short stories, including "The Man in the Black Suit," which won the O. Henry Prize in 1996. The collection features stories by Richard Russo, Alice Munro, William Gay, T. C. Boyle, Ann Beattie, and others.

ISBN-13: 978-0-618-71347-9 • ISBN-10: 0-618-71347-6 $28.00 CL
ISBN-13: 978-0-618-71348-6 • ISBN-10: 0-618-71348-4 $14.00 PA

THE BEST AMERICAN NONREQUIRED READING™ 2007. DAVE EGGERS, editor, introduction by SUFJAN STEVENS. This collection boasts the best in fiction, nonfiction, alternative comics, screenplays, blogs, and "anything else that defies categorization" (*USA Today*). With an introduction by singer-songwriter Sufjan Stevens, this volume features writing from Alison Bechdel, Scott Carrier, Miranda July, Lee Klein, Matthew Klam, and others.

ISBN-13: 978-0-618-90276-7 • ISBN-10: 0-618-90276-7 $28.00 CL
ISBN-13: 978-0-618-90281-1 • ISBN-10: 0-618-90281-3 $14.00 PA

THE BEST AMERICAN COMICS™ 2007. CHRIS WARE, editor, ANNE ELIZABETH MOORE, series editor. The newest addition to the Best American series—"A genuine salute to comics" (*Houston Chronicle*)—returns with a set of both established and up-and-coming contributors. Edited by Chris Ware, author of *Jimmy Corrigan: The Smartest Kid on Earth,* this volume features pieces by Lynda Barry, R. and Aline Crumb, David Heatley, Gilbert Hernandez, Adrian Tomine, Lauren Weinstein, and others.

ISBN-13: 978-0-618-71876-4 • ISBN-10: 0-618-71876-1 $22.00 CL

THE BEST AMERICAN ESSAYS® 2007. DAVID FOSTER WALLACE, editor, ROBERT ATWAN, series editor. Since 1986, *The Best American Essays* has gathered outstanding nonfiction writing, establishing itself as the premier anthology of its kind. Edited by the acclaimed writer David Foster Wallace, this year's collection brings together "witty, diverse" (*San Antonio Express-News*) essays from such contributors as Jo Ann Beard, Malcolm Gladwell, Louis Menand, and Molly Peacock.

ISBN-13: 978-0-618-70926-7 • ISBN-10: 0-618-70926-6 $28.00 CL
ISBN-13: 978-0-618-70927-4 • ISBN-10: 0-618-70927-4 $14.00 PA

THE BEST AMERICAN MYSTERY STORIES™ 2007. CARL HIAASEN, editor, OTTO PENZLER, series editor. This perennially popular anthology is sure to appeal to mystery fans of every variety. The 2007 volume, edited by best-selling novelist Carl Hiaasen, features both mystery veterans and new talents. Contributors include Lawrence Block, James Lee Burke, Louise Erdrich, David Means, and John Sandford.

ISBN-13: 978-0-618-81263-9 • ISBN-10: 0-618-81263-6 $28.00 CL
ISBN-13: 978-0-618-81265-3 • ISBN-10: 0-618-81265-2 $14.00 PA

THE B·E·S·T AMERICAN SERIES®

THE BEST AMERICAN SPORTS WRITING™ 2007. DAVID MARANISS, editor, GLENN STOUT, series editor. "An ongoing centerpiece for all sports collections" (*Booklist*), this series stands in high regard for its extraordinary sports writing and topnotch editors. This year David Maraniss, author of the critically acclaimed biography *Clemente,* brings together pieces by, among others, Michael Lewis, Ian Frazier, Bill Buford, Daniel Coyle, and Mimi Swartz.

ISBN-13: 978-0-618-75115-0 • ISBN-10: 0-618-75115-7 $28.00 CL
ISBN-13: 978-0-618-75116-7 • ISBN-10: 0-618-75116-5 $14.00 PA

THE BEST AMERICAN TRAVEL WRITING™ 2007. SUSAN ORLEAN, editor, JASON WILSON, series editor. Edited by Susan Orlean, staff writer for *The New Yorker* and author of *The Orchid Thief,* this year's collection, like its predecessors, is "a perfect mix of exotic locale and elegant prose" (*Publishers Weekly*) and includes pieces by Elizabeth Gilbert, Ann Patchett, David Halberstam, Peter Hessler, and others.

ISBN-13: 978-0-618-58217-4 • ISBN-10: 0-618-58217-7 $28.00 CL
ISBN-13: 978-0-618-58218-1 • ISBN-10: 0-618-58218-5 $14.00 PA

THE BEST AMERICAN SCIENCE AND NATURE WRITING™ 2007. RICHARD PRESTON, editor, TIM FOLGER, series editor. This year's collection of the finest science and nature writing is edited by Richard Preston, a leading science writer and author of *The Hot Zone* and *The Wild Trees*. The 2007 edition features a mix of new voices and prize-winning writers, including James Gleick, Neil deGrasse Tyson, John Horgan, William Langewiesche, Heather Pringle, and others.

ISBN-13: 978-0-618-72224-2 • ISBN-10: 0-618-72224-6 $28.00 CL
ISBN-13: 978-0-618-72231-0 • ISBN-10: 0-618-72231-9 $14.00 PA

THE BEST AMERICAN SPIRITUAL WRITING™ 2007. PHILIP ZALESKI, editor, introduction by HARVEY COX. Featuring an introduction by Harvey Cox, author of the groundbreaking *Secular City,* this year's edition of this "excellent annual" (*America*) contains selections that gracefully probe the role of faith in modern life. Contributors include Robert Bly, Adam Gopnik, George Packer, Marilynne Robinson, John Updike, and others.

ISBN-13: 978-0-618-83333-7 • ISBN-10: 0-618-83333-1 $28.00 CL
ISBN-13: 978-0-618-83346-7 • ISBN-10: 0-618-83346-3 $14.00 PA

HOUGHTON MIFFLIN COMPANY www.houghtonmifflinbooks.com